THE LITTLE SHIPS

ALEXIS CAREW #3

J A SUTHERLAND

THE LITTLE SHIPS
Alexis Carew #3

by J.A. Sutherland

Newly commissioned lieutenant Alexis Carew is appointed into *HMS Shrewsbury*, a 74-gun ship of the line in New London's space navy. She expects *Shrewsbury* will be sent into action in the war against Hanover; instead she finds that she and her new ship are pivotal in a Foreign Office plot to bring the star systems of the French Republic into the war and end the threat of Hanover forever.

For Aryn,

Made you wait for the third book — I suppose that's torture enough.

Whatever influence I had on you is the best thing I've accomplished in life, sweetheart, and I could not be prouder of you.

*Oh ... and **call your grandmother!***

And to the men and ships of The Little Ships of Dunkirk, 26 May to 4 June 1940.

And gentlemen in England now abed
Shall think themselves accursed they were not here,
And hold their manhoods cheap whiles any speaks
That fought with us upon Saint Crispin's day.
Henry V, Act 4, Scene 3
William Shakespeare

ONE

"*Fire!*"

Alexis Carew, sixth lieutenant aboard *HMS Shrewsbury*, stepped back from the gunport quickly and added her own voice.

"*Fire!*" she yelled.

Her vacsuit's radio crackled with static as the order was passed on by the two midshipmen with her on *Shrewsbury's* upper gundeck. The crews of the fourteen guns that lined the ship's port side stepped back and the gun captains slammed their hands down on the buttons that fired the guns. The crystalline tubes of the guns flashed and, even before the afterimage had faded from her eyes, the crews were in motion to reload the guns with fresh shot.

Alexis ducked her head back to the port and watched as the shot from her guns joined the rest of *Shrewsbury's* broadside on its way to the enemy ship. Fourteen more from the guns of the main gundeck below them, along with seven from the quarterdeck guns and two from the forecastle, all flashing across the space between *Shrewsbury* and the other ship in the odd way things behaved in *darkspace*. Even light was affected by the presence of so much dark energy and dark matter, with the bolts of the lasers becoming condensed and fore-shortened in their path between the ships.

The bolts of light seemed to slow and condense as they moved, until they struck the other ship and the shot splashed against its hull. The light from the bolts illuminating the gases and droplets of vapor-ized thermoplastic from the other ship's hull.

"Faster, lads!" Alexis yelled to her reloading crews. "Captain'll want two broadsides in three minutes, or he'll know the reason why!"

The carefully choreographed dance of reloading the guns went on.

Before the guns' tubes had even darkened, the gun captains threw open the breeches to expose the gleaming casings of the gallenium-cased shot. The other two men of each crew knelt and ran their eyes over the gun tubes, checking for any obvious damage from the last firing. A cracked or hazed tube could burst, sending the next bolt in deadly splinters of energy throughout their own gundeck.

The gun captains pulled the spent shot canisters from the breeches and flung them to the far side of the gundeck, then selected new shot from the racks that ran down the middle of the deck. They ran practiced eyes and fingers over the shot to see that the casing was well-sealed. It was early in the action and the gallenium-mesh nets covering each gunport kept out most of the radiation effects of *dark-space*, but that wouldn't last. More and more would creep in the longer the action went on. Enemy shot would damage the nets, or even hole the hull, allowing in even more. That radiation affected all electronics, save those protected by enough gallenium, and if the shot casing wasn't sealed well enough the gun wouldn't fire.

Alexis smiled with a certain pride. She loved the guns. The way her voice and breathing echoed inside the helmet of her vacsuit, the hot, heavy work of hauling shot canisters from the racks to the guns, she even loved the risk.

She knew it would take only one shot, even from the smaller frigate *Shrewsbury* now faced, to end her. Though the hull was thick, it could be breached, and the gunports only had the thin nettings, meant to keep out the *darkspace* radiation and not as any sort of protection for the crews.

But still she never seemed to feel so alive as in action, pitting her lads against those on another ship.

Her crews were working well. The runners were collecting the spent shot canisters for return to the well-protected magazine below, where the capacitors would be quickly recharged. Her two midshipmen, Walborn and Blackmer, were assisting the crews where needed, or at least had the sense to step back out of the men's way where not.

The guns' tubes had been checked and the facings inside the breeches, where the shot's lasing tubes would meet the tubes of the guns, were even now being wiped clean.

Alexis was dimly aware of the other ship firing, but none of their shot penetrated *Shrewsbury's* hull. She spared a moment's worry for the spacers working the ship's masts, then returned to her more immediate concerns.

One by one, the gun captains shoved new cannisters into the guns, slammed home the breech, and raised their arms to signal their readiness. Some of them took a moment to adjust their aim, having their crews roll the heavy gun carriages into a new position or crank the wheel to change its elevation. The work had to be done by hand because no electrical motors or controls would work once the *darkspace* radiation began entering the ship.

"Ready forward!" Walborn yelled, his arm going up in concert with his last gun captain's.

That's twice he's ready first, Alexis thought. *There'll be a shilling or two changing hands if Blackmer's crews don't show better.*

Walborn was an inveterate gambler, though for small stakes, and had roped Blackmer into his bets. The younger boy had likely lost a month's pay since joining *Shrewsbury*. It was a practice Alexis discouraged, but couldn't stop. Not because of Blackmer's losses, but because they were betting on the actions of their crews.

As though they were nothing more than horses in a race.

The last gun captain's arm went up, Blackmer's following quickly.

"Aft ready!" Blackmer's voice sounded over the radio.

"Upper ready!" Alexis called, her own arm going up. The quarterdeck would hear her report, but if the radios became inoperable due to radiation creeping inboard there was a spacer at the aft hatch to relay the signal as well.

"*Fire!*" came the order from the quarterdeck.

Again shot flowed across the space separating the two ships and struck the enemy.

Alexis eyed the damage to the other ship. There were several holes in the frigate's hull where *Shrewsbury's* shot had penetrated. Three masts projected outward from the ship's bow, not quite equidistant, as the Hanoverese preferred to rake their fore and mizzen masts a few degrees closer to the mainmast that projected straight up from the bow.

Metal mesh sails on the main and mizzen masts gleamed with the azure glow of the charged particles that allowed them to harness the dark energy that flowed through *darkspace* like winds.

Most of the foremast, though, was missing, shot through and cut away early in the action.

The Hanoverese frigate was much smaller than *Shrewsbury,* a 74-gun third rate, and no frigate had any business tangling with a ship of the line. It was just the Hanoverese captain's bad luck that had allowed the engagement.

The frigate had been trailing the convoy of merchantmen *Shrewsbury* was escorting for some time, always staying far enough astern or to windward so that *Shrewsbury,* a much larger and slower ship, couldn't bring it to action.

Then it had tried sneaking in on the convoy of merchantmen *Shrewsbury* was escorting under cover of a *darkspace* storm, hoping to make off with a prize or two. But the storm had cleared with the two ships surprisingly close together, putting paid to the frigate's plans and leaving it no choice but to engage *Shrewsbury* at least long enough to escape. Though that hope for escape hadn't survived the first broadside, when *Shrewsbury's* fire had shot through the other ship's foremast and left its rigging a deplorable mess.

The action had really been decided then, but the frigate's captain had refused to strike his colors and surrender.

Another broadside or two and he'll have no choice but to strike, Alexis judged.

The frigate's hull was pocked with holes where *Shrewsbury's* guns had eaten away at it. Four of its gunports were merged into a solid line of open space, where the hull between them had been burned away by *Shrewsbury's* guns. The frigate fired and Alexis noted that at least three of the other ship's guns were no longer firing, though they were still attempting to fire in broadside.

Soon now, and Captain Euell will have a prize to join the convoy.

"Load, lads, *load!*" she yelled. "They're all arse-up and begging for it!"

She straightened from the port just as the other ship's broadside arrived. Perhaps the frigate's guncrews had adjusted their aim, or perhaps just bad luck, but the shot found *Shrewsbury's* upper gundeck for the first time.

One bolt flashed through the number two gun's port, narrowly missing a spacer examining the gun's tubes. The man froze for a moment, as though not believing what had just flashed between his face and the tube, then resumed his examination as though nothing had happened.

The other shot, though, struck through the number nine port aft. There was a flash of vaporizing metal as it came through the netting that covered the port, then it struck Midshipman Blackmer full in the chest.

The energy of the heavy laser burned a hole the size of Alexis' hand through the boy's vacsuit, body, and out the other side to finally strike and dissipate against the darkly colored starboard bulkhead.

Alexis rushed to Blackmer's side, but saw that there was no point. The vacsuits could seal against something small that pierced nothing vital, but this had killed Blackmer outright. She grasped his body by the arms and dragged him to the starboard side of the gundeck where he would be out of the way of the gun crews.

"Ready forward!" Walborn's voice echoed in her helmet.

Alexis watched the aft guncrews, waiting until the last gun captain flung his hand up.

"Upper ready!" she yelled.

"*Fire!*"

TWO

"WINE, SIR?"

"Thank you, Littler." Alexis nodded her thanks as Captain Euell's steward filled her glass. Hers was the last, she being the junior officer at the captain's table. The men at the table quieted as Littler stepped back with the wine bottle and looked expectantly at Captain Euell.

"Gentlemen," he said, raising his glass. "Fine work and a successful action."

"Fine work and a successful action!" they all chorused, Alexis included. She raised her glass and took a sip.

The captain's day cabin seemed almost spacious with just the seven of them. Captain Euell, his steward, Alexis, and four of *Shrewsbury's* other lieutenants were the only occupants.

Lieutenant Slawson, the second lieutenant, was off with the prize crew getting the Hanoverese frigate in hand. The others, Lieutenants Barr, Brookhouse, Hollingshead, and Nesbit, in order of their seniority, had been invited to dine with Captain Euell in celebration of taking the Hanoverese frigate.

"A shame about young Blackmer, Carew," Euell said. "He had the makings of a fine officer."

Alexis nodded. "He did, sir," she said, her throat a bit tight.

"Bad luck, that," Lieutenant Barr, the first lieutenant, added. "Not another man lost but him."

The others murmured agreement and Alexis raised her glass as she knew was expected.

"Absent friends," she said.

The others raised their glasses in turn and there was a moment's silence.

"A fine lad and he'll be missed," Captain Euell said.

And that will be the last said of him, Alexis thought, a bit bitterly.

She understood the need; with the war on so many men fell in bloody actions that it was best not to think on them too long. Not from callousness, but because there were still the living to care for.

The other midshipmen in the berth would have their own toasts to Blackmer tonight. The best of his friends in the berth would go through his things and select a memento or two before his kit was sealed and struck down into the hold to be sent back to his family. His body would be reduced to ash in the fusion plant and those ashes packed away in his kit as well. It was a sad package to think of sending home.

"We'll cover a bit of business before dinner, I think," Euell said, "as Carew will be dining elsewhere again."

"Thank you, sir," Alexis said. "I'm sorry about that."

Euell waved her apology aside, but Alexis could tell he didn't find the situation aboard *Shrewsbury* at all to his liking.

No more than I do, she thought.

"What do you suppose your dinner will be tonight, Carew?" Lieutenant Brookhouse asked, grinning.

"Yes," Lieutenant Nesbit said. "I can't wait to hear your description of the next dish that Eades fellow feeds you."

"I shudder at the very thought, sirs," Alexis told them. "He's not told me what's next and I daren't ask. But after that last one ...

well, I suppose that's the reason we call the French 'Frogs', after all."

Brookhouse laughed and gestured at her glass. "Fortify yourself well, is my suggestion."

Alexis took a healthy swallow. "There are some things that shouldn't be faced sober," she agreed.

The others laughed and Alexis took another drink of wine to hide a sudden emotion. How different the laughter aboard *Shrewsbury* was from that on her previous ship, the ill-fated *Hermione*, with her tyrannical Captain Neals and a midshipmen's berth full of toadying bullies.

"I'll have Littler send a plate to the wardroom for you," Euell said. "In case you can still stomach good, planet-raised beef after whatever Mister Eades places in front of you."

"Thank you, sir," Alexis said. "That will be welcome, no matter what Mister Eades' cook has prepared for us. It seems the French are incapable of serving a simple bit of any meat without they cover it in some sort of ... goop."

The others laughed again, but the laughter turned to amused looks at Alexis as her tablet pinged. She grasped it through her jump-suit, frowning because she was certain she'd turned it off before coming into the captain's cabin. No officer wanted a meeting with the captain interrupted by a midshipman asking questions.

"I'm sorry, sir," Alexis said, pulling her tablet out. "I'm sure I turned it —" She broke off and clenched her jaw at the sight of the message. "Mister Eades requests my presence, sir. I'm certain I turned the tablet's alerts off, though. I've no idea how he manages it, but he seems to regard our communications systems as his personal playground."

Euell pursed his lips. "And *Shrewsbury* as his personal transport, come to that." He sighed. "I can't fault you for not controlling the man when that's beyond me as well. Tell him you'll be along shortly."

"Aye, sir."

"If I didn't have orders to offer him and that Courtemanche

fellow 'every accommodation', I'd have his accommodations in the bloody brig."

"And no one would be more glad of it than I, sir," Alexis agreed as she sent the requested message and turned off the tablet's speaker again.

Captain Euell took a sip of wine and set his glass down.

"To business, then," he said. "Now that we've done away with that frigate that's been dogging us, I believe there are no other Hanoverese ships in a position to threaten the convoy. If there were, they'd certainly have come in with the frigate to attack during the storm, or to its aid at the end there. So we should have a clear, two days' sail to the border. Unless we run across some other ship by happenstance, of course.

"Once in French Republican space, the convoy will begin to disperse, and we ourselves shall sail directly for *Nouvelle Paris* with our charges, Mister Eades and *Monsieur* Courtemanche."

"And may we soon be shut of them," Lieutenant Barr said, giving a mock toast.

"At least until the return trip," Captain Euell reminded them. "We are to remain at Mister Eades' ... disposal —" He curled his lip on the last word. "— until such time as he has finished with whatever it is he does there."

Alexis looked down at the table as all eyes turned to her. All of the other officers were curious about their mission, but Eades had instructed her — threatened, really — not to speak a word of it. She could only be grateful that *Shrewsbury's* other officers, and captain, were being so understanding that their most junior lieutenant knew more about their purpose than they themselves did.

"Regardless," Euell continued, "we'll likely have some weeks idle in orbit around *Nouvelle Paris*." He waited for the grins and excited murmurs to subside. "Yes, I'm rather looking forward to weeks of leave on a Core World myself. And they've a proper, naval station to grant the crew leave, as well, without the worry of them running."

With the war had come the return of the Impressment Service

grabbing merchant spacers and even some civilians up in the Press for service in the fleet, not to mention those crewmen who'd come from the assizes with the choice of either Naval service or prison before them.

Given the harsh conditions of sailing the Dark, the poor food, consisting mostly of a daily half kilo of "beef" grown in the purser's nutrient vats, and miserly pay, often paid months in arrears, it was a wonder men didn't jump ship in the midst of *darkspace* itself.

The French naval station at *Nouvelle Paris* would have the pubs, shops, and other, more prurient, establishments the crew would be looking forward to, but in a sealed environment with guards at the planet-bound boats and around any merchant shipping. The added difficulty, and the certainty of losing what portion of their pay was in arrears, would make most of the men think twice about attempting to run.

"Will the ships of the convoy not be running a risk when they disperse, sir?" Lieutenant Brookhouse asked. "Some of their destinations are quite near the Republic's border with Hanover."

"To date," Euell said, "the Hanoverese have limited their aggression to us. It's an odd, disturbing turn of events, given their past propensity for attacking everyone in sight all at once. For the moment, though, New London appears to be their only target. We've heard nothing of conflict with the Republic, *Deutschsterne*, or *Hso-Hsi*." He frowned. "Though why those others haven't come to our assistance yet is beyond me, as well. Our shared history of conflict with Hanover, after all ..." He shrugged. "It is beyond me."

"Perhaps, with such a long peace as we've had," Brookhouse suggested, "they're hoping New London will settle Hanover before the Hannies set their sights on other targets."

"Perhaps," Euell allowed, "though even a cursory review of history should put paid to such hopes. In any case, we have a last bit of ship's business before we bid our Lieutenant Carew good luck in her evening's trials." He raised a glass to her and the others followed suit.

"With Mister Blackmer's death, we are a midshipman short and, since we'll be some time in Republican space, will have to look to other means of replacing him. Please give it some thought, gentlemen, and put forth the names of any of our master's mates you think might have the makings of an officer. Lieutenant Carew?"

"Sir?"

"I should like to place Mister Artley with you on the upper gundeck. Do, please, see what you can make of him."

"Aye, sir," Alexis said automatically, but inwardly wincing.

Artley was the youngest midshipman aboard *Shrewsbury* at just twelve years old. It was his first time aboard ship and most of the officers were already despairing at his future.

The boy was timid, almost mouse-like, with both the other midshipmen and the crew. She wasn't sure what Captain Euell might expect her to "make of him", given that she was the most junior lieutenant aboard herself.

And with every waking moment I'm not on watch spent closeted with Eades and Courtemanche.

"Better you than me, Carew," Lieutenant Hollingshed said with a grin and a raised glass. "I wish you luck."

THREE

"Choose, Miss Carew! Quickly!"

Alexis looked at the array of items on the table before her with a wary eye. Mister Eades, of the Foreign Office, was seated across the table from her with a similar array and she could detect just the tiniest indication of impatience in his expression and voice.

"This one?" she asked, tentatively picking up a four-pronged fork.

Eades sighed and shook his head. "No, Miss Carew, we've been over this. That is a salad fork." He picked up an instrument with two long prongs. "*This* is for *escargot.*"

Alexis set the fork down on the table with the others and eyed her plate with distaste. How Eades' cook had managed it, with the limited space aboard ship to cook in as well as store provisions, she didn't know, but he'd managed to produce yet another meal that she was certain even *Shrewsbury's* hardest man would turn his nose up at.

"If I must stab a giant snail, Mister Eades, I shall want something a bit more formidable, I think."

"One does not *stab* at a fine Court dinner," Eades said. "One uses the tines to gently tease the meat from the shell."

Alexis grimaced. "Could we not, perhaps, leave the snails in their shells? Safe in the garden?" Alexis felt her stomach roll a bit at the thought. "And simply have the butter and garlic over toast?"

"We may not, Miss Carew," Eades said.

Alexis sighed. After the morning's battle and Blackmer's death, then a long day of herding the convoy's merchantmen back into a semblance of order, she longed for nothing more than a bit of rest. Perhaps even a small amount of time in the wardroom to speak to the ship's other officers, men she had to work with, but had been given little opportunity to come to know.

Instead she was once again in Malcom Eades' cabin, being asked to learn what she considered utter silliness.

"Should I wake Courtemanche, Carew? For another dancing lesson?"

"No!" Alexis said quickly. "No, that won't be at all necessary. It's the two-tined fork for snails, you say?"

Vachel Courtemanche, representative to Her Majesty's Court from *La Grande République de France Parmi les Étoiles*, The Grand Republic of France Among the Stars, shared the cabin with Eades. It was his task to teach her some particularly French things, such as the dances currently popular at the French Court, and he was, so far as Alexis' limited encounters could discern, a prototypical Frenchman — an outrageous flirt and certain that he was the universe's greatest gift to women.

This Alexis would have been able to accept with a tolerant smile, were he not also some four times her seventeen years of age and ... well, the man had an odor about him. An unpleasant, almost unbearable, odor. That Alexis thought this after spending more than two years aboard ships — *Shrewsbury* herself having a complement of over eight hundred men, all limited to no more than a quart of water per day for washing — said much.

How Eades could stand to spend his days in such close proximity to the Frenchman was something Alexis couldn't fathom. *Shrewsbury* had been built as a fleet flagship and boasted a spacious admiral's cabin, in addition to her captain's, which Eades and Courtemanche had taken for their use. They'd divided the sleeping cabin between them and used the absent admiral's day cabin for their teaching of Alexis.

Torment, rather.

Eades smiled the infuriating little smile that always had Alexis' teeth clenching. The man loved to get his own way and was intolerably smug about it when he did so.

"Good, Miss Carew."

"As I've said before, the proper form of address, Mister Eades, would be 'lieutenant' or 'mister', if you please. The Navy makes no distinction for my gender."

Eades shrugged. "I am not a part of your Navy, Miss Carew, nor, I assure you, are the French. Perhaps you should respect their customs, as you'll be with me there for some time."

Alexis fought down a flash of anger, but not before snapping. "Perhaps you should respect the customs of the Service that's providing you transport, sir."

"I much prefer that *you* learn the customs of our soon-to-be hosts," Eades said. "The French are an odd lot, and easily offended."

Alexis took a deep breath and calmed herself. Sniping with Eades did no good at all.

"I fear I'll never remember these things. At home on Dalthus, we only ever used a single fork at any meal." She stared at the glittering array of utensils laid out before her. It would have been unthinkable to send that much silverware back to the kitchen and expect their cook, Julia, to wash it after every meal.

"Yes, well, the French Republican Court is not a colonial pig-farm, now is it?"

Alexis raised her gaze to stare at Eades. Dalthus might be a colony and her grandfather proud to name himself a farmer, but he, along with the three thousand other First Settlers owned the entire star system of Dalthus.

"If those at this Court are as ill-mannered as yourself, Mister Eades, I believe I shall prefer the pigs."

"And I would happily send you back to them," Eades said, "but if this plan is to succeed, your presence is required at the Court. Not only your presence, but that you *impress* the Court."

"I almost wish you would send me back, Mister Eades, or at least allow me my Naval career in peace." Alexis gestured at the table setting. "I do not find *this* impressive."

Eades glared at her, his normally impassive face actually showing disapproval. "You know Commodore Balestra of the Berry March fleet; you've met her, spoken to her. The French will listen to you and your opinion of her, and of those worlds, *only* if you are able to seem, yourself, of some note. Something more than a young girl from a barely civilized colony world."

"For a diplomat, Mister Eades, you are far from diplomatic."

Alexis sighed again. Her time spent with Eades was always trying, perhaps because he was always demanding she learn the most absurd things without ever explaining the whole reason. Why was it so important that she impress the French? Why did they need to impress the French at all? She understood so little of his reasons, or even the reasons for the war New London found itself in, that she found it difficult to care about more than her ship, the crew, and distant friends.

Yes, she'd met Commodore Balestra, commander of a Hanoverese fleet in the worlds known as *La Baie Marche*, the Berry March. Though the worlds were part of Hanover, with whom her own nation of New London was at war, the worlds themselves had once been part of the French Republic, and the people there still thought of themselves as French.

Alexis had spent some time on one of those worlds as a prisoner of the Hanoverese and had grown to know the commodore. Something Eades hoped to take advantage of in his plans to convince the French Republic to declare war on Hanover and attempt to regain their former possessions.

"I am no diplomat at all, Carew," Eades said. For the first time since she'd met him, Alexis noticed something distinctive about Malcom Eades — his eyes suddenly became the most frightening thing she'd ever seen. "I am, in fact, the very opposite of a diplomat. No, Carew, I make things happen for my Queen — and in this case, what I shall make happen is that the Republic of France shall join the war against Hanover, Commodore Balestra and the worlds of the Berry March shall revolt against Hanover, and the Republic of Hanover shall find itself ... no more."

Alexis licked suddenly dry lips. She'd never heard such utter, certain hatred expressed in so calm a tone.

"I don't understand," she said, almost whispering. "I don't even understand why we're at war with Hanover to begin with."

Eades' brow furrowed. He cocked his head to one side and opened his mouth, closed it, then opened it again. He sat back and regarded her as though seeing her for the first time.

"That is a shocking degree of ignorance."

Alexis clenched her teeth to keep from snapping at him. *God help us if he were a diplomat ... the kingdom would be doomed.*

"Mister Eades," she said instead, "I was raised roughly on a colony planet, as you know. There was quite enough for me to learn on Dalthus about running my grandfather's lands, so you must forgive me for not following whatever events led to this war. My time in the Navy has consisted of some months tracking pirates aboard *Merlin* and some time more aboard *Hermione*. My encounters with the Hanoverese have consisted of Commodore Balestra and her staff, who were quite kind to me and, as it turns out, are French and not Hanoverese at all, and a Hanoverese lieutenant whose ship I took with a ruse — he, though a bit lecherous, was more a buffoon than the evil you seem to see in them.

"Moreover, I have a bare three years in Naval service. It's been all I could do to learn the *Navy's* ways, much less anything about the wider universe. And, in case you had not noticed, sir, the Navy itself is not at all prone to *explaining*."

Eades was silent. "No," he said finally. "No, I suppose it is not." He poured himself a glass of wine and took a sip. "Do you know a thing about New London's history at all?"

Alexis flushed, feeling a bit foolish, for she would have to admit that she did know only a very little.

"The price of *varrenwood*, the shipping rates for grain ... the times to plant and harvest, even the assay process for a new mine, Mister Eades," she admitted finally. "These were always far more important than some dry history that would never ..." She closed her eyes, realizing how silly it sounded. "Would never have an impact on my life."

"If you wish a career in the Navy, Carew," Eades said, "rather than simply a position, I suggest you begin paying history more heed." He ran a hand over his chin. "Very well, then, I will explain. At least as much as one can in a short time.

"I'm sure you know, at least, that the systems we call the Core Worlds — the longest settled and most developed — were once colonies themselves?"

Alexis nodded.

"Good. Well, the entire history of mankind in the stars is likely too much to cover this evening, but ... do you at least know your ship's history? Perhaps that will give you the correct perspective."

"*Shrewsbury's?*"

"Yes." He shook his head. "No, I can see from your eyes that you don't, and that surprises me. There is a reason this particular ship was selected for this particular mission. That bronze plaque near the airlock, where they do all the folderol of coming aboard, do you know what it means?"

Alexis was reasonably certain that no one aboard *Shrewsbury* would care for the ceremony of piping officers aboard and saluting the ensign at the airlock being referred to as 'folderol', but she had to admit she didn't know the plaque's purpose. There were so many Naval traditions and their meanings that she didn't yet know. She'd seen the plaque in question — it bore the ship's name, *HMS. Shrews-*

bury, and the names of several hundred men, along with the odd inscription *We Who Stood*. She'd assumed it might be the ship's first crew, but now felt she'd been very mistaken. She was certain, however, that she'd have had a chance to learn it if Eades had not been so jealous of her time.

"*Shrewsbury* is a Named Ship, Carew," Eades said, "I chose her for this visit to the French Republic as carefully as I chose you. Perhaps more so." Eades cleared his throat.

"At the end of the Second Colonial Independence War, when we — that is to say the major Core Worlds, New London, the French, *Ho-Hsi*, and *Deutschsterne* — were able to knock the forces of Earth, Terra Nova, and *Nueva Oportunidad* back and retain our independence, a large portion of the *Deutschsterne* fleet and dozens of systems rebelled." He met her eyes steadily. "This was hundreds of years ago, of course, but the ramifications are felt today. The rebellion was led from the Hanover system. Hanover was a political colony, with all that it implies, you understand?"

Alexis nodded.

After *darkspace* was discovered and travel to other star systems became possible, the first attempts at colonization had been disasters. The first colony worlds, Terra Nova and *Nueva Oportunidad*, had been an odd attempt to mix all of the cultures of Earth into some sort of utopian ideal. The result had been years of factional battles and bloody civil wars as different groups tried to gain superiority on the new planets.

In the interim, exploration went on and it was discovered that habitable planets were not so rare as originally believed.

The second wave of colonization, much, much larger than the first, had consisted of homogeneous groups. Religious and political groups fleeing to set up their own versions of utopia were among them, along with groups that simply wanted a bit of room between them and their neighbors.

The result on most of the cultural colonies, as the political and religious settlements were referred to, had been years of factional battles and bloody civil wars as those supposedly homogeneous groups fragmented points of doctrine and philosophy.

Humanity, it seemed, very much enjoyed killing each other.

"Settling new lands has always been a safety valve to get rid of those with extreme or unpopular beliefs," Eades continued, "and it generally works well to this day — at least from the perspective of those of us in the Core who don't have to deal with them anymore. If a group can pay the survey and transport costs to claim a system, good riddance to them and let them run their world as they see fit. They often fall to quarreling amongst themselves over some obscure point of dogma and leave their neighbors well alone until they come to their senses and want services only the Core can provide."

Eades sighed.

"Hanover was an exception," he said. "That particular group settled several systems close together and managed to spread their ideas to their neighbors. It was *Deutschsterne's* bad luck that those systems comprised quite a large part of their industrial worlds. When Hanover rebelled it was a complete surprise to *Deutschsterne* — and it was coordinated in such a way that ..." He paused.

"The goal of those systems, Miss Carew, was not simply their own independence from *Deutschsterne*. That might have been understandable, but they wanted more. They intended to not only rebel, but to conquer." He raised his eyebrows. "Conquer *everything*, it seems. They believe, truly *believe*, that they're meant to rule all of humanity. A horribly ambitious goal, but they were well on their way to succeeding, and by the most ... dishonorable means."

Eades poured her a glass of wine and set it in front of her. Alexis raised it and took a small sip.

"You're aware of the Abbentheren Accords?"

Alexis shook her head.

"No, of course not," Eades muttered. "Why should I expect you know a thing other than —" Eades shook his head in disgust. "A bit of study would do you no harm, Miss Carew.

"In any case, the Abbenthern Accords go into great detail about how warfare may be waged and the actions of Hanover in that war were the catalyst for Abbentheren," Eades said. "It is unthinkable today to bombard a planet from orbit in any way. That is because we've already seen what such warfare can do. Hanover struck the *Deutschsterne* capital world first ... their entire political leadership wiped out, along with seven million people in the capital city ... all with no more effort than nudging a rock out of its orbit and dropping it into the planet's gravity well."

Alexis gasped at the thought of the destruction such a thing would cause.

Eades nodded. "Hanover took a very ... pragmatic view toward conquest after that success. The ancient Romans had a policy in their own warfare ... *Murum Aries Attigit,* they called it, the ram has touched the wall. If an enemy city capitulated before the battering ram touched their walls, they'd be spared. After? No. Hanover would demand capitulation and accept surrender, but —" Eades shrugged. "— once the rocks were in motion, well, *murum aries attigit.*"

Alexis stared at Eades, unable to believe such an act would ever be committed.

"Abbentheren was a beautiful world, if the preserved images are to be believed," Eades said, taking another sip of wine. "But the ram touched the wall there, Carew." He snorted. "Many, many rams.

"All of this, of course, was against *Deutschsterne* — a civil war, of no concern to New London or the French King." He smiled at her look of shock. "Yes, Carew, a monarch. The Grand *Republic* of France Among the Stars was once the Grand *Kingdom,* you see.

"Perhaps Hanover couldn't find a suitable rock, I don't know, but they changed tactics and chose assassination when they decided to expand their list of enemies. Virtually the entire royal family of the Grand Kingdom was assassinated overnight."

Eades drained his glass and filled it again.

"As was New London's," he said. He gave her a bitter smile. "It was not the Foreign Office's finest hour to have missed that bit coming. Nor the Palace Guards' for allowing it to happen. To fail your Monarch in such a way, Carew ... it is a thing that burns through generations." Eades took a deep breath. "It sounds a bit like a fairy tale, I suppose, but both kingdoms had clear claimants — the *last* clear claimants, mind you — to their thrones safely where they could not be reached by assassins ... aboard ship, in *darkspace*, serving in their respective navies.

"Both kingdoms were in utter disarray, of course, with no clear chain of command or leadership. The Hanoverese began rolling over systems one after the other. Once word spread of what happened to those systems that resisted ... well, one cannot blame people for wanting to live, I suppose.

"You're wondering, of course, what all this has to do with *Shrewsbury*? Well, I'm getting to that." He filled her glass, though Alexis did not recall having drunk the wine. "Someone, it's unclear who, felt that it was necessary to get the two crown princes together so that they could discuss an alliance against Hanover — princes, still, you see, for there'd been no way to stage a coronation for either. I suppose someone might have thought to just have a ship's captain do it, things being what they were at the time." He shrugged. "As I said, all was in disarray.

"In any case, both fleets were in such a state that when the ships the princes were on came together, the rest of both fleets were nowhere to be found. Either not yet arrived or not having received the message to gather. And so it was just the French ship, *Belle Nuit*, and New London's ... HMS *Shrewsbury*." He drank again. "I told you I'd get to it.

"The New London and French fleets may not have been able to find the meeting place at the appropriate time, but the same cannot be said for the Hanoverese. No sooner had meetings begun between the two princes, than seven Hanoverese ships arrived in-system. At the time, our Prince Henry was aboard *Belle Nuit* chatting with the French fellow, I forget his name.

"So, then, there was *Shrewsbury's* captain, Merewode Shetley — *his* name I remember, you see — with his Crown Prince aboard a

French ship, seven Hanoverese ships bearing down on them. A good mix the Hanoverese sent, at least according to those who'd know about such things — enough fast ships so that they couldn't escape and enough guns so that they couldn't fight. A bad business all around.

"Captain Shetley sent one signal to *Belle Nuit*, Miss Carew — *We Shall Stand*.

"Then he put *Shrewsbury* about, sailed into the Hanoverese, and damned if he didn't stop them ... or at least damage and delay them long enough for *Belle Nuit* to get well away. The French logs show *Shrewsbury* still firing hours later when *Belle Nuit* finally sailed out of sight." He took a sip of his wine. "And that is the last record of *Shrewsbury*, Captain Shetley, or any of his crew. So *Shrewsbury* became a Named Ship. One of seventeen in New London's history. If this particular incarnation were to be destroyed today, the very next ship launched would be so christened, for there is *always* a *Shrewsbury* in Service to Her Majesty."

Eades raised his glass and nodded to her. "I may not respect all of your Navy's customs, Miss Carew, but I do, never doubt, respect its deeds."

Alexis stared at him, unsure of what to say or if he was done speaking.

Eades sighed. "We got Henry back, of course, our Queen's many-times great-grandfather. The French had the poor judgment to misplace their prince some few years later in a battle, and he'd had the even poorer judgment to not spend that time rantipoling with every girl he could lay hands on and generating an heir or six — so they had no clear heir to the throne. Had the unexpected good sense, though, not to start a dynastic struggle in the middle of a war, and somehow managed to make themselves a republic in rather short time.

"We — New London, the French, and what was left of *Deutschsterne* — managed to stop Hanover and force them to the treaty table. Word of Abbentheren and other systems had spread and they were faced with nearly the entire bloody universe coming in against them, so they agreed to stop the war, give back what systems they'd taken, save those of *Deutschsterne*, and sign the Abbentheren Accords. That was ... oh, I don't know exactly, seventeen or so wars with them ago?" He shrugged. "My family has served the Monarchy since that time, Miss Carew. Since my own many-times-great grand-father failed to recognize the danger Hanover represented to them."

Eades picked up the wine bottle and appeared puzzled when he found it empty.

"I will see Hanover ended, Miss Carew."

He met Alexis' eyes and she shivered at his look.

"That's enough history for today, I suppose," he said. "I believe I hear *Monsieur* Courtemanche stirring and lord knows you require more practice at dance."

FOUR

ALEXIS LEFT EADES, Courtemanche, and the flag cabin sometime later with much to think about. Eades' tale — and the emotion he'd shown, far different from his usual smugness and disdain — had shed new light on this mission. She wondered, though, if the man wasn't placing too much importance on her and her ability to convince the French to join with New London against Hanover.

She'd explained to him more than once that she did not know Commodore Balestra well. She'd only met the woman a handful of times while she was a prisoner on Giron, one of the worlds Hanover had taken from the French Republic a century before.

That the people of those worlds, and Commodore Balestra who commanded the fleet drawn from there, still thought of themselves as French was indisputable. But Alexis doubted whether the leaders of the Republic would take her word for it.

And if they do, she thought, *how will Balestra even know?*

The last reports Eades had said the fleet from the Berry March, *La Baie Marche* as the French called those worlds, had been ordered deep into Hanover space and replaced with ships from Hanover proper.

At least that places Delaine far from the fighting.

Delaine Theibaud was the Frenchman Alexis knew far better than the commodore, and Alexis smiled at the memory. The flamboyant lieutenant could make the most outrageous statements and then beg her forgiveness with a grin and, "You must forgive me ... I am French."

Odd as it sounded even to her, her time as a prisoner on Giron had been the happiest she'd known since leaving her home on Dalthus, solely because it was time spent so much with Delaine.

So, we must convince the French, then find the Berry March fleet, then somehow get a message to Commodore Balestra which convinces her of the Republic's intent ... and even then we must still convince the various worlds of the Berry March of all this.

Alexis shook her head. It all seemed quite complicated and more than they could hope to accomplish with just the one ship, Named or no.

She slid the hatch to the wardroom open and entered. Lieutenants Hollingshed and Nesbit were there at the wardroom's table, sharing a bottle of wine with Major Howey, who led *Shrewsbury's* marines.

Isom, a spacer who'd attached himself to her as a sort of personal servant during her captivity on Giron, stood by the wardroom cupboards with Bonsall, the wardroom's regular steward. He raised his eyebrows in enquiry and she nodded slightly.

Alexis seated herself at the table with the others and Isom brought her a cup, which Hollingshed filled for her, drawing a glare from Nesbit who usually assigned himself that task. The bottle ran out, though, leaving her with less than half a glass.

Isom returned in a moment with a warm plate of beef. Real beef, as the captain had been as good as his word and sent a plate from his own table for her.

"Bring us one of the reds we brought aboard at Hartleigh, will you Isom?" she asked. Lord knew after an evening with Eades she'd need more than a glass.

"Aye, sir."

Strictly speaking, lieutenants did not bring their own servants aboard ship. Oh, they could, but usually only if their name ended with a peerage. One or more of *Shrewsbury's* regular crew typically performed stewards' duties in the wardroom and gunroom, receiving a small remittance from the officers. Isom, though, had apparently found some way to follow Alexis aboard *Shrewsbury* and then made some arrangement with Bonsall. She supposed that so long as he performed other duties aboard ship and his remittance for the extra work came from Alexis herself, there was no cause for anyone to complain.

Isom returned with the bottle and Nesbit took it from him with a wink before filling Alexis' glass. It mixed the two wines, but none of the wardroom residents had bottles so fine left aboard that mixing would do them harm.

Alexis took a sip of her wine.

"Does it meet m'lady's approval?" Nesbit asked.

"Anything that dulls my senses and sears my nostrils would meet with my approval after the last few hours work."

"Then my day is complete. I live but to serve your whim, you do know."

Alexis chuckled. Nesbit was a match for her own age of seventeen and *Shrewsbury's* fifth lieutenant. Since she'd first come aboard, he'd treated her with outrageous courtesy and flirted extensively. At first she'd been concerned. Not only was any fraternization aboard ship forbidden by the regulations, but her experiences aboard her last ship, HMS *Hermione*, had left her leery of her peers. She'd been a midshipman aboard that ship, not a lieutenant, and the other midshipmen had been both lecherous and cruel toward her.

She'd quickly determined, though, that Nesbit was in no way serious about his attentions. He seemed to be doing it mostly to relieve his boredom and entertain himself; at worst he thought of her as a foil to hone his wits for runs ashore.

"If you've a mind to serve," she said, "taking a scrub brush and cake of soap to *Monsieur* Courtemanche wouldn't go amiss. Barring that, waylay him some evening and dunk him in a tank of rum until it's killed whatever it is must be growing somewhere on the man?"

She'd caught Hollingshed in mid-drink and had to grin at the coughing and choking that came from behind his suddenly raised hand.

"More of his dancing lessons?" Major Howey asked, face showing his amusement.

Alexis gave a mock shudder. "Interminably more. I fear I'll never have the way of it."

"Nonsense!" Nesbit said. "Surely you must move across the floor with the grace of a swan."

Alexis raised an eyebrow. Harmless as Nesbit was to her, she did wonder if he ever achieved his ends with the ladies on-station.

"Do swans dance, then?" she asked. "I was quite unaware."

"I have faith you will stun the gentlemen of *Nouvelle Paris,* as you have laid waste to *Shrewsbury's* wardroom."

Alexis eyed him for a moment. "Laying it on a bit, aren't you?"

Nesbit frowned. "Do you think so?"

"I've been flirted with by the French before, you know," Alexis said. "I fear you'll have your work cut out for you on *Nouvelle Paris.*"

Nesbit gave her a hurt expression. "Are you saying I don't measure up?"

"Well —" Alexis smiled at the memory of her time on Giron, possibly the most pleasant prisoner of war experience one could have. "They do have a certain way about them."

Nesbit narrowed his eyes, drawing his brow down. "Then I shall be the brooding New Londoner and the girls will find me all exotic."

Alexis laughed. "A plan for all contingencies?"

"Of course," Nesbit said. "One must go into action prepared for any eventuality."

"Still," Hollingshed said, "I've heard these dances the French hold go all night a'times. Do you truly find it so distasteful?"

"For those dances with set movements, I'll allow myself adequate." Alexis shook her head. "But these partnered dances where ... where I must follow another's whim, it seems, I find I have no ability."

Alexis realized even as she spoke the words what she'd just let herself in for, but she was too fatigued to stop her mouth. Nesbit was on his feet before she'd finished speaking, hand extended.

"Utter nonsense. Come, show me this lack. I believe you not." He gestured at Hollingshed. "Music, please."

"Of course, yes," Hollingshed said immediately with an evil grin for Alexis. "Certainly if such a lack exists, it is our duty to assist a fellow officer in her deficiency."

Alexis sighed. She was horribly tired after such a long day, but now the idea was in their heads, especially Nesbit's, there'd be no getting it out. She could only hope that if she played along now and let them have their fun they'd forget about it — better just the two lieutenants and Major Howey to witness her embarrassment than if they brought it up again before the entire wardroom. Likely then she'd wind up with all five of the other lieutenants vying to show her how it was done.

It wasn't as though they singled her out for the teasing, of course. Nesbit was a constant target for his schemes to meet ladies while on leave, Barr took more than his share for being the wealthiest of those in the wardroom, and Slawson's ears ... well, Alexis would much rather be singled out as the prettiest of the wardroom, rather than for those ears. It was almost affectionate.

No, this teasing is how they show affection for one another, rather than simply say it.

"I think I want no part of this," Howey said with a smile and a nod. "I'm off to my bed."

With another sigh Alexis took Nesbit's hand and rose, while Hollingshed played appropriate music on his tablet. At least Nesbit didn't stink, though he was taller than Courtemanche and that was awkward as well — he towered over Alexis' bare meter and a half by a full thirty centimeters or more and Alexis found herself staring at his chest. The reach to place her hand on his shoulder was uncomfortable, and Nesbit flushed as his own natural placement of his hand found something quite a bit higher than her waist.

Didn't think of that, did you? I'm simply not built for this sort of thing.

Nesbit cleared his throat and slid his hand down to where it belonged.

"So, then, now —" he said, nodding in time to the music and starting to move her through some steps. "It's not so — ow, bloody! No, no, it's quite all right, just let's try again. Simply move with — damn! Not that way, *with* me. Stop trying to — ow! Are you bloody *stomping* on me? Just turn to the right — no, my right, damn your eyes! *Ow!* You don't bloody weigh enough for it to hurt that mu — *ow!*"

Nesbit stopped, released her, and held up his hands. He gave Hollingshed a wounded look at his barely contained laughter and shook his head.

"You're a bloody menace!"

"I did warn you," Alexis said, resuming her seat.

Nesbit limped back to the table. "It's dance, Carew, not bloody wrestling!"

Alexis poured him a fresh glass of wine and slid it across the table to him. "I'm not at all certain why I have such trouble with it."

Nesbit drained his glass. "If a simple dance is such a struggle, I shudder at the thought of what an effort bedding you would be ..."

He froze, glass halfway to the table, and blanched. Hollingshed was equally silent, staring from Nesbit to Alexis.

"Oh, hell, Carew, I'm sorry for that." He set his glass down and spread his hands. "I wasn't thinking —"

Alexis cut him off hurriedly. "I'm not one to take offense at what's clearly a jest, Nesbit," she said, "even a crude one." She laid her hand on his arm. "I know the sorts of jests young men make amongst themselves, at least those of an age."

She nodded at Hollingshed who was only a year older than she and Nesbit. She didn't include Lieutenants Barr and Slawson, the first and second lieutenants in that. They were both much older more properly restrained. But Nesbit and Hollingshed, even Brookhouse to a certain extent, were only a little ways from midshipmen themselves, and no matter their upbringing they had little more couth than the village youths when their elders weren't around.

"And I'd rather you made them," she continued, "rather than being forever on your guard to avoid offending me." She squeezed his arm. "I'll draw my own lines, if you please, and that was nowhere near one. In fact, I think that may be the first time you've given up playing the gallant and simply spoken as yourself and, dare I say, a friend?"

"In my tongue-tied colleague's defense," Hollingshed said, holding the wine bottle to the light before pouring, "we've only seen a little of you off-watch. Difficult to know someone that way."

Alexis nodded.

Damn Eades for that as well, she thought. She'd been aboard *Shrewsbury* for nearly two months, but he'd taken so much of her time that she'd truly not had the chance to know the other officers, and that was good for neither herself nor the ship. *They've seen me on watch and may trust my skills, but they don't truly know me.*

"Well now you know, and I'm quite able to tell you if you cross a line, without it becoming some sort of dire event."

"That's good to hear," Hollingshed said. "We were a bit unsure what to think when you came aboard. *Shrewsbury'd* just come from the Core, you know, and we'd had several women aboard there, but we'd heard the Fringe was, well, different, I suppose."

"The Fringe or Fringe women?" Alexis asked with a smile.

"Both, to be honest," Nesbit said, finally speaking again. "I'd expected all the girls out here to be locked away in cloisters."

"Skirts never above the ankle," Hollingshed added.

Nesbit nodded. "Veils."

"Virtue guarded every moment."

"And none too bright, truth to tell."

"Vaporish," Hollingshed said with a gleam in his eye.

"Prone to hysteria."

"Not to be bothered with such things as voting or finance or property matters, of course."

"Horrid dancers."

Alexis had been looking from one to the other as they'd laid out their expectations, sad that, much as they were teasing her, there were plenty, if not most, of the Fringe Worlds that were exactly like they described. Perhaps not all of them, nor all the same, but of all the prejudices on the Fringe Worlds, women tended to be the most universal target.

Part of that was due to the natural divisions of work in a developing colony, she knew, and part to a certain over-protectiveness when a new colony's limited medical care made childbirth a surprisingly dangerous proposition for those raised in the Core, but there was also something else to it that bewildered her.

She'd encountered it in her former captain, Neals, aboard *Hermione*, and couldn't entirely dismiss the man's attitudes as coming solely from what she was certain was insanity. Still, she'd seen not a bit of that in the officers or crew of *Shrewsbury*.

Nesbit's final comment registered and she shoved his shoulder, laughing. "Beast!"

"So did you enjoy your evening with Mister Eades otherwise?" Hollingshed asked.

"I'll allow I did learn some things, but enjoyment isn't in it," she answered. "You gentlemen are awake quite late."

"I have the middle," Hollingshed said with a grimace, referring to the middle watch which ran from midnight to four a.m. "Not much point in trying to sleep until then."

Nesbit raised his glass with a smile. "And I couldn't leave the poor man to drink alone."

Alexis smiled in return.

"And worse than the middle alone," Hollingshed went on, "I've to share it with our young Artley."

Nesbit shook his head sadly. "That one'll never make an officer."

"Is he truly that bad?" Alexis asked. She'd had little contact with Artley. Not surprising since there were more than a dozen midshipmen aboard *Shrewsbury,* along with the ship's crew of over seven hundred men.

Hollingshed grimaced. "You'll see for yourself soon enough," he said. "He's not a bad lad, truly, but he's timid as a mouse and clumsy." He shrugged. "The hands are starting to lose respect for him, I think."

"I see," Alexis said. That would, indeed, be bad. The men aboard were willing enough to take orders from midshipmen, even the youngest of them. They'd even take a likely youngster in hand and help him along if they thought he'd make a good officer one day.

Lord knows what I'd have done myself, she thought, *without the good opinion of* Merlin's *crew.*

But if the crew lost respect for him, even the little bit they might have for a very young midshipman, then Hollingshed was likely right and the lad would never make an officer.

And I'm to rely on him for my gundeck in action.

Alexis took another sip of wine and grimaced. Perhaps it would be best to take the lad's measure earlier, rather than later, and the quiet of the middle watch might make a fine time to do so.

"Would you be at all interested in trading watches, Hollingshed?" she asked. "I have the first dog tomorrow, if you like."

"A full night's sleep and a shortened watch tomorrow?" He nodded. "Aye, I'll take that trade and thank you for it. Wish to get a better look at the bad bargain our captain's given you?"

Alexis shrugged. "I'll not call it a bad bargain until I've worked with the lad, but I'd rather have the boy's measure before next gun drill ... or, worse, an action."

"He's not seen an action from the gundecks," Hollingshed warned her. "Captain's kept him on the quarterdeck."

Alexis winced. The quarterdeck was one of the safest places to be in action, with the thicker hull that protected it. That hull could be breached by enemy shot, but *Shrewsbury* hadn't encountered such an action since either Alexis or Artley came aboard. If the lad hadn't been to the gundecks, even during drill, how would he react to the chaos and danger?

FIVE

THE MUTED TONE of the ship's bell began sounding as Alexis slid the hatch to the quarterdeck open. Lieutenant Barr looked up from the circular table of the navigation plot that comprised the center of the compartment and raised an eyebrow.

"Hollingshed and I have exchanged watches," Alexis said, crossing to his side.

Barr nodded.

Alexis studied the plot to familiarize herself with *Shrewsbury's* course and speed, as well as the positions of the merchant ships in the convoy. Those positions were plotted based on images of the other ships brought inboard from *Shrewsbury's* hull by a complex series of optics that kept the radiations of *darkspace* at bay. None of the ship's other sensors were functional in the odd realm filled with dark energy and dark matter — they'd have to wait until they transitioned back to normal-space at a Lagrangian point in some star system before those could tell them anything.

The spacers who'd be standing the middle watch with her were already present, waiting beside the consoles they'd be manning, some whispering with those going off watch to pass along anything important. Not that there would be much of that since they'd taken the frigate that had been dogging the convoy's heels.

All of the spacers for the next watch were present, Alexis noted, save Artley, but just as the final note of the bell sounded, the hatchway slid open and he rushed onto the quarterdeck smoothing his uniform and trying to control his gasps for breath.

Barr gave Alexis a small grimace and Alexis fought down a surge of irritation. She was torn between sympathy for the lad having to make his way in a strange environment and irritation that he couldn't manage to find his way to his watch station until the very last moment.

Was I ever in such a state? she asked herself, struggling not to smile at the thought.

"I have the deck, Lieutenant Barr," she said.

"The deck is yours," he agreed. "There are no changes to the standing orders." He nodded to her, and glanced at Artley who was murmuring to Thedford at the signals console. Everyone else from the previous watch had already left the quarterdeck. He gave a little sigh and shrugged to her before leaving.

Alexis reviewed the state of the navigation plot, noting the positions of the ships in the convoy. She settled into her place to enjoy the quiet for a time. She'd always liked standing the middle watch best, running from the ship's midnight to four a.m. when the hands would wake and *Shrewsbury* would begin to bustle and echo with the sounds of the day's activity.

In the quiet of the night, with the other officers and Captain Euell all asleep, *Shrewsbury* was truly hers. Barring a storm or significant change in the winds, she could order sail and course changes, even issue orders to the entire convoy, without anyone questioning her. She caught her lower lip between her teeth to keep from grinning.

Until morning when the captain reviews the log and asks why I've sent his convoy zig-zagging about to my whims.

"Mister Artley, a throw of the log, if you please," she said. "I'd admire an update to our course."

"Aye, sir."

She made a point of watching surreptitiously as he worked the signals console to send her order out to the spacers minding the sails. *Darkspace* was a featureless void, with not even stars to navigate by — only a constantly roiling mass of shadowy storms were visible in the distance. Once a ship was out of sight of a system's pilot boat, assuming there was one, the only way to navigate was through dead reckoning.

One of spacers would have to take the log to the ship's keel and launch the weighted bag outside of *Shrewsbury's* field, where it would stick in the morass of dark matter that permeated *darkspace*. The bag was attached to a line and timed. How much line was pulled out in that time would tell Alexis how fast *Shrewsbury* was traveling and the angles to the bag at the end would give her an idea of the ship's speed, course, and drift.

What made the whole system work was the odd effect *darkspace* had on distances. The farther a ship traveled from a star system, from any normal-space mass, really, the faster or farther it traveled in *dark-space*, but to the ship itself, the speed appeared constant and quite slow. So though the thrown log might only strip a few hundred meters of line off the log's reel, *Shrewsbury* herself might have made light years of normal-space distance.

Or not ... I never have been sure if we're traveling faster or farther or what.

Since a ship could only transition back to normal-space — and that only in star systems and at particular places called Lagrangian points — there was no way to tell how the distances between matched up.

Of course, none of that would happen if Artley didn't relay her order to the crew outside.

Alexis frowned as the time dragged on and Artley pecked at the signals console. It was a simple, common order, given four or more times each watch, and this was not Artley's first time at the console. In fact he'd spent all his watches there, as it was often the assignment given to the most junior midshipman on watch.

Artley finally reported that the order had been relayed to the spacers outside via the ship's fiber optics, no electronics being functional outside the hull in the *darkspace* radiations.

Once the log had been thrown and the information relayed back inside, Alexis bent over the navigation plot to update the ship's course. She ran her own calculations, then allowed the plot's computer to do so. She grinned as she saw that hers was not too far off the computer's — it had been a long time since she'd once plotted her ship's position all outside of known space, but the mental hoops required for *darkspace* navigation still tripped her up from time to time. That she and the rest of *Shrewsbury's* crew relied on what were essentially guesses of the ship's speed and direction for their safe arrival did still make her a bit queasy.

When she was done, she displayed Artley's records on the navigation plot to review them. The time he'd taken to relay a simple, expected order, and the uncertainty he'd shown, troubled her. She'd have to rely on him to command or even help man half her guns in the next action, and what she'd seen of him so far made her far from confident.

Artley was new to *Shrewsbury*, she saw, with not very much more time aboard than she herself had. He'd come aboard just as the ship left the Core Worlds for the Fringe. That in itself wasn't unusual. *Shrewsbury* had transferred to the Fringe from Core Fleet just before she'd come aboard and fully half the crew and officers were new to the ship.

True, *Shrewsbury* was Artley's first ship and he'd been in the Navy no longer than he'd been aboard, but midshipman recruits in the Core Worlds were most often from families with a Naval tradition. Artley's lack of confidence and knowledge didn't speak of someone from a Naval family and his records confirmed it. It seemed he'd had no prior contact with the Navy at all.

Alexis' frown deepened. From most Fringe Worlds the Navy was a step up for a young lad who didn't want to follow in whatever work his father performed, especially if one could become a midshipman, an officer in training, rather than as common crew. But Artley had come from the Core, where there were far more opportunities and options available. Why, the lad hadn't even finished the basic schooling available in the Core. True, there were ample opportunities for him to study with *Shrewsbury's* systems, but it was still odd. What could have made him sign aboard ship? And more so, what could have convinced his family to allow it?

Whatever the reason, his records didn't say. She closed them and crossed to stand next to him at the signals console.

"Mister Artley?"

Artley jumped, as though he'd been unaware that Alexis had approached, and turned to face her. "Sir?"

"I'm given to understand that you'll be joining my division on the upper gundeck, in place of Mister Blackmer."

Artley nodded. "Yes, sir."

He swallowed and Alexis thought she saw his eyes glisten.

Were they close, then? And has anyone thought to comfort him after Blackmer's death?

It was hard to know. *Shrewsbury* had eighteen midshipmen aboard, ranging in age from Artley's twelve to a practically ancient one of twenty-three — who'd failed to pass for lieutenant so often that he'd likely resigned himself to being a midshipman forever — and their berth was a chaotic one. Alexis had visited once, then left and thanked her fate that she'd been promoted lieutenant without having served aboard a ship so large as *Shrewsbury*.

It was hard enough being the only girl of six aboard Hermione. She shuddered at the thought of what *Shrewsbury's* midshipmen's berth might be like for her, though none of the lads aboard were near so vile as *Hermione's* had been.

Still, the Navy did tend to forget that the midshipmen were little more than young lads, or, as in Artley's case, barely more than children. *Shrewsbury* had seen little action since leaving the Core Worlds and Blackmer had been the first death aboard, save by accidents Outside on the hull. Artley had likely never lost a friend at all, much less by so violent circumstances.

Alexis laid a hand on Artley's shoulder.

"He was a good lad, Blackmer was."

Artley nodded, swallowing again.

"You'll have a time of it filling his shoes, but I've confidence you'll do him proud."

There was little else she could say. Not on the quarterdeck with other hands about to hear. She made a mental note to speak to the boy more later, though, and to ask Slawson about the matter when he returned. As second lieutenant he was nominally in charge of the midshipmen's berth. When she'd have time to do so she wasn't sure, though.

Alexis returned to the navigation plot and noted that one of the merchantmen in the convoy was drifting from the projected course.

"Mister Artley," Alexis said, "*Imperial Rose* has been sailing a point or two to leeward and is falling away from us. Make a signal to request she come up a bit and rejoin the convoy."

Artley spun around and looked at her with wide eyes. He gulped visibly. "Aye, sir."

Alexis watched him out of the corner of her eye while appearing to stare at the navigation plot. Artley pecked at his console for a long time before she saw the signal go out, lights on *Shrewsbury's* masts and hull flashing and changing color to signal the other ship. Alexis sighed. Far too long, but the other ship did see the signal and firmed up her course to remain with the convoy.

SIX

SHREWSBURY SAID goodbye to the last of the merchant vessels as expected, but added a fast packet from New London that was waiting at their last stop before entering French space. They were within sight of the pilot boat for the Caillavet system, but still in *darkspace*. As the merchants were leaving them and *Shrewsbury* had adequate supplies, Captain Euell saw no need to transition. Instead he passed a message back via the pilot boat and waited while the packet joined them in *darkspace*.

The packet made fast to *Shrewsbury's* starboard side, matched docking tubes, and passed along its messages.

Eades quickly closeted himself with Courtemanche; there'd apparently been some last minute priority instructions for him aboard the packet.

All through *Shrewsbury's* wardroom, the officers' tablets *pinged* as messages were processed through *Shrewsbury's* system and delivered. Alexis felt a moment's anxiety, as she had ever since her time on *Hermione*.

On that ship one of the midshipmen had placed a filter in the messaging system that had prevented any of her messages from being sent or delivered. She knew that *Shrewsbury* — that most ships, even — was far different than *Hermione* had been, but the experience had still left her with scars.

Scars on mind and body, she thought, as her own tablet *pinged* and she felt her body release the tension.

She worried every time *Shrewsbury's* messages caught up with them that hers were going astray again. Sometimes, not always, certainly, but sometimes, when Captain Euell ordered a change in *Shrewsbury's* sails, she would tense, waiting to hear the echo of *Hermione's* captain call out, "And flog the last man down from the yards!"

The scars on her back, where that same Captain Neals had ordered her flogged, had healed well. *Shrewsbury's* surgeon had even performed some work on them that had eased the tightness when she stretched too far. They were still visible — thin, white traces across her skin, some of them raised — but bothered her little.

I could wish my mind had healed so completely. Living in constant fear for near six months leaves a mark as deep as any lash.

She scanned through her messages quickly. There were several from her grandfather back on Dalthus and she opened the last of these, relieved to read his first words assuring her that everyone was well.

That was the most important thing, and she'd read them in detail at her leisure. She hoped there might be word of his attempts to gain support for changing Dalthus' inheritance laws to allow her to inherit his lands, but the situation was unlikely to have changed from the last she'd heard. It was a slow process, trying to garner support first to place an amendment to the colony's charter on the ballot for the next conclave of the settlers, then trying to get enough votes to pass it.

There was a message from Mister Grandy, the solicitor she'd consulted with in the Penduli system about Isom's situation. Isom had been a legal clerk and was taken up by the Impress Service. Thrown aboard ship with no knowledge of the Navy and with a still-bleeding tattoo to "prove" he was a spacer. With *Shrewsbury* not only away from Penduli but about to leave New London space entirely, there was little Grandy could do about the matter, though he was still trying to get Isom's impressment records sent to him.

Alexis was somewhat surprised at Isom's attitude toward the whole matter. He seemed to have given up on any hope of challenging his impressment and become resigned to being aboard *Shrewsbury*.

"Passing the word for Lieutenant Carew," Midshipman Slayden called from the wardroom hatch. "Lieutenant Carew, sir?"

Alexis looked up from her tablet and realized that she'd been lost in thought for some time and not looking at her messages at all. In fact, she'd not fully read a single one.

"Yes, Mister Slayden?"

"That Mister Eades is asking for you, sir," Slayden said.

Alexis sighed. "Of course he is. Thank you, Slayden."

She made her way to Eades' cabin and knocked, entering at Eades' shout of acknowledgment from within.

"Come in, come in," Eades called.

He and Courtemanche were hunched over the table in their day cabin. The table's surface displayed a star map and several messages. Courtemanche was frowning and running his fingers over several systems, measuring distances.

"Come over here, Carew," Eades said, not taking his eyes from the table. "Look here, we've just received word of the forces being assembled for our efforts."

Alexis approached the table. She could make out the worlds of the Berry March highlighted on the starmap. Eades tapped a system quite near the border.

"Here at Alchiba," he said. "A fleet of forty warships and over a hundred transports."

"Sixty thousands of men," Courtemanche said, grinning widely, "cavalry, air ... all that will be needed."

Alexis frowned. "Should you be telling me this, sirs?"

Eades waved his hand in the air. "It isn't as though the

Hanoverese could have a spy aboard this ship, Carew. Just don't you go blabbing it about."

Alexis ignored that, concentrating instead on what Eades had said of the forces being assembled. "Did you say only a hundred transports?" The transports would be smaller than *Shrewsbury* and, though they'd have a smaller crew as well, wouldn't be able to transport nearly as many men. She thought the usual number was to place three hundred men aboard a troop transport and had no idea how much space these cavalry or air forces would require.

"I'm assured its enough. Possibly more than one round-trip required," Eades said. "Top men were involved in this planning. Top men. In any case —"

He was interrupted by the sound of bosun's pipes over the ship's speakers, followed quickly by the drum signaling that they beat to quarters.

Eades frowned. "Isn't that what they played just before we attacked the Hanoverese frigate?"

"It is," Alexis said, "but this will be only a drill. Captain Euell said that he wished to exercise the guns as soon as that packet was off with our dispatches."

"Hmph. And I suppose you must join the rest of the crew for this nonsense?"

Alexis tried to keep her face impassive and not smile. In truth the opportunity to exercise the guns again thrilled her and that it interrupted more of Eades' company was a pleasant bonus.

"I'm afraid so, sir," she said. "If you'll excuse me?"

SEVEN

"Ready forward!"

Alexis peered through the nearest gunport at the short tube of hull material *Shrewsbury* would use as a target for gunnery drill. It was being towed on a long line by the captured Hanoverese frigate. As she waited for the aft guns to be ready, bolts of light flew toward the target from the main gundeck, blasting great holes in the target.

"Read ... ready aft!"

"*Fire!*" Alexis called almost immediately.

Captain Euell had set the decks in competition against each other for this drill, and they weren't so far behind that they couldn't catch up, if only Artley and his teams would speed things along a bit.

Alexis stepped back and watched the teams working to reload. Forward the work went as efficiently as she could hope, but the aft guncrews were frequently in disarray. Loaders found themselves having to check their pace on the way to the breech, gun captains found access to their gun's breech blocked, men examining the barrels were jostled out of position and forced to begin again, and all, as nearly as Alexis could tell, a result of Midshipman Artley placing himself in the wrong place at the wrong time.

How on earth can a single boy find himself under so many feet?

"Mister Artley!" she called. "Stand clear of the guns unless your assistance is required!"

She turned to the fore guns as Artley's "Aye, sir!" crackled over her suit radio. Walborn's crews were moving with the smooth motions she'd come to expect. The more senior midshipman stayed out of his crews' way, stepping in only when needed and knowing where to stand so that he'd not impede their work.

Captain Euell had taken advantage of the last merchantmen departing to exercise *Shrewsbury's* guns on a daily basis, and Artley should have gained the knack of at least staying out of the way by now.

"Ready forward!"

Alexis peered out through the nearest port. Shot flashed from the main gundeck below to strike the target.

"Ready a-aft!"

"Fire!"

Her deck was a full ten or more seconds behind the others now. She had a sudden urge to rub her forehead at the frustration of it, stopped only by the helmet of her vacsuit.

Shouts of alarm sounded over the radio. Alexis drew back from the port and looked around, then rushed aft as she saw the crowd of spacers around the eleven gun struggling with something. She couldn't make out what was wrong until she got there; the shouts ran over each other.

She shoved her way through the crowd of men from the other guns and found Artley. The eleven gun's captain and crew were struggling to free the gun's breech where the sleeve of Artley's vacsuit was caught. A jet of vapor streamed from his suit where the breech torn it, and Artley was struggling to pull himself free. As she watched, his struggles lessened and the jet of vapor trailed off. At first, Alexis thought that his suit had finally sealed against the tear and he had calmed as his suit reaired, but then saw his right hand go to his helmet's collar.

"No!" Alexis leapt forward and grabbed his arm before he could release his helmet.

Something must have gone wrong with his suit and it hadn't sealed. Artley was out of air and trying to remove the helmet, not caring in his desperation that the entire deck was in vacuum. One of the spacers grasped Artley's upper arm and pressed tightly, trying to keep any remaining air in the suit. Artley's struggles against Alexis' grip on his arm continued.

The gun captain grabbed a discarded shot canister and slammed it against the breech, which moved just enough to free Artley's suit.

As he was freed, the surrounding spacers grabbed his limp form and rushed him to the aft companionway's airlock. One of them had a roll of vacsuit repair tape out and was winding it around Artley's arm, but Alexis could see that it would do no good — the rest of Artley's suit was limp and unaired.

Alexis rose and rushed after them, sliding inside just as the hatch shut and keying her radio.

"We've a decompression on the upper gundeck! Mister Castell to the aft companionway!"

She clenched her teeth as she waited for the lock to cycle. Surely the boy would be all right. She tried to think of how long it had been since the last of the air jetted from Artley's suit and how long it had taken to get him to the airlock. It couldn't have been more than thirty seconds in total that he'd been in vacuum.

Castell, *Shrewsbury's* surgeon, met them as they descended the ladder to the orlop deck and his surgery. Alexis followed, but once on the orlop Castell's mates rushed Artley into a compartment and shut the door behind. Alexis and the men from the gundeck were left standing outside.

Alexis pulled Caris, the gun crew's captain aside.

"Did you see how this happened?"

"Saw the what, not sure as to how," Caris said. "We was rushin' and the breech stuck some. That gun does a'times. Have to slam it, forceful like. So we slams it shut and Mister Artley he goes to stand, but he jerks halfway up. Like he's held down, you see? But then he throws his other arm and shouts 'Ready aft', only stuttering as the lad's wont to do when he's nervous. So then you yells fire an' he yells fire an' it's only then that I sees his suit's all caught in the breech, but it's too late, you understand, a'cause of I've already slammed down on the button and all."

Alexis winced. Artley must have known his suit was caught in the breech and called ready regardless. She shook her head. There was a constant demand for faster and faster broadsides in gun drills in preparation for real actions. Two ships might be evenly matched in their number and weight of guns, but the one that could fire faster and more accurately had the decided advantage. A smaller, even much smaller, ship could defeat a larger one if her gunnery was sufficiently better. Still, Artley should not have taken the risk — perhaps in a real action it might have been worth the chance that his suit wouldn't be damaged, but certainly not in a drill.

"You did well getting him down here so quickly, Caris." Alexis squeezed his shoulder. "You and the lads go on up and help set things right after the drill. I'll wait here and send you word as soon as there is any."

"Aye sir." He gestured to the others of the guncrew who'd gathered. "He's a ... well, he's a likable enough lad, he is."

Alexis watched the men file out of the sick berth.

Aye, 'likeable'. Not 'a good lad', nor a 'promising' one, nor even 'likely', which says much about how the crew sees him — and I can't much argue myself.

EIGHT

"A BAD BIT OF BUSINESS, Carew. Will the boy be all right?"

Alexis joined Nesbit at the wardroom table and nodded thanks as Isom set a glass of bourbon before her without her having to ask — he must have suspected that she'd want more than wine. She took a sip and rubbed her forehead.

"Castell says he will be," she said. "I've just been to see the captain and report. Artley's resting now, but should be up and about by the end of the watch. He started breathing on his own before we'd even got him to the orlop and Castell says that's a good sign. He's dreadfully swollen, though that should be gone by the end of the watch as well."

"Swollen?" Nesbit asked. "How so?"

Alexis grimaced. A vacsuit's liner was designed to fit snugly, keeping everything but one's face safe from swelling in the event of decompression.

"His suit liner was as ill-fitting as the suit itself." Alexis took another drink. "All but useless. Whoever fitted him out for his kit did a criminal job of it. Aside from the size, the suit itself is substandard.

It's naught but what one would expect in some ferry's emergency locker, there for show and good for little else."

Nesbit frowned. "Why would his family send him off so ill-equipped?"

"I've no idea, but the suit failed to seal at all — neither at the tear nor the emergency seals farther up his arm — and so all of his air simply vented."

"Why was he near the gun's breech to begin with?"

"Who knows?" Alexis sighed and drained her glass. "Perhaps he thought the shot was misaligned? I despair of understanding what that boy is thinking at times. One might as well tie a note to a rock and throw it to another ship when he's on the signals console and he's forever underfoot of the gun crews. I fear the lad will never make a spacer and, worse, that he or someone else will die of it before he's done."

There was a strangled sound from the wardroom's hatch and Alexis turned to see Artley there with Caris, the eleven gun's captain. Artley was still in the sweat-soaked underthings he'd worn under his vacsuit, his hair disheveled, hands and feet swollen and painful-looking, with red-rimmed, bloodshot eyes.

Alexis' heart fell as she took in the look on his face and realized that he'd heard her every word.

"Artley —"

The boy sobbed again, turned, and fled.

Caris cleared his throat and looked down at the deck, scratching the back of his head.

"Was helping the lad back to his berth to rest," he said, "but he'd not go until he'd seen you, sir. Said he wanted to apologize for disappointing you."

NINE

SHREWSBURY'S HOLD was well-lit but still full of the nooks and crannies a twelve-year old boy would find useful as a hiding place. Alexis had spent a good deal of time in such places aboard her last ship, *Hermione*, and so had begun searching the hold after seeing that Artley wasn't in his own berth.

She wasn't at all certain what she'd say when she did find him, though. She regretted that he'd heard her intemperate words, but that made her evaluation of him no less true, and it was past time someone had a serious talk with the boy about his place in the Navy.

It was possible he simply wasn't suited to life aboard ship and should be put ashore. That might be a disappointment to his family if they'd hoped to start a Naval tradition with Artley's service, but Alexis couldn't imagine them sending Artley to space so ill-equipped and unprepared if they did. Still, better they were disappointed by his not becoming an officer than by his death.

Alexis dropped to her knees to crawl through the low space between two towering vats of the weak beer served to the crew in lieu of recycled water. The curving sides of the vats met, but formed a sort of tunnel at the floor. It was a tight squeeze and awkward even for her small frame. Artley could manage it under normal circumstances, she thought, but might have trouble with his current injuries. Still, she knew there'd be an open space at the end where these vats backed against the next row and their curving sides formed a sort of small, low-ceilinged room.

The light back there was dim, as it was blocked from above and only came in through the low tunnels that gave access, but Alexis was still able to see Artley. It seemed she'd found a place he came often, not just today, for he had a ship's blanket and pillow there with him, as well as a litter of crisps wrappings that spoke to many visits.

He was hunched over, still in his sweat-soaked underthings but wrapped in the blanket, hair disheveled from his suit helmet, and hugging his knees.

Alexis eased herself out of the tunnel and cleared a space amongst the crinkly wrappers. She rested her own back against the vat, knees drawn up so as not to encroach too much on Artley's space, and was silent for a time.

"Mister Artley," she prompted finally.

Artley simply hugged his legs to him more firmly and buried his face in his knees.

Alexis frowned. She was sorry for the boy, but this was still the Navy and such behavior wasn't tolerated. Artley faced a hard decision, and harder work if he chose to stay aboard and not resign his place.

"In another ship, with another officer, Mister Artley, such dumb insolence would find you sent to seek out Mister Huben and put to kissing the gunner's daughter."

The ship's gunner was tasked with discipline of the younger midshipmen. In addition to mastheading, being sent to the very top of the ship's mast and left there for an entire watch, if the offense were grievous enough, they'd find themselves bent over one of the ship's guns and thrashed. Nothing like the floggings the crew faced, but threat enough for a young midshipman.

Artley raised his face and Alexis saw the tears. "I'm sorry, sir."

"No. No, I'm the one who's to apologize, Artley." She sighed. "Not for the meaning of what I said, mind you, but the way it was uttered and that you heard it the way you did." She met his eyes and saw fresh tears, but went on. "I should have spoken to you long before this."

Part of her wanted to blame Eades and his damnable lessons, but the fact was that Artley had become her responsibility when he'd joined her division and she'd failed to pay as much attention to the boy as she should. Eades might cause her to have less time, but it was up to her to still perform her duties — one of which was to see to the midshipmen who reported to her. She'd just been lucky with Walborn and Blackmer, that they were experienced and required little in the way of her time.

"What prompted you to join the Navy, Mister Artley? What did you hope to find here?"

"I don't know, sir."

"I'd expect such an answer from a new hand, half drunk and the other half addled by the Press' cosh, Mister Artley, but young gentlemen do not arrive aboard in that condition. I may reasonably expect that you were both conscious and sober when you came aboard *Shrewsbury* and can make some account of the circumstances. Please do."

"I truly don't know why I'm here, sir," Artley said, looking, if possible, even more miserable. "I never thought to join the Navy ... I always thought that I'd work in my Da's shop. That's what he always said to me."

Artley was silent for a time and Alexis prompted, "The circumstances of coming aboard *Shrewsbury*, Mister Artley?"

He nodded. "I woke one morning and my Da ... not my real Da, he died a year or more ago, but the man my mum took up with, you understand? He said I should call him Da, too, though I didn't want to." He paused again and Alexis nodded for him to continue. "Well, he woke me and said I was off to someplace that would make a man of me. Mum was all crying and carrying on, and I thought I was being

53

sent away to school. Da ... the man Mum married ... well, he took me off with not a thing packed and then he sent me aboard a shuttle with a Navy captain. First I heard of being in the Navy was when we reached his ship and he showed me a chest and bag he said were my things. He had me put on a midshipman's uniform and next I knew I was back in a boat and on my way to *Shrewsbury* ... and barely an hour aboard here before we were making way for the transition point and Lieutenant Slawson was shoving me out the hatch onto the hull and demanding I name for him all these parts of a ship I'd never seen before!"

Alexis blinked. The story had come out in such a rush that she wasn't sure she had the full of it.

"Tell me if I understand," she said. "Your father, your real father, owned a shop and told you it would be yours one day?"

Artley nodded. "I'd work with him every day after school. It's a fine shop."

"But he died? And your mother's met a new man?"

Artley nodded again. "I don't like him."

"I should think not," Alexis said. "And they, neither of them, spoke to you of the Navy ever?"

"Never, sir. He talked of sending me away for schooling, but never the Navy."

"I see," Alexis said, quite afraid that she did. "Do you know at all what arrangements your father made? Your real father, I mean. For the shop and for you and your mother upon his death?"

Artley shook his head and Alexis frowned. Artley might not know, but she certainly had her suspicions. A fine shop left to another man's son and a new husband who might wonder what would be left for him when the son came into his majority. What better way to have it for himself than to send the boy away to the Navy? Especially with a war on and the very real possibility of Artley being killed.

"What a vile business."

"Sir?"

Alexis studied his face, but it seemed Artley was oblivious to his stepfather's possible motives. He seemed innocently bewildered by what had happened to him. If being put aboard ship had come as such a surprise, might that have something to do with how he performed his duties? Alexis hesitated, looking at the lad. He was obviously still shaken by his close call and she wondered if it was the best time to be having this conversation. Still, perhaps it was the perfect time to drive home the seriousness of life aboard ship, regardless of whether it was the life Artley would choose for himself.

"Is it safe to say that you've never wanted to be in the Navy?" she asked.

Artley shook his head. "Never thought of it, sir."

"And safe to say that the Navy's still not where you wish to be?"

Artley hesitated, perhaps afraid to answer, and Alexis raised an eyebrow.

"I just want to go home."

"Mister Artley, I will allow you just this one meeting for a whinge like that." Alexis fought to keep her face stern as his expression fell. Perhaps he'd wanted some sympathy and she longed to give it to him, but the truth was he was in the Navy, aboard ship, and very far from home. If he didn't give it his best efforts, then the prediction she'd made in the wardroom would come true and someone, likely Artley himself, would be dead of it. "You are aboard this ship. Perhaps you'll one day return home, but while aboard I'll have your best efforts in your duties. Your very *best* efforts, Mister Artley, which I suspect no one aboard *Shrewsbury* has yet seen."

"I —"

"Think on this," she said, interrupting him. "Had this morning's incident happened during an action, you would surely be dead."

Artley looked at her eyes wide. "But —"

"That entire guncrew came to your aid — in an action, you'd have been shoved to the side for Mister Castell's loblolly boys to take below in their own time. I would not have come to your aid myself, and stopped you taking your helmet off in a full bloody vacuum.

55

Moreover, there are eight hundred men aboard *Shrewsbury* who depend upon those best efforts of yours for their own lives."

Artley winced and looked away.

"If your father — your real father — truly intended to leave his shop to you then you must have previously exhibited some degree of competence as yet unseen aboard this ship. I need to see that competence, Mister Artley. I need you to apply yourself to *Shrewsbury's* work as diligently as I'm certain you did in your Da's shop. Study your signals and use your bloody head at the guns, do you hear me?"

"Aye sir."

"Though about this little hidey-hole here, Mister Artley."

"Aye sir. I'll stop coming down here."

"No, you needn't stop completely. There's nothing wrong with wanting a bit of time to yourself — Lord knows it's hard to find a moment's quiet to think aboard ship, but do try to spend some time with your berthmates. They're not bad lads at all."

"I will, sir, thank you."

Alexis shoved a pile of crisp wrappers to the side. "But when you are here, I'll have no more this, do you understand? I plan to start inspecting this space and if I find it anything but as tidy as your berth it'll go poorly for you."

"Aye sir."

TEN

"DAMN HIM. DAMN HIM TO HELL."

"Sir?"

"Roger Corbel, Carew. *Captain* Roger Corbel of *Feversham*. He's the one sent me Artley, you see." Euell rose and began pacing. "Never would have believed he'd be in a business so vile as you've just described, though. Damn the man. And damn me."

"You, sir?"

"For not paying enough attention when the lad came aboard." Euell sat again, his nostrils flaring in anger. "Corbel told me that Artley was a distant relation in need of a berth — it's not uncommon. A captain might not want a relative aboard his own ship for any number of reasons and so he asks a fellow captain to take the boy. And *Shrewsbury'd* just been through the bloody Purge, so I had need of more midshipmen."

"The Purge, sir?" Alexis asked, frowning.

Euell glanced at her. "That's what we of Core Fleet call the pointless reshuffling of crew we go through when we have to sail for the Fringe. Fully half of *Shrewsbury's* crew was replaced before we were allowed to sail, so as not to offend the delicate sensibilities of whichever Fringe Worlds we were likely to be stopping at. It's a bloody nuisance at the best of times and with the war on ... well, not enough replacements for them all." He grimaced in distaste. "It's why you were such a surprise when you came aboard."

Alexis flushed. From Euell's tone she hadn't been a pleasant surprise either.

"Not your fault, Carew. It's just that I left two fine lieutenants and a midshipman behind in the Core for no better reason than their gender might offend some Fringe worthy's thoughts on how the world should be. Half my crew shuffled off to other ships with destinations where they'd not be found offensive for one reason or another. One man's religion, another's preferences." He paused while his steward returned with the wine and took a long drink. "I'll tell you, Carew, there's no few in Core Fleet who are tired of the whole mess and think it's past time Her Majesty told the entire Fringe to by God suck it up and accept the men and women of the Fleet as they are. With a war on, you'd think they wouldn't be so bloody particular about who stands between them and the Hanoverese, would you?"

"No, sir," Alexis said, face fixed and hoping to show no reaction. She wasn't sure what shocked her more, the thought of fleet captains discussing so blatantly what they thought Her Majesty should do or the image of the Queen telling anyone in any way to 'suck it up'. She did know that when faced with a captain of such strong opinions, the best course of action a lieutenant had was to react as little as possible, whether she agreed with him or not.

Which she found she did, come to that.

Euell regarded her for a moment, then laughed. "Drink up, Carew. One of the prerogatives of command, you'll someday find, is the privilege to go on a right good rant while junior officers sit there wondering whether it's best to agree or simply behave like they're part of the chair." He drained his glass and gestured for more. "It's grand fun."

"I'm sure it is, sir."

Euell sighed. "But enough of that — this business with Artley merely brought it to mind again and it's irksome still. Does he suspect the full nature of why he was sent away?"

"I don't think so, sir. It doesn't seem he's thought through the implications his absence will have on his inheritance." She caught her lip between her teeth. "Do you suppose we can find some way to send him home when we reach the French capital?"

Euell blinked as though shocked and shook his head. "No, that's simply not possible. Firstly, it's three months travel, at best, to his home, but more difficult is that he's in the Navy now. With the war on, he can't just resign — oh, they'd allow it, I suppose, but how would it look? A young gentleman resigns in the midst of war? There'd be talk of cowardice being the reason. A judgment which would follow him in all he tries to do."

Alexis nodded, her hopes for Artley falling. Such a thing would indeed follow him, and haunt him. Possibly not if he were to gain his own shop back, but certainly if he ever wanted to do something else with his life, such as university or a position in government.

"And more troubling," Euell went on, "what happens to him should he return home?"

"Sir?"

"Well, Carew, if this man was willing to send him away once, and into the midst of a war at that, he'll certainly do so again, and possibly to someplace worse."

Alexis stopped herself from asking what could possibly be worse than the Navy for a lad such as Artley, but the question must have shown on her face.

"If this truly was some plot to get the boy out of the way so that this man might somehow steal his inheritance, then it's a cold fellow we're dealing with. To send the lad aboard ship in time of war, there had to have been some hope that he'd never return." Euell paused to let that sink in. "Thwarted in that, might he not turn to some plan with a more certain outcome?"

"Do you think he'd do the boy harm?"

"He wouldn't have to, not directly at least. There are any number of schools an unwanted lad might be sent away to, some of them quite harsh. And some, I'm sure, where a hope may be made a certainty if the proper sum is paid."

Alexis' shock must have shown on her face for Euell nodded confirmation.

"Oh, they exist, I assure you. For all most schooling is best done through a tablet and proper learning core, there are still some who prefer a more traditional means. And where there's coin to be had for a vile deed, you'll find men willing to get at it. All of which is moot, for we've no way of getting the lad out of the Navy without harming him in the first place, and no safe way to send him home in the second. No, the lad's stuck and we're stuck with him." He sighed. "Would you like me to transfer him to another division? Hollingshed's, perhaps?"

"No, sir," Alexis said immediately. "I suspect he'd find that more of a rejection and there'd be harm from it." She frowned. "If our speculations are correct, sir, then I assume the stepfather will have provided him no funds, nothing on the ship's account? To purchase a new vacsuit, I mean — a proper one."

Euell shook his head. "I don't recall that he came aboard with anything but the most basic kit." He sighed. "Damn me, but it was a hectic time and I wish I'd paid more attention to the lad."

Alexis nodded. She felt much the same.

"I'll speak to Mister Grummer, sir? About the suit?" *Shrewsbury's* carpenter would be able to cut down a spare spacer's vacsuit, one of the suits the ship carried for the crew, for Artley to use in the meantime, but those suits had all seen long, hard wear.

"Yes," Euell said, "he'll need something better until we get to *Nouvelle Paris*, at least." He frowned, brow furrowed. "And well past *Nouvelle Paris*, come to that. I doubt there'll be a solution for our Mister Artley other than for him to make the best of a bad berth. He wouldn't be the first officer for whom the Navy wasn't a first choice."

ELEVEN

SHADOWS CLOSED *in on her from every side. Dark, flowing masses, reminiscent of the darkspace clouds outside the ship.*

Alexis spun around and tried to run, but knew it was hopeless. The shadows were behind her too, and to all sides.

She turned and figures began to coalesce out of the darkness.

Heads and faces simply masses of shadow, with barely the hint of features, but she could imagine them well enough.

Alexis clenched her eyes shut, murmuring to herself. The phrases and explanations from books she'd read told her that these figures weren't real, that they sprang from her own guilt.

She whispered that to herself over and over, but still when she opened her eyes, what she saw were the figures of men she'd killed or, worse, failed to save still closing in around her.

"You're not real!"

She opened her eyes, but they were still there. She squared her shoulders and faced the central figure. They were all known to her, at least the ones at the forefront, even though they had no faces. This one though, was the one that always drew her attention.

Horsfall, a pirate captain and the first man she'd killed.

He raised his arm to point an accusing finger at her.

"Not real at all," she said. "You're my bloody Id or whatever it's called, that's what the books say."

The shadows remained unimpressed with her books, they never were.

Alexis felt her own arm rising to point and fought to keep it at her side. That was another thing the books said, try to alter the sequence of the nightmare, but again she failed. Her arm leveled with Horsfall's figure, a pistol heavy in her grip.

"I had to," she whispered, as her finger tightened and her arm jerked upward.

Horsfall's figure disappeared in flowing mist and Alexis found her hand empty.

She braced herself. Now the other shadows would come for her as they always did.

Only this time it was different. The others remained where they were while only one stepped forward.

This figure was smaller, only a little taller than Alexis herself.

"Who are you?" she whispered.

ALEXIS WOKE THRASHING in her bunk. Her blanket was tangled and knotted around her and her pillow had been tossed onto the floor sometime in the night. The compartment lights came on as she sat up, dim at first then adjusting slowly brighter. She leaned back against the bulkhead, breath coming in ragged gasps.

The dream wasn't new; she'd had it off and on since the end of her time aboard her first ship. She'd even come to understand it a bit, or at least think she did after reading on the meaning of dreams and some psychology.

She knew well enough that she expected a great deal of herself and suspected, from her reading, that the dream represented that — her feelings that she'd failed the men those figures represented. Even Horsfall, the pirate she felt was the central figure of the dream — he'd have been doomed to hang if she hadn't shot him, and yet she felt that she should have done something different, even though she couldn't think what that might be.

The smaller figure was new, though, and she couldn't think of who it was, who it might represent.

It could be Blackmer, she supposed, but she truly felt no guilt herself for his death. It was only a fluke of that particular action that he'd been killed, not any of Alexis' doing or a result of her orders.

The possibility that it might be Artley, something she was becoming more certain of as she thought about it, disturbed her more, for she'd always before been certain that the shadowy figures were not only men she'd failed, but those who'd died as a result.

If that small figure was Artley ...

The boy's not dead. True, I've failed to teach him as I should these last weeks, but he's still alive. Even the accident with his suit was more his stepfather's doing than mine. She scrubbed her face with her hands and rested her head against the bulkhead. *What's enough? And what does it mean?*

She had a sudden dread that it did mean something, that it meant Artley would die.

"That's foolishness," she muttered, standing. "Utter foolishness."

She slid open the drawer under her bunk and pulled out fresh clothes. Her cabin was much the same as those she'd had as a midshipman aboard other ships. Two meters square with a bunk along one wall and a desk that folded down in the corner. It even had a second bunk above hers and a second corner desk, both of which were folded up against the bulkheads. An advantage of being a lieutenant was that she had the cabin all to herself. The extra bunk was there in case circumstances, such as unexpected passengers, forced some of the lieutenants to share a berth.

At least I've privacy, so no one can hear me when I have that bloody nightmare.

She checked the time on her tablet. It was just shy of six bells in the middle watch, not quite three in the morning. The morning watch would start in an hour and she'd have to be up and about anyway. She grabbed a towel along with her clothes and made her way to the wardroom heads. Another advantage of her lieutenant's commission was a larger water ration than she'd had to make do with as a midshipman. Not as much as she could wish, but enough so that she wasn't feeling forever itchy.

A hot shower usually washed away the remnants of the nightmare, but her concerns over the small figure lingered. She couldn't shake the feeling that it was Artley, and it frightened her no matter how she told herself it was foolishness. It meant that she was going to fail him and cost him his life.

She told herself it was impossible to know such a thing, but stories her grandfather told came to mind. Stories of the grandmother she'd never known — a proud, fiery Scots from New Edinburgh — and her claims to have what she called the Sight.

If New London's founders, with their hereditary aristocracy and insistence that the shilling and farthing were fine ideas, had been eccentric, then New Edinburgh's founders had been barking — they'd seemed intent on bettering every bit of New London's insanity.

Where New London's aristocracy was relatively small, relative to the population, New Edinburgh seemed to have decided that noble rank should be the norm, not the exception. The head of every family styled himself a lord. New London might have instituted a rather liberal *code duello* to settle grievances, but New Edinburgh had elevated the feud to an art form all its own.

Her grandmother had come from that environment. Fiery, proud, short-tempered, and fiercely protective of her clan — her grandfather's stories had painted quite a picture, and Alexis had always regretted that she'd never known her grandmother. Those tales, also, had made it clear that her grandmother was only half-joking when she teased her grandfather about having the Sight.

Alexis shut the water off and dragged her thoughts back to the ship.

"Foolishness and rubbish," she muttered. "The dream's misplaced guilt and Artley, if it is him, is in it because I'm worried for the boy."

She dressed and dried her hair, thinking once again that she should cut it short so that it would dry faster. Instead she pulled it back into a ponytail and checked her uniform in the mirror.

Well, I can fix the worry, I suppose.

If Artley was stuck in the Navy, and it appeared he would be, then she could do her best to give him the tools he'd need to survive, possibly even thrive if he could resign himself to his new life.

There are worse ways for him to make his way in the world, if he can't go home.

She dropped her old clothing back in her cabin, balling up her bedclothes as well. Isom would see to laundering the lot for her and arrange for fresh bedding.

She lay down on the bare mattress and waited until the ship's bell sounded eight times over the speaker. Loud enough to wake the men and not muted and dim as it was overnight. That was the end of the middle watch and start of the morning. The men would be up and about soon and set to cleaning the ship after a brief time for their necessary business.

Alexis left her cabin and made her way down to the hold. At the purser's office, she waited while Plant, the ship's cook, and his assistants gathered supplies for the crew's breakfast. For the men it would be bread and eggs, though the eggs would be from powder reconstituted with the ship's water. Alexis wasn't sure which of the two benefited least from the association.

"Good morning, Mister Grayson," she said as the others left.

"And to you, Lieutenant Carew, sir. What can I do for you this fine morning?"

Alexis glanced away from the purser's counter after the departing cook. She'd learned to have a healthy skepticism of ship's pursers and Grayson's cheerfulness so early in the morning made her wary.

Likely he just got away with shorting the cook on the breakfast breads and looks forward to pocketing the difference.

"Midshipman Artley's had a mishap with his suit," she said. "I'm to see about him using one of the crew's spares for a time."

Vacsuits were expensive and far beyond the means of a common spacer. At between ten and twenty pounds for a decent suit, they could cost a year's pay for a spacer. Officers, of course, purchased their own, but the crew were issued theirs by the purser — and charged a usage fee against their pay. When a man mustered out of the Service or the ship paid off after its commission he returned the suit to the purser — and was charged a fee for any unusual wear and tear, of course.

"Aye, I've some spares, I'll allow," Grayson said, "but is the lad's suit not up to repair? I heard what happened of course, but —"

"Mister Artley's suit is entirely inadequate." She nodded toward the storage cabinets behind Grayson's counter.

"It's only that the boy's so small," Grayson said, spreading his hands. "Once it's cut down for him, who'll we ever have aboard again to wear it?"

"I have every confidence in your ability to find some use for it once we reach *Nouvelle Paris* and can obtain a proper suit for him." She frowned. There was still the question of how Artley might pay for a new vacsuit once they reached that system.

"It's only that —"

"Mister Grayson, a vacsuit for Mister Artley, if you please." Alexis kept her voice level, though she found dealing with pursers and chandlers tiresome. "One of your newer ones, as it's for an officer."

Grayson scowled, but said, "Aye sir," and turned to his cabinets.

Alexis accepted the vacsuit he selected and looked it over briefly. It wasn't what she considered new at all. It was scuffed, stained, and showing more than one place where it had been repaired after a tear from either work or enemy action.

Some, perhaps many, of those repairs would mark where the suit had come back into Grayson's stock with its previous owner marked DD, for Discharged Dead, in *Shrewsbury's* muster book.

Still it was sturdier protection than what Artley had come aboard with. She suspected Grayson had something better back amongst his shelves, possibly even one or more suits new in the box.

Pursers, unlike the other warrant officers aboard ship, paid Admiralty for their warrants and received no salary. They made their wage on the difference between what they paid to supply the ship and what Admiralty would reimburse them for. As such, they were notoriously parsimonious with their supplies and often suspected of dishonesty by the crew.

As *Shrewsbury* had come from the Core, Grayson had likely had the opportunity to buy in new items like vacsuits at a very low price and could trade them at a profit in the Fringe. If he were to trade a new, Core-built vacsuit to a Fringe ship for an older suit and some other supplies, he'd be able to pocket the profit for himself.

Alexis ran a finger over a particularly long patch in the vacsuit's arm.

"And when Mister Artley steps onto the quarterdeck in this, we'll tell Captain Euell it's the very best we have aboard, yes?"

Grayson opened his mouth, closed it, and swallowed hard. Without a word he gathered the suit up and went off amongst his shelves for a moment, returning with another vacsuit.

This one was better, though still not new. Alexis examined it carefully. She considered pushing more, but Grayson was correct that it would be no use to anyone else aboard once it was cut down for Artley's use.

Well, I suppose I could likely fit in it. Her own first vacsuit had been one of full size that was cut down by her first ship's carpenter. Since then she'd been able to replace it with one that was better made to her own small frame.

She nodded and gathered up the vacsuit.

"Thank you, Mister Grayson."

"And Mister Artley will be visiting me to sign for it, will he?"

Alexis sighed and nodded again.

"I'll see that he does."

Grayson would likely see that the cost of the suit was deducted from Artley's pay and he'd get no credit for returning it. Perhaps he could keep it as a spare, as Alexis had with her first vacsuit.

She took the vacsuit across the hold to the carpenter's berth. Grummer was already hard at work fabricating parts for the repairs and replacements that would be done on *Shrewsbury* that day. Behind him a half dozen materials printers hummed and spun, laying out layers of plastic and metal to build up the requested parts.

Grummer met her at the counter and she passed over the vacsuit.

"For Mister Artley?" Grummer asked as he spread the suit out on the counter to examine it.

"Yes," Alexis said. She wrinkled her nose in distaste as Grummer opened the suit and the scent of its previous wearers wafted up. No matter the suit liners that could be removed and washed, the nature of crew's hard work had them sweating right through into the suit itself. Her own smelled no better, but at least it was all her own.

"I've repaired his old one as best I can," Grummer said, "but this will be a sight better."

"Might it be ready by the start of the morning watch tomorrow?"

"Oh, aye, no problem at all."

TWELVE

The next morning saw Alexis awake early again, though the night had spared her any shadowy dreams.

She retrieved Artley's new vacsuit from the carpenter's shop and made her way to the main gundeck, then aft to the gunroom where the midshipmen and warrants berthed. The gunroom was a bit of a madhouse in the morning. The warrants were already up and about the ship, leaving the midshipmen to ready themselves for the day. Alexis stepped through the hatchway to be narrowly missed by a sopping wet towel thrown at Trigg, a lanky boy who'd dodged past the hatch just as she opened it.

The towel struck the bulkhead beside her and drops of water spattered her uniform.

"Gentlemen!" she yelled.

The horseplay ceased immediately at her call, leaving the dozen or so midshipmen who were present scattered about the compartment in various states of dress, all staring wide-eyed at the compartment hatch. Alexis flushed as she caught glimpses of hastily covered bits, but held her ground at the hatchway.

It wasn't the first time she'd caught sight of something she'd rather not have, but that was a part of life aboard very crowded ships. At least she encountered such things less as a lieutenant in *Shrewsbury's* wardroom than she would if she were still a midshipman.

Alexis had never served in a ship of the line as a midshipman, so had never had to deal with a berth so crowded with young men. Her first ship, *Merlin*, had been a sloop-of-war, with only herself and two others. *Hermione*, her second ship, had a complement of six midshipmen, but they were a surly, cruel lot, mirroring the ship's captain. *Shrewsbury* was generally a happy ship and it was reflected in her crew and officers.

She'd often wondered what it might be like to have served in such a berth, but a quick glance around the gunroom convinced her that she might be better off for lacking that experience.

Apparently she'd interrupted some sort of towel battle, as half the midshipmen held towels twisted into whips and the other half stood near those they'd hastily dropped. She looked down at the soaked towel piled on the deck beside her. They must have taken the towels into the head's shower with them, given the low daily water ration midshipmen received.

At least it wasn't a waste of the water. Ships were a closed system. No matter if it went down the drain or evaporated into the air, the water would eventually make its way to *Shrewsbury's* recyclers.

Face impassive, she scanned the assembled midshipmen but didn't see Artley amongst them. With a glance down at the towel that had almost struck her, she walked to the gunroom table and set Artley's new suit on it.

"Is Mister Artley about, Mister Trigg?" she asked the hapless midshipman who'd been the target of the towel that almost hit her.

Trigg was pale and wide-eyed. While a certain amount of horse-play was acceptable in the midshipmen's berth, or even a bit of skylarking through the rigging, it was best kept out of sight of lieutenants and certainly not to be done around the captain. If she'd been struck by the towel, no matter their intent, she could have ordered dire consequences. Even on a happy ship such as *Shrewsbury*, some lieutenants wouldn't abide such an act.

If anything, Trigg went paler at her question and she wondered why.

"I —" Trigg began.

"I'm sorry, sir," Champlin, the senior midshipman, said. "Mister Artley's in his cabin ... may I pass your request on to him?"

Alexis frowned. She looked around the gunroom and each of the midshipmen suddenly found the deck or bulkhead quite fascinating as her gaze passed over them. Not a one would meet her eyes, including Champlin. They were up to something, no doubt. She had a sudden worry for Artley, then forced that thought down. No, none of *Shrewsbury's* midshipmen were cruel or would harm the lad, but still ...

"Is the boy sick, Mister Champlin?"

"No, sir," Champlin said, still looking down at the deck.

"Then I should wish to speak to him."

Champlin's shoulders slumped.

"Aye sir."

He nodded to two of the others, who went to one of the cabin hatches and slid it open. A pile of towels almost as tall as them toppled out to the floor and they bent to pick it up. It was only as they got the pile upright that she saw it wasn't all towels. There was a thin slit at the top, through which she could see a pair of eyes peering out at her.

Thin, towel-wrapped appendages stuck out to either side and two more below, and the entire mess was wrapped round and round with vacsuit repair tape, the sort one could wrap around a holed suit in an emergency.

"Mister Artley?"

The pile shuffled forward, its legs and arms unable to bend. A muffled sound emerged. Alexis was torn between laughter and concern. She fought to keep her face impassive.

"It weren't but a game, sir," Champlin said quickly, quieting when Alexis glared at him.

"Are you quite all right, Mister Artley?"

More muffled sounds emerged.

"Oh, for heaven's sake! Will one of you not free his mouth?"

One of the midshipmen who'd opened the hatch hurriedly tugged at the towels around Artley's head until his mouth was visible. This had the unfortunate effect of covering Artley's eyes, however, and he began slowly swaying back and forth as though unable to keep his balance.

"I'm fine, sir!" Artley called out.

"Hold him steady, will you?" Alexis said. "So that he doesn't topple over." She turned to Champlin. "What exactly is the meaning of this, Champlin?"

"It's as Mister Champlin said, sir!" Artley called out loudly. He shuffled forward again and turned, whacking his toweled arms into the midshipmen around him. "Naught but a game!"

"A game?"

Champlin stepped forward. "It's, well, you see, sir ..." He trailed off.

"Go on, Mister Champlin, I am all a-tingle to gain acquaintance with this new game."

"They all raised the coin to buy me a new vacsuit!" Artley yelled.

"You do not need to yell, Mister Artley, I can hear you quite well."

"What?"

"Gentlemen, can you uncover his ears, as well?" Alexis turned to Champlin again. "Out with it, Mister Champlin."

Champlin squared his shoulders. "Sir, after we saw the real state of Artley's suit, well, we took a bit of a whip-around ... the whole berth put in, you see, even the bosun gave a bit." He shrugged. "It's a tidy sum and'll go most of the way toward a proper suit."

Alexis nodded, happy to see that the gunroom had rallied around Artley in that way. He might not have fit in perfectly since coming aboard, but she was pleased to see she'd been right about *Shrewsbury's* midshipmen. They were a good lot at heart. Still, there was the whole matter of Artley's current state.

"I remain singularly unenlightened, Mister Champlin."

Champlin cleared his throat and scratched his neck. "Well, then someone said —"

"It was me, sir," Trigg said, stepping forward. "It was just that, well, we were looking at that sum — and it's a tidy bit of coin — so I mused on as how we should just build Artley a new vacsuit and spend the lot on a bit of fun when we get to *Nouvelle Paris*."

It was all Alexis could do to keep from laughing.

"And so you built him a suit out of towels and sealant tape?"

"Aye sir," Champlin said, flushing and looking around the berth. "Things deteriorated a bit after that, though."

"So I see."

"I'm quite all right, sir!" Artley yelled, still apparently unable to hear properly. "It weren't but a game, really!"

He waddled forward a few steps, then toppled over to rest on the deck, limbs waving feebly.

Alexis closed her eyes and shook her head slowly. She rested her hand on the vacsuit she'd brought.

"As you can see, gentlemen, I've brought Artley a suit ... a *proper* suit, he can use until we reach *Nouvelle Paris* and he can avail himself of your generosity." She looked down at Artley. "Mister Artley, I'd admire it did you meet me at the sail locker immediately after breakfast."

"What, sir?"

Alexis sighed.

"I'll see he's there, sir," Champlin said.

"Thank you."

Alexis made her way back to the gunroom's hatch, then paused and bent to retrieve the wet towel from the deck. She turned back to look at Trigg, who flushed and swallowed hard. The other midshipmen shifted nervously and Alexis wondered if she hadn't missed out on something after all, something important, in being promoted so quickly and after serving on only two ships.

The other lieutenants spoke with great fondness of friends they'd made as midshipmen. For Alexis' part, she could count only one of those she'd served with as truly a friend, and the count of those she'd relish never meeting again, the midshipmen of *Hermione,* was quite a bit higher.

She kept her face still and stared at Trigg for a three-count before throwing the towel and catching him full in the face.

"As you were, gentlemen," she said as she left and slid the hatch shut.

THIRTEEN

ARTLEY JOINED Alexis at the sail locker hatch carrying his new vacsuit. Alexis had donned hers already and waited while he put his on. Then they entered the lock.

"What are we doing, sir?"

"I thought we should have another talk," Alexis said. She sealed her helmet, as did Artley, and she cycled the lock.

The crew was still at their breakfast and *Shrewsbury* was sailing easy. The captain wouldn't be ordering any course or sail changes until after they'd eaten, unless some sort of emergency came up.

Alexis often went out onto the hull at this time. Much like the middle watch, it had a quiet, peaceful feel to it that she enjoyed.

Once on the hull, she made her way down the bow to the ship's keel. She looked behind her once to make sure Artley was following and that he'd clipped on a safety line to the guidewires that ran along the hull. She'd read more of Artley's record the night before and noted that he'd spent very little time Outside, whether in *darkspace* or normal-space. Lieutenant Slawson, the second lieutenant, who was nominally in charge of the midshipmen had even made a note that Artley didn't join the others in skylarking amongst the rigging in his off-time.

Shrewsbury's keelboard was extended, as she was sailing close-hauled to the wind. It was a thin, telescoping plane that ran the length of the keel and, at the moment, extended over twenty meters from the hull. As the keelboard contained no gallenium, it caught in the morass of dark matter that made up *darkspace*, causing drag that allowed *Shrewsbury* to offset the force of the winds and sail against them.

Alexis pulled herself along the guidewire until she reached *Shrewsbury's* stern, then stopped and waited for Artley to catch up.

When he arrived, she grasped his shoulder and touched her helmet to his. The suit radios were useless outside the hull in *darkspace*, as the dark energy radiations made all electronics inoperable. That also made it the most private way to speak aboard ship, which was why Alexis had brought him here. Artley'd had enough of his business butted about the ship.

"I like to come back here of a morning." Alexis gestured past the stern and the ship's massive rudders. "Are you quite recovered from your vacsuit fitting this morning?"

Artley laughed, his voice echoing oddly as it was transmitted from his helmet to hers. "Yes, sir. It was a mess to get all the tape off, but we managed."

Alexis nodded, though he couldn't see her. She was glad that Artley had taken it well and it seemed to have been a good-natured venture. Especially with the other midshipmen having done a whip-around to raise the funds for a new vacsuit.

"I thought it was quite kind of them to put together that much coin for me," Artley said, echoing her own thoughts. He seemed to be on the verge of saying more so Alexis waited him out. "I talked with Walborn and Champlin quite a bit last night, sir. Pulford and Adley joined us for a time, but mostly Walborn and Champlin." He paused again. "I believe I had a bit too much to drink."

Alexis bit her lip to keep from laughing. Artley might be young yet, but a midshipman's berth would teach one to drink, if nothing else.

"Was it a good talk?"

"Yes ... what I remember of it, I suppose."

"Well, it sounds like you've made a good start, with the gunroom at least." She tried to keep amusement out of her voice. "We've a fine set of lads aboard *Shrewsbury*. You'll find staunch, sturdy friends there."

Artley was quiet for a time and Alexis again waited him out.

"I'll likely never have my Da's shop, will I? That's what they think."

Alexis considered her answer. She didn't want to give the boy false hope, but neither did she want to quash it entirely. He'd have options, after all, though they'd be a difficult road.

"It's not entirely out of the question, Mister Artley, but things do appear that way."

"I never wanted to do anything else ... certainly not the Navy."

"I never wanted to join the Navy myself," Alexis said.

"You didn't?"

"No. All I'd ever hoped for was to inherit my family's lands and go on as he has, taking care of the land and the people."

"And now you don't want to do that anymore?"

"Sometimes yes and sometimes no, Mister Artley ... there's something to be said for the Navy." She gestured off the stern of the ship. "What do you see out there?"

Artley was silent for a moment, then, "The Dark?"

Alexis smiled. She looked off into the distance. Yes, the Dark — full of its roiling clouds of black that seemed to be fighting some battle. Flashes that weren't light, but were somehow blacker than the Dark itself. She wasn't sure how to put her feelings into words for Artley.

"How many people are there on your home world, Artley?"

"Nine billion, I think."

Alexis raised an eyebrow. She'd known *Shrewsbury* and her crew had come from the Core Worlds and what that meant, but the figure was still astounding to her. What must a single planet with nine billion people on it be like? Would there be any space left at all? Dalthus had not a fraction of that number, even if one included those still indentured.

"How many of them, do you suppose, have ever been off the planet? Out of atmosphere?" She thought of her first time stepping through the outer hatch on *HMS Merlin*, her first ship. "How many have seen their own sun except filtered through air? Or seen the stars from behind a planet, where that sun's light doesn't dim them?"

She gestured off the stern again.

"And that out there's an even rarer sight. You've joined a select few, Mister Artley, to look out on the Dark. Even the rich toffs who buy passage between systems and never leave their sealed ships haven't seen it. Just us spacers."

"The men are afraid of the Dark," Artley said.

"And should be," Alexis agreed. "It's harsh and unforgiving, both the Dark itself and life as a spacer, especially the Navy's version — but there, again, you've joined a select few, you know. The Navy's all that stands between the Fringe Worlds and the pirates who'd prey upon them. In this war we stand between Hanover and all of New London."

"Like a wall, sir?"

"Aye, very like a wall. New London's worlds — Fringe and Core, both — are filled with farmers and merchants and families all going about their business. Mister Eades has told me some of what Hanover's done to worlds it wanted ... I'd not have that happen to my world nor yours, not if I can help to stop it."

"I suppose it would be grand to be in some heroic action. Like the ones they strike medals for."

Alexis could almost hear him grinning.

"Or to be made captain ... or admiral even," Artley went on. "Wouldn't that show him?"

Alexis smiled tolerantly. She could tell the 'him' Artley was speaking of would be the stepfather who'd sent him off.

"My Da'd be proud of me for that," Artley finished.

Alexis gripped his shoulder.

"I'm sure your Da would be proud of you regardless, Mister Artley. Live a good life and be happy in what you do, that's what my grandfather always told me would make my parents proud."

Artley was silent for a moment. "What about you, sir? Wouldn't you like to be an admiral someday and have a great cabin all to yourself like that Mister Eades is in?"

Alexis laughed. "Oh, can you see that, Mister Artley? All meter and a half of me dressed up in an admiral's uniform and covered with gilt and medals? The hat itself would be half my size. No, I doubt I'll ever be so grand as that." She gazed off into the Dark, watching the clouds roil against each other. "Though I should like to be made commander one day, I think, and have a ship of my own. Not a 74 like *Shrewsbury* nor even a frigate, but a ship of my own and a willing crew. I think there may be no grander thing."

FOURTEEN

SHREWSBURY CROSSED into French Republic space without incident. They met a pair of French frigates escorting a convoy of their own shortly past the border and received word that Hanover had still made no move to include the Republic in their latest war, though the French had made it clear they were not entirely neutral and no Hanoverese warships would be permitted in French space.

Though they still kept a vigilant watch, the news lessened the anxiety Alexis and *Shrewsbury's* other officers felt. The convoy itself began splitting up, with one or two merchant vessels leaving for their destinations each day. By the time they neared the French capital system there was only *Shrewsbury*, the two French frigates, two merchantmen, and the captured Hanoverese frigate left in the group.

Alexis was with Eades when they arrived at *Nouvelle Paris*. He looked up as the ship's speakers rang with the call for *all hands* to prepare to take in sail as they approached the Lagrangian point that would allow them to transition from *darkspace* into the system.

"Have you ever been to a Core world, Miss Carew?"

Alexis stifled a sigh. He well knew she hadn't, as he'd pointed it out to her often enough in chastising her lack of proper knowledge and behavior. "I have not."

"Well, let's to the quarterdeck, then. That great circle thing in the middle will have the best views from outside the ship and you'll want to see our approach, I'm sure."

"The navigation plot, you mean?" Surely he didn't mean to push his way onto the quarterdeck and stand around the plot? Captain Euell would surely have the deck for their entry into the system and he wouldn't want his passengers cluttering the place up. "I'm not sure if that's wise —"

Courtemanche slid the hatch to his sleeping quarters open and peered out.

"This sound, does it mean we are arrived?"

"It does," Eades said, rising. "Come, Carew."

"Ah!" Courtemanche said. "I have been too long from home. I must see."

"Mister Eades," Alexis tried to protest, but the other two were already at the hatch and she had no choice but to obey Eades' come-along gesture. "Mister Eades, *Monsieur* Courtemanche, it is not customary for passengers to enter the quarterdeck, especially during transitions. The captain —"

Eades made a dismissive sound and waved her objections away. "Captain Euell has been tasked with providing this mission every assistance and accommodation. Surely a bit of space around his precious table is not too much to ask."

"It's a navigation plot, not a bloody table," Alexis muttered, but followed along behind the two.

They made their way to *Shrewsbury's* quarterdeck. The marine stationed there looked uncertain as they approached and Alexis hung back. Perhaps he'd stop them and she didn't want her presence to make him assume they had permission to enter. But Eades and Courtemanche had so often taken advantage of *Shrewsbury's* hospitality that even the marine was unsure of whether they could come and go as they pleased. He took the middle road of sliding the hatch open and announcing them before they'd fully arrived.

"Misters Eades an' Cortmunch, sir," he called through the hatch.

Alexis heard a muttered oath followed by Euell's resigned, "Oh, very well, let them by."

She followed the other two onto the quarterdeck and gave Euell as apologetic a look as she could muster.

Eades and Courtemanche went immediately to the navigation plot, but Alexis held back. Eades motioned to her.

"Come, Carew, you'll want to see this."

Alexis looked to Euell, who nodded.

At first, Alexis was unsure of what she was seeing. The navigation plot was displaying images from all around the ship, but the space ahead of them was full of lights, not just the swirling black of *darkspace*. Alexis frowned. There were so many of them. She'd known a Core World would be larger than any she'd seen, but she hadn't expected there to be this much shipping visible in *darkspace*. Then she frowned further as the scale struck her. Some of the lights were so small that they couldn't possibly be ships — unless they were, but then what would the larger be?

"*Les Étoiles de Paris*," Courtemanche said proudly.

"'The Stars of Paris'?"

"Twelve planets, seventeen moons," Courtemanche said with a smile. "One hundreds and forty-five points of transition. Each protected by the guns of *les Étoiles de Paris*. The most massive installation in *darkspace*."

"You've built forts in *darkspace* at every Lagrangian point?" Alexis couldn't even begin to ponder the cost. Each of the forts appeared to be three or even four times larger than a ship of the line and it wasn't even just one of them at each Lagrangian point. Some points had three or even four of the installations around them, with guns pointing in all directions.

"New London's fortifications have more guns," Nesbit whispered in Alexis' ear.

"The guns of *les Étoiles* may be less numerous, but they are larger," Courtemanche said, having heard.

"Compensating," Nesbit whispered.

Alexis covered her mouth with her hand as Courtemanche flushed.

"Lieutenant Nesbit," Euell warned, but Alexis thought his face held a suppressed smile of his own.

THE REST of their arrival stunned Alexis as much as the *darkspace* forts of the system had. She, along with Eades and Courtemanche, stayed on the quarterdeck, despite the hours-long approach under conventional drive. The space around *Nouvelle Paris* teemed with ships. A steady stream of them sailed to the planet's L4 point for transition to normal space, streamed under conventional drive to the planet, and then from there to the L5 point and back to *darkspace*. To Alexis, used to much less traveled systems, it appeared as though space itself was crisscrossed with busy thoroughfares.

Normal space at the Lagrangian point contained several permanent structures as well. More fortifications surrounded the transition point, so that any ship that made it past the *darkspace* forts would face additional guns immediately after it transitioned. Alexis marveled at the extent of the fortifications.

So many. The expense of that much gallenium for the darkspace *forts alone ... and then the crews to man them.*

For Alexis, coming from Dalthus where the population was still less than a million, worlds like Zariah and Penduli, where there were single cities with that many people, had been a shock. Her first glimpse of *Nouvelle Paris* left her speechless.

As *Shrewsbury's* course took her outside the planet's orbit to turn and close with the traffic patterns, the night side of the planet came into view.

"It's like a jewel."

It was only when she noticed Courtemanche beaming at her that she realized she'd spoken aloud, but even the realization that she'd likely just given Eades more ammunition for his colonial pig farmer taunts couldn't dampen her wonder.

Without the system's sun to dampen it, the planet glowed like another star. Lights covered its surface in a delicate, lovely lattice, like luminescent lace.

More than that, though, she now noticed the size of some of the ships, far larger than any she'd seen before and larger than she thought was possible. She edged over to the tactical console and looked over the shoulder of the spacer manning it.

"What is that ship there, Carpenter?" she whispered.

The spacer ran fingers over the console to magnify the ship and display information about its class. "Intrasystem cruiser," he said.

Alexis read the ship's stats with wide eyes. Larger by far than any ship she'd ever seen, too large to ever transition and travel in *darkspace*, for the sail area to move that much mass would be impossible to manage. But its size and armaments would make it quite useful for its purpose — defending the system against invasion by the smaller ships that *could* travel the Dark.

So many guns ... and directly powered, rather than having to load shot protected from darkspace. She read on. *And missiles ... yes, I suppose that would be no problem at all with a developed star system to resupply in whenever you like, instead of having to worry about space in the hold for months on end.*

And it wasn't just the one, she saw. There were several of the cruisers around the system, and some ships even larger.

How would one ever be able to attack a system defended like this?

"If you're quite through gawking, Miss Carew," Eades called from the quarterdeck hatch, "I suggest we prepare to debark."

Alexis noted the reactions of *Shrewsbury's* officers and crew on the quarterdeck. All of them, from the helmsman to Captain Euell himself, had stiffened at Eades' words — whether at the affront to her personally or the disrespect he showed her rank and, therefore, the

Navy at large. She wondered if the man sought to antagonize others intentionally — much as she disliked him, she had to admit he seemed far too perceptive to be blind to the effect of his words. Regardless, the entire ship was at his disposal and Euell's orders were to provide Eades with "the utmost in assistance and accommodation". Those orders applied to her as well.

"As you wish, Mister Eades. I'll have my man gather my things — it should take me no more than a bell."

Alexis suppressed a grin at the look on Eades' face. He seemed to have not mastered the ship's system of keeping time by the number of bells in a watch, and she could see him struggle with the desire to ask her just how long that might be. Finally Eades nodded and turned to Euell.

"Captain, thank you for such a fast passage. I'm sure your crew will enjoy leave at the French naval stations, but I do request that you remain prepared to sail on the very shortest notice."

"Of course. *Shrewsbury* is ... at your disposal, Mister Eades."

"Thank you, captain. I expect we'll be here no more than a week, perhaps a fortnight at most."

FIFTEEN

"EIGHT BLOODY WEEKS!"

Alexis threw her beret across the room and shrugged out of her uniform jacket.

Isom retrieved the beret from where it had landed. "More of the same then, sir?"

Alexis swung her jacket onto the bed with a resounding *thump*.

"Meeting after meeting. Meetings with this ministry and that official. All just to arrange yet more meetings. I suspect we'll meet with the Directorate for Bloody Thumb-twiddling on the morrow!" She paused and rubbed her forehead. "'No more than a fortnight', my arse."

"Well, least it's evening now and you can enjoy yourself at those parties they have."

Alexis inhaled deeply and rounded on him, ready to let loose more of her frustrations, but forced herself to stop. None of this was Isom's fault and he'd been patient to a fault with her expressing it.

Be honest, he's put up with my bloody tantrums for weeks now.

She watched as he smoothed the fabric of her beret and set it carefully on the dresser.

And repaired the damage.

She knew it wasn't fair to him, but there was no one else she could complain to. Eades merely smiled tolerantly and told her to remain patient, not even acknowledging that he, himself, had said they should be in-system no more than a fortnight, or that Courtemanche had assured them the French were primed to join the fight, primed to free their brethren in the Berry March.

If that were truly the case, Alexis had yet to see signs of it in the daily meetings. Meetings where she sat at the back of the room waiting to be asked to speak to her experiences on Giron and with Commodore Balestra. Things Eades had assured her the French would want to hear, but of which, to date, she'd spoken not a word. Instead, Eades, Courtemanche, and whichever officials they were meeting with discussed everything from trade to the state of the succession in *Hso-Hsi*, far on the other side of *Deutschsterne* space.

In some ways the evenings were worse, though.

The French might not have been a monarchy for several hundred years, but they seemed to have made up for it with an elaborate, bureaucratic Court. The Ministries and Directorates of the government had replaced the aristocracy and there were nightly gatherings around the capital city, some with thousands of attendees and all the pomp and ceremony one would expect of a royal palace, complete with a majordomo announcing each new arrival's place and distinction within the government.

Eades swore that it was at these that the real business of government was conducted, but she'd been asked nothing about the worlds of the Berry March or Commodore Balestra at these either. She'd only either been asked to dance or had to smile politely at comments which were nothing more than thinly veiled expressions of contempt for New London.

Even her delight with the wonders of a Core World was palling in the face of her frustration.

With a sigh, Alexis retrieved her uniform coat from the bed and handed it to Isom. She went to the window and looked out, head swimming a bit as she looked down, barely able to see the ground far below. She and Eades had been given a suite of rooms in Courtemanche's residence which had impressed even Eades. Apparently height in the towers was some sort of sign of status and Courtemanche's rooms were very high indeed.

Aircars streamed by outside and Alexis shook her head in wonder. It seemed everyone on this world either flew from place to place or took one of the ubiquitous capsules that ran through tubes crisscrossing the city. Both moved at speeds which made Alexis uneasy, though moreso the tubes, which Alexis found horrifying. No one seemed willing to walk so much as half a kilometer for themselves, and Alexis hadn't seen a single horse since she'd arrived.

I miss horses.

She turned from the window and found Isom readying a change of clothes for her. He'd laid everything out on the bed and was brushing her jacket. Fresh trousers and tunic, the dress sword that went along with a lieutenant's uniform, even clean underthings — that last still gave Alexis pause, but Isom seemed to be not the least bothered by it. He treated her like any other officer. Alexis couldn't help but smile — she'd never have suspected it of herself, but she found his assistance immeasurably helpful.

"Thank you, Isom. I'll just wash up and then off to more parties. Perhaps tonight someone will give me cause to speak about what I came here to say in the first place."

Isom left and Alexis proceeded to the one thing on *Nouvelle Paris* that still managed to delight her even after eight weeks. Her room's bath, with unlimited hot water and a tub she could fairly swim in, was the one bright spot to the time she'd been on the planet.

I may never adjust to shipboard life again after this, she thought as the hot water cascaded over her.

Alexis dressed and then called Isom in to give her uniform his approval. She shrugged her shoulders to settle her uniform jacket in place. Isom moved from behind her to tug on the jacket's hem and eye it critically. He brushed a few imaginary pieces of lint away and nodded in satisfaction.

"Masts square and rigging tight, sir," he said.

She laughed. "You're too long a'space, Isom. You're starting to sound like a seasoned tar."

Isom shrugged. "Have to make the best of what we can't change, sir."

Alexis nodded, smile fading. "Indeed."

She knew Isom was referring to the fact that he was in the Navy only because he'd been falsely gathered up by the Impressment Service, their officers even going so far as to mark him with a spacer's tattoo while he was still unconscious from their stun rods. He'd been a legal clerk with no connection at all to space or ships, but there was little he could do about it now. Perhaps if he'd managed to stay with a ship near Penduli where there was a solicitor working on the issue for him he might have had a chance, but he'd chosen to follow Alexis. He seemed to have accepted what he couldn't change and determined to make the best of things with her.

So should she make the best of what she couldn't change. The days and now weeks of sitting idle while the French talked and pondered and ... well, generally drank themselves into oblivion before starting afresh the next day. She was so bloody tired of the wait. She'd rehearsed and rehearsed what she'd say until the words were rote, but she wanted her chance to be perfect — if the Republic might really join the war for the chance to free the worlds of the Berry March, she owed Delaine and Commodore Balestra her best efforts to convince them.

But after the talking, and lasting far longer each night, were the parties, and these were what the French seemed to prefer. Hours and hours each evening, full of drinking, dancing, and dining ... and the endless "*Mais non, mademoiselle,* no talk of war ... tonight we dance, *oui?*"

Alexis was sick to death of it and ready to scream — not least because the damned French would not allow her to decline when asked to dance. They pressed the issue with an insistence that bordered on rude, then gave her quite wounded looks when the dance was done.

It's not as though I don't warn them. It's their own fault if they have to limp away.

She had never in her life felt so utterly useless as she did here. While other officers were leading their men in the war, she was reduced to smiling prettily at the most foppish courtiers she could ever imagine. She clenched her jaw and raised a hand to adjust her rank insignia, squaring it properly with her collar as regulations required.

They're complacent. Need something to spur them to action ... short of a flechette to the arse, perhaps, but not far off.

She regarded herself in the mirror, though Isom would have ensured she was presentable. The French were even more concerned about a proper uniform than the Royal Navy's regulations — anything out of place would be noticed and remarked on, probably as further proof that the New Londoners were vulgar and uncivilized. She suspected the common folk of the Republic were more serious and less judgmental than those at Court — *Probably much like the people of Giron, and Delaine himself* — but the attendants at Court were ... a chore.

She eyed her uniform again, eyes falling on her rank insignia, and her lips curled upward.

Perhaps a flechette to the arse is what they need after all. Her eyes strayed to her baggage. *Something to spark a conversation, at least.*

SIXTEEN

"Lieutenant Ca..." The majordomo at the Great Hall's doorway broke off, eyes widening then narrowing as he took in her uniform collar.

Alexis had never heard him pause or hesitate before. He seemed to know at a glance everyone who might attend the night's festivities — their rank, their lineage.

Probably knows their bloody ancestors to the fourth generation.

He looked her over again, shrugged, and slammed the butt of his staff into the marble floor forcefully — more forcefully than she'd heard him do so any night before and four times in rapid succession. The sharp *crack* of the impacts echoed through the room, cutting across conversation and drawing eyes to the entrance.

"*Lieutenant d'Honneur* Carew!" he announced loudly.

Alexis blinked. That wasn't at all what she'd expected and she wasn't sure what to think of it. She'd hoped that by exchanging her own rank insignia for those given to her by Delaine — an archaic set of gold lieutenant's bars, similar to New London's, but crossed with the *fleur de lys* instead of a fouled anchor, that she might start some sort of conversation. A question or two about their source that might give her the opportunity to tell these people about Delaine, about Commodore Balestra, and the people of a dozen systems who still thought of themselves as French, no matter how long they'd been occupied by the Hanoverese. Surely if they were aware, they'd want to help? Do *something* to free them and bring them back to the Republic?

What she had *not* expected was such a change in the announcement of her arrival, nor to be greeted with blank, silent faces and narrow, almost menacing, looks.

Alexis made her way into the hall, trying to remain calm. She met the dark looks with a nod and a pleasant smile, all the while wondering just what she'd done.

I thought they were just outdated.

"Can you use that sword at all, Miss Carew?"

Alexis jumped, gasping as Eades appeared at her shoulder. The man had the infuriating ability to appear as if from nowhere, no matter how alert she thought she was.

"Sir?"

"Your sword?" Eades nodded to the blade. "Is it ornamental only?"

"I ... I am not unskilled, Mister Eades." To herself, though, she began to curse her decision to accept the ornamental sword that came as part of the uniform and to have put off finding one that would make a more serviceable weapon. She'd been so rushed since her promotion, what with being shipped off first to meet *Shrewsbury* and then the trip to *Nouvelle Paris* that she'd had little time to think about such things.

Now, looking around at the glares of those in the crowd, she could wish that New London's formal dress called for officers to wear sidearms, as she'd heard Hanover's did. She'd feel far more comfortable with a rapid-fire flechette pistol at her side.

Eades grunted. "Good, then I'll not lose future entertainments from you." He retrieved two glasses of champagne from a passing waiter and handed one to her. "The French have a slightly less liberal *code duello* than New London, but they are willing to settle differences with the blade. Most of these fops *are* unskilled, though, so do try not to kill anyone important when the firestorm you've just invited arrives, eh?"

"Sir," Alexis whispered, "what exactly have I done?"

Eades eyebrows rose. "You don't know?" At her shaken head he threw his head back and laughed. "Oh, you are a treat, Carew! Well, imagine your reception in the wardroom if you'd just wiped your arse with the battle ensign while farting *God Save the Queen* ... off-key. That will give you an idea of what you're in for." He took a sip of champagne and backed away from her, raising one finger in admonition. "No one important, remember ... and not *too* many bodies on the floor, please."

"Sir?"

Eades turned and walked away, still laughing.

Alexis took a gulp of the champagne, wishing it were something quite a bit stronger.

Perhaps I should leave ...

"Do you mock us, *anglaise?*"

One of the courtiers had stepped forward into the empty space that surrounded her. Others watched from nearby as he placed a hand on his sword hilt and tilted his head back to look at her down the length of his nose.

"Pardon me?" she asked.

The man's nostrils flared and he tossed his head, sending long, curly hair flying over his shoulder.

"Ah, now it is *pardon*." He shook his head. "Do. You. Mock," he repeated, slowly and distinctly, nodding at her collar and the offending insignia.

Alexis inclined her head, choosing to ignore his attitude. She truly hadn't expected to anger or offend anyone.

"I do not mock, sir, I assure you."

"You wear *le Fleur*," he said. "By what right?"

Alexis raised a hand to touch the insignia gently, drawing gasps and looks of astonishment from those watching.

Oh, bloody ... are you not even allowed to touch the thing?

"Sir," she said, keeping her voice level and calm. The crowd around them was growing as more and more people came to watch the confrontation. "I was given these by a friend upon my promotion. I did not know their import to you —" *And still don't.* "— and did not mean to offend you."

"Ah, I understand now" the man said, nodding. Alexis had a moment to think that the whole thing might be settled before he continued. "You are stupid."

"Sir!"

"You wear those here? Without knowing the meaning?" He snorted. "Stupid." There was a twitter of laughter from the crowd. "And some friend gives? *Très stupide!*"

That was too far, too much. It was one thing to call her stupid for not thinking or bothering to find out the full meaning of the insignia before wearing them, but how dare this popinjay speak so of Delaine!

"You go too far, sir," she said, voice low.

"*Moi? Le Fleur* is for *le héros*, the Hero of the Republic! Leave to wear it is granted not these last seventy years! To no one! But you ... you *Bloody*, you *Bifteck*, you wear it here among us? *I* go too far?"

"Seventy years, sir?" Alexis snapped, her temper flaring.

He had a point, she supposed, and perhaps she shouldn't have worn the insignia, but, damn him, they'd been eight weeks in the Republic and no closer to an agreement.

All the while men were dying. New London men, Hanoverese, and men of the Berry March, possibly even Delaine.

All while this dandy and his like drank their champagne and prattled on.

"That's quite a long time, isn't it?" She took a step toward him. "Produced no heroes in seventy *years*, you haven't?" She looked him up and down. "I can see why."

The man made to speak, but Alexis cut him off.

"This insignia was given to me by a good and decent man on Giron in *La Baie Marche*," Alexis said.

"*Le Hanovre!*" the man spat. "Those worlds are no more *Français!*"

"You utter fool," Alexis said. She knew she should probably shut her mouth and back away. Eades had told her repeatedly how important it was for her to impress these people, but she was simply fed up with their inaction. "The men and women of those worlds are more French than you, you strutting, little peacock!"

She advanced on him, fuming.

"Three bloody generations under Hanover and they *still* think they're French and long to come home — though what they'd make of you lot I shudder to think on.

"The man who gave me these, sir? They came from his many-times great-grandfather, who fought *le Hanovre!* To his *grand-père* who fought *le Hanovre!* He would fight *le Hanovre* himself, if given the least bit of support from you lot! And I, sir, I, and the rest of us *Bifteck*, will fight *le Hanovre!*" She looked him up and down, putting as much contempt as she could manage into her stare and voice. "You, sir, will drink champagne."

The man stared at her, eyes wide. He'd alternately flushed, then paled as she spoke. His lips curled in a snarl and his hand tightened on the hilt of his sword. "*Merde!*"

Alexis steadied herself in case he drew, but she wouldn't back down now. She looked him over again and wrinkled her nose in disgust. "Indeed."

The man seemed to stop breathing entirely, staring at her. In fact, she noticed, the entire hall was deadly quiet and the crowd around her had grown to include, she suspected, everyone in attendance. All of whom were equally still and staring at her. She flexed her fingers, making no move toward her sword's hilt, but prepared to draw if he did.

There was a sharp *tap* from somewhere in the crowd, then another, followed by the rustle of cloth as people began to move and slide aside. The *tapping* grew closer and Alexis saw an old man coming forward. He walked with a cane, something rarely seen, and wore a French naval uniform, chest as gaudily covered as any of the French officers she'd seen. As he reached the edge of the crowd she ran her eye automatically over his rank insignia, letting out a gasp of astonishment. Not just one, but three admiral's rosettes adorned his collar, indicating that he had, at least once, for he was certainly retired at his age, commanded not just a fleet but the entire French navy. And each rosette bore the *fleur de lys* that crossed her own lieutenant's bars.

The admiral stopped at the edge of the crowd, took two, tottering steps further toward her, and stopped again. He raised his cane a few centimeters off the floor, swayed, and steadied himself.

He's going to strike me and I bloody well deserve it. Alexis watched him sway again as he raised the cane a few more centimeters. *I only hope he doesn't fall and die in the doing ... he's likely one of those important ones Eades would rather I not kill ...*

A young woman hurried out of the crowd to the admiral's side and grasped his elbow to steady him. He said something, far too low for Alexis to hear, and the woman took his cane from his grasp. He raised his hands and pressed them together, or as much as he could with fingers gnarled with age and clearly unable to fully straighten. A bit apart and then together again.

Is he ... ?

He was. Clapping, or thumping, at least, as it seemed he couldn't make his palms meet in a sharp clap. Alexis raised her eyes to his and found them surprisingly sharp and alert, though pale blue and watery with age.

"*Brava, mademoiselle, brava et bien dit.*"

Alexis straightened her back unconsciously and doffed her beret, the closest thing the Royal Navy had to a salute. She had a sudden, absurd wish that she could salute ... or bow ... or something to show greater respect. The man's presence was so formidable.

"Sir," she said, "I truly meant no disrespect —"

The admiral snorted and reached for his cane, settling it on the floor before turning his gaze to the courtier who'd accosted Alexis. "*Tu!*" he said before switching to English. "Puppy! Worry she wears a bauble? What have you done to earn one for yourself?"

"Sir, I —"

The admiral snorted again and looked around the crowd. "I wear *le Fleur!* I fought *le Hanovre!* I will share *le Fleur* with any who do the same!" He returned his gaze to Alexis and smiled. "Even *le Bifteck.*"

He made a shuffling turn to walk back through the crowd. "'*Merde*' ... 'Indeed' ... Ha!"

SEVENTEEN

ALEXIS SIPPED a glass of champagne in an alcove between two pillars trying to remain as unobtrusive as possible. No one else had approached her and the dark looks had lessened somewhat, but she still felt unwelcome in the hall. Both Eades and Courtemanche were nowhere to be found.

Likely hiding in their rooms so they'll have no association with me.

"I owe you an apology, Miss Carew."

Alexis jumped, startled, and leaned out of the alcove to find Eades standing on the other side of one of the pillars.

I do wish he'd stop that.

His words registered and she stared at him in shock.

"An apology, Mister Eades?"

"Yes, Courtemanche and I have received no fewer than seven invitations to meetings since your little speech out there." He gestured at the crowd with his glass, then looked at her. "I was worried bringing you here that your colonial ways might offend the French. Now I begin to wonder if you're not a better asset when you're allowed to just run about and do as you will. Come, let us go to meet Admiral Reinier."

"Admiral Reinier?" Alexis asked, puzzled and still trying to determine how she felt about being described as an asset. She rather thought Eades had not used the word in sense that was entirely complimentary.

"The old man who came to your defense," Eades said. "He's one of three living holders of that bauble you decided to wear and the only one still able to get out and about. Come."

Alexis followed Eades who led her to where Courtemanche was waiting. They left the hall and made their way to a lift that took them down several levels to where the city's transport tubes intersected the building.

"Mister Eades," Alexis said, hesitating. "Might we take an aircar instead?"

Eades pressed the button to call for a capsule and laughed. "Still not comfortable with the tube, Miss Carew?"

Alexis swallowed and shook her head, but the capsule had already arrived and Eades motioned her toward the open door with an amused look. Reluctantly, she entered and took her seat. She clenched her teeth as Eades and Courtemanche entered. The capsule had seating for six and was shaped like nothing so much as a bullet.

She didn't mind aircars. They were a technology she well understood, not too much different than the antigrav haulers on Dalthus. She even enjoyed flying in them and seeing the world from high up, even in the pilotless versions they had on *Nouvelle Paris*. It had taken her a trip or two to grow accustomed to the fact that there was no pilot, but she'd adjusted.

The tube was different. Where aircars might reach speeds of a thousand or more kilometers an hour going cross-country, they kept to more limited speeds within the city where there was more traffic. The tubes did not.

The capsules' inertial compensators allowed them to accelerate and decelerate almost instantaneously, without any effect on the occupants and, as the capsules traveled within a closed system of tubes kept in vacuum, there was no real theoretical limit on how fast they could travel.

Their capsule launched itself from the boarding station into the main system and Alexis swallowed hard as her stomach lurched.

They'd boarded at the fifty-story level and she had a moment to wish they'd at least entered underground. The maniac who'd designed the system had thought it wise to build the tubes themselves out of a clear material and place windows in the capsules. Underground, at least, she couldn't see the blur of the city's buildings and aircar traffic passing at insane speeds. She closed her eyes tightly and swallowed again.

I do miss horses so.

"Are you unwell, Miss Carew?"

"You needn't concern yourself, Mister Eades," Alexis said, eyes still closed. She forced her hands, which were clenched on the seat's armrests, to relax. Eades was, she was sure, much amused by her, but she was less concerned by that than by surviving the next bit of the ride.

Alexis opened her eyes to see if they were at least out of the city yet, but they weren't. There was another capsule about a hundred meters ahead of them in the tube, which wasn't so bad. It was a stable, unmoving reference point she could keep her eyes on and ignore the lights of the buildings flashing by beside them. Then in an instant there was another capsule directly in front of them, a bare two or three meters away from the front of theirs. They must have passed a boarding station and the tube's system had chosen the spot in front of theirs for it to enter.

"Horses," Alexis whispered, clenching her eyes closed again.

They were soon out of the city and crossing open countryside, the tube now supported by pylons spaced hundreds of meters apart. At least away from the city's lights it was harder to see the landscape pass by. Alexis opened her eyes but kept her gaze fixed far in the distance, certainly not to the left where a second tube for the opposite direction was visible. The occasional blur of a capsule's lights flashing past was worse than the landscape.

Alexis saw the sky lighten ahead of them and swallowed hard. That they'd sped their way to the planet's dayside was only another disturbing reminder of the capsule's speed. What would happen if even a tiny bit of the tube's structure gave way and compromised the vacuum? She was certain the designers had taken that into account, but going from vacuum to air at this speed would do very bad things she didn't wish to contemplate. She closed her eyes again, but opened them again a moment later when Eades nudged her.

The world outside seemed to jerk to one side as their capsule switched from the travel tube to one leading to a boarding station. Their capsule slowed to a more reasonable pace as they approached the station, as though the designers wanted to give passengers time to appreciate their arrival.

The tube curved gradually down to a large building on a lake with a view of mountains on the far shore. The building itself seemed to blend in with the landscape, though it was large, at least by Alexis' standards. Two three-story wings swept away from a five-story main building.

"Where are we?" Alexis asked.

"*Amiral d'Honneur* Reinier's home," Courtemanche said.

Alexis looked at the beautiful structure. "He has rooms here?"

Courtemanche shook his head. "*Non*, this is *Amiral d'Honneur* Reinier's home."

Alexis looked from the building, amazed that such a thing belonged to one man, to the tube which led to its front steps. "He has his own tube station?"

Courtemanche shrugged. "*Amiral d'Honneur* Reinier is much admired."

Eades leaned forward in his seat. "Admiral Reinier's fleet took a great many prizes in the last war."

They were met at the door by the same woman who'd attended

Admiral Reinier at the reception. Alexis realized that she and the admiral must have left the reception before them.

"Ah, Marguerite!" Courtemanche called, rushing to embrace her.

Alexis winced in sympathy. Courtemanche's odor had not improved since they'd left *Shrewsbury* and it was only a bit less unbearable in the more open spaces to be found planetside, but the woman gave no sign that she noticed.

"*Monsieur Courtemanche! Il a été trop longtemps,*" the woman said in return. She turned to Alexis and Eades as Courtemanche stepped back to introduce them. "Yes, the guests *mon grand-père* he has said will come." She smiled at them. "Come, I will speak to you within the English, yes? I have the needs of practice."

Eades stepped forward and took her hand, raising it to his lips. "Your English is exquisite, *Mademoiselle* Reinier."

Is he flirting with her? He's twice her age if a day.

"*Non* ... no, you are kind, *monsieur*, but I be ... am to be, ah, the diplomat one day. I must learn the languages." She gestured them inside. "Come, please, *mon grand-père* is awaiting you."

She led them down a long hallway to a wing of the house that overlooked the lake and into a large room with floor-to-ceiling windows. The view of the lake and mountains beyond was spectacular, but the room was cold and Alexis shivered as they entered.

"*Pardon, Mademoiselle Carew,*" Marguerite said. "*Mon grand-père,* he wishes it always to be as Autumn and to sit by the fire."

Indeed, at the far end of the room there was a large fireplace with a roaring fire and a number of deep, leather chairs arranged around it.

"Marguerite, something to drink for our guests, *s'il vous plaît,*" Admiral Reinier said once they were all settled into seats by the fire.

Alexis did have to admit that the contrast between the cold room and the warmth of the fire was pleasant. She supposed that if one liked these conditions and was of a certain age, it might not be wise to wait until they occurred naturally. She took another look at Reinier. If the last *fleur de lys* had been awarded over seventy years ago, then

Reinier must be over a hundred years old, even if he were the last recipient, which she didn't know he was.

"So!" Reinier said when they'd all been served a glass of wine. Marguerite stationed herself beside his chair instead of sitting, as though readying herself for his next request. "You have been to *La Baie Marche, Lieutenant* Carew? How does it go with those who have been so long apart from us?"

Alexis licked her lips, suddenly nervous. She hadn't expected to be the first one asked to speak. Surely Eades or Courtemanche should take the lead in this. But she saw that everyone was looking at her expectantly.

"I spent some two months on Giron, sir," she said finally, "and that only in one village, but what I saw of it has convinced me that the people do not think well of Hanover."

She paused as she saw why Marguerite had remained near him. His hands were too gnarled to grasp a wine glass, so instead she set a small straw in it and raised it to his lips. Alexis flushed as he met her gaze and she realized she'd been rudely staring.

"I think that you were well to have been taken by a fleet of *La Baie Marche, Lieutenant* Carew," Reinier said. He held up his hands. "I have *le Hanovre* to thank for these — a gift from my own time with them long ago. The damage was not so much in my youth, but has become worse with age." He barked laughter and smiled. "Like so much does, *oui?* The doctors, they say to replace them, but —" He shrugged. "— I am an old man and soon I will go to my rest. I would like it to be as whole as I may be."

"Shush, *pépère,*" Marguerite said, patting his shoulder.

"She thinks I will live forever." He gestured for Alexis to continue.

"The fleet there, Commodore Balestra's fleet, is made up almost exclusively of men from the Berry worlds — I didn't hear a word of German spoken by them the entire time I was there, only French."

She went on for some time, telling Reinier everything she could remember and answering his questions. She had the most trouble talking about Delaine and what she'd learned from him — she found it difficult to keep her feelings for him out of her voice, especially when she told of him giving her the lieutenant's insignia she wore, but thought she managed it fairly well. Finally Reinier sat back and frowned.

"And so," he said, this time to Eades and Courtemanche, "you wish *la République* to join in this war, to convince this Balestra and her fleet to join in this war, for *La Baie Marche* to make *la révolution?*"

"My thoughts are known," Courtemanche said. "*Le Hanovre* has held our people too long."

"New London stands ready to assist," Eades said. "A fleet is being gathered as we speak. We have troops and transports made ready, as well."

Reinier nodded. "To do this thing, it would be good to have *Deutschsterne* act with us. To force *le Hanovre* into guarding another border."

"The *Deutschsterne* are worthless, *grand-père*," Marguerite said. "They have not fought *le Hanovre* for three wars now. They simply move a ship or two about at most."

"There are few worlds of *Deutschsterne* that do not bear craters, Marguerite," Reinier said. "They have cause to fear. And each ship or two must be matched, *oui?* A ship watching *Deutschsterne* is a ship not in *La Baie Marche*."

He frowned and eased himself in his chair.

"*La République* has known peace for too long," he said. "The senate is large and there are worlds far from *le Hanovre* who will not wish to fight. They have no dog to the hunt, as you say, *oui?*" He gestured and Marguerite held the glass for him to sip again. "For them it must be made a personal affair, one of honor, you understand? Else we must deal with them as *lâches dégénérés* ... degenerate cowards."

The three men — Eades, Courtemanche, and Reinier — spoke for a time about whom to approach. Reinier seemed to think little of most of the names Courtemanche mentioned, punctuating his opinions with, to Alexis, shocking commentaries on the individual's honor or personal habits.

"*Non,*" Reinier said at last. "If these are the sort you have approached, it is no wonder."

He pursed his lips and thought for a long time, then looked at Alexis.

"This Theibaud —" He raised a hand to his own collar where his rank insignia was. "The one who gives you *le Fleur.* Your young man, *oui?*"

Reinier grinned and Alexis flushed as she realized she obviously hadn't kept her feelings for Delaine out of her voice.

"I did want to thank you, sir," she said. She raised her own hand to her insignia. "For coming to my aid over these."

The admiral waved a hand. "No family with those would give them lightly. Or where undeserved."

Alexis flushed again.

"There are Theibauds in *La République* still who are known to many and we will speak with them," Reinier went on. "Balestra ... hmm ... I knew a Balestra in ... *un moment s'il vous plaît.*" He frowned. "*Oui.* Ah, Marguerite, will you bring my journals — ah, *Lieutenant quatre, peut-être cinq. Capitaine neuf.*"

Marguerite nodded and started to leave.

"*Mademoiselle* Carew?" she asked. "Would you assist me in this?"

"*Lieutenant,* Marguerite," Reinier chided her.

Marguerite ducked her head in apology to Alexis, who followed her from the room.

EIGHTEEN

"*Pardon*," Marguerite said as she closed the door and led Alexis down the hallway.

"It's quite all right."

"*Non, mon grand-père*, he is correct. Just as I must learn to speech ... *speak* your English, I must pay more care to ... ah, *le rang*, rank and position?"

Alexis nodded.

"*Merci*." Marguerite smiled. "These things will be important to me."

"So you intend to become a diplomat?" Alexis asked.

"*Oui*. My father is the consul on Cannich, a New London world near the border. I grew up with *maman* here, but think I will follow his path, yes?" She glanced back the way they'd come. "But that is for tomorrows. For todays I work with *mon grand-père* on his ... the book of memories?"

"Memoirs?"

Marguerite frowned. "This is our word *mémoir*, but in the English?"

"The same."

Marguerite grinned. "Hmph. You steal our word?"

"A great many of them, if I'm not mistaken. We're rather good at that."

Alexis followed Marguerite to another room and stopped in the doorway, staring.

"*Oui*," Marguerite said, smiling. "Such is the reaction of many."

The room was not large, perhaps four meters on a side, but its walls were lined with shelves and those shelves were filled with books. Real, physical books.

"*Mon grand-père's* writings," Marguerite said. "His ... journals?"

Alexis nodded that she understood. "What are those?" she asked, noting several bare shelves.

"Ah, those are the times his ship is lost. At times I ask him for stories of those days and record what he says to me." Marguerite looked around the room. "There is so much of his life here." She perused the shelves. "*Grand-père's* memory, *mademoiselle*." She shrugged. "He does not think in our years, only in his rank. And so I must find his journals from four and five years of a *lieutenant* and his nine year ... *non*, ninth, *oui*? His ninth year of a *capitaine*."

Alexis stared at the shelves in awe, both at the dedication it must have taken to write so many words by hand, and the devotion the old man must feel to his service to mark time in such a way.

"As," she said, taking Marguerite at her word. "'As a captain', not 'of'."

Marguerite smiled. "*Merci*."

She pulled an antigrav tray from a corner of the room and began loading volumes on it.

"Those, there," Marguerite said, pointing to the far side of the room where the journals were behind clear, locking fronts. "From his time of ... *as* —" She smiled. "— *amiral* and *amiral de la flotte*, they are secret. But I think better they should make secret those of him as the *aspirant et lieutenant*, before he learned to watch his words, *oui*?" She gestured to the other side of the room. "As *amiral* one must, even in his journal ... um, to see the hidden words?"

Alexis grinned. "Read between the lines, do you mean?"

Marguerite grinned back. "*Oui*. 'Atween the lines', I like this. For his *amiral* journals one must read 'atween the lines to see his thoughts. As *lieutenant* he simply write, 'this man is the *connard*'."

"His discretion improved with age, then? You'll pardon me, but he seemed outspoken enough just now."

Marguerite nodded. "*Oui*, with rank, more discretion ... until now." She grinned. "Now he is retired, he simply tell the man to his face."

Alexis laughed.

They made their way back to the others and Alexis found herself with little to do.

Reinier asked Marguerite to review the journals for mention of the Balestra he remembered serving with, and then to search the Republic's naval records to determine if that family might be related to a commodore in the Berry Worlds. Eades and Courtemanche continued to speak with Reinier about how to proceed. Who to speak to and in what order, whether they should attempt to bring *Deutschsterne* into the plan, and what preparations New London was making already.

Alexis thought to help Marguerite with the journals, but they were not only in French, but in an unsteady hand. She wondered why, with the damage to his hands, Reinier had insisted on hand-writing them.

With little to do and no questions directed at her, Alexis settled back in her chair and perused her tablet. She'd set herself a course of study after her meetings with Eades aboard *Shrewsbury*, determined to learn as much of New London's history as she could, and not be caught out by him again. To that she'd added naval tactics and strategies, especially around attacking and defending fortified systems from *darkspace*. The sight of the French fortifications and the massive ships in-system had piqued her curiosity.

The talk, and her studying, went on until late into the night. As their journey via the tube had raced from night into daylight, Alexis found herself nodding off over her tablet. Eventually Eades was shaking her awake for their trip back to the city, something Alexis would have much rather slept through the trip in its entirety.

It seemed as though she'd only just returned to her rooms and laid her head down before Isom was at her side to tell her that Eades and Courtemanche were waiting for her.

If her first eight weeks on *Nouvelle Paris* had been frustrating, the days that followed were equally exhausting. It seemed as though every bureaucrat in the city could simply not hear enough of their plans and excitedly led them to some superior who simply must, of course, hear the whole thing from the beginning — including all Alexis could remember of her time on Giron in the Berry March.

She thought things were going well. At least they seemed to be meeting with those who had more interest and more power to make decisions, though she still had no real idea of what those decisions were. Once she'd told her story and answered any questions to their satisfaction, she was usually sent off to her rooms while Eades and Courtemanche continued the discussion — only to be trotted out again for the next meeting.

It came as quite a surprise, then, when Eades announced that they'd be returning to *Shrewsbury* the next morning.

"Has anything been settled then?" Alexis asked.

"Of course. We've just been working out the details."

"So they'll really do it? The French will join us in the war?"

"A fleet is assembling as we speak to harass the Hanoverese along the border," Eades said, "and there are transports full of uniforms and weapons, along with a French admiral and field marshal, preparing to sail for Alchiba and join with our troops there."

"Uniforms and weapons?"

"To equip those of the Berry March who rise up and join us."

"So it's done then." Alexis took a deep breath and closed her eyes in relief. "It shall be very refreshing to return to *Shrewsbury* as nothing more than an ordinary lieutenant, Mister Eades, I must tell you." She offered him a small smile. Frustrating as it had been, she supposed it was worth it now that it was over. "I cannot say I envy you this business of yours."

"You'll not miss our dinners together, Miss Carew?"

"I will certainly not miss those French dishes. Though I will say that your influence has set me to studying history more than I ever thought I would." She supposed she could allow him that victory at least.

"I suppose you'll have a bit of time for that on the way to Wellice."

"Wellice?"

"Our next stop," Eades said. "I'll have to notify Captain Euell that we'll be stopping there on our way to Alchiba to drop you off."

Alexis felt a chill. "Drop me off?"

Eades gave her an odd look. "For your transport into Hanover to communicate with Commodore Balestra. Surely you haven't forgotten that?"

The chill intensified. "Into Hanover? Me?"

"The third leg of our strike against Hanover, Carew." Eades' eyes were intense. "The Berry Worlds revolting with a New London army on the ground, the French coming in alongside us in the war with their fleet harrying the Hanoverese border, and Commodore Balestra's fleet — a *Hanoverese* fleet — in revolt as well and joining us in the Berry March. The Hanoverese will not know where to turn next — other worlds they've taken may rise up as well. It will be the beginning of the end for them."

"But —" Alexis paused. Eades seemed so certain, so sure of himself and his plan, but she couldn't share his certainty. Hanover controlled hundreds of systems. Surely their control over them wasn't so fragile that these few worlds would spell doom. Or, perhaps, the Hanoverese control over those systems was more fragile than Alexis suspected. Eades, after all, did seem quite certain.

The full import of Eades' words struck her.

"Mister Eades," she began carefully, "when you say I'm to go into

Hanover and that *Shrewsbury* is to 'drop me off' ... how then am I to go about it?"

It would be one thing to sail into Hanover as part of an invading New London fleet, or even on *Shrewsbury* alone, with the might of 74 guns to back her up, but Eades seemed to be saying that *Shrewsbury* would not be making that trip.

Eades waved his hand dismissively.

"I've just the man for getting you in to speak to Balestra, never fear. You'll sail with him, find Balestra, and pass along our messages." Eades smiled and patted her on the shoulder. "Nothing to it, and your *Shrewsbury* will be waiting for you at Alchiba when you return."

NINETEEN

ALEXIS UNHOOKED her vacsuit from the air and water lines in the sail locker, then checked Lieutenant Hollingshed's suit valves before turning her back to him so that he could check hers in turn. The two of them, along with the twelve or so spacers in the locker, were the last of the crew to replenish their vacsuits before heading back Outside.

Once all of the crew's vacsuits were checked, Hollingshed slid open the hatchway and they made their way onto the ship's hull. Alexis ran an eye over the set of the sails.

Shrewsbury was on the starboard tack, possibly for the last time before reaching the more variable winds outside the influence of the *Nouvelle Paris* system. The sails were aligned well, full and bright with the azure glow of the particle charge that allowed them to harness the *darkspace* winds, but she thought she could detect the first bits of a shudder that indicated the winds were not so steadily blowing toward the system's center as they had been.

At the least, she thought there'd be no sail changes ordered for several bells, not unless something untoward happened.

That would give her time to relax a bit.

Whatever sense of urgency Eades and Courtemanche had failed to exhibit during their stay on *Nouvelle Paris*, their hurry to leave once they had agreement made up for. With the agreement of the French to enter the war and assist in the liberation of the Berry March, Eades had taken up packing and returning to *Shrewsbury* as though he wanted to be well away before they could change their minds. Courtemanche had been equally hurried, ordering the packing of his baggage and having it sent aboard a French ship as rapidly as possible.

Alexis made her way off *Shrewsbury's* bow and paused a moment to look off into the distance. She could just make out the lights of Courtemanche's ships, four transports and two frigates on their way to Alchiba with the first load of French uniforms and weapons for the troops they hoped to raise in the Berry March.

Shrewsbury wasn't keeping company with those, as she'd be making the stop at Wellice, something Alexis was more than a bit unsure of. Eades seemed to think it would be a simple matter for her to sail off into Hanover on a strange ship and make contact with Balestra's fleet, but Alexis doubted it would be so easy.

She wasn't at all pleased at the thought of leaving *Shrewsbury* again. This ship was her proper posting and she felt she'd neglected her responsibilities quite enough, what with all of Eades' meetings and then weeks and weeks on *Nouvelle Paris*. Time enough to worry about that later, though.

She latched a safety line onto a new guidewire and started pulling herself along *Shrewsbury's* keel toward the stern. She'd at least have a bit of time to relax before the next order to change sail came. There'd been little opportunity since coming back aboard. Eades' insistence that they make all possible speed for Wellice had her suited and onto the hull to oversee the foremast hands before Isom even had her baggage safely returned to her cabin.

Since then, it had been tack and tack again as *Shrewsbury* beat to windward.

Nearing the stern, she caught sight of a figure already there, clipped on to the last guidewire and floating free of the hull while facing aft. The figure's vacsuit bore a midshipman's markings, and its small size could only mean it was Artley.

Alexis eased herself to a stop next to him and let herself float beside him for a moment before leaning toward him and touching her helmet to his.

"It's a fine view from here this morning, Mister Artley," she said.

Normally the view from the ship's stern in *darkspace*, away from most of the lights on the masts at the bow, was of the roiling masses of *darkspace* in the distance. Here, though, they were still close enough to *Nouvelle Paris* that they could make out the lights of the forts and even some of the shipping. She thought the sight was quite magnificent, if not unique, though somehow not as peaceful as the sheer emptiness of *darkspace* away from a system.

Les Étoiles de Paris, *indeed.*

"It is, sir." Artley hesitated. "Would you like me to leave, sir? So you can have the place to yourself, I mean?"

Alexis chuckled. She supposed she did have a reputation for enjoying the solitude of the ship's stern.

"You were here first, Mister Artley. Perhaps I should be asking you that?"

"Oh! No, sir!" He hesitated. "I do like it back here, though. Even in normal-space it's quite peaceful."

"It is," Alexis agreed. She noted Artley's vacsuit, which was new and good quality. She'd heard from Lieutenant Nesbit while on *Nouvelle Paris* that the midshipmen had quite a time on the station. Rushing from chandler to chandler and back again while they bargained for the best deal on a new vacsuit for Artley, then having a fine start to an evening with what was left of the whip-around funds. Even the bosun had gone along to take part in the bargaining.

They must have bargained hard to have a bit of coin left, she thought, eyeing the suit, which was obviously high quality. *He'll have a chore to replace it with similar quality when he outgrows this one.*

Another thought came unbidden that sent a brief chill through her. *If he has the chance to outgrow it.*

That damned nightmare had come again more than once in the enforced idleness of her stay on *Nouvelle Paris*. Always ending with the new, small figure at the forefront standing as though to accuse her.

Stuff and nonsense, she told herself again.

"I see that you've managed to find a proper vacsuit," she said, trying to shake her feeling of unease.

"Oh, yes! The others all came along and saw I wasn't cheated, and I've still the one from the purser as a spare — though this new one hardly smells at all!"

Alexis laughed. "I'm sure you'll remedy that soon enough."

Artley laughed in return, then sobered. "I ... I don't think anyone's done so kind a thing for me since my Da died. I'll have to repay them somehow."

Alexis frowned. "It was my understanding it was a whip-around, Mister Artley, a gift. I'm certain they expect no repayment."

Artley was silent for a moment. "My Da always told me there are some debts a man keeps in his own ledger book, sir, even if the other fellow doesn't."

Alexis wasn't certain how to respond to that. It was a surprisingly mature comment to come from Artley, even if it was only something his father had said that stuck with him.

There was a sudden blur of motion and bodies began streaming past them on both sides. Past and then over the stern of the ship, whipcracking at the end of safety lines as the guidewires caught them, then arcing back to *Shrewsbury's* stern between the massive rudder and planes that extended off past the hull's field into *dark-space*. All of the figures were in vacsuits colored as midshipmen and Alexis had to laugh out loud after the initial shock.

Some of them fumbled more than others with their lines, but in a moment they were all on their way up the ship's stern toward the top of the hull.

Alexis saw Artley frozen in place, hands on his own safety lines, one where it was clipped to *Shrewsbury's* hull and the other at his waist. She laughed again.

"Do go on, Mister Artley. Don't let me keep you from joining in."

"Thank you, sir!"

In an instant, Artley was off over the edge the hull, pulling himself rapidly up the stern after the other midshipmen.

Alexis' laughter died and she took a deep breath. There was a part of her that wanted to join in the game, whether it was a simple race or some complicated game of tag, but she knew she couldn't. Those were games for the midshipmen — they taught the boys the ship's lines and how to best move about — and not for lieutenants.

THE LIEUTENANTS GATHERED around *Shrewsbury's* wardroom table were a bedraggled, exhausted mess. Hollingshed and Slawson, the second lieutenant returned to *Shrewsbury* when the Hanoverese prize he'd commanded was turned over to the *Nouvelle Paris* prize court, had managed to bathe, but the rest, Alexis included, had, at best, managed to throw on fresh clothing before coming to table.

The winds had, indeed, become more variable outside the influence of the *Nouvelle Paris* system, but they hadn't varied to be fair for Wellice. Captain Euell had kept the crew hard at work in an effort to accommodate Mister Eades' call for all possible speed, but he'd finally called them in for a late supper and, Alexis dearly hoped, a night of easier sailing.

"I hear we've you to thank for this, Carew," Barr said, easing himself in his seat.

"Not mine and I see no sense in it," Alexis countered. "It's Eades that wants the speed put on."

"It's a month's sail to Wellice," Hollingshed said. "Does he think a few moments here at the start will make a difference?"

"I don't know," Alexis admitted. "He was simply in a rush to leave as soon as ..." She trailed off. *Shrewsbury's* purpose, and her own, was still something of a secret.

"I hear you'll be leaving us again at Wellice, though?" Hollingshed asked.

Well, as much a secret as one can have aboard ship.

She nodded.

"I'll be shut of the gundeck for a few weeks at least," Hollingshed said. "At least there's that."

Alexis had to smile despite her fatigue. Hollingshed's dislike of the chaotic gundecks was well known. He much preferred the order of the quarterdeck during an action.

"Has it been so terrible?" she asked.

"Listening to him whinge about it after every drill has been terrible," Barr said.

Hollingshed huffed.

"All that running about," he muttered, then raised an eyebrow at Alexis. "Your protégé has come along, though."

"Protégé?"

"Young Artley," Barr said. "The lad's improved a good deal all around."

"I certainly can't take any credit for that," Alexis said. "I've hardly been here."

"Hm," Nesbit said with a glance at Hollingshed. "You know, Artley's not only improved on the gundeck. He's put it about that he's in the Navy to stay."

Alexis had to raise an eyebrow at that.

"Oh, yes," Hollingshed said. "Says he's going to be just like the, ah, how does he put it?"

"Be just like the finest officer he's ever seen," Nesbit said with a grin.

Alexis sighed with relief. If Artley had settled with himself that he was in the Navy and determined to make the best of it, then that was one worry off her shoulders. As for patterning himself after a favorite officer, well, she often did the same. If there came a situation she was unsure of how to handle, she'd often consider what her first captain, Captain Grantham, or even his first lieutenant, Caruthers, might handle it.

"Captain Euell's a fine officer," she said. "Artley could certainly choose a worse man to model himself after."

Hollingshed and Nesbit shared a look. Nesbit shook his head.

"You're a wonder, Carew. You really are."

"So who are you to meet on Wellice?" Hollingshed asked. "Sure to be a letdown after running about with the French."

"I'm not at all sure," Alexis said. "I'd never think there was something worse than the French bureaucrats, but any time I ask Mister Eades about this mysterious meeting he simply says, 'I've just the man for it,' and then — and it's most disturbing — he smiles."

TWENTY

AVREL DANSBY WAS the epitome of a New London gentleman. Well-dressed, well-groomed, well-spoken — not titled, certainly, but clearly the holder of so much wealth that marrying a title would not be entirely out of the question at some point. He was, perhaps, fifty years of age, but a full head of dark hair still framed a handsome face with a well-tended mustache and goatee to match. His dress was conservative, and spoke of dark, quiet shops where one certainly never left with one's purchases that day, for they would be run up especially for you and delivered to your home.

Alexis distrusted him immediately.

It was something about the man's eyes. A distance, a hardness that went beyond what she'd expect to see even in a new hand sent straight from the gaols. Her first sight of the man reminded her, unsettlingly, of the pirate captain Horsfall she'd encountered aboard her first ship, and she sensed something in him that was far at odds with his dress and manners.

Though able to afford a better dentist than Horsfall, at least.

"Lieutenant Carew," Dansby said as Eades introduced them. He held out his hand and Alexis forced herself to take it.

"Mister Dansby," she said.

Some of her thoughts must have made their way into her tone, for Dansby's eyes narrowed and he looked her up and down as he released her hand.

Eades looked from one to the other and smiled thinly. "Yes, I can see this will go swimmingly, won't it?" He gestured to the table. "Let's have a seat, shall we?"

Alexis and Dansby went to opposite ends of the table, seemingly by some unspoken agreement, and sat. Eades took a seat along one of the table's longer sides. He pressed a spot on the table to summon the pub's waitstaff. "How remarkable," he said, looking again from one end of the table to the other. "Rather like sitting down to sup with a mongoose and a cobra."

"And which do you name me, Eades?" Dansby asked, never taking his eyes from Alexis.

"The snake," Alexis said without thinking.

Dansby smiled. "Yes, I suppose you are the cute, cuddly one."

Alexis flushed as a servant entered. Eades asked for wine to be served and a spare bottle left, then privacy. She resisted the impulse to grasp her glass and drain it immediately in an attempt to settle her nerves as Dansby continued to stare at her.

"Perhaps, Mister Dansby," she said, "but with teeth still, I'll trust you to remember."

"Children," Eades chided as the servant left. He tucked his nose into his glass and inhaled deeply. "Your natural and understandable animosity aside, please, do attempt to behave in a civilized manner, will you?"

"'Natural and understandable', Mister Eades?" Alexis asked. It sounded like Eades had expected her and Dansby to dislike each other, which begged the question why he'd introduce them in the first place.

"Of course, Miss Carew. What else would one expect of a Naval officer and a pirate?"

"I prefer *entrepreneur*, Eades," Dansby said. "And that particular enterprise was long ago, in any case. A bit gauche for me these days."

Alexis looked at Eades in surprise. The Foreign Office had dealings with pirates? Even former pirates? Though at least now she understood her dislike for Dansby. She thought of the pirates she'd encountered aboard *Merlin*. The image of a merchant spacer's crew, bodies stacked like cordwood came to mind.

"Well you shall both set aside your differences," Eades said, "as Her Majesty has need of your services."

"I've long since paid that debt, Eades," Dansby said. "I'm a respectable man of business these days."

"I rather doubt that debt is paid, Mister Dansby," Alexis said, "as I see no noose about your neck."

"Her Majesty's Government found other, more important, uses for me, Miss Carew. The debt was paid long ago." He turned his gaze to Eades. "In full and more, as I recall."

Eades cleared his throat. "Attend to me, children, and stop your bickering." He pulled out his tablet and set it on the table. "Her Majesty has some additional requirements of you, Dansby."

"Then tell me what it is and we'll discuss my fee," Dansby said. He sat back in his chair and smiled. "I've a full pardon for all that went before."

"Yes," Eades said. He smiled thinly. "All that went before — and though piracy may no longer be in it, there are still, shall we say, undertakings of a less than strictly legal nature." He scanned his tablet. "*Celeste*, currently bound for Fieldbank. *Maria*, for Springdell. *Katherine*, for Northby." As Eades spoke, Alexis saw Dansby's eyes narrow and he sat forward again. "Should I continue, Mister Dansby? And should those ships, perhaps, be visited by a Naval inspection, rather than local customs officers?"

Dansby echoed Eades' smile. "I am, of course, entirely at the service of Her Majesty and Her Government."

"Indeed," Eades said.

Dansby drained his glass. "So what is this business?" he asked.

"We simply wish you to transport Miss Carew to a certain place and return her safely here."

"Where?"

"First your assurances that you understand this is not to be spoken of at all. This task will, I'm afraid, be bound by the Official Secrets Act."

"Of course," Dansby said, waving a hand. "Yes. It usually is, isn't it? Where am I going?"

"Somewhere in Hanover."

"I assumed that, Eades. They're the only ones we've a war on with at the moment. Where in Hanover?"

Eades grimaced, looking uncomfortable.

"Unfortunately, that is information we do not have at this time. You are to use your own contacts to determine the whereabouts of a certain Hanoverese fleet, the Berry March fleet commanded by a Commodore Balestra. You will then put Carew in a position to make contact with certain officers of that fleet."

Dansby laughed. "Oh, so I'm to just sail into Hanover and start asking about their fleet movements, am I? You're mad."

"That is the task required of you, Mister Dansby."

"And you?" Dansby looked Alexis up and down. "I can play a smuggler easy enough. I bring a load of goods the Hanoverese want and they'll welcome me. But you?" He snorted.

"Mister Eades and I have already discussed my role, sir," Alexis said. She had her own doubts about the entire enterprise, but didn't want to voice them. No matter if she agreed with Dansby that the risk was great, the thought of voicing agreement to the vile man irked her. "I shall be a lady from the Berry March who's taken passage on your ship to find a brother serving with the fleet. C'est une ruse crédible, n'est ce pas?"

"No," Dansby said. "No, it is not a believable ruse at all." He nodded at Eades. "He come up with that?" He drained his glass. "No. No girl from the March would take passage on my ship with my crew. Lord, girl, you'd have to play at being the dimmest bulb in the bunch to make that story stick. Any half-sensible girl would run screaming from my crew. No." He frowned and rubbed a finger along his lips. "No, you're not from the March at all. In fact, you're my niece. A distant niece, mind you. And come aboard to learn the trade. That'll explain your presence and allow me to keep watch over you."

Alexis bristled. "I've no need of a watchman, Mister Dansby. I'm quite capable of taking care of myself."

Dansby looked her over, an irritatingly smug grin on his face. "You haven't met my lads yet, girl."

Alexis met his gaze, attempting to display a calmness she didn't truly feel. "Nor have they met me, sir."

Eades shook his head. "*Children!*"

Alexis and Dansby looked at Eades, then back at each other, and Alexis felt a disturbing instance of kinship with the man. Not enough to offset her dislike, but she felt certain Dansby would join her in beating Eades senseless if she suggested it.

The enemy of my enemy is not my friend, but he might be willing to hold the bastard down while I kick him, and there's something to be said for that.

Dansby raised an eyebrow, as though sensing her thoughts, and turned back to Eades.

"And the cost of this farce?" he asked. "Who's to cover that?"

"Her Majesty will, of course, reimburse you for all proper expenses you incur."

"Up front."

Eades frowned. "Are you suggesting that Her Majesty is not, as your peers would put it, 'good for it'?"

"Her Majesty I trust," Dansby said. "Her Buggering Clerks who view the paperwork, I do not. Ten thousand pounds ... up front and no accounting."

Alexis gasped. Ten thousand pounds would buy an entire ship and more. Apparently Eades felt it was an outrageous demand as well.

"We wish to hire one of your ships, Mister Dansby, not purchase your entire fleet. Five *hundred* pounds and an accounting at the end."

"Nine thousand. I've a crew to pay, as they won't be able to go about their normal business." He took a long drink of his wine. "And they're not stupid. They'll know this is some odd bit of doings and want more for it."

"Are you suggesting they're untrustworthy?" Alexis asked, becoming even more nervous about what Eades was getting her into.

Dansby laughed and even Eades grinned a bit.

"'*Course* they're untrustworthy. That's why I have to pay them."

"Mister Dansby's crews are pirates, smugglers, thieves, and murderers, for the most part, Miss Carew. Trust is not a factor."

"Former," Dansby said. "Well ... for the most part."

"Mister Eades," Alexis said, "I find myself becoming a bit more concerned about this business. Surely there's some other transport —"

Eades grunted. "We exaggerate, I assure you." He reached over and patted her hand, making Alexis shiver. She began to feel a bit like a small rodent caught at dinner with a serpent and a crocodile, only wondering which of the two would make a meal of her first. "A bit of bargaining, no more."

The two finally settled on a sum that Alexis still felt was ridiculously high, but Eades seemed satisfied with, and no accounting, which satisfied Dansby.

"Now we've settled that —" Eades pulled a bag from under the table and slid it toward Alexis. "— you'll want to change into these."

Alexis opened the bag and found the sort of ship's jumpsuit she was quite used to, but this one worn, a sort of light brown color, and decidedly not Navy issue. She'd had doubts about this entire plan from the beginning and nothing she'd heard had eased her mind. She sighed. Whatever her feelings, though, she had her orders.

"Yes, I suppose I must."

TWENTY-ONE

ALEXIS FOLLOWED Dansby down the station corridor. She felt very out of place without her uniform and fought the urge to stare at passersby who, she was sure, were carefully noting her. She'd spent over two years in the Service, wearing nothing but the Navy's dark blue ship's jumpsuit or her more elaborate dress uniforms, and everything about the jumpsuit Eades had provided seemed wrong. It was the wrong color, the wrong material, certainly the wrong fit, as her proper uniforms had been tailored to her small frame by a variety of hands aboard ship. Most distressing was how bare her head felt from the lack of the beret she'd worn every day for so long. Though she knew it wasn't so, she was convinced that everyone aboard the station could tell at a glance that she belonged in different garb.

Dansby gestured at her impatiently.

"Hurry along now, Rikki. I haven't got all day."

Alexis bristled. "I should like to know where we're going, before I blindly follow you, Mister Dansby." She frowned. "And what do you mean by calling me that?"

"Rikki?" Dansby asked, as though surprised she didn't understand. "Tavi? Kipling?" He sighed. "Did they teach you to read at all on your pig farm?"

Alexis started to retort, but Dansby cut her off.

"Oh, very well." He stepped close to her and whispered. "Will you at least slouch a bit, Miss Carew? You walk as though you've a yardarm up your arse."

Alexis glared at him, but let her shoulders fall a bit lower as they resumed walking. That only increased her self-consciousness, for it forced her to think about how she was walking, and surely any onlooker would be able to tell it wasn't her natural gait.

I must get better at this before we reach Hanover.

Dansby glanced over at her and shook his head. "Something *between* a Queen's Officer and a chimpanzee if you can at all manage it?"

She bit back a retort but straightened her back. They walked along and Dansby led her down several levels until she noticed that it was he who now looked out of place. Her bearing might not be as casual as that of those around her, but at least the low quality of her jumpsuit fit in better. Dansby, in his tailored suit and clearly expensive grooming, was drawing speculative looks from those around them — looks that Alexis noticed quickly turned away when Dansby met them with his own glare.

Out of place or not, they see him as a danger.

"Perhaps, Mister Dansby," Alexis said, "as we're to play these parts, it were best if we decided upon what we're to call each other?" She set her feet and glared at him. "And it shan't be this 'Rikki', or what have you."

Dansby grimaced. "Oh, very well, yes, the parts," he said. "In truth, I find it a silly bit of business, but you're too young — and look younger — for me to have any other reason to have you aboard my ship."

"That is not a part I believe I would willingly play in any case, Mister Dansby," Alexis said.

Dansby cast her a sidelong glance. "Meant you're not old enough to be someone I'd hire aboard," he said. "Not old enough to have made any reputation to speak of that would warrant it."

Alexis flushed. "I see."

His eyes moved over her. "'Course it's a long trip," he said, "and if you were to get lonely …"

Alexis ground her teeth for a moment. "If you were the last man alive, Mister Dansby, we might, perhaps, discuss which species should best replace humanity … but no more, I assure you."

Dansby laughed. "Perhaps the snakes, Carew?" He paused. "But you're right, really. 'Uncle', I suppose, is best for you to call me, but for you … is there some endearment your family uses?"

Alexis felt her gorge rise at the thought of Dansby using any endearment at all, much less one her grandfather might have called her. "You may use my given name … *uncle*. And no more. We are not close relations, after all, and the charade is that we've only recently met, yes?"

"Very well. Alexis it will be then."

Alexis shuddered. Even that allowance was far more familiar than she wished to be with Avrel Dansby.

Dansby stopped them at a disreputable-looking chandlery and motioned for her to enter. It had none of the order and organization she'd grown accustomed to in chandleries catering to Naval ships. Dark and dirty, with samples scattered everywhere and little order that she could see. Dust rose from the shelves as they passed and tickled her nose.

They were met by an abrupt, "What do y'want?" from the proprietor as they entered.

"To take my money elsewhere, if that's how I'm to be greeted, you surly sot!" Dansby yelled.

Alexis looked at him in shock, as did the chandler. There was a long pause, then the chandler cocked his head to one side.

"Dansby?" he asked. He smiled widely and hurried out from behind his counter to embrace Dansby. "Damned if it ain't! Good lord, man, look at ya! Y'do clean up proper nice!"

Alexis waited, prepared for Dansby to introduce her, but the two men simply continued chatting. She moved on to browse the items for sale. She would have to, effectively, outfit herself from scratch, as none of her Naval gear would be appropriate — even the underthings she'd kept on after changing into the jumpsuit Eades had given her would have to go, she realized. They were clearly Navy issue and would certainly raise the suspicions of a smuggler's crew if seen. At least this chandlery, as it catered to civilian crews, had ... *How was it the Navy chandler, Doakes, described it when I was going aboard* Merlin? *'Items of a feminine nature.'* She would even need a new vacsuit. *Sizes, though ...*

"Excuse me," she called. "*Uncle?*"

Dansby paused his conversation and smiled. "Yes, dear niece?"

Alexis inhaled deeply and stopped her first response before smiling as sweetly as she was able. "Would you please ask your friend, to whom you've failed to introduce me, if he might have any smaller sizes in the back?"

Both the chandler and Dansby looked at her oddly. "Those're the ready-mades, miss," the chandler said. "For spacers in a grand hurry, you might say. Just pick out what y'like an' it'll be made up for your size." He turned back to Dansby. "Bit provincial, is she?"

"Colonial, even," Dansby said, grinning. "Likely expects a needle and thread to be involved."

Alexis flushed, but went back to examining the shelves, quite convinced that Dansby had expected her question and been waiting for it just to discomfit her.

Well, at least I've not to worry about the cost, she thought, moving to what appeared to be the most expensive ship's jumpsuits in the shop.

She fingered the fabric, which promised to be quite a bit more comfortable than those the Navy issued. The Foreign Office might never see the funds Eades had advanced to Dansby again, but with him footing the bill for her outfitting she'd not feel at all bad about spending his money.

Alexis continued to shop while the two men talked quietly over the counter. At first, she thought to worry what they were discussing, but she overheard snippets as she moved about and it seemed to be no more than two old friends catching up after some time apart.

She moved the last of her selections to the shop's counter and waited while Dansby and the chandler continued to talk. She had to admit the pile was quite impressive, even with only one of each item being on the counter itself. She assumed, like most chandlers, this one would take the order and quantities and have most of the items delivered directly to the ship.

After a time, the two men wandered over.

"All ready, dear niece?" Dansby asked.

Alexis nodded, determined to have some words with Dansby about his form of address. She thought they'd agreed he'd use her given name.

"I am," she said.

"This is my niece, Alexis, Bickham," Dansby said, finally introducing her.

Bickham nodded to Alexis, then returned his gaze to Dansby. "Thought y'had no family?"

"A distant relation," Dansby said. "Grandfather's brother's line, really. Quite forgotten about them, until dear Alexis contacted me." He grinned. "She was about to be married off to a pig farmer on some colony world, you see, and fair begged me to become her savior. Isn't that right, dear niece?"

Alexis kept her thoughts off her face as much as she was able. "For the most part, uncle," she said, "though I'm sure Mister Bickham isn't at all interested in such things."

"Nonsense," Dansby said. "Bickham's an old friend of mine and always one for a tale." He rested his elbows on the counter and leaned toward Bickham. "I sent her some money, of course, for though I've had no contact with that branch of the family, I felt my obligation to her sorely, and dear Alexis here hopped aboard the very next merchantman to make her way to me." He shook his head. "Not too much for planning, though, the dear girl. Fled with naught but the clothes on her back and what money I'd sent her. Had her pockets picked at the first station they stopped at and lost all the coin. Lucky she'd paid in full for her passage or she'd have been stuck there, isn't that right dear niece?"

"Yes, uncle," she said, staring at him. "It was quite naive of me to be so trusting. I shan't make that mistake again, I assure you."

"See that y'don't, miss," Bickham said, nodding. "Lots o'untrust-worthies around."

"Indeed," Alexis agreed, not taking her eyes from Dansby.

"Had to sell even the clothes she'd fled in," Dansby went on, seemingly oblivious to Alexis' growing anger. "So as to have even a few pence to supplement the ship's meals, you see, and so arrived with nothing at all but this second- or third-hand jumpsuit. Not quite the sight I expected when I met her ship, I can tell you."

"No doubt," Bickham said. He patted Alexis' hands where they rested on the countertop. "Well, yer uncle'll take care o'ya now, miss, y'just wait and see."

"I'm sure he will, Mister Bickham." The corners of her lips curled up a bit. "Uncle Dansby was quite distraught when I arrived and he saw the state I'd been traveling in for so long. He was most profuse with his promises that I suffer no such deprivations now that I'd arrived." She slid the first pile of items — jumpsuit, underthings, and boots, all the finest and most expensive she'd found in the store — toward Bickham. "I shall never be able to express my full gratitude for Uncle Dansby's generosity." She saw Dansby's face tighten. "A round dozen of each of these, I think — save the boots, of course. A single pair of those."

The norm aboard Navy ships and most merchantmen was six, and Alexis saw Dansby frown and begin to speak.

"I know, uncle, but ..." She ran a hand over the jumpsuit she wore and looked up at him with wide eyes. "After so many weeks with just the one ..."

Dansby cleared his throat, made as if to speak, and then shrugged.

"We'll just get yer sizes, then, miss," Bickham said.

He gestured to a hatch behind the counter and Alexis went through it to find herself in a small room with a raised, circular platform in the center. Bickham had slid the hatch shut behind her and left her alone, so she stood silently for a time, waiting. Eventually she slid the hatch open and peered out.

"Excuse me, Mister Bickham," she said, "but what am I to do?"

Alexis flushed as Dansby laughed out loud and Bickham looked at her curiously. "Be measured, miss?"

"Stand on the platform," Dansby said, still laughing. "It'll tell you what to do." He turned to Bickham. "Colonial."

Alexis slid the hatch shut, face burning, and stepped onto the platform. The room's lights dimmed and she jumped as a series of lasers shone through the room, playing over her body, then again as a voice sounded.

"Please remain still for proper measurements," the voice said, a female voice, though clearly generated.

Alexis snorted as she realized what it was, no more than a larger version of the device that could scan a part for replication aboard ship. She stood still and the lights played over her again.

"Please remove all clothing for proper measurements," the voice said.

Alexis glanced once at the hatch, which was shut but didn't seem to have a lock. She shrugged and undressed, shivering in the chill station air. The hard plastic of the platform was even colder on her feet. She resumed her place and the lights played over her again. The voice gave a series of instructions — where to stand, how to stand — and Alexis followed them. She sighed with relief when she was finally done and the voice said, "Measurements have been completed and transferred to your tablet. Have a nice day."

"Thank you," Alexis said automatically as she stepped down from the platform.

"You're welcome."

She dressed quickly and slid the hatch open.

"Order'll be no more'n an hour," Bickham said. "Here or delivered straight t' yer ship?"

"I've taken lodgings," Dansby said. "Have them sent to The Glaive, if you please."

Bickham raised an eyebrow. "The Glaive, is it? Yer doin' better'n I thought."

"Well enough," Dansby said.

"Excuse me," Alexis said, not sure if she'd heard properly. "Did you say the whole lot would be run up in an hour's time?" A dozen jumpsuits and underthings, plus boots, all to her size and in only an hour?

Bickham laughed and shared a look with Dansby. She was quite certain they were both thinking the same thing, *colonial*, but it was a surprise to her. Clothing on Dalthus was still mostly hand-made and she'd had no need for anything but uniforms since joining the Navy — those were bought ready-made from the Naval chandlers and altered for her by the hands aboard ship. Many of the crew were dab hands with a needle and thread, for they'd much rather mend a torn uniform than purchase new — why waste the cost of a good beer, after all?

"The manufactory for these is here on-station," Bickham said. "Order's already in their queue to be made."

"Of course," Alexis said. Indeed, of course, for why shouldn't there be a machine to make the clothing to order just as the carpenter aboard ship could tap a few things into his tablet and have a new halyard or pulley, or even an entire mast, printed by the replicators? Once a system's infrastructure became large enough to support such a thing it would be common-place. But clothing had always been such a utilitarian thing that she'd never considered it. A thought began to form, but Dansby spoke before it became fully realized.

"We'll need to see your special room, as well, Bickham," Dansby said.

The chandler raised an eyebrow. "Really?"

"If she's to come aboard ship with me, it's probably best."

Alexis looked from one to the other, but neither paid her any attention and she didn't want to seem "colonial" again, so she simply followed. They went behind the counter and through another hatch, then down a dim corridor to where Bickham stopped facing a seemingly blank bulkhead. He tapped in a particular place and a portion of the bulkhead slid back to reveal another compartment.

She followed them in and stopped, staring around in amazement as lights came on. Weapons of all sorts and sizes littered the walls and counters. Blades, from tiny knives to elegant dueling swords, chemical-propellant pistols, laser pistols, flechettes.

What a bounty of potential mayhem ...

Dansby and Bickham were muttering together again, but this time Alexis felt no need to join them. She was far too fascinated with the surroundings and wandered the room take in all that was on offer. She'd thought for some time that she should purchase some personal weapons — all of the other lieutenants had something more than the dress sword they wore with their uniform — but hadn't found the time.

"Alexis? Dear niece?" Dansby was calling. She looked up from a display of lasers that were not only sold as matched sets for dueling, but whose capacitor cartridges were made of gallenium for use in *darkspace*. Despite the shocking price, she was sorely tempted to have a pair — to be able to fire lasers during a boarding action would be decisive. But the thought of dropping one or more of those cartridges, priced at nearly twenty pounds, while reloading with a vacsuit's gloves on, was daunting.

"This might be appropriate for you," Dansby said, holding his hand out to her. "It will give you some means of defense and it isn't too great to handle."

Alexis stared at his hand for a moment, thinking it was empty, until she saw the small flechette gun he held. It was a tiny thing. The darts must be no more than five centimeters. In fact it was almost smaller than her own hand and was dwarfed in Dansby's. As a weapon it would be deadly enough — tiny darts would be stripped off a solid block of plastic embedded with metal and impelled by magnets at the target — but it was still so small that Alexis felt a surge of irritation that Dansby simply assumed it was all she could handle.

"Uncle Dansby ... *dear* uncle," Alexis said. "Perhaps this might be the proper time to have a word or two about assumptions."

In the end, Alexis had to prove to Dansby that she could, indeed, use the items she'd selected. The look on his face when they crossed practice blades was only slightly less satisfying than that he had when she demonstrated her marksmanship.

No more than half of those in the station's corridors were openly armed, though, so it was with no little self-consciousness that she stepped out of Bickham's shop. The sword on her left hip was a bit longer and much lighter than the cutlasses a Naval crew might use in a boarding action. Not so long as a gentleman's sword for dueling, but long enough to make up for her shorter arms in action against another ship's crew. The chemical-propellant pistol on her right hip would look too large in her hands, but it was powerful enough to punch through even a Naval vacsuit, and its recoil wasn't so great that she'd be unable to use it in vacuum or if a ship's gravity were cut, provided she was able to brace herself against something.

Bickham had convinced her to take a shorter blade as well. She'd been reluctant, as she'd never used one, and the marines she'd trained with aboard ship had always been quite clear that there was never a winner in a knife-fight — only one who was bleeding somewhat less than the other. But if she were to find herself hard-pressed in close quarters, a smaller blade might be useful. She had two now. Both short and slim, but very sharp. One strapped to the inside of her left forearm and one in the outside of her right boot. Bickham had altered the orders for both her jumpsuits and boots to make accommodations for them, so that they'd be easier to draw.

Lastly the tiny flechette pistol Dansby had selected was tucked into the small of her back. Bickham had changed the jumpsuits she'd ordered for that as well, giving her a small, unobtrusive pocket that sealed the pistol in place without being at all noticeable.

All in all, she was better armed than she'd ever been — even aboard ship with a boarding imminent.

"It's not as though you'll be fighting battles aboard *Marilyn*, you know," Dansby said, his voice sour.

"I simply wish to be prepared for any eventuality, uncle," Alexis said. In truth, she'd been wanting some personal weapons for some time — to have them paid for out of Dansby's purse was simply icing on the cake. "*Marilyn?* Is that your ship?"

Dansby nodded. "Her name'll change when we enter Hanoverese space, but that's what she's called now."

Alexis remembered the litany of ships' names Eades had read off. "Are all your ships named after women?"

Dansby leered. "Amazing what a lady'll do if she thinks you've named a ship for her."

Alexis sighed. Life aboard ship with Dansby was going to be a chore, no doubt. She thought of the idea she'd had before being distracted by Bickham's armaments room. Civilian clothes would not be at all amiss, if they were to be had as readily as her jumpsuits.

"I believe our next stop should be a civilian clothier — for something other than shipboard attire."

Dansby scowled. "Now what do you need that for, *niece?*"

Alexis looped an arm through his and pulled him into motion. "Well, *uncle*, a man may wear the same three suits day after day, but if I'm to meet who I plan to, then I should be prepared to dress for any occasion or venue." She scanned the storefronts for someplace that looked likely. Her dress uniform was appropriate attire for any event, but she couldn't very well wear it in Hanover. Nor could she wear a simple, ship's jumpsuit in any but the most common of station pubs. "After all, there's no telling where he'll be. There may be many meetings necessary to settle the proposal, and they could occur over dinner, at a club, perhaps a ball, anywhere at all."

"A *ball?*" Dansby asked, nearly choking.

"Of course." Alexis patted his arm, already planning what she'd need. Clothes had never been very important to her. On Dalthus, denim trousers and a linen shirt would suffice for most days. She'd owned one dress that she wore for special occasions — she did *not* include the horrid, pink concoction her grandfather had seen fit to buy her for courting. Since she'd entered the Navy, it had been nothing but uniforms. Even at liberty, a uniform would suffice. But meeting Delaine in Hanover, she'd have to appear as something other than a simple spacer — especially a foreign spacer. No, civilian dress was the thing, and fine enough that no one would think twice about seeing her in conversation with a young lieutenant. "Don't worry, uncle," she said. "We'll only need a few things here. The rest we may purchase at our destination."

"*Rest?*"

TWENTY-TWO

"And for yourself, miss?"

Alexis glanced up from the menu displayed on the table's surface to the hovering server. Hovering, indeed, for it was simply a thick, round tray floating in the air beside the table. She blinked once, then caught the smirk on Dansby's face. He seemed to take an inordinate amount of glee in her reaction to any technology she hadn't encountered before. A glee which irked her both for him looking down on her and because it caused her to dampen her own enthusiasm.

I should be able to enjoy these things without being laughed at.

"Do you have Scotch?" she asked. She saw Dansby frown, likely at the price, for real Scotch whiskey was produced in only three systems and cost of transport made it dear indeed.

Dansby cleared his throat, but the menu in front of Alexis had already changed to display The Glaive's selection of whiskeys.

"The Auchindoun Reserve, please," Alexis said. It wasn't the most costly on the list, but the price was high enough to sting.

"Very good, miss." The server floated away.

"I should have taken you straight to my ship," Dansby said, "and saved my purse."

"And have me come aboard in some spacer's castoffs, uncle?" Alexis smoothed the front of her dress. "That would never do, I think."

Dansby frowned. "Wouldn't have thought you such a clotheshorse, coming from the Navy as you have."

"And I would have thought you'd speak with more circumspection, considering your line of work." Alexis glanced around the dining room to see if anyone was close enough to overhear.

"The privacy field's on," Dansby said, tapping a red light at the center of the table. "No one can hear us."

"If there's one thing my association with Mister Eades has taught me, *uncle*, it's that no system is entirely secure."

Dansby grunted.

Alexis smoothed her dress' skirts and had to admit to herself that he had a point about the clothes. She'd not have thought it of herself, either, but the remainder of the day's shopping had been ... enlightening. The first civilian clothier they'd stopped into had completely changed Alexis' perception of both clothing and herself.

The shopkeeper had taken her in hand and she'd found that the scanner in Mister Bickham's shop had stored on her tablet not only her sizes, but a complete three-dimensional rendering of her. The clothier's systems could show her a life-size image of herself wearing virtually anything the shop offered. Alexis had merely to react to seeing it and the system would quickly move on, using her expression of approval or dislike to determine what she was presented with next, and doing a quite creditable job of learning her tastes.

The outcome of which was that the longer she stayed in the shop, the more she liked what was presented to her. There were even, she discovered, some ... structural enhancements, as the shopkeeper described them, that made the most of what little she had, and she found herself judging each outfit presented to her by what she thought Delaine might make of it.

In the end, it was only Dansby's insistence that they had barely enough time to return to The Glaive and dress for supper that had convinced her to leave the shop. She'd settled on only four outfits, varied to be suitable for a wide range of occasions. The most delightful, and expensive, being the dress she wore now.

The dress was a rich, deep purple, accented in black. Its skirts didn't billow like the dresses that had been in fashion when she left Dalthus, but instead fell in straight lines that made her, somehow, seem taller. In fact every aspect of the dress seemed to be perfectly designed for her, accentuating those attributes she had and, she had to admit, enhancing those she did not.

No, I'd never have considered myself to be one to care about such things, but ...

She slid her hands over the skirts again, delighting in the feel of the fabric. She caught Dansby staring at her and flushed.

The server returned with their drinks, which slid off its surface and onto the table without spilling a drop. Alexis took a small sip of hers, and then another, and made a mental note to remember this one. It was really quite good.

"Will you be having wine with the meal?" Dansby asked. "Or will you be swilling my guineas the entire evening?"

"Perhaps I should have a bottle sent to our rooms, uncle? To celebrate our new enterprise?"

Dansby looked pained and Alexis almost had a moment's sympathy for the man. She hadn't looked at the cost of a single thing she'd bought that day, only smiled at Dansby's look of outrage when presented with the reckoning. On the other hand, he'd once been a pirate and was now a smuggler, and seemed to have done well for himself at both, even leaving aside what Eades had paid him.

Two servers appeared and slid plates onto the table in front of each of them. Dansby dug into his with gusto.

"Enjoy the meal, Carew. There'll be nothing like this once we reach Hanover."

"Do you not care for the food, then?" Alexis asked, glad to be hearing even a little about where they'd soon be going.

"The cakes are wonderful, but they have an unnatural penchant for pork and sausages." He chewed a mouthful of food thoughtfully. "Should you be offered anything called *currywurst*, I suggest you refuse. Neither Hanover nor *Deuchsterne* are able to put on a proper curry ... and there are some things that simply shouldn't be prepared that way. That's one reason I chose to stay at The Glaive tonight, instead of going directly aboard *Marilyn*." He raised another forkful to his lips. "And I plan to see a play after supper, before we head off into the hinterlands. I find Hanover's entertainments no more to my liking than their curries."

"What play is that?" Alexis asked with some interest. She'd rather not go with Dansby, but she'd found she enjoyed live performances, though she'd only been to a few.

"*Henry V.* It's one of the histories."

Alexis sat back and pursed her lips. "I realize that you and Mister Eades at least found common cause in ridiculing my colonial origins, Mister Dansby, but I did learn some of New London's history and I well know we've only had three Henry's in the Monarchy."

Dansby stared at her for a moment, unmoving, and Alexis thought she'd put him at a loss for words until he suddenly barked laughter that actually sprayed food onto the table. He laughed more, then started coughing and grasped for his wine.

Alexis flushed.

If he falls over and turns blue, I'll not lift a finger to save him.

"Oh, dear lord," Dansby said finally, alternating between drinking and clearing his throat. "That may be ..." He coughed violently. "I suggest you learn your classics, Carew. It will give you something to pass the time on our voyage."

THE PLAY, Alexis allowed as she and Dansby left the theatre and made their way through the station's corridors back to The Glaive, had been quite good, and she was rather pleased with herself for wrangling her way to see it along with Dansby. She hadn't fully understood it, but it was captivating enough to make her want to. And she understood Dansby's amusement at her a bit better, now that she'd seen the play was based on a different kingdom than New London.

She knew little of Earth's history — what little history she'd studied had more to do with New London than anything before that ruling system was founded — but thought now she might be well-advised to learn more.

Between histories, strategy texts, and these 'classics', I may be studying the rest of my life.

"I suggest you get a good night's sleep," Dansby said as they neared The Glaive. "I expect to be aboard *Marilyn* and making sail midway through the morning watch, and remember that I'll have you keep to yourself for most of the voyage. As my 'niece' it will be your first journey with us and it's reasonable you'd simply remain silent and observe."

Alexis fought down a sigh. Perhaps one of the most enjoyable things about the play had been that Avrel Dansby had remained silent throughout.

"Tell me about the ship and crew," Alexis prompted, hoping to pry a bit of solid information from the man, "and your plan for finding Commodore Balestra's fleet."

"Plan?" Dansby gave her a bemused look. "I have as much plan at this point as Eades does, which is to say none. He's turned the whole mess over to me with no more plan than 'go find them'."

Once again, Alexis was struck that their only common ground seemed to be a mutual dislike and distrust of Mister Eades. She eyed Dansby.

I suppose even a snake can recognize something slimier than himself.

"There's a system called Baikonur," Dansby went on, "a bit inside Hanoverese space. No habitable planets, but there's a mining outpost with a less than thorough bureaucracy. We'll head there first —

someone will have heard of where this Balestra's fleet has been stationed."

Alexis grimaced in distaste. "Some other pirate or smuggler, I presume."

"Someone with reason to keep track of the Hanoverese navy's comings and going, and willing to answer questions while not speaking of what's been asked." Dansby shrugged. "This system, Baikonur, does tend to attract an unsavory sort. If it offends your sensibilities, you're welcome to stay here and tell Eades you refuse to go. I've been paid either way."

Alexis sighed. "I suppose I'll have to get used to the idea. And your crew?"

Dansby shrugged. "They'll do as they're told and not ask questions."

TWENTY-THREE

"'Niece', my arse, Dansby! What're you getting us into now?"

Alexis widened her eyes at the woman's outburst and took a half step back, placing Dansby firmly at the forefront on his ship's mess deck and bearing the brunt of the woman's ire.

The crew of Dansby's ship, *Marilyn*, was the scruffiest, surliest looking group Alexis had ever encountered. Naval crews often had hard men, men taken straight from the gaols and given the choice between the Navy and imprisonment, transport, or even hanging. She was used to that. These, though, were different. Alexis had the sense that these were men who'd done all the things that might warrant imprisonment, transport, or hanging ... but had been smart enough to not get caught.

And women, she thought.

The crew consisted of twelve men and two women, and any elation Alexis had first felt about being aboard ship with other women for the first time was quickly quashed.

"Now, Anya," Dansby said, holding up his hands in a placating gesture. "There's nothing more to it than I've said already."

"Bollocks! Bollocks in a vice!"

Dansby winced visibly. He'd gathered *Marilyn's* crew on the mess deck and introduced Alexis to them as his niece, much removed, who'd had some issues with her family's shipping company. Issues that made it prudent for her to remove herself far from the systems in which they traded — and which led all concerned to believe she might be better suited for the work Dansby's side of the family engaged in.

Alexis tried a tentative smile, but the woman glared at her. Anya Mynatt was *Marilyn's* first mate, something Alexis had been thrilled to discover until the woman began talking.

"You promised me I'd have this ship when Tarver left it! Now he isn't captain any longer, but you're in his cabin instead of me, and brought this bedwarmer aboard!"

"Mist ... Miss Mynatt!" Alexis objected. She cursed herself for the slip, but wasn't used to addressing anyone aboard ship except as mister or by rank. The rest of the crew would be addressed simply by last name, as on a Navy ship, and the only other petty officer, a master's mate named Bowhay, was clearly a 'mister' with his bald head and massive beard, but she was at a loss as to what to call a female petty officer on a civilian ship.

"Shut your gob, you little trollop!"

Alexis' temper flared, but Mynatt advanced on Dansby.

"Anya," Dansby said again. "I have a special, *profitable*, run to make that I want to oversee personally. When we're done, Tarver will still be gone and you'll have *Marilyn*, I assure you."

Mynatt scowled at him then pointed at Alexis. "And the tart?"

"My *niece*," Dansby insisted.

Mynatt stared at him for a moment, nostrils flaring. She looked Alexis up and down, then stormed off.

Dansby sighed. "Will you get us underway, please, Bowhay? I'll have a course for you once we're in *darkspace*."

"Aye, sir," Bowhay said. "Hands t'make way! Be about it lads!"

Dansby sighed again as the crew dispersed.

"Do you allow all your employees to speak to you so, uncle?" Alexis asked.

Dansby grunted and gestured for her to follow him toward *Marilyn's* quarterdeck. The ship was a small sloop, which accounted for the size of the crew. Alexis had been more than a bit relieved at seeing how few crew members there were. The small number lent some credence to Dansby's contention that his ships no longer engaged in piracy, for a pirate would have more men aboard. A bit of smuggling was easier for her to stomach.

"Anya's a special case," Dansby said.

"Perhaps she'll have a better opinion of me once it's seen I know my way about a ship?"

Dansby snorted. "No, I rather doubt that will be a help at all." He gestured for her to follow him. "Come along then. There're two cabins for the occasional passenger — both smaller than Anya's or Bowhay's, unless you'd like to speak to her about giving up the first mate's cabin?"

"No," Alexis said. "No, I'll be quite satisfied with whatever is available."

"Fine choice."

ALEXIS' tablet woke her at her usual time aboard ship, just before the start of the morning watch. She dressed quickly and spent a moment looking for her beret before remembering that she would not be wearing the Navy's customary headgear aboard this ship.

Then she exited her cabin to find the rest of *Marilyn* dark and silent, not the bustle of activity she was used to at this hour. Farther down the mess deck she could make out the shadowed shapes of the crew still in their bunks. With a frown, she made her way to the quarterdeck, expecting to find, at least, Dansby up and preparing for the day.

Instead she found a single spacer drowsing at the helm.

The man snorted and jerked awake as she entered, looked her over once, and then settled back into his place with half-closed eyes.

"*On your feet!*" Alexis barked without consciously deciding to. The man jumped, staring at her with wide eyes. Her jaw was clenched with anger. It was one thing to keep a different watch schedule, which was why she assumed the rest of the crew was still abed, but to be asleep on watch certainly couldn't be the norm for Dansby's ships.

"Bugger off, girl," the spacer replied, relaxing and closing his eyes again.

Alexis opened her mouth to yell at the man again, but paused in shock. She'd never been spoken to that way aboard ship, even the first she'd ever served on. It was suddenly driven home to her that *Marilyn* was not a Navy ship and that the rules could be quite different aboard her.

"Is it ..." She struggled to keep her voice level. "Is it common then, to sleep during one's watch aboard my uncle's ships?"

The spacer sighed. "Captain Tarver didn't care and Dansby's not said different." He grinned broadly. "Likely won't see that one afore noon, himself, is my guess." Alexis started to speak again but he cut her off. "Look, you, the helm's set, we're not carrying any cargo to worry about being inspected, there's no pirates near the borders, what with all the warships, and we're far enough in New London space still that there'll be no Hannie hunting around for a quick prize." He pointed at the navigation plot. "There're no ships in sight and the computer'll wake me if it suspects one, so ... bugger off then."

He closed his eyes.

Alexis blinked. She longed to call for the bosun, but *Marilyn* had none and no Captain's Mast to bring the man up on charges either.

And no Articles to charge him under.

She looked around the quarterdeck. Aside from there being only a single spacer on watch, and him asleep, *Marilyn* was not at all well kept. The decks and consoles were grimy, and there were bits of trash in odd places — it looked a great deal like the Hanoverese merchant

Trau Wunsch she'd stolen to escape Giron, and that ship had been in such poor condition mechanically that it had been sent to the breakers instead of the Prize Court.

She left the quarterdeck confused as to how to proceed. One thing was certain, though, she realized. Dansby had not made her position clear to the crew. They might know she was his niece, but not how she fit into the ship's hierarchy, if at all — something which would have to be corrected immediately.

Alexis left the quarterdeck and made her way to the master's cabin where Dansby slept. Abed until noon he might plan to be, but she'd see him out of it and dealing with his responsibilities.

She rapped on the cabin's hatch.

"Dansby? Uncle?"

She rapped again, harder this time. There was a sound from within but no answer.

"Uncle Dansby?"

She grasped the hatch's handle, intending to rattle it, but the hatch unlocked at her touch and slid smoothly open. Dansby had apparently not been at all particular when he'd given her the same access to the ship that he possessed. The cabin was dark, but Alexis heard another noise. She stepped inside switching on the light.

"There's no use hiding from me, uncle. I've some things to disc ..."

Marilyn's master's cabin was a single space, not the separated day- and sleeping-cabins Alexis was used to aboard larger warships. Dansby was, indeed, abed as the spacer had predicted. Also abed, and astride him, was Anya Mynatt.

"If you've come to join us, girl," Mynatt said, turning toward the hatch but not bothering to stop her movements, "you should know I'm partial to a bit more in the way of curves on a lass."

Alexis flushed. Yes, the rules were apparently quite different aboard this ship. She resisted the urge to bolt from the compartment, not wanting to give Mynatt the satisfaction of seeing her run.

"Uncle," she began, but then saw that Dansby wasn't looking at her. Was, possibly, still quite unaware of her presence at all. She cleared her throat. "Miss Mynatt, would you be so kind as to inform my uncle that I wish to speak to him on the quarterdeck? When he is not otherwise ... occupied."

Alexis backed out of the cabin without waiting for Mynatt's response. She slid the hatch closed and leaned forward to rest her forehead against it, then realized what was still going on behind it and leapt back as though the hatch itself were somehow associated. She looked at her hands and started toward the head to wash, feeling suddenly quite dirty.

Dear heavens, but I already miss the Navy.

ALEXIS WAITED for Dansby on the quarterdeck, studying the empty navigation plot and ignoring the amused glances of the now awake helmsman.

Certainly now *he's decided to remain awake.*

She caught her lower lip between her teeth, forced herself to stop it, then found her hands going to her head to straighten a nonexistent beret. Arms crossed and jaw clenched to keep from further fidgeting, she saw the helmsman openly grinning at her. Not the sort of grin at all that she'd experienced from spacers on Navy ships, no matter how hard the men were, but something else entirely.

Alexis glanced around the quarterdeck, but they were alone. There was no other officer, no marine sentry, no bosun for her to call on. The helmsman was now running his eyes over her in a way that made her feel decidedly greasy.

She wondered if she should leave and retrieve Dansby, whether he was quite finished or not, but dismissed the idea quickly. She'd be aboard some time and couldn't rely on him to always be near. No, she'd have to set some of her footing with the crew herself, and not in the Navy way with a bosun or the marines to back up her authority. Even aboard *Hermione* the captain wouldn't have allowed the common spacers to treat her this way; it would have undermined the authority of all his officers.

She thought about Mynatt, who must have some of this crew's respect to be first mate and expected to become captain. How had she come to be accepted as a leader among such a crew?

Certainly not by pretending to be a man.

Neither Mynatt's dress nor attitude implied that, and she certainly knew there were no secrets aboard ship, so she must expect to retain the crew's respect even after they found out about her and Dansby. Alexis suspected no amount of skill in ship handling or other spacer's skills would turn the trick, either.

The helmsman caught her eye again and leered. The look made Alexis shudder and want to leave the compartment, which, she realized, would be exactly the wrong thing to do. More so even than the hardest men aboard a Navy ship, Dansby's crew acted by a different set of rules than most. They preyed on others, one step above piracy and who knew what they went about on their own in ports, and would judge others to be predators as well, or simply prey.

No, she couldn't be a Naval lieutenant aboard *Marilyn*. She'd have to be something else, something harder. She thought she had it in her to be that, but the possibility did frighten her.

Her thoughts ran to Midshipman Timpson of *Hermione* and how she'd tried to goad him into challenging or attacking her while they were prisoners on Giron. True, he'd been the one to install a filter in *Hermione's* signals console that had trapped all of her messages from being delivered or sent for nearly a year, but part of Alexis had imagined simply walking into the cafe and shooting him. She worried what those impulses might lead her to, without the restraint of Naval discipline.

Alexis sighed. Worry she might, but she had little choice in how to deal with this crew.

She stepped close to the helmsman and leaned in, reaching behind her back for the hidden pocket where her new flechette pistol was kept. She had to rise up on her toes to get her lips next to the man's ear.

"What's your name?" she whispered.

"Embry," the man said, pressing closer to Alexis, but then freezing in place as he came in contact with the flechette pistol she'd moved between them at a particularly pointed height.

"Do you look at Miss Mynatt in that way, Embry?" Alexis asked, no longer whispering and voice hard.

Embry swallowed. "Um, no."

Alexis nodded. "Should I feel a need to prove my place aboard *Marilyn*, Embry, I'll do so in a way that makes Miss Mynatt look quite kind and forgiving in comparison. Do you take my meaning?"

Embry stepped back from her, nodded quickly, then locked his eyes on his helm and cleared his throat.

"Endearing yourself to my crew, niece?" Dansby slid the quarter-deck hatch shut behind him and crossed to the navigation plot.

"Establishing boundaries, uncle," Alexis said. She stepped back from Embry and slid the flechette pistol back into its hidden pocket. She clapped him on the shoulder with a friendly smile. "Isn't that right, Embry?"

Embry stared at her for a moment, eyes wide, then relaxed and shrugged, as though she'd settled firmly into a different slot in his mind. "Fair enough."

Dansby grunted.

Alexis nodded to Embry and went to Dansby's side. If this crew gossiped amongst themselves half as much as a Naval crew did, then she might at least have put an end to that particular bit of nonsense.

"Which would have been clearer and less dramatic if you had made my position and role clearer when we came aboard," Alexis whispered.

"I was a bit busy dealing with Anya, if you recall."

"As you were this morning, uncle."

Dansby flushed. "You wanted to speak to me about something?"

"Well, yes, several things, in fact. The state of the ship, for one."

Dansby frowned. "What about it?"

Alexis gestured around the quarterdeck, wondering if Dansby truly didn't see it. "Have *Marilyn's* decks had even a single bristle set to them since you acquired her?"

Dansby rubbed his eyes as though pained. "I realize that ... your side of the family trades in higher class of goods than I might," he said, "but most merchantmen don't. *Marilyn* looks as she does for a reason." He knelt and unscrewed the fasteners on a panel beneath the plot. "Look, what do you see?"

Alexis knelt and looked inside. The components were spotless and the wiring was neatly tied up. Even the inside face of the panel Dansby had pulled off was practically shining, unlike the dingy outer side.

"What —"

"Most merchantmen are small, ill-kept, and one failed trade away from debtors prison," Dansby said, standing. "When *Marilyn* is inspected at some port, I want the customs man to see exactly what he's seen on the last dozen ships and what he expects to see of the next dozen. She is to be, in all respects, unremarkable."

TWENTY-FOUR

"Beets?" Alexis watched the crates of roundish vegetables being carted through the hatch from the boat alongside. "Of all things, beets?"

Dansby shrugged. "They don't grow on Diebis — something in the soil." He tapped his tablet as a crewman pushed an antigrav pallet with another four crates through the hatch and toward *Marilyn's* hold. "We'll make a nice bit of profit on this cargo."

Alexis crossed her arms and waited until the rest of the pallets had come aboard and she was alone with Dansby at the hatch.

"You've stopped us at every world we've passed ... more than every world. Our course has zigged and zagged for weeks now. I thought we were sailing for this Baikonur place?"

Dansby touched his tablet a last time and looked down the tube to the station. He waved to one of the station workers there and slid *Marilyn's* hatch shut.

"Neither this system, nor any of the others we've zigged and zagged to offer much in the way of what Baikonur demands," he said. "Diebis, on the other hand, requires beets, and is quite close to Kennet."

"And?" Alexis asked, knowing there must be more.

"Kennet produces items of a, shall we say, intimate nature ... much in demand by the miners of Baikonur."

Alexis started to ask what products those might be, then decided that she truly didn't want to know.

"Then why didn't we simply sail directly to Kennet?" She shook her head. "Come to that, why not sail directly to Baikonur?"

Dansby gave her a pained look.

"We've had similar discussions before, I believe. *Röslein* is a merchant ship, dear niece, or must appear so. It would be odd, indeed, if she sailed straight from New London space to Baikonur, especially with a bloody war on."

Röslein was the ship's new name, changed in the signals console and all her registrations as the former-*Marilyn* had crossed the border to stop at the first system on Dansby's list to trade with.

"You've forged your ship's name easily enough," Alexis said. "Why can't you just forge these stops then and quit wasting time?"

Dansby rubbed his face. "I'm perfectly willing to falsify every bit of it, but the truth is so much more effective. If some overzealous local does happen to check things further than our logs, I'd prefer that as much as possible be the truth. Once someone's been overloaded with truth they stop looking for a lie, you see."

Alexis closed her eyes and nodded. She didn't like the delays but could see the sense of it.

"Please don't try to teach me my business. We're now an Hanoverese trader doing lawful business in Hanoverese systems. It's why my crew speaks fluent German ... and why I'd much prefer you stayed in your cabin while we're in port." Dansby shook his head. "I can't believe Eades sent you aboard without your having learned the language."

"I have a bit," Alexis said, "but found French much easier."

Dansby gave her a dubious look. "I don't see how. German's quite precise and logical — properly spoken French is indistinguishable from being asphyxiated."

"Still ... beets?"

Dansby double-checked that the hatch's lock was engaged and motioned for her to follow him to the quarterdeck.

"Do you think a smuggler carries nothing but what he smuggles?" He made a derisive noise. "Legitimate cargoes cover the illicit ones — they're what justifies our travels from system to system."

Alexis had a sudden thought and grabbed Dansby's arm to stop him.

"These 'legitimate cargoes' we've been carrying," she whispered. "Are you saying they're not all?"

"All what?"

"You know full well what I'm asking. Are there smuggled goods aboard this ship?"

"I'm not generally a produce hauler."

"But you're on a mission for the Crown!" Alexis kept her voice low, but she was furious. It was one thing to rely on Dansby knowing that he'd been a pirate and was a smuggler. It was quite another thing for him to endanger their mission with his activities. "What if the ship is searched?"

Dansby sighed. "I've been at this business a rather long time, you know. Besides, I'm known to the Hanoverese and they generally leave my ships alone. The subterfuge is more for the local system agents."

"Known to them?"

"Yes, known. They know that I smuggle and make use of my services on occasion to get a man into New London or information out." He waved a hand as she started to object. "Oh, Eades knows all about it. His men pick up the Hanoverese agents where I drop them off and keep them under surveillance."

"And the Hanoverese don't suspect this?"

Dansby shrugged. "They may, which is why Eades provides me with just enough true information to keep them guessing." He grinned at her. "It's a deep game we play when leaping into this particular rabbit hole, Carew. We can only hope it's our side who owns the bottom."

His words didn't put her any more at ease, as she was still not convinced that Dansby's side was the same as hers.

TWENTY-FIVE

Röslein née Marilyn finally arrived at Baikonur. The system itself was remarkable only in that it had no remaining planets whatsoever, just a series of asteroid belts, as though some long-ago cataclysm had shattered every planet that formed.

Those asteroids, though, were remarkable in that they contained a great deal of gallenium, and so Hanoverese miners flocked to the system in a rush to extract the wealth.

The system's only station was a hodgepodge of traditional station modules cobbled together with the remains of ships that were too decrepit ever to risk *darkspace* again, yet solid enough that they could be used as habitats instead of being sent to the breakers.

That they were being used this way was a further testament to the gallenium ore in the system. Despite those hulls having valuable gallenium embedded in them, they were being used as habitats in normal space instead of being broken up for scrap. In Baikonur, it was easier and cheaper to mine fresh ore than to melt down an otherwise useless ship.

One entire section of the station seemed to be made up of

nothing but a large loop of station corridor, with decrepit ships permanently filling the inside of the loop and temporary docking for visiting merchants along the outer edge.

Dansby docked *Röslein* along this stretch, as the place he'd meet his contacts was deep in the middle.

Alexis followed him through the maze of interconnecting corridors and ships.

"I've brought you along with me at your insistence, niece, but you simply can't join me at the table."

"I'd only like to hear for myself."

"And this sort of man won't speak with someone he doesn't know at the table. Especially a stranger with too much English in her German. Most of those on station won't care — this is the sort of place in Hanover that someone fleeing New London for a misunderstanding would head for. The Hanoverese authorities care about nothing here, save that there's no gallenium smuggled out. But this particular man takes more care than most."

"'Fleeing a misunderstanding'?"

"Discretion being the better part of not being hanged, yes."

"Such wonderful places you take me to, uncle."

They left the main corridor into the maze of interconnected ships' hulls that made up the center. Some were stitched together with more sections of station corridor, while others had their hulls and locks welded directly to the next, and still others had lengths of flimsy ship's boarding tubes stretched between them.

"Perhaps I should have worn my vacsuit," Alexis murmured.

"You'd look too out of place," Dansby answered. "Risk assessment is not amongst these men's more prominent traits." He grinned at her. "Else they'd not have had those misunderstandings to flee from."

They entered a long length of station corridor that stretched between two hulls, with other hulls to either side. It appeared the corridor had become the dumping ground for all those connected to it, with stacks of shipping crates and piles of refuse strewn about.

There was barely enough room to walk side by side between the refuse and only a few places where they could see the corridor's bulkheads at all.

"Here," Dansby said, gesturing to the next alcove in the trash and crates. This one led to a hatch, behind which was a mid-sized merchant hull turned into some sort of pub. The messdeck, on which they entered, was a large common room, full of tables and bustling with activity. The servers were human, not automated, and based on the girl who set down her tray of drinks, grasped a miner's hand, and led him laughing to the aft companionway, both they and the deck above were available for more than simply food and drink.

Dansby led her to an empty table, gestured for a server, ordered wine for the both of them, and waited until they'd been served before speaking again.

"I see my man in the back — and, no, I won't point him out to you. Don't go looking, either, and don't stare when I go to meet him. I'll tell you all he tells me as soon as I return."

Alexis drained her glass. She'd grown more and more nervous the farther they went into Hanoverese space. With every throw of the ship's log, her growing dependency on Dansby had gnawed at her. That he'd done nothing untoward failed to ease her fears. After such a long time aboard ship with him, she suspected he had a bit of integrity, at least that he'd like to think so, and that he'd stick with the job he'd been paid to do so long as he could. It was what circumstances might convince him he could no longer fulfill the terms of his contract that concerned her. She'd be far more comfortable if she heard for herself what their destination might be.

Dansby leaned close and whispered to her, as though having read her thoughts. "I've never failed Eades in a task, Carew, and I'd not want to learn what might happen were I to do so."

Alexis studied his face. She found trusting hard enough when the recipient was worthy. She forced her jaw muscles to relax.

"Very well."

Dansby grunted and rose. He left, walked to the other table, and sat, making no show of greeting. Soon he was bent over head close to the other man, whispering. Alexis watched them for a moment, but realized her scrutiny would only draw attention to Dansby as others wondered what she found so interesting. She forced herself to look away, not wanting to draw too much attention to Dansby's meeting. She poured herself another glass of wine and scanned the rest of the pub.

Dansby had described Baikonur as a vile hub of smugglers and piracy, and the pub, from what Alexis could see, was the worst of the lot. Looking around, she thought he hadn't gone nearly far enough in his description.

The clientele made her want to spin around in circles so as to never allow any of them at her back for too long, and she found, as she looked around, that the other patrons were as aware of her gaze as she was of theirs. One in particular seemed to raise his eyes to meet her whenever her gaze moved in his direction — or eye, rather, as he sat in profile to her. She could only see half of his face, and that so scarred and disfigured that she found the sight uncomfortable.

"Kann ich dich begleiten?"

Alexis spun her gaze around and found a man standing at her table. He smiled and repeated himself, but Alexis had no idea what he'd said. For a moment, she panicked at how to respond, but then remembered Dansby's assurances that Baikonur was so near the border and had so varied a clientele that English would not seem suspicious here.

"I'm sorry. I don't understand," she said.

The man smiled broader. "Ah, English." He pointed at the chair across from her. "I to sit?"

Alexis frowned. "You want to borrow the chair?"

The man shook his head, laughing. *"Nein."* He pointed at her then at the chair. "Pretty girl. I to sit?"

Alexis glanced around. Dansby was still hunched over the table talking to the man he'd come to meet. The disfigured man glanced away again as her gaze passed over him and a chill went through her for some reason. She looked back at the man by her table.

"You want to join me?"

The man smiled. "Very pretty."

"Thank you," she said. "But no." She tried a tentative smile so as not to offend him.

The man frowned. "So alone. Pretty girl should not be alone."

Alexis took a deep breath. "I ..."

Is it so inconceivable that I should be at a table alone?

She glanced around again. The man was keeping her from seeing what Dansby was doing, but she still didn't want to be rude.

"I'm waiting for someone," she said finally.

"Ah," the man nodded and walked away.

Alexis frowned. She wondered if this sort of thing was common. She'd never encountered it before, but she'd never really gone anywhere on leave except in her uniforms. She shook her head.

As though I couldn't possibly stand being alone, but so long as I'm claimed by another ...

She glanced around again and saw the disfigured man staring at her again. She found her own eyes drawn to him as well. There was something about him — she frowned. Was it a familiarity?

As her eyes passed over him again, he raised a glass to his lips and Alexis saw that it was not only his face that was disfigured. His arm had been replaced by a crude prosthetic. It moved well enough for him to grasp his glass, but its covering lacked the more lifelike hue she'd expect even from one made on her homeworld or printed aboard ship.

Perhaps Baikonur lacked the facilities to manufacture better, but the clientele of this pub were supposedly spacers, who'd travel widely and surely make stops where he could receive better care.

She started to avoid looking at him directly, but he still drew her attention. She kept her eyes always to the side, but tried to keep him in sight. Then the man turned, stared at her fully for a moment, revealing the undamaged side of his face, then rose and walked toward the back of the pub.

Alexis stayed where she was, jaw clenched in sudden recognition from the moment's glimpse of the unscarred half of the man's face. He was familiar for a reason, but she couldn't believe it was him. Had, in fact, spent the years since their last meeting certain that she'd killed him.

TWENTY-SIX

DAVIEL COALSON, *alive and here, and sure as certain he's recognized me as well.*

The last time that she'd seen Coalson had been on the signals console of her first ship, *Merlin.* Captain Grantham had left her in command of the ship and a skeleton crew while he assaulted the illegal gallenium mining operation Coalson ran, in addition to the piracy and smuggling Grantham had begun investigating him for.

Coalson had fled in a ship's boat and Alexis had pursued in *Merlin.* He'd been on his way to reaching a ship and escaping when she'd ordered a full broadside fired into his boat. He'd dropped something in *Merlin's* path, though. She suspected it was a nuclear mining charge of some sort. *Merlin* had come close to being destroyed, it was only her order to roll ship and take the blast on the ship's heavy keel that had saved them, and it had taken some time to repair the damage. By the time they'd been able to search, the other ship had fled and the wreckage of the boat had drifted and dispersed so greatly that they'd been unable to recover it all.

A voice spoke near her and she spun around, startled. A man was standing near her table, smiling expectantly. Not the same one as before. He spoke again, but so rapidly that Alexis couldn't follow what he said at all.

"What?"

He spoke again, slower, but still smiling and pointed to the chair.

Oh, for the love of ...

"No," she said.

The man sat.

"I meant, 'No, you may not join me,' not, 'No, the seat's not taken,' or whatever it is you were asking."

The man smiled.

"You can't understand a bloody word I'm saying, can you?"

The man nodded and smiled wider.

"And yet, you're still sitting at my table ..."

Alexis looked around hoping to catch Dansby's eye or catch some sight of Coalson at the rear of the pub so that she'd at least know where he was.

The man at her table said something and reached across the table to take her left hand in both of his. He stared at her intently and said ... something.

"I'm certain that was quite complimentary and I'd be incredibly flattered ... if I understood a bloody word of it. But I didn't and I'm not and I'm busy —" She waved her free hand at him in a go away gesture. "So would you please bugger off then?"

The man laughed and ran his fingers over her palm in a way that made her want to rush off to the head and wash herself.

Alexis ground her teeth together. She took a deep breath, started to say something more, then shook her head.

"No," she muttered, "I've had quite enough of this."

With her free hand she pulled one of the blades Dansby had bought her from her left sleeve and held it up in front of her. The man froze and his eyes widened. She waved the tip of the blade back and forth.

"Look, you, this knife?" She pointed it through the table in the general direction of the man's lap. "Your bollocks." She flicked her wrist in a cutting motion, then raised her eyebrows. "Savvy that, at least, do you?"

The man released her hand and stood up, then took a step back from the table. He scowled at her and squared his shoulders, then muttered the first word she understood before walking away.

"Bitch."

Good lord, even with a whole other language at his disposal that's the still best he can come up with?

Alexis watched him go, then slid her knife back into its sheath. She glanced around, but no one else in the pub seemed to have noticed the exchange. Either that or such things were so common that the clientele paid no heed.

She turned in her chair so that she could see the table the man she thought was Coalson had been at. How could it be him? Coalson's body was never found, but they'd always assumed that he was among the dead.

His boat took a full broadside. It was shredded to bits and I think the fusion plant must have gone as well.

But he wasn't dead. She was certain it had been him at that table. He was here on Baikonur and he'd recognized her as surely as she'd recognized him.

She looked over to Dansby, willing him to finish so that they could leave or at least to look at her so that she could communicate some sense of urgency. Whatever Coalson would do, having recognized her, would not be to her benefit, and she wanted nothing more than to reboard *Röslein* and be gone from Baikonur entirely.

She almost cried out with relief when Dansby rose and gestured for her to follow him. They left the pub and she waited until they were some distance down the corridor before she grasped Dansby's arm.

"We must speak. Quickly."

"I'll tell you what I've learned when we reach *Röslein*. Patience, niece."

"No, damn your eyes, this is a different matter!"

"What —"

Dansby's head jerked sharply to look down the corridor, then he shoved her to the side into a pile of trash between stacks of crates and leapt backward himself. As quickly as he moved there was a loud *crack* and shouts.

"Four of them!" Dansby yelled. "To either side, maybe more." He already had his weapons drawn. Chemical pistol in one hand and laser in the other.

Alexis drew her own pistol as more *cracks* sounded and the crates around her shook. She had her flechette pistol in its hidden holster as well, but didn't think those tiny darts would be of much use with all the cover in the corridor. Dansby raised a hand above the crates he was sheltering behind and fired off two quick shots, then fired the laser in the opposite direction. More shots struck the crates.

"Fire back at them, damn you!"

Alexis, eyes wide and not quite believing that she was being shot at on a station, leaned around the edge of the crate to find a target. She managed a quick glimpse of two men, behind crates themselves, farther down the corridor, before seeing them adjust their aim toward her and ducking back.

"Don't look to aim, just bloody shoot!" Dansby yelled at her. He had his tablet in hand and began speaking into it rapidly while trying to fit a new capacitor into his laser with the other.

"What if someone comes out a hatchway?" she demanded, thinking of the crowded pub and not wanting to shoot an innocent by mistake.

"No one'll come to investigate this nonsense!" Dansby yelled at her, firing again. "And if they're foolish enough to do so they deserve to be shot!"

Alexis did as he said, simply pointing her pistol over the crates and firing twice rapidly, then doing the same in the other direction.

"I've no quarrel with you, sir!" a voice called. "It's that bitch, Carew, I want!"

Alexis recognized the voice now too, and no doubt it was Coalson. How he was here, how he was even alive, she didn't know, but it was him.

Dansby looked at her across the corridor, his mouth open with astonishment.

"I left you alone for ten bloody minutes!" More shots rang out and Alexis and Dansby returned fire. "What did you do?"

"Send her out!" Coalson yelled. "Or throw out your arms and I'll let you walk free!"

"Run, whoever you are!" Dansby called back. "And you might live out the day!"

He fired his laser again and was rewarded with a cry of pain from down the corridor. He turned to Alexis with a wide, feral grin as he slammed a new capacitor into the laser's grip.

"Worth every bloody pence."

"Can't have many more charges for that!" Coalson called.

More shots struck the crates near them. Alexis flinched as the impact knocked the crate above her off the stack and she had to bat it away as it fell.

"It's only a matter of time!"

"How many magazines do you have?" Dansby whispered.

Alexis did a quick pat of her pockets and boottops to ensure she had all she thought she did. "Six and what's left in the pistol."

Dansby blinked and shook his head. "Don't believe in going half-prepared, do you? Never mind." He glanced around the crates quickly and ducked back as more shots were fired. "What's left in your pistol that way," he said, pointing. "On three and reload quick."

Alexis nodded.

"One. Two. Three."

They both stood fired rapidly over the crates, Alexis one direction and Dansby the other. Alexis ducked back down as the slide on her pistol locked back and reloaded, but Dansby ducked down and then stood again. Laser one direction and pistol the other, he fired both, then dropped and quickly reloaded.

"There's always some want to rush when they think you're reloading," he said with another grin. "Might have got both."

There were cries and moans to either side and more shots rang out. Bullets and flechettes slammed into the crates, over and over.

"I believe you've angered them, Mister Dansby." Alexis couldn't help but grin back. Her heart was pounding and her body felt chilled, but she was also exhilarated. Everything around her was bright and clear, the edges sharper than she thought normal.

"Seeing a friend take a laser to the groin has that effect." He raised an eyebrow. "Does little for the groin owner's disposition, as well."

Alexis fired several shots, again not looking, just wanting to keep their attackers at bay. There was a sharp cry and the calls for help from that direction cut off.

"Shoot a man who's injured, Carew?" Coalson called out. "That's the cowardly behavior I'd expect of you!"

"Don't bloody shoot the wounded, Carew," Dansby said.

"I wasn't aiming, I'm sorry." Alexis shrugged. She felt little compunction about it, truly. Perhaps later she might, but for now he'd been trying to kill her and might have been still firing, wounded or not.

Dansby met her eyes and grinned. "I'd gutshot that one and his cries were putting his fellows off. They'll rally now he's silent."

Alexis found herself grinning back. Outnumbered and surrounded they might be, but she felt very much alive.

"Nothing to say, Carew?" Coalson called. "Have I finally silenced that tongue of yours?"

Alexis and Dansby fired over the crates again.

"I've a fine serpent here to do my speaking, Coalson." She grinned at Dansby. "He's more than a match for a rat like you."

"Does your serpent know you're Navy, Carew? Or does he wear that absurd blue of yours as well?"

There were shots and shouts of alarm from the other side, away from Coalson.

"That way," Dansby said, pointing toward Coalson, "and keep firing. Now!"

Alexis rose with him, not understanding why, but oddly trusting him. She fired rapidly and heard footsteps behind her, but Dansby never turned so she kept on until spacers from *Röslein* charged past, led by Mynatt. Alexis and Dansby stopped firing as their foes turned and ran. Alexis caught sight of Coalson at the rear, or rather at the front of the retreat, before he scrambled to the side and disappeared into some ship's hull. His men were close behind him, with Mynatt and the *Rösleins* on their heels.

Dansby leaned back against the corridor wall. He slid the capacitor cartridge from his pistol and inserted a fresh one, then looked over at Alexis. He pressed a hand to his side, probing, and winced. Blood soaked his jacket beneath his hand.

"You're hurt!" Alexis crossed the corridor and grasped his arm, seeking to pull his hand away and see the damage.

"Grazed," Dansby said. "Barely struck at all." He stared down the corridor in the direction Coalson had run and shook his head in disbelief. "Who was that?"

"Should we not be going?" Alexis asked. "Before the station patrol arrives?" In truth she was surprised they hadn't already.

"Patrol?" Dansby laughed. "Be lucky if the bodies don't rot where they lie. Now tell me what this was about."

Alexis did so, as briefly as she thought he'd accept.

How Coalson was from her home planet and had always hated her family. How her first ship, *Merlin*, had discovered he was involved in piracy, smuggling, and illegal gallenium mining. And how in the final chase she'd been in command of *Merlin* and given the order to fire a full broadside into Coalson's boat as it ran for another ship and before whatever he'd dropped behind had detonated.

"By the time we repaired *Merlin* and could return to search the wreckage it had dispersed far and wide, so there was little left," she concluded. "We recovered some of the bodies, but not his, and the other ship was long gone. We simply assumed he was among the dead

... a full broadside into so small a boat, and every shot struck. No one should have survived."

"Piracy and smuggling and a secret gallenium mine all at once? This Coalson believes in a pie for every finger, now doesn't he?" Dansby winced. "Still how? How in bloody hell?"

"I'm sorry, Mister Dansby. I ... I've been certain he was dead and how he's managed to be here ..."

"Oh, not that." Dansby waved it away. "Baikonur is where you come to run into his sort. If there was any system where you'd find the man again it would be here. No it's just that ..." He gave a derisive laugh. "You're a mere slip of a girl. Thirty *bloody* years I've been sailing, man and boy — piracy, smuggler, every damned dark bit of business I could find." He shoved his pistol into its holster. "And the first damned time I'm ambushed and shot is over a man *you* failed to kill properly?"

"Again, Mister Dansby, I'm sorry this happened."

Dansby shook his head. "If you're inspiring this much hate so young, Carew, you might consider a change in occupation."

"I'll give that due consideration."

She stood and looked up and down the corridor to see that it was, indeed, still clear. She wondered just how much Mynatt had heard of the last part of the confrontation and what she'd make of it.

Dansby pushed off the wall. "Let's be off back to the ship." He looked down the corridor in the direction Mynatt had followed Coalson. "Anya will find us there after she's tired of the chase." He shook his head. "I'd have you safely aboard before you're seen by anyone else who'd like you dead." He winced again and glared at her. "Not that I'm entirely unable to see this Coalson fellow's point, mind you."

TWENTY-SEVEN

"Navy? She's bloody Navy!"

"Damn it, Anya! Keep your voice down!" Dansby made a frantic shushing gesture and went to his cabin's hatch to ensure it was closed.

Alexis stepped back from the two. She and Dansby had managed to get back to *Röslein* before Mynatt and the others returned. Dansby insisted they both wait in his cabin, where he had a sturdy hatch and an override of the ship's systems, until they learned just what had been overheard by the crew. When Mynatt and the rest returned, she demanded entrance and Dansby let her in after confirming it was only her outside his cabin.

Mynatt was, to say the least, displeased with her new knowledge and Dansby's explanation of the situation had done nothing to placate her.

"You're going to get us all killed, Avrel!"

"Shh!" He spread his hands. "It's a fair job. It'll be all right, you'll see. Did any of the others hear?"

Mynatt paced rapidly back and forth, jaw clenched and breathing loudly.

"No, I don't think so," she said. "I was closest and I barely heard it myself." She put her hands to her head and pulled her hair. "Nor could I *bloody* believe it until I came back to the ship and found you locked in here! *What* were you thinking?" She held up a hand. "No! I know what you were thinking, or thinking with, rather. Your damned purse and nothing more! What if the crew had heard? What if this Coalson tells someone on the station?"

"We'll deal with it," Dansby said.

"'*We*'? Word gets out you brought the New London Navy here and your ships will never dock again! Who'll sell to us? Who'll buy from us?"

"Anya, please calm down, I'll —"

"I'm tired of your damn promises, Avrel!" Mynatt advanced on Dansby, backing him up until he was against the bulkhead. "You promised me a ship years ago and I've held up my end of the bargain more than once! What'll you promise now? That your latest stupid scheme won't get us all killed or worse?"

Alexis frowned, wondering what the worse might include, but didn't dare ask. Dansby looked like he was terrified of Mynatt and Alexis couldn't blame him. She'd found herself edging toward a handy corner as well, hand on her pistol in case things turned violent.

"Damn you! You can't do this to your crews, keeping them in the dark like this! Unlike *her* —" Mynatt flung her arm wide to point at Alexis. "— we're not just to follow orders! We have a say in things!"

"Miss Mynatt," Alexis said, trying to calm her, "if you'd listen for a moment and let us explain, please. My presence has nothing to do with your regular business and needn't —"

"And *you*!" Mynatt spun and advanced on Alexis. "I should have bloody known you were Navy, with your damned ways and all."

Alexis felt the bulkhead against her back and tightened her hand on her pistol, then released it and slid her hand behind her to where her flechette gun rested. If things did turn violent, then the flechette would be quieter and possibly less lethal. She wasn't certain of what the best way to handle Mynatt was, but she knew the rest of the crew couldn't know her true identity or the mission was doomed. She needed this ship to carry her to wherever Commodore Balestra was or there'd be an entire fleet and tens of thousands of troops waiting in vain on Alchiba.

"This is my crew!" Mynatt yelled, a bit of spittle spraying from her mouth and landing on Alexis' face. "You'll not put them in this kind of danger! You'll not get away with it!" Mynatt's eyes narrowed and she started toward the cabin's hatch. "The crew'll not —"

The high-pitched whine of the flechette gun cut her off and was quickly followed by her shrill screams of pain. Mynatt grasped her leg and fell, but it was an awkward fall because her left foot remained flat to the deck. A dozen or so thin flechettes protruded from her boot top. More had penetrated farther, going through boot, foot, and boot sole before lodging firmly in the deck. Mynatt thrashed from side to side while her foot remained firmly nailed to the deck.

Alexis opened her palm and regarded the tiny flechette gun with raised eyebrows. She'd hoped it would have the power to penetrate Mynatt's boot top at best.

Small, yet mighty.

Dansby stared at her open-mouthed. Alexis stepped forward and stood over Mynatt.

"I've had quite enough of you," Alexis said. "This irrational hatred you have of me seems to have driven you beyond all reason."

"Damn you!" Mynatt yelled. "I'll tell the rest of the crew and they'll —"

Mynatt screamed again as flechettes penetrated her knee.

Alexis knelt down and placed the barrel of the flechette gun against Mynatt's midsection. While her foot and knee would likely be fine in a only few days after the flechettes were removed, having the tiny darts tear through her organs would be quite another matter.

"You've discovered who I am, Miss Mynatt. Surely you understand that I have a duty to perform and will brook no opposition?" She prodded forcefully. "The Navy does have a certain veneer of civility to it, but, I assure you, underneath we are as brutal as our duty dictates, do you understand?"

Alexis prodded again, harder.

Mynatt looked to Dansby, wide-eyed, and opened her mouth to speak, but Alexis cut her off.

"Not another word until I say," she said. "Simply nod if you understand, please."

Mynatt nodded.

"Excellent." Alexis met Mynatt's eyes and for the first time saw fear there, mixed with the hatred. And perhaps a little uncertainty, as well.

Surely the woman had realized that the cause for her initial distrust and hatred of Alexis, the fear that Alexis would be given the ship she so desired, had been misplaced. If so, then possibly the situation could be salvaged. If not, she'd have to kill Mynatt and how would that be explained to the crew? She and Dansby could find themselves facing a mutiny, no matter if Mynatt was able to tell the crew that Alexis was a Naval officer or not. Not to mention that she had no clear idea how Dansby would react — the man's dealings with Mynatt seemed to go hot and cold at a moment's notice.

Alexis rose, but kept the flechette gun trained on Mynatt's torso.

"You do see now, Miss Mynatt, that my presence aboard *Röslein* is no threat to your being given her captaincy? That was your fear at the start, yes?"

Mynatt's eyes narrowed and she started to nod, but Dansby spoke.

"She's bloody well not getting one of my ships now!"

Alexis sighed.

No, it wouldn't be enough for me to have to make just one of them see sense, now would it?

"Uncle —" She shook her head. "Mister Dansby, will you please —"

"She tried to mutiny!" Dansby pointed at Mynatt. "I'll see she never gets a ship from anyone!"

Alexis sighed again.

"Oh, do calm down Mister Dansby. This can all be settled —"

"Nobody threatens me like that on my own bloody ship, Carew." His hand settled on his own sidearm. "In fact I'll —"

Alexis stepped back from Mynatt so that she could see both of them and transferred the flechette gun to her left hand. With her right she drew the pistol from her side and pointed it at Dansby.

"You —"

"Both of you be still and listen to sense," Alexis said. "I've met your crew, remember, Dansby. If either you or Mynatt kills the other, there'll be more than one of the men who starts to wonder why he shouldn't come to command himself. And if I have to worry about that with the crew, then I might as well shoot the both of you and deal with them myself."

She watched as Dansby's hand relaxed and fell from his belt.

"Now, Miss Mynatt, surely you can look on this discovery of my identity as the opportunity it is, and not a difficulty?"

Mynatt's eyes narrowed and Alexis could see that she was thinking now, instead of simply reacting to the news.

Finally Mynatt chuckled. "Wish you'd thought to say all that before you shot me."

Alexis flushed. "You gave me little chance to get a word in."

Mynatt tried to sit up, winced and lay back down again, settling for propping herself up on her elbows. "Fair enough."

"What are you two on about?" Dansby asked.

"Oh, do shut up, Dansby," Alexis said. "You had your hand in driving her to this as well."

"What? I —"

"Will you tell me you didn't hold that captaincy over her head from the time we came aboard? That it had nothing at all to do with her coming to your bed?"

"Well —"

"Nor that it was the first time?" Alexis demanded.

Dansby shut his mouth and cleared his throat.

"Very well, then. As to what we're about and my being a Naval officer ... Miss Mynatt, you must know after all your time in his employ that Dansby is not a complete idiot?"

"What?"

"Not so far as business goes, no," Mynatt agreed, eyes narrowed more. "There must be enough profit in this for him to be taking the risk."

"Exactly," Alexis said. "He wouldn't be going along himself if the risk were so great, either. So you simply carry out this voyage and when we're done, Mister Dansby will return to managing his business and you will have the captaincy of *Röslein*." She motioned for Dansby to be quiet. "Which is what everyone wanted to begin with, yes?"

"I suppose," Dansby muttered finally.

"No," Mynatt said.

Dansby and Alexis stared at her.

"As you pointed out, the crew will grow restless and curious if you kill me." She shifted and winced. "Besides, you shot me."

"What more could you want?"

"A thousand pounds to start." Mynatt's eyes narrowed. "You're right that he wouldn't come himself if the risk were so great, but he wouldn't either if the pay weren't great enough. There's more coin in this than he's let on and I want a piece."

"Never!" Dansby yelled.

"Be quiet, Mister Dansby," Alexis said. "I'm negotiating. What else?"

"A five year contract as *Röslein's* captain," Mynatt said. "I'll not be dismissed in a week's time at his whim. And half the owner's share of profits for those years."

"*What?*"

"I was shot!" Mynatt yelled back. "And I ... with *you* ... and I'm not bloody sure which was worse!"

Dansby's face went red.

"All things have a price, Mister Dansby," Alexis said. "A contract so you can't be dismissed out of hand is fair and a thousand pounds

—" She ignored Dansby's sputtering. "— but half the owner's share for a year only."

"Four."

"Half for two and half of whatever more than the ship's current average you bring in for three."

"Your word on it?"

"It's Mister Dansby's ship," Alexis reminded her. "I'll be going back to the Navy when this is done."

Mynatt nodded. "I've dealt with your type of Navy before. You've your honor shoved so far up your arse I can see it in your eyes. I shouldn't think Dansby would very much enjoy being the one to break your word."

"Mister Dansby?" Alexis asked.

"Oh, I've a say now, do I? Fancy that."

"You can agree or we can settle things some other way," Alexis said. "I suppose I could just shoot whichever of you I'm most irritated with at the moment."

"Should've never bought you those guns," Dansby muttered. "Oh, very well. I'll have the contract drawn up as soon as we return to New London space."

Alexis shared a look with Mynatt. "You'll have the contract drawn up and under seal in the ship's systems before the end of the watch."

Dansby shrugged. "Very well."

Alexis lowered her guns, wary, but Mynatt seemed to be satisfied and Dansby, for all his griping, seemed to have calmed down and seen the sense of it.

"Now we simply need to get Miss Mynatt some medical care ... and explain to the crew why she needs it."

"FELL?"

Bowhay was watching two spacers help Mynatt to her feet and through the hatch to have her wounds tended.

"Yes." Alexis looked up as Mynatt turned at the hatchway. Despite her wounds, Alexis couldn't help but think the grimace on her face was more suppressed laughter than pain. She glanced over at Dansby who was making no effort at all to hide his own amusement. The two seemed quite willing to put aside any lingering animosity once it was time to come up with a story for Mynatt's foot being nailed to the floor.

"I was showing Miss Mynatt the fine flechette pistol my uncle purchased for me and ..." She shrugged. "... well, I fumbled it and it fell. Struck her foot and discharged."

Bowhay nodded. He looked at Dansby then back to Alexis. "And the knee then?"

Alexis flushed. "Well, you see, when I went to pick it up I was quite distraught at what had happened to Miss Mynatt's foot. I thought to engage the safety, but I must have ..." She closed her eyes unable to believe she was forced to admit to such a thing. "I must have pulled the trigger instead."

Bowhay nodded. He looked at Dansby.

"That's the way of it, Mister Dansby, sir?"

Dansby nodded. "Yes. See that the crew knows what happened, and that Anya will be back at her duties shortly."

"If you'd like, miss —" Bowhay glanced at Dansby. "— and with yer uncle's permission, of course, there's room in the hold if you'd like a bit of practice and training and such. I'm a fair shot and could, well, teach some safe handling and all."

Alexis clenched her teeth. "I —"

"I think that's an excellent idea, Bowhay," Dansby said. Alexis glared at him, but he went on. "I knew she was a poor shot — rounds went all over the range when I bought that for her, and all over the corridor during that bit of business aboard the station — but I did think she knew how to handle the bloody things without shooting someone in the foot. Just glad it wasn't worse." He grinned. "Yes, why don't you set up a bit of a range in the hold and see if you can at least get her to hit the target? Might take some time, mind you."

Alexis glared at him. She'd have to shoot as poorly as he'd described and accept Bowhay's instruction just to keep their story plausible.

"There's a man at the hatch," a spacer said, easing his way past Mynatt and into the compartment. "Says he's a message from some fellow name of Coalson?"

TWENTY-EIGHT

"Of course it's a trap, Mister Dansby ... uncle, whatever," Alexis said. "I'm no fool."

Dansby grunted. He took a moment to ease Mynatt's leg where it rested on a pillow. The three of them were in Dansby's cabin where he'd ordered Mynatt brought once the flechettes were removed and her wounds dressed.

Now she reclined on Dansby's own bunk, her bandaged leg elevated, and, to Alexis' surprise, Dansby was hovering around her like a mother hen, despite the fact that the injuries were, indeed, minor.

Once the flechettes were out, it had been seen that Mynatt didn't even have any broken bones. The tiny darts had simply punctured them cleanly. She'd be in pain for a day or two while things healed, but there was no serious damage.

Not an hour past I had to draw on him so he'd not shoot her dead. I do not understand these two.

"Best stick with 'uncle' even though it's just the three of us and Anya knows the truth of it," Dansby said.

Alexis nodded.

"As to whether you're a fool, well, heeding this Coalson would be a fine sign of one. He's simply goading you, trying to draw you in."

"Perhaps."

"A certainty." Dansby adjusted Mynatt's cup of grog on the bunkside table, as though to ensure it was within her easy reach. "It was an overturned buggy, you said. What more could he have to say about it?"

Alexis thought of the short message Coalson's man had brought. Simply a location and the words:

Come alone and I'll give you the truth of the day your father died.

"I DON'T KNOW."

"Was there ever any suspicion around it?"

Alexis shook her head. "Not that I ever heard. I was only ... three years of age, I think, when it happened. They'd gone to Port Arthur for a time and their buggy was found on the road back. Too fast into a turn and it had gone off the road and down an embankment." She shrugged. "Never a hint of anything more to it."

"There you have it, then. Nothing more to it and nothing for this Coalson to tell you. He's simply thrown it out there to reel you in."

"But why choose something I've no questions about to begin with?"

"She has a point," Mynatt said. "Why choose something from so long ago? If he were going to lie about having information, why not use the war? Or piracy? Or something more current?" She reached for her cup, found it moved, and rolled her eyes at Dansby before drinking. "It makes no sense."

"It makes perfect sense." Dansby rose and paced to the far side of the room. "She shows up, Coalson yells 'buggy accident!', then shoots her in the head. She dies knowing she was a fool and he has his revenge." He crossed to the sideboard and poured himself a drink. "It's exactly what I'd do." He paused. "Well, I'd have killed you the first time you crossed me, but if you'd managed to maim me as you did him then I'd want you to die knowing you were an utter fool."

"Would you pour me one of those?" Alexis waited, thinking, while Dansby did so. Certainly it was a trap. Coalson wanted to kill her, no doubt. But was there some way to get his information without springing it? Or to turn the trap back on him?

"Eades will not take kindly to your risking yourself on this, either." Dansby handed her a glass and shook his finger at her. "We've his goals to accomplish here, don't forget."

"Eades?" Mynatt asked.

"Our sponsor in this endeavor. The source of your thousand pounds and not a man you'd like to cross."

"There is that," Mynatt said. "Doesn't do to leave a paying job for something personal."

Alexis drained half the glass, relishing the burn in her mouth and throat. Seeing Coalson again, the firefight, the confrontation with Mynatt, all of it had drained her. She felt numb and wanted to sleep, but Coalson's message nagged at her. If she left without hearing what he had to say, would she ever have another chance? Was there something about her parents' death that had been kept hidden from her, or that her grandfather didn't even know?

Dansby and Mynatt were right, though, that their task from Eades was more important. Did she even have the right to jeopardize it for personal satisfaction? And how to convince the two of them if she did? She'd need their help, to be sure.

She drained the rest of the glass and held it out to Dansby. No, they should just sail away, forget about Coalson and resume their mission as though they'd never encountered him ...

No ... no that won't work at all, now will it?

"We have to deal with Coalson," she said. "There's nothing else for it." She saw that she had Dansby's and Mynatt's full attention. "We're to just sail away and think he'll leave it at that? No, he'll dog our heels every step of the way and what then? Have him appear on some other station, a proper Hanoverese one, when we need to be secret and unnoticed?"

"It's *your* heels he's after."

"And we're all in the same footsteps for the duration, aren't we? He hates me — if he's access to a ship, and I think he must, then he'll be after us."

"We can outsail him. Easily."

Alexis crossed her arms. "There's money in it."

Dansby raised an eyebrow.

"How much?" Mynatt asked. "And from where?"

"Had the Navy not assumed Coalson was killed by *Merlin's* broadside, there'd be a price on his head. Piracy, smuggling, murder, and his illicit trade in gallenium — how much do you think the bounty would be?"

"Five hundred pounds at least," Mynatt said, giving Dansby a speculative look.

"More," he said. "The gallenium with a war on?" He looked at Alexis. "The war was on when this occurred?"

Alexis nodded. "We had yet to hear of it on Dalthus, but yes."

Dansby smiled. "Profiteering, possibly trading with the enemy — Hanover's a large buyer on the black markets. A thousand just for that." His smile fell and he sat on the edge of the bunk. "But he was assumed dead and there's no bounty on offer, so how do you get by that? And how am I to be seen to collect it? Who'd trust me thereafter? And how is it all to work? There's no guarantee such a bounty'd be issued for him dead or alive, and if it's issued for him only alive then we'd have to turn him over to the Navy. How are we to do that in the middle of —"

Alexis raised her hand to stop him.

Dansby frowned. "I don't think —"

Alexis cut him off again. "The Navy represents the Crown on distant stations, if there's no civil authority," Alexis said. "This station is quite distant, I think, and I've seen no magistrate for some time." She shrugged. "I am, after all is said and done, a Naval officer."

"You plan to claim you represent the Crown in this?" Mynatt asked. "We take Coalson and then ... what? Turn him over to you as the Crown's representative? And you'll do what with him? We can't keep him aboard the entire trip."

"He receives the same treatment he would have, had *Merlin* plucked him from space in Dalthus," Alexis said.

Mynatt drew in a sharp breath. "You plan to hang him? Just like that?"

"That's a dangerous game, Carew," Dansby said. "If your Navy decides you didn't have that power. Usurping the Crown's authority is a hanging offense itself."

"It provides at least some legal fiction," Alexis said, "and gets us on our way to finish this mission without worrying about Coalson forever at our heels. Unless you'd like to rid us of him without attempting to collect a bounty?"

"Not now that you've mentioned it, no," Dansby said. "Five hundred pounds or more certainly wouldn't go amiss." He grinned. "And it's you who'll face the consequences if your superiors disagree, not us. Of course there's a chance we won't be paid, either."

"There's a risk they'll not pay," Alexis admitted. "As for the other, rely on Eades for secrecy and I'll rely on him to smooth things over — I can't believe I said that, but I suspect he'll not want this mission known, still, so it must be a small matter to keep the award to you secret and gloss over any imperfections in my authority."

Mynatt touched Dansby's hand and they shared a look.

"She's right about having to deal with him, even if there's a chance there's no profit in it."

"I still find your motives suspect," Dansby said to Alexis. "It's personal for you more than anything."

"I have little memory of my parents, Mister Dansby, and those mostly from images and tales, I suspect. My earliest genuine recollection is sitting in my grandfather's lap and seeing his tear-covered face as he tried to explain to me that my mother and father were never coming home." She nodded. "If Coalson knows aught of that, then it is quite personal."

Dansby took their glasses and filled them, remaining silent until he'd returned to the bunk and passed them out.

"All right then," he said. "And what's your plan to deal with him and remain alive yourself?"

"That's where my serpent comes in." Alexis raised her glass to him in mock toast. "Surely you're not prepared to admit that Daviel Coalson is cleverer than you?"

TWENTY-NINE

ALEXIS' back itched as she entered the pub. It was a different one from where she'd first seen Coalson, but no less seedy and disreputable. She felt vulnerable and exposed despite their plan.

Seven plans, actually, for Dansby wasn't one to make assumptions. They'd thought out every possible move of Coalson's and had contingencies for all.

Save the one where he shoots me in the head immediately. That we've no plan for.

It was a risk, but she felt she knew Daviel Coalson well enough to be confident he'd wish to gloat for a time first.

There were few patrons in the pub and she saw Coalson immediately. He sat at the rear of the compartment with his back to the bulkhead. There were, perhaps, a half dozen other patrons and she suspected they were all his men.

One of them rose to block her path and gestured.

"Arms up," he said. "I'm ter search yer."

Alexis held her hands out to her sides and the man ran his hands over her, lingering in places that made her want to drive a knee into him. As his hands ran over her left arm, near the cuff where her ship's jumpsuit was frayed, she fought the urge to tense. Most of the plans relied on what Dansby and his crew did, but one relied on what was concealed in that cuff. He moved on, though, and did find the hidden pocket at the small of her back, making her glad she'd left the flechette pistol behind. Finally he nodded and backed out of her way.

She made her way to Coalson's table and sat. He had a glass of wine before him, bottle on the table, and an empty glass near where she sat. Up close his injuries were worse than she'd thought. The right half of his face was deeply scarred and the prosthetic he wore seemed to start above the elbow.

"I'm surprised you had the courage to come, Carew."

"Let's get on with it, shall we?"

Coalson pulled his tablet from a pocket and set it on the table. "Oh, do allow me my moment, yes? I plan to record this and send it to your grandfather along with the news of your death. It will be a last, fitting bit of my family's revenge against him."

Alexis shook her head sadly. She could understand if Coalson wanted revenge against her — she'd been aboard *Merlin* when his schemes were discovered and she'd given the order to fire into his boat. She'd caused his gruesome injuries, and yet he was still, after all that, fixated on revenge against her grandfather.

By all accounts his father, Rashae Coalson, had been mad. A paranoid well past the point of delusion. When the colonists to Dalthus were choosing lots, the properties they'd own based on their shares in the colony, Alexis' grandfather had by chance chosen several that Rashae wanted. Instead of bad luck, Rashae Coalson had seen it as a plot — that her grandfather, Denholm, had some knowledge of what Rashae wanted and had chosen specifically to thwart him.

Rashae had hated Denholm until the day he died, then passed that hatred, irrational though it was, on to his sons.

Alexis scratched her left wrist, transferring the capsule in her cuff to her hand, then took the wine bottle from the table and poured herself a glass. She was relieved to find it was a new bottle and let the capsule fall into it. She raised her glass and drank.

"No protestations, Carew? No going on about how your grandfather was innocent and misunderstood?"

"I've given up trying, Mister Coalson. I cannot convince crazy."

Two men entered the pub. They were from *Röslein*, though Coalson wouldn't know that. Dansby had brought along almost the entire crew, though not through the main hatch. They'd assumed Coalson would have men watching the ship to see that only Alexis left it, but Dansby had brushed the concern aside.

"I'm a *smuggler*, dear niece," he'd said. "Getting things on and off this ship without notice is a thing I've a bit of experience at."

Two of Coalson's men approached the new arrivals and ushered them out, saying that the pub was closed, but they'd planned for that. The men had only to enter so that they could relay information about the layout to Dansby.

"Station a man outside," Coalson ordered. "I don't wish to be interrupted." He gestured at his face with the prosthetic and scowled. "This is your doing, you know. Firing into my boat." He clenched the fingers of his prosthetic, grinding them together. "Can't go to a decent clinic in New London space for fear of being identified — and proper Hanover systems are out, what with the war on."

"Any of *Merlin's* officers would have fired into your boat. The outcome's your doing and you have only yourself to blame."

"But I blame you."

"Of course you would — you're as mad as your father."

"Mad? Mad to see the truth of your family's vendetta against mine? How else to explain your presence here with the very man I've been waiting for?"

"What —"

"Dansby, damn you!" Coalson slammed his prosthetic onto the table. One of his men glanced their way, but then went back to watching the door. "After I recovered, after I got fitted with this —" He held the prosthetic up for her to look at. It was a crude piece of work, all metal without even the semblance of artificial flesh. "The best that could be done in the primitive systems I could safely visit. I've been to every pirate haunt and smuggler's den I could remember since ... and everywhere it's the same answer: If you want to go that deep into Hanover, deep enough for proper medical care, then it's Avrel Dansby who can get you there and back again."

Coalson pointed at her.

"Weeks I waited on Baikonur for one of his ships, so as to send a message to him and arrange passage. Then word that the man himself was meeting in that bloody pub." He shook his head, snorting in disbelief. "And who do I see with him? A bloody Carew. And you claim I'm mad? That you're not pursuing me? No, I'm no more mad than my father was."

Alexis remained silent. She could see how such a coincidence might appear, but as Dansby had said, if there was a system where she'd encounter a man like Coalson, it was Baikonur.

"Rashae, my father, was a great man, Carew. You have no idea. He saw the promise of Dalthus and the gallenium ore in the belt there, arranged to bury the survey report, and founded the colony. In another generation the Coalsons would have been the wealthiest family in the Fringe if you'd not interfered. All my life I lived in his shadow, nothing good enough to please him. But this —" He tapped his tablet and smiled. "— when your grandfather gets this and knows the whole truth, along with the news that the last of his line is dead, then I'll have surpassed Rashae. I'll have made our revenge complete."

"What truth, Coalson? You grow tiresome."

"Such bad luck the Carews have had on Dalthus. First your grandfather's Highlands whore perishes, then your father. Pity about Katlynne, though — seems she'd have been better off with me, after all."

Alexis felt sick to her stomach to hear Coalson speak about her family, especially to speak so about her mother, Katlynne. Coalson seemed to be implying that he'd been a suitor, something Alexis had never known.

"What do you know of your grandmother's death, Carew?"

Alexis frowned. Coalson's message had mentioned her parents, not her grandmother. Lynelle Carew had died before Daviel Coalson was just a child.

"She died in childbirth. My father came early, there was a storm ..." She'd heard the story more than once. How in the early days of the colony there'd been just the one antigrav hauler capable of flight. Port Arthur, still called Landing then, was where the only doctor was and it was a half-day's travel by horseback. The storm came and Lynelle, her grandmother, had gone into labor. Something was amiss, but no one was terribly worried — until they'd called for the hauler to fly her to the doctor and found that it had been damaged. And by the time the doctor had finally arrived, having ridden horseback through the storm, it was too late.

"Oh, yes, it was a grand opportunity that storm, and my father took it. Grabbed it with both hands." Coalson filled his glass and drank before pouring more for Alexis. "He had recordings, you know, of the radio calls your grandfather made throughout the night, begging for that hauler to come and drag his precious Lynelle to be cared for." He smiled. "What? Never knew whose lands that hauler was on?"

Alexis felt a chill. She stared at Coalson, unable to move and not wanting to hear his next words.

"We had bright sun on the coast that day, I'm told. The hauler was half-loaded, right there in the yard near our old house, before my father had the proper estate built. Half-loaded, did I say? Couldn't fly in that state. The pilot knew the urgency and they all rushed to unload." He frowned. "Our foreman was generally a far better fork-lift driver than he was that day, truly. Perhaps he was shaken after my father took him aside and impressed on him the urgency of the situation? No matter but that it took weeks to repair the hauler from the damage his clumsiness wrought."

"You're mad," Alexis whispered. Could Rashae Coalson have really hated her grandfather that much? To have the colony's only hauler damaged just to cause her grandmother's death? All for spite at some imagined slight? "You're all mad."

Coalson smiled and drank more. Alexis could feel the drug she'd dropped into the wine working on her and Coalson had drunk far more than she. She wished that it would work on him quicker, for she now thought this meeting had been a mistake and didn't want to hear more.

Done away with him, yes, but it was a mistake to allow him to speak this poison.

"Do you know, Carew, that it was that very same hauler my father let me fly to Port Arthur some years later? He'd bribe the pilots, you see, and give them a break from their work, to let his sons fly the routes. He had the vision that we'd soon have enough coin to ship in our own hauler and even a personal aircar — he wanted us to be skilled in their use." He drained his glass and poured more, emptying the bottle into his glass. "I only meant to startle them, really."

Alexis froze, unable to tear her eyes away from Coalson.

"Horses, you know, never do seem to get used to something coming at them out of the sky. No matter how much they're around things that fly, if a thing comes straight at them they simply bolt."

"No," Alexis whispered.

"Oh, yes." Coalson leaned back in his chair and smiled. He drained his glass and replaced it on the table, then looked at his hand and frowned before returning his gaze to Alexis. "Imagine my surprise when the buggy went off the road and overturned."

Alexis longed for a weapon or to simply launch herself over the table at Coalson's throat, but she could feel the drug she'd dropped into the wine working on her. Her muscles were weak and her limbs leaden. She could see that Coalson was affected as well. His flesh hand on the table clenched and unclenched slowly. She tore her eyes from him and glanced behind the pub's bar to the doorway leading farther back. One of *Marilyn's* crew looked back at her.

They never watch the back, just as Dansby said.

She returned her gaze to Coalson.

"No words for me, Carew? My father beat me for that, you know. Quite soundly — oh, not for their deaths, but for doing it in daylight when I might have been seen. I suppose he was correct and it's only luck that's kept my secret until now." He frowned and looked down at his hand on the table, the prosthetic fingers clenching and unclenching as though at random. He licked his lips and shook his head sharply, then glanced at the wine bottle.

"What?"

Coalson started to rise, but Alexis reached across the table and grasped his arm. It was a struggle, her own movements were difficult, but Coalson fell back into his seat. Alexis had one hand holding his prosthetic to the table and the other wrapped in his collar. She heard shouts and bodies rushing about, but couldn't turn, simply looked into Coalson's eyes, then they both toppled to the floor, unable to remain upright in their chairs.

"You drank too," Coalson whispered.

A shot rang out.

"I have men I trust at my back," Alexis replied.

It seemed odd to speak so of Dansby, much less *Röslein's* crew and Mynatt, but she did trust them in this. He and his men had come in the back way, taking Coalson's by surprise. The drugged wine was an addition to the plan, Dansby feeling that it would add to the confusion of Coalson's men if they saw him helpless. Her vision darkened and she no longer felt her hands where they gripped Coalson, but she saw with satisfaction that it didn't matter as his eyes were closed as well.

THIRTY

ALEXIS CAME aware quickly and far more painfully than she'd expected.

Her skin felt as though tiny insects of flame were burrowing their way under her skin. They flowed through her, then quickly dissipated and were gone, while she became fully aware.

"What was that?" she asked Mynatt who was pulling an injector from her arm.

"Stimulant."

"I've taken any number of stimulants on the quarterdeck — none of them made me feel like ants of fire were burrowing through me."

Mynatt smiled. "Avrel didn't specify what to give you, so I got to pick."

Alexis shuddered at the brief but intense sensation.

"Well give Coalson a double dose of it then." She swung her legs over the bunk and was happy to find her head was clear despite the drug in the wine. "Are we well away? Did it all go as planned?"

"In *darkspace* and nearly out of the system. Your friend is still drugged, and bound as well. *His* friends were, perhaps, not so much his friends when it came down to it. They ran out the front of the pub as soon as they saw that Coalson fellow down and may not have stopped running yet."

"He's certainly no friend of mine," Alexis said. She'd had no real hatred of Coalson before. Oh, she'd despised him for his involvement in piracy, but that was a distant feeling. Now, after hearing what he and his father had done, she felt she truly did hate him.

Mynatt took a step back and narrowed her eyes. "That's sounding more personal than before. What did the man say to you?"

"Nothing that need concern you or the ship. Nothing of interest at all, really." Alexis hadn't fully processed what Coalson had told her, but she was certain it was nothing she wished to share with Mynatt or Dansby. "And there is no sign of pursuit?"

"None at all." Mynatt frowned. "Avrel doesn't like this next bit and neither do I. I know we discussed it, but we should just shoot him and dump him out a lock."

Alexis shook her head. "If you want a chance at a bounty on him, it has to be done a particular way. I can't guarantee the bounty would have been for him just dead. Explain it to the crew however you like, but it's best if we're able to say you turned him over to the Navy, me, and he was hanged."

She met Mynatt's eyes and then looked away. The Regulations and Articles allowed a captain to summarily hang pirates if it was 'not in the Interests and Safety of Her Majesty's Ship and Crew' to return them to port for trial. Others who took pirates — privateers or the rare merchant who was able to fight back — were supposed to turn them over to the nearest Naval ship or port in order to collect any bounties on record. It was a stretch to think the Crown would pay any bounty for Coalson, and Alexis was far from a captain, but there was a chance. The pair would apparently try anything for the chance at a bit of coin.

The truth was that she felt a bullet or laser to the head was too good for Coalson and she wanted to see him hang. She wanted the ceremony of it — to watch as the ship's line was attached high on the mast and the noose looped around his neck below the vacsuit's helmet. And she wanted to see Coalson's eyes as a pair of crewmen lifted him free of the ship's hull and flung him high. He'd float free of the ship until he exited the hull's field and was captured by the morass of dark matter that permeated *darkspace*. If he was lucky, there'd be enough slack in the line and the ship would be traveling so fast that his neck would snap when it finally went taut — if he was unlucky, the noose would simply tighten and slowly strangle him as he was dragged behind the mast.

She followed Mynatt to the quarterdeck and waited for Dansby to arrive with Coalson. He had the man's hands bound behind him and his feet were shackled so he could take only short, mincing steps. He was also gagged and in an emergency vacsuit, save the helmet which Dansby carried.

"Bowhay'll be along with a line soon," Dansby said. "I'll take the helm, Embry. You go and have a drink with the rest of the crew." Dansby waited until the helmsman had left and it was just the four of them on the quarterdeck, then he shoved Coalson into place before the sail locker's hatch. "I've Bowhay and another man who'll do it, but they don't like the idea." He returned to the quarterdeck's main hatch as though to see that no one from the crew was near. "There's muttering." He raised an eyebrow at Alexis. "And they're wondering on you."

"That I'm ..." Alexis started, concerned that the crew might suspect she was Navy.

Dansby shook his head. "Not that, just that this is unusual and they know you're the source of it. This —" He gestured toward Coalson. "— him. It doesn't fit with the fiction of your being my niece. Not at all."

Coalson started to say something through his gag and Dansby shot him a look.

"Quiet, you. My side's still tender where one of your bastards shot me, so I've no wish to hear from you."

"I'm curious what he has to say," Mynatt said. Before Alexis could protest, she reached out and pulled the gag away from Coalson's mouth.

"I'll scream she's Navy as soon as your bloody crew comes near!" Coalson yelled. "You're working for the bloody Navy, you hear me, you —"

Mynatt shoved Coalson's face hard into the hatch, shutting him up.

"It's my experience threats like that have a way of getting one shot on this ship, so I suggest you keep it to yourself." Mynatt jerked him back and then slammed him forward again. Coalson's forehead bounced off the bulkhead and his look grew dazed for a moment.

Mynatt shrugged and left Coalson to join Dansby by the helm.

"Still we must have something to tell the crew about this."

"Some old grudge?" Alexis asked. "He did attack us, after all. As for the noose, tell them I've simply a harder heart than you, *uncle.*"

Dansby snorted. "You're a cold one, Carew, no doubt. Perhaps we got it wrong, which of us is the snake and which the mongoose."

Alexis turned away, not wanting him to see her face. She went to Coalson's side.

"I'd already sent off a message to my son, Carew," Coalson said. "Edmon will know I saw you here and when word comes of my death he'll know it was you to blame. He and my other sons will know what to do and they'll end your whole damned line once and for all! Do you hear me? The message'll come for you that your dear grandfather's gone to meet his Highlands whore and their whelp!"

Alexis' felt herself grow hot at the threat. She stared at Coalson for a moment, then retrieved his vacsuit helmet from the deck. She glanced over to where Dansby and Mynatt were. They'd moved to the hatchway into the rest of the ship and Mynatt was whispering something to Dansby.

She looked back to Coalson and wondered if he really had sent such a message. If he had, there was little she could do about it. Dansby might have some way of getting a message back to New London space, but it was likely they'd have to return to Baikonur to do so. She met Coalson's eyes and it occurred to her that even hanging was too good for the man.

A chill replaced the heat and she found herself acting without really thinking.

"Do you suppose Bowhay will be long?" she called to Dansby, struggling to keep her voice calm. As she hoped, they both looked out into the companionway. Alexis slid the sail locker's hatch open and drove her knee into the back of Coalson's.

His legs buckled and he stumbled into the lock, Alexis close behind. She slammed the hatch closed and locked it. Dansby or Mynatt would be able to override it from the quarterdeck, but by the time they did she'd be Outside. She slammed Coalson's helmet onto his suit and latched it, then shoved him toward the outer hatch. She donned her own helmet.

"What are you doing?" she heard Dansby demanding over the suit radio.

What am I doing?

Coalson was struggling to regain his feet, but Alexis shoved him back down. With his hands and feet bound he could gain no leverage.

Yes, what am I doing?

She stared at the outer hatch for a moment, teeth clenched and breath coming in short, rasping gasps. The Coalsons and their lunatic, irrational hate had taken so much from her and now this one was threatening to take more. She stared at the hatch longer, almost hoping that Dansby would open the inner hatch and stop her, as she finally admitted what she intended.

Her grandfather wouldn't approve, she knew, and neither would her father, she was certain. Her mother would be horrified, for Katlynne had been, by every story she'd ever heard, the gentlest and kindest of souls. But mother and father were dead, taken by the man who knelt before her, and her grandfather would never know.

Alexis knew she would never, ever, tell her grandfather of what Daviel Coalson had admitted. She didn't think he'd be able to bear the thought that his actions, no matter they were filtered through the Coalsons' insanity, had played a part in those deaths.

Her grandmother, though — Alexis had heard all the tales of that one. Her grandfather never tired of the telling, no matter that the memories broke his heart. It was as though he kept her alive, at least for himself, in the stories. And it was a telling measure of Denholm Carew's inadequacy in raising a young girl that the stories Alexis had heard most often about Lynelle were those that centered around her temper. What Denholm would often describe as "her Scots was up and loose that day", and then repeat something she'd said in his truly horrible attempt at a Highlands burr. Alexis could almost hear her, could almost tell what she'd be saying now.

It's a feud they want? Can ye nae hear the pipes, lass? They call the clan.

Alexis held Coalson on his knees and knelt down herself so that she could see his face through the helmet. He'd been silent since they entered the lock, but she could see the confused look on his face as Dansby's voice still called over the radio asking what she was doing.

She unsnapped one of the safety lines from her belt and hooked it to the inside of the hatch, then grasped the latch.

Coalson's eyes widened as he realized her intent and he finally spoke.

"No!"

Alexis tested the bonds on his hands to ensure he'd not be able to get them loose and dump his air.

"You can't! Carew! For God's sake, shoot me! Hang me if you must! Don't —"

"Carew?" Dansby's voice interrupted. "What are you doing, damn you!"

Alexis leaned close to Coalson, so that their helmets touched. She wanted to be sure he heard her words. She wanted him to suffer and she wanted him to feel the same fear she did now for her grandfather's safety. She hesitated a moment, knowing this wouldn't be the last she'd see of Daviel Coalson. If she did this, he'd be joining the parade of accusing figures in her dreams for certain. Then she fixed her thoughts on the parents she could just barely remember and the grandmother she'd never known.

"Think on this, Daviel Coalson, as you go and meet the Dark. If I'll do this to you, what fate awaits your sons?"

She flung open the hatch and Coalson's scream was cut off as the radiation of *darkspace* rendered their suit radios useless. The lock was still aired and it rushed out, taking Coalson with it. Alexis braced herself for the short time it took and watched Coalson float away.

He struggled and twisted as he floated forward along the bowsprit, propelled by the outrushing air from the lock. Soon, though, his momentum slowed as he left the ship's field and *Röslein* began to catch up. Alexis stepped out onto the ship's bow, ready to fend him off or untangle him if he managed to snag any of the rigging, but he'd exited at a fine angle and remained just out of reach of the hull no matter how he tried to reach for it.

Alexis pulled herself along the hull, following him to the stern as *Röslein* steadily made way. At the stern she stopped, watching as Coalson was left far behind.

It was a spacer's greatest fear, to float free of the ship in *darkspace*. Those who were taken back aboard said that their limbs became leaden, that they could feel their blood slow, dragged to a stop by the dark matter that permeated everything. That their very thoughts slowed. They'd dump their air and suffocate if their ship didn't immediately turn back for them, rather than suffer that fate, but Coalson wouldn't be able to dump his air and his tanks were full.

Four hours or more he'll last, grandmother. It's the best I could manage.

THIRTY-ONE

Alexis made her way back along *Röslein's* hull from the stern, pulling herself forward along one of the guidewires that crisscrossed the hull.

She wasn't sure how much time had passed. The ship was still firmly within the winds that blew directly toward the system's center, though Baikonur had no pilot boats whose lights could be used to judge distance. Beating to windward to leave the system, their speed was not so great. It had taken some time, she thought, for Coalson's form to fade from view in the distance.

Perhaps an hour?

None of the ship's crew were on the hull still. Dansby must have kept the helm locked all that time. Her eyes automatically took in the set of *Röslein's* sails against the direction of the wind. They were not on the best point of sail at all, so, yes, Dansby must have kept the crew inboard, waiting for her to be done with Coalson.

She closed her eyes and let the wire run loosely through her hands as her momentum carried her forward.

Her thoughts about the sails weren't enough to keep her mind from what she'd just done. It was as though two voices had warred for control of her and, now Coalson was out of sight, the one that wanted him spaced and drifting behind the ship had settled into quiet satisfaction, leaving her with only the one horrified at what she'd done for company.

Not voices, no, but parts of my own soul.

She still felt satisfaction at Coalson's fate, but it was deep and distant, not at the forefront of her thoughts, and its presence only horrified her more. She felt her gorge rise and began pulling on the guidewire again to reach the sail locker faster.

She forced herself to think of nothing while the locker aired, then took a deep breath as she grasped the inner hatch's handle. She didn't think it would be wise to show weakness or regret to *Röslein's* crew after what she'd just done — and Dansby, as well as Mynatt, would likely be displeased. There was no telling what her act would do to their chances of collecting a bounty on Coalson.

She entered the quarterdeck. Bowhay had joined Dansby and Mynatt, and there was a spacer at the helm as well.

The four of them stared at Alexis, but said nothing, and she tried not to look at them as she passed. Neither did she look at any of the crew on the messdeck as she made her way to the ship's cabins and the single head those who berthed there shared. She could feel their eyes on her, though, and how they paused and went still as she passed.

She started to run a bit of water in the sink, thinking to splash her face, then lurched for the toilet as her stomach rebelled.

Some time later, there was a tapping at the hatch. Alexis ignored it. Her stomach was empty, but still convulsed and she felt too weak to move. If Dansby, Mynatt, or Bowhay needed to use the head, they could go aft to the crew's. *Röslein* wasn't a Navy ship where she might have to answer to a superior officer.

The hatch slid open.

"I'm busy," Alexis said, trying for as much dignity as she could, being sprawled on the deck with her head over a bowl. She didn't look up, as she had no desire to speak to anyone.

"Oh, no doubt," Mynatt said, sliding the hatch shut behind her. "You've been busy, aye."

"I would prefer some privacy, Miss Mynatt," Alexis said. Whatever the woman had to say, whatever recriminations, could well wait a bit. She was sure she'd hear from Dansby as well.

And the Navy will have its say, when it comes time for Dansby to ask for his bounty and recounts these events.

"No doubt," Mynatt repeated. She set a bottle on the sink, then eased herself down to sit on the deck, back to the hatch. Her injured leg, still in a brace, barely had room to extend across the small space of the head. Mynatt winced as she settled herself.

Alexis winced too, thinking of how close she'd been to pulling her chemical pistol instead of the flechette when she'd shot Mynatt.

"I am sorry about that," Alexis said.

Mynatt grunted.

"At least it wasn't a bullet to the head, I've that to be thankful for," she said, echoing Alexis' thoughts. She paused and frowned, staring at Alexis' face. "Oh, it was a close-run thing, was it?"

Alexis flushed.

"Doubly thankful, then, that you paused to think ... with me at least." She reached up and took the bottle from the sink, holding it out to Alexis. She nodded at the bowl. "To get the taste from your mouth."

Alexis took it gratefully. It was rum, not her favorite unless mixed into ship's grog, which she'd acquired a taste for, but it might burn away a bit more than the taste. She rinsed her mouth, spat, and then took a long drink.

"The crew is disturbed," Mynatt said, waving away Alexis' offer of the bottle. "What you did ..." She shook her head.

"He —"

"I heard his threats. Still ..."

Alexis took another drink, glad that Mynatt had cut her off. She and Dansby had heard Coalson's threats, true enough, but they hadn't heard what the man had confessed to Alexis. She'd been about to say, and was just as glad that she hadn't, now she had a moment to think on it. Mynatt wasn't her friend and there was no reason to share such confidences.

"You've a temper needs taming," Mynatt went on. "I've served with hard men since coming to work Avrel's ships, some not so much removed from a pirating cruise as I'd like, but even they'd not do as you did to that man."

Alexis took another long drink. Her self-recriminations were difficult enough to take; to be reproved by the likes of Anya Mynatt was harder to put up with. Still, the woman had a point. Her temper had got the better of her more than once and it had been only luck that things worked out.

"I've my own battles with hasty action," Mynatt said. "Had an officer's berth with the Marchant Company once."

Alexis raised an eyebrow. The Marchant Company held exclusive shipping rights to *Hso-Hsi,* and their profits were legendary. The shares ship's officers received in a single voyage could leave them set for life.

"What happened?"

Mynatt narrowed her eyes and grabbed the bottle from Alexis, taking a long pull before handing it back.

"That's not to the point," Mynatt said, "only that my temper got the better of me and I acted without thinking through the consequences." She waved a hand at the bulkhead. "Now I'm here and prospects with Avrel Dansby are not nearly so bright as with Marchant. And don't think I'm telling you this from any care for yourself. It's only that Avrel's told me you're key to this voyage and he's loath to see it fail. For yourself, I could give a fig, but if your temper harms our chances more than it already has —" She took a deep breath and pushed herself up. "Master yourself, girl."

Alexis nodded.

Mynatt paused, her hand on the hatch.

"Do you really intend to harm his sons?" she asked.

Alexis winced. She should have assumed Dansby and Mynatt would have listened in on the events in the lock.

"No," she said. "No, I wanted Daviel Coalson to die with that thought in his head —" She caught Mynatt's eye, acknowledging that it was a cruel desire. "— but I've no grudge against Edmon or his other sons. So far as I know they're blameless in all of this. This feud, one-sided as it's been, has caused enough bloodshed."

Mynatt grunted. "Of course you've just killed their father for a second time ... the lads may take exception to that."

THIRTY-TWO

Alexis kept to herself in the weeks that followed.

The ship made its zig-zag pattern from system to system, picking up cargo after cargo, both aboveboard and illicit. Dansby put her on the watch schedule, primarily, Alexis thought, to get her out of her cabin from time to time. Their ruse of calling her Dansby's niece, never too firm to begin with, had clearly collapsed completely. *Röslein's* crew was certain that she was not some far-removed relative learning Dansby's business and that *Röslein's* journey was not their norm.

They seemed to accept, though, that both Dansby and Mynatt were of the same mind now, and further accepted Alexis as the source of their voyage's profits. That was enough for them, so long as they were paid. They were not, however, very accepting of Alexis herself.

There was no overt hostility, but Alexis didn't feel the looks of fear she got from the crew were an improvement. They cast nervous glances her way whenever she was about the ship. Those who shared the quarterdeck with her during watch remained silent and jumped whenever she spoke. It reminded her of nothing so much as how the crew aboard *Hermione* had acted toward Captain Neals, and Alexis kept to her cabin partly to avoid their looks.

Part of her wanted to explain to the crew the circumstances of Coalson's death and what he'd done. She suspected many of the men might sympathize with her at least a bit. Still she wasn't sure how she'd feel if they didn't. She wished, frequently, that she could have brought Isom along with her on *Röslein*. She hadn't realized just how much she'd come to rely on his steady presence and assistance.

Dansby and Mynatt asked her to dine with them from time to time, but the two seemed to have grown inordinately closer since their confrontation over Alexis. They were openly sharing the master's cabin now, something the crew was more easily with than Alexis' own actions. It was an acceptance that would never occur aboard a Navy ship, and Alexis didn't understand it.

She rarely accepted the invitations, in any case, finding herself both uncomfortable at the couple's displays of affection and, to tell the truth, a bit jealous.

The closer they came to Dietraching, the system Dansby had discovered was where the Berry March fleet was now based, the more impatient she became. Aside from it marking the end of their voyage, she longed to see Delaine again. It felt like being with him again might help her make sense of her own feelings.

When they finally did arrive, they found that most of the Berry March fleet was in-system, along with more than a few other Hanoverese naval vessels. Once docked, Alexis fretted about the ship while Dansby and his crew roamed the station, gathering information about the fleet and its officers' habits.

"You can't just go blundering about crying his name through the corridors, Carew," Dansby said in response to her latest complaint that she wanted to leave the ship. "Not least because your German sounds like a poor New London vidshow of the last war. Let my crew do their job — they know we want this man, they'll track him down."

"And why haven't they yet?" she demanded. She poured another glass of wine, but found the bottle empty and set it on the common table between the cabins. "Is it so very difficult to determine what ship a man is on and which pubs he frequents? I'd think that would be far easier information to gather than finding illegal goods to fill your holds."

"When that man is a naval officer in time of war, yes, it is more difficult. At least if one wishes to remain out of an Hanoverese prison, that is." Dansby frowned as she rose and crossed to the shared pantry that stored their wine. "And would you want to cut back a bit on that? You'll want your wits about you when we do locate him."

Alexis stopped. Despite his tone, Dansby did have a point. A crewman could return at any moment with word of where Delaine was and she might have very little time to come up with a plan for meeting him.

"Perhaps you're right." She returned to her seat, picked up her half-filled glass, then set it down again. She had been drinking more than was usual even for a spacer these last weeks. She knew it was an effort to avoid thinking about what she'd done to Coalson. Moreover, it was an effort to avoid the nightmares that had come back with renewed force — she thought that might have more to do with her idleness than anything else, though. "Have your men found out anything at all?"

Dansby sat. He took her half-filled glass for himself, as though he didn't want her to have even that little bit more drink, and drained it.

"Some," he allowed. "There've been some changes in the Berry March fleet." He held up a hand to forestall her questions. "Let me tell it, not pester me with questions.

"Those worlds have never properly assimilated into Hanover, we knew that or we wouldn't be here for this purpose to begin with. It's why they've been allowed that fleet in the first place, a 'local defense force' that's a sop to their sensibilities. With this war, though, Hanover seems to be more concerned about them already. They've never brought that fleet this deep into Hanover before, and these explanations they make about 'exercises' with the Hanoverese fleet proper aren't sitting well with the Berry March spacers aboard station.

"Nor are some changes in the command structure. Balestra's still in overall command, but some Hanoverese officers have gone aboard some ships, and every ship now has a sort of political guide who's Hanoverese."

Dansby rubbed his face.

"I can't believe I'm saying it," he went on, "but I could wish Eades were here to better read the politics. If the Berry March spacers are unhappy with these things, it's certain those on the worlds themselves are as well. That would seem to bode well for Eades' mad plan. Still ... these political officers worry me. I've dealt with them before in Hanover and don't like it. They're a bit frightening and it will make this Balestra's task of revolt much harder. I'd prefer we had *Röslein* well away from here before she begins her little fun, if you can manage that at all once you speak to her."

Alexis nodded. She could understand that. Dansby had signed on to help her deliver the message, not get involved in whatever might come after.

"And of Delaine? Lieutenant Theibaud? Is there any word?" she asked.

Dansby nodded. "We should have a place you can make your presence known to him soon."

"Where?"

Dansby waved her back into her seat. "Calm yourself, Carew. Please. It's a pub he frequents, but always in the company of other officers — some from the Berry worlds, but others are these new Hanoverese officers in the fleet. You'll have to be careful about approaching him there."

Alexis took a deep breath. It felt like a huge weight had been lifted from her. After all the weeks of travel aboard *Röslein*, they were almost at the end.

THIRTY-THREE

ALEXIS WATCHED the group of officers at the table around Delaine. She wasn't sure which would be better, to approach him here or follow when he left. The pub was crowded with Hanoverese naval officers and any conversation here could easily be overheard, but if she followed him one of the other officers might notice and how would she explain that? Perhaps it would be better to wait until another time. But that would entail finding Delaine again. It had taken some days of observation by Dansby's crew, far more versed in that sort of skullduggery than Alexis, to spot him leaving his ship and tail him to this pub where Alexis might have a chance of catching his eye.

She glanced toward Dansby, who'd taken a table near the pub's entrance to watch over her. She moved farther in, pressing through the slight crowd to find a table from where she could observe Delaine. She fought the urge to look around, as she felt out of place and certain she was being watched. Not only because she was surrounded by Hanoverese, no few of them naval officers, but because she was in civilian dress and still not used to it. Despite the shopping she'd forced on Dansby, she'd worn none of the items save ship's jumpsuits for the entire trip, preferring their comfort and familiarity.

The pub's clientele was a mix of civilian and Hanoverese navy personnel, and more upscale, catering to lieutenants and commanders, and those with more than a bit of spare coin, she assumed, given the dress of the civilians present. Delaine was at a table with four other lieutenants and they seemed engrossed in conversation, paying little attention to the rest of the pub.

The table before her lit up with drink and food choices as she sat down. She sighed a little, thankfully that Dietraching was a sufficiently advanced system that she wouldn't have to ply her limited German simply to order from a human server. She could recognize enough to read the menu and order a glass of bourbon and a few moments later a floating server lowered onto her table and delivered it.

"*Fräulein, darf ich sie kaufen ein getränk?*"

Alexis looked up from her drink to find a man at the other side of the table gesturing at an empty chair with a hopeful smile on his face.

"*Nein, danke, ich warte auf jemanden,*" she said with a smile. While she'd mastered little more of German, despite lessons with Dansby, that was a phrase, and several like it, she'd practiced to recognize well enough, expecting to be approached if she spent much time sitting alone. Thankfully the man simply nodded and moved on, accepting that she was waiting for someone instead of pressing his suit.

She glanced once more toward Delaine's table, hoping he'd look her way, when he looked up, laughing at something one of the other men at his table said. His eyes passed over her, then returned. He blinked, frowned, then looked away and back again.

Alexis' breath caught as their eyes met. It had been so very long and she hadn't thought to see him again, possibly not ever. She caught her lower lip between her teeth and raised her eyebrows slightly. Now that he'd seen her, she'd leave the decision on where to approach up to him.

The officers at his table had noticed the change in his expression and followed his gaze to her. One of them said something and the others laughed. Delaine said something in return, not taking his eyes from her, and they laughed again. More words were exchanged and more laughter. Delaine kept glancing her way, until finally he stood, said one last thing to the other officers, then straightened his uniform tunic and walked toward her.

"*Ma biche*," he whispered when he reached her table.

Alexis grinned, though there was a deep pain in her chest. She hadn't realized how much she longed to hear his pet names for her again. She wanted to throw her arms around him, but that could be dangerous here, as it would have to be explained.

"Not *bichette?*" she asked with a small smile, remembering what he'd called her via ship's signals when she was fleeing Hanoverese space.

"In that dress, *non*. It shows you ... the word, grown up, *oui?*"

Alexis felt her face heat and tried to turn the conversation.

"Well, calling me that almost got you in a great deal of trouble last time, before I explained to Mister Lain that it means 'little doe' and not what it sounds like. It is better than cabbage, though." That had been the last thing he'd called her, the very last thing before sailing back to Hanoverese space from Penduli Station. My little cabbage.

"*Mon choux*," Delaine said, then grinned. He held up a hand, thumb and forefinger a short distance apart. "It is also the tiny pastry filled with the sweetest of cream. I like them very much."

Alexis felt her face heat more and knew she'd just flushed bright red.

How does he do that? He didn't say anything the least untoward and yet I'm ... damn me, but Naval officers on secret missions for the Queen do not blush!

"May I sit?"

She nodded, unsure of how to start. Encouraging revolt and mutiny wasn't the sort of thing one could just blurt out in a pub where others might hear, so they'd have to find some excuse to leave for a more private setting.

As Delaine sat, Alexis noticed a commotion at the table he'd left. One of the men was grinning widely and the other three were grimacing and sliding coins across the table to him. She frowned and looked back to Delaine.

"Are your friends *betting* on whether I'd allow you to join me?"

Delaine shrugged. "*Henri* is my friend. The others, they are *le Hanovre* and do not know me well." He nodded toward the pub's door. "Should we leave together, *Henri* will know much wealth."

Alexis struggled not to smile.

Well, no, I suppose we'll not need much excuse to leave this place and seek privacy after all.

She leaned forward over the table so that they wouldn't have to speak as loudly and felt a little satisfaction when she saw that Delaine's eyes were not meeting hers.

Mister Dansby's money was well-spent on this dress, it seems, if it can make the most of what little I have — there's a bit to be said, it seems, for structural enhancements. I wonder how much wealth Henri would come into if I were to wrap my arms around him and kiss him as I long to.

Instead she forced a stern look on her face.

"And is this how you've spent our time apart? Approaching strange women and betting with your friends on the outcome?"

Delaine raised his gaze and she realized as she spoke that she was only half teasing. When they'd parted after her court martial on Penduli, she'd never expected to see him again. With the war, especially with them being, ostensibly, on opposing sides, she'd thought it impossible, despite their promise to seek each other out after the war was over. Even messages would have been impossible.

She'd been approached by other men since — none of *Shrewsbury's* officers, of course, but the time they'd spent in ports offered opportunities — and she'd spent pleasant enough evenings with some. No more than suppers on-station and the occasional show in port —

there'd been little enough time to get to know someone and less, she admitted, interest on her part. Still she knew it was different for the male officers. She'd seen their disappointment often enough when she'd thanked them for a pleasant evening and ended things.

Delaine's face looked stricken, and Alexis realized she must not have had such a teasing note in her voice as she'd thought. Or, perhaps, there had been a great deal of that sort of thing. And, perhaps, it was unfair of her to feel the way she suddenly did, as though she'd been betrayed, when in truth she had no hold on him.

It's been nearly two years since I last saw him, but perhaps I don't care if it's fair at all and would happily strangle any number of those unknown women at the moment.

Delaine started to speak, but she held up a finger to stop him.

"If you say 'I am French' we shall have words, I think."

"I had thought I was never to see you again," he said quietly.

Alexis swallowed hard and caught her lip between her teeth, thoughts running away with her.

Damn me, but he's done nothing I didn't do myself ... well, perhaps more, but I certainly had the opportunities. And it's only by the slim chance of Eades' plotting that we're even meeting again and I have no hold on him, but fair or not I want one, though we never did more than kiss — and don't I wish I'd taken that opportunity on Giron and let him ply me a bit more when we had the chance. I wonder if it's been any of the women in this room since we've been apart ... and wouldn't they look fine as a pile of strangled corpses?

She took a deep breath and tried to settle herself.

This is all so very confusing.

"*Alexis*, how are you here?"

The question drew her back from her thoughts, reminding her of her duty. No matter her sudden confusion over her feelings, she had another, clearer, purpose here and concentrating on that would give her time to ponder the other.

"We have much to talk about. Do you know a private place where we can do so?"

Delaine nodded.

"Then let's be off." She glanced at the table he'd left where the four officers were paying a great deal of attention to them. "And leave Henri with a much-filled purse."

———

DELAINE'S IDEA of a private place turned out to be an establishment that offered private rooms to officers on station. Not just the sleep pods commonly available to spacers, but real rooms with full beds and a bath shared with only one other room. Alexis was a bit put out that he seemed to know the place so well. She was well aware of why male officers kept rooms on-station instead of sleeping aboard ship. Nor was she pleased with the look she received from the establishment's owner and the thought of what he must think of her.

None of that was enough, though, to dim her enthusiasm as the room's hatch slid shut and left them alone for the first time. She wrapped her hands around Delaine's neck and pulled his face down to hers.

It was only some time later, after she felt they'd made a proper greeting after so long apart, that Alexis finally explained how she'd come to be on Dietraching.

"*La République,* they will come for us? Truly?"

Alexis nodded. "There's a French admiral and general ... field marshal, you call them, I think? They're on their way to Alchiba — may already have arrived — with uniforms and supplies. New London has assembled a fleet and troops. It's all being prepared."

Delaine rose from his seat beside her and started pacing.

"I know that this has been thought of," he said. "My commodore, she sometimes says things that make me think there is even a plan." He stopped pacing and looked at her intently. "You are certain of this?"

Alexis smiled. "I have messages for Commodore Balestra from

admirals and generals in both New London's and the Republic's forces. When I met with Admiral Reinier on *Nouvelle Paris*, he —"

Delaine was suddenly on his knees before her, grasping her hands. "You have been to *Paris?*"

Alexis had to laugh at the look on his face. "I was there for almost three months."

"Is it as wonderful as they say?"

Alexis thought of the days spent in drab offices waiting for some petty bureaucrat to bother speaking to them and night after night of interminable parties that all ran together in her memory, then saw the hope and expectation in Delaine's eyes.

"What I saw of it was quite grand," she said finally. "Admiral Reinier's home is lovely ... they have very impressive forts."

They talked for a time about how to go about getting Alexis in to meet with Balestra. It would have to be done covertly, so that the Hanoverese security officer aboard the commodore's flagship caught no suspicion of what was happening. Delaine could speak to her privately easily enough, but meeting with Alexis would be more difficult. Finally they realized that there was no more they could do until such a meeting was arranged.

"*Alexis*, I cannot tell you how I feel. Always I have wanted my world to rejoin *La République,* and since I left you I have wished to see you again ..." He grinned. "You are like some *génie* to make my wishes come true."

Alexis caught her lip between her teeth and looked down. Now that she'd fulfilled at least part of her duty in coming here, she could finally think of more personal things. She'd spent the nearly two years since she'd last seen him regretting what they hadn't done, and didn't wish to make the same mistake again.

"You do have one wish left, you know." She glanced up quickly to watch his face. "By tradition, I mean."

Delaine's brow furrowed.

To hear the other officers talk, this sort of thing comes so easily to them. I wonder if the Navy hasn't issued some instruction manual I've yet to read.

"It occurs to me," she said, wondering how direct she'd have to be, "that you did take this room for the entire night, and it would be a shame for Henri to come by all those winnings dishonestly."

Delaine eyes widened. He cupped her face in both hands and tilted it up.

"Are you certain, *mon chaton?* I should not wish you to have regrets."

Alexis forced herself to breathe, hoping her voice wouldn't tremble as so much of the rest of her was. Regrets were what she'd had since she'd last left him and she had no idea when they'd have another opportunity. Once her messages were delivered to Balestra, she'd be back aboard *Röslein* and sailing for New London space. Delaine and Balestra's fleet would be close behind, but when they did reach New London she'd be back aboard *Shrewsbury*, which might not even participate in the Berry March revolt.

"I actually am capable of knowing my own mind, Delaine. Still, to be safe, you shall have to do your very best to see I have no cause to."

THIRTY-FOUR

ALEXIS WOKE with her head still resting on Delaine's chest where she'd lain before falling asleep, one arm and leg draped over him and a rapidly expanding pool of drool wetting her cheek. She winced at the sight, then licked her lips and shifted slightly.

Perhaps if I move very slowly I can wipe that off before he wakes.

"*Bonjour, mon ange.*"

Alexis closed her eyes and sighed.

Do men never sleep? Or do they simply lie there and watch us?

She sat up and pulled up the sheet to her chest, clutching it there with one hand while she used the other to daub at Delaine's chest. She stopped at the look of amusement on his face and flushed.

"I cannot imagine that you have never drooled in your sleep," she said, turning her back to him.

Delaine laughed and ran a hand over her bare back, making her shiver. She felt the sheet move as he grasped it and wiped his chest.

"And so," he said. "There is no sign of it to embarrass you."

She felt his hand stop caressing her and he ran a finger along one of the scars that crisscrossed her back.

"This is from *Capitaine* Neals?"

The anger in his voice made her turn. She lay back down and rested her face on his chest. "That's over. I barely notice the scars anymore."

Delaine held her tightly. "I would wish more was done to him."

Like throwing him off a ship in darkspace?

Alexis shuddered, this time from the thought, not Delaine's touch. She'd almost told him the night before of what she'd done to Coalson, but stopped. She did want to talk to someone about it, someone she trusted, but feared what he might say — more so what he might think of her for it.

"I doubt he'll ever return to duty," she said. "If he should, it will be at a desk with a port admiral examining his every decision and no power to flog a soul."

"It is not enough."

"It was what could be had." The captains making that decision had not wanted to risk the embarrassment of a court martial for Neals and the risk of his actions being exposed. Even in a Service with such strict discipline, Neals was one to be ashamed of.

He also has powerful friends, Alexis reminded herself. Friends might have stepped forward to protect him from anything more.

Delaine cupped her cheek and raised her face to his.

"Let us move to pleasanter things," he said. "Later I will speak to my commodore and arrange a meeting for you, but this morning is still ours."

THE STATION CORRIDOR HELD A SUBDUED, early morning crowd. Though stations ran twenty-four hours a day for visiting ships, most fell into a somewhat normal rhythm of day and night — at least for those who lived aboard the station full time. Alexis took Delaine's arm as they left the hotel.

"I have time for breakfast, and then I must return to my ship, *ma chèrie*. I will speak with my commodore as soon as I may —"

Behind them, someone called out, then again, louder. Alexis couldn't tell what was said, but Delaine looked and scowled.

"*Merde.*"

Alexis looked also and saw an Hanoverese officer hurrying toward them. Others in the corridor moved aside as he came on. He called out again, waving his arm.

"*Leutnant Theibaud!*"

Delaine leaned close to her and whispered, "This man is dangerous. Speak only *Français*, and little of that."

He straightened and smiled as the man drew nearer. Alexis wondered at the warning, for the man seemed cheerful — smiling and round-faced, with red patches on his cheeks. Pale, thin hair covered his head.

"*Herr* Reinacher," Delaine said, smiling, when the man reached them.

"*Leutnant* Theibaud."

Then came a string of German so fast and guttural that Alexis had no hope of following it. Delaine responded in kind. Alexis only realized that they had begun speaking of her because the man gestured at her. Delaine looked at her and squeezed her hand in warning before responding.

The man looked at her and held out his hand, speaking very slowly and loudly.

"*Ahchanting, maidmosul* Aubert."

It took Alexis a moment to realize what he was saying, or trying to say, and that only because it was so obviously a greeting.

He's trying to say 'enchanté mademoiselle', but what a horrid accent — and what on earth is an aubert?

"*Merci, monsieur,*" she said, remembering Delaine's instruction to speak only French and giving him her hand.

She repressed a shiver as he bent and kissed her hand, then another when he straightened and met her eyes.

Smiling and cheerful, but with dead-cold eyes.

He addressed Delaine again and Alexis tried to follow the

conversation, but it was too rapid for her limited knowledge of the tongue. Delaine shook his head several times, but the man persisted and eventually Delaine seemed to agree reluctantly. With a wave and a nod to Alexis, the man walked off.

Delaine took Alexis' arm and hurried her in the opposite direction.

"Who was that?" Alexis asked.

"A moment," Delaine said, voice low and tense. He waited until they were several intersections away and spent the time darting glances at those around them until finally he pulled Alexis into a side corridor. "*Herr* Reinacher. He is with my fleet as ... ah, *la police politique?*"

"Political police?" Alexis asked. "What did he want?"

"This disturbs me, *Alexis.*" Delaine frowned. "He has asked me to attend *l'opéra* and the reception after. I have told him you are a friend, ah, *Mademoiselle* Aubert, traveling from my home. His French is ... *affreux*, frightful, and he cannot understand it spoken quickly, so he will not expect to speak with you. This invitation, though, it disturbs me very much."

"Well, if he's attached to your fleet, would this not be a simple courtesy?"

"*Non.* Not to me, I am but a *lieutenant.* My commodore, she has trust in me, but I am below the notice of such as he. And *Herr* Reinacher, he was most insistent and asked for you to attend as well." He looked around. "*Alexis,* I think that you should return to your ship, this *Röslein,* and leave. I do not like his interest."

"But I must meet with Commodore Balestra," Alexis said. "I have the messages from the Republic and the plans —"

"Then give to me this message and I will pass it to my commodore."

"They're on my tablet."

Delaine pulled his tablet from his pocket. "And transfer it to mine and I will give it."

Alexis sighed. "I seem to recall you making a quite thorough search of me last night. Perchance did your hands encounter my tablet in their travels?"

Delaine grinned. "*Non*, nothing but you." His grin faltered. "*Herr* Reinacher is not to laugh at, *Alexis*. He is a dangerous man, much to be feared. You have told me of these plans — I will inform my commodore and you should leave."

"If I disappear, just sail off, will that not appear more suspicious to him? And draw more suspicion to you and Commodore Balestra in turn?"

Delaine sighed. "It would be difficult to explain," he said.

"Then I should attend this, this opera and the reception. Perhaps he is simply showing a courtesy. If you and the other officers from the Berry March fear him so much, he must surely know it, mustn't he? Perhaps he saw you with a girl and decided to take the opportunity to do something kind, something to, I don't know, improve relations with the officers of your fleet?" She saw Delaine's skeptical look and shrugged. "I don't want to be the cause of trouble for you or Commodore Balestra."

Delaine looked at her and quirked one corner of his mouth up. He looked around and leaned close to her.

"You come to ask us to make *la mutinerie*, to take our ships home, and to raise *la révolte* against *le Hanovre* ... this is not trouble?"

"LONG NIGHT, CAREW."

Alexis was, perhaps, halfway back to *Röslein's* berth at the station's quayside and jumped with an audible gasp as Dansby appeared at her elbow. She'd thought she'd been quite good about keeping her wits about her and her eyes scanning the crowd in the corridor, yet he'd approached to within touching distance without her noticing.

"Did you take lessons from Eades to be able to do that?"

"Who do you think taught him?" Dansby said. He grasped her

elbow and got her moving down the corridor again. "May I assume our work here is done and we may make haste to leave?"

"No, it is not. I've yet to meet with Commodore Balestra."

"All night closeted with one of her lieutenants and you couldn't pass the bloody messages along?"

"I didn't have my tablet with me, now did I?"

Dansby stopped and turned her to face him. He looked her over.

"No, I suppose you didn't ..." He frowned. "You look different somehow."

Alexis flushed.

Dansby raised an eyebrow. "Oh, I see. Well, at least one of us had a productive evening." He started back toward *Röslein*. "For myself, I spent the night moving from place to place in a rather exposed corridor so that I could keep an eye on where you'd gone." He glanced at her again. "I'd have sought entertainment for myself, if I'd known you were in such good hands."

THIRTY-FIVE

"You are well, *ma belle?*"

Alexis shook her head. They were stopped in a side corridor a few intersections from the theatre where the opera had been held on their way to the reception. Alexis' head was still pounding from the performance — some sort of epic filled with winged women, horned helmets, and a score that she suspected consisted of invisible trolls roaming the audience to strike the watchers' heads with stone mallets.

She raised a hand to her temple, rubbing gently. "Will the pounding ever stop?"

Delaine chuckled. "Be glad it was only the one."

Alexis' eyes widened. "There's *more* of it?"

"*Cinq*, five, I think. These are almost the national event of *le Hanovre.*"

She shook her head in wonder.

"If you are not well, perhaps this is not wise. I will make your excuses to *Herr* Reinacher."

She'd seen Reinacher before the performance and at intermission, but briefly both times as he merely said hello and rushed off. But he'd said, through Delaine, how much he looked forward to seeing her at the reception. The attention was unnerving, given that he'd said so very little to her and who he was. She was beginning to wonder if Delaine hadn't been correct and she should have boarded *Röslein* and sailed that morning. On the other hand, if Reinacher's interest was innocent — or, at least, more prurient than suspicious — she would only draw attention to Delaine and Balestra by running. Attention they could ill afford as the Berry March fleet was already under some suspicion.

"What can happen at a reception?" she asked. "A bit of food, a bit of drink, and then we'll say good night." She laced her arm through his and hugged it tightly to her. "Perhaps a few words with Commodore Balestra, and I may transfer the messages to her." She felt her tablet through the thin material of the small bag she carried. She had a moment's regret that her dress, like the one she'd worn the night before, was ill-suited to concealing a weapon.

"I worry about *Herr* Reinacher's interest."

"We've discussed that — my failure to attend and disappearance would pique his suspicions more."

Delaine nodded. "Still, I worry."

The reception was held in a large compartment near the opera. The space took up two levels of the station and was large enough that Alexis thought she could see a hint of the station's curve in it. The balcony around the second level was less crowded and had many alcoves and rooms branching off it for privacy. The lower level was crowded with people and small tables around a central dance floor.

Dancing. Why must there always be dancing?

Alexis and Delaine wandered through the crowd on the lower level. Alexis caught sight of Balestra several times, but she was always surrounded by a group of other officers and Delaine shook his head, whispering, "Too many of *le Hanovre* about her. She will find a time to leave them and will meet us above. Much business is discussed here" He nodded at the balcony. "There are rooms above for discussion or —" He raised an eyebrow. "— more intimate things."

Alexis flushed. Much as she longed for a repeat of the more intimate things of the night before, she was quite certain she wouldn't be able to appreciate them properly with a hall full of people right outside the door, no matter how private the rooms were.

Delaine laughed. He leaned close to her ear and whispered. "Too much of New London, still. You should be more *Française*." He stepped back toward the dance floor and held out his hand. "Instead will you dance, *mon cœur?*"

Alexis snorted. "I've two or more left feet, I'm afraid."

"Surely not." He took her hand. "Come, please."

Alexis shrugged and took his hand, muttering, "On your own head."

Delaine led her to the dance floor just as the music stopped.

Alexis raised an eyebrow. "A sign that this is a poor idea, do you think?"

Delaine smiled as the music started again, a slow number. He pulled her close, hand on her hip. "Signs and signs, *oui?*" He started her into the dance. "You see?" he whispered. "It is not so — ow. *Ma cocotte,* you must move where — simply follow, yes? Ow. *Non.*" He laughed. "You do not like to follow."

"I did warn you."

Delaine stopped and looked her in the eye for a long moment, then leaned close to whisper in her ear, the feel of his breath sending a shiver through her. "Do you trust me, *Alexis?*"

Not trusting herself to speak, she nodded.

"Close your eyes." Delaine pulled back so he could see her face. "Close them." He leaned in again as she did so. "Move with me, *mon amour.*"

THE MUSIC ENDED FAR TOO SOON for Alexis. Delaine slowed to a stop and she with him, eyes still closed and held tightly to him.

There may be something to this dancing business after all.

It certainly was nice once she let go and got the hang of it. Not nearly so nice as how she and Delaine had spent the night before, but it could be done in public. Odd that once she'd relaxed and simply trusted Delaine she'd had no trouble with it at all. She'd have to think on that once she had a moment.

Alexis felt Delaine tense and opened her eyes to find Reinacher approaching, a wide, toothy smile on his face.

"*Leutnant* Theibaud, *Fraulein* Aubert —" she heard, and that was all she understood as Reinacher and Delaine exchanged words. Once or twice Reinacher gestured to her and she smiled in return, but other than that she was completely in the dark as to the topic of conversation.

Alexis scanned the hall while the two talked, Delaine clearly only responding to Reinacher's prompts. The crowd, for all that they were Hanoverese, seemed normal and happy to her, not the rampant warmongers described by Mister Eades. If anything, they seemed far more relaxed and easygoing than a similar gathering in New London, at least in the systems Alexis had experience with, though not nearly so much as the French on *Nouvelle Paris*.

Then again, it would be quite difficult to outdo them, I think.

A sharp *ping* cut through the thrum of nearby conversations and drew Alexis' attention. Delaine frowned and pulled out his tablet, frowning more as he read from it. He put it away and spoke to Reinacher again, smiling shrugging apologetically. He grasped Alexis' arm and started to step away. Alexis assumed he'd received some message from his ship and was making his excuses to Reinacher to have to leave, which, frankly, relieved her, but then Reinacher laid a hand on her arm and spoke, smiling more broadly. A chill ran through Alexis and she could imagine what was being said.

I'm sorry, Herr Reinacher, but I'm called to attend my ship and we must leave.

Nein, Leutnant Theibaud, surely Fraulein Aubert would prefer to remain here.

Delaine was speaking again and then Reinacher. Alexis could tell that they were simply repeating themselves and worried that Delaine's insistence that she leave with him would seem odd. She laid a hand on Delaine's arm and spoke quickly as he'd told her too, stumbling a bit over a word or two and hoping Reinacher wouldn't notice.

"*Prenez soin de votre bateau bête, Delaine. Monsieur Reinacher me divertira.*" *Take care of your silly boat, Delaine. Reinacher will entertain me.*

Delaine looked at her shocked and she willed him to understand. If they argued too much, it would only incite more suspicion. She could spend a time pretending she didn't understand a word Reinacher said and then excuse herself. She'd make her way back to *Röslein* and retire for the night, then try to contact Balestra the next day.

Je ne comprends pas, *will be the most Reinacher gets from me. A useful phrase, that.*

Delaine paused, then nodded. He said something to Reinacher, leaned close to Alexis on the side away from the other man, and whispered.

"*Fais attention á toi.*" *Take care.*

Alexis kissed his cheek as he drew back, smiled assurances she didn't entirely feel, and patted his arm. She watched Delaine walk away, her heart beating faster and faster as he disappeared into the crowd, then turned back to Reinacher with a smile that quickly faded.

Reinacher was no longer smiling, no longer jovial. His face was set, eyes narrowed and cold.

THIRTY-SIX

Reinacher took Alexis' arm and another man she'd never seen before took the other. Their grips were tight to the point of being painful. She started to speak, to ask what they were doing, but Reinacher squeezed her arm harder and she took the hint. The two men steered her off the dance floor and up the stairs to the balcony level, having to support her and almost drag her when she stumbled.

She looked around frantically, hoping to see Delaine or even Balestra, though what they'd be able to do she didn't know.

They turned into a corridor off the balcony, one almost hidden from view by plants and decorations. It was nicely appointed, not a service hall as she'd assumed, and it soon met another corridor in a T-intersection.

Behind those alcoves and meeting rooms Delaine mentioned.

"*Que faites-vous?*" Alexis asked quietly. She was trying to think how Marie Aubert from the Berry worlds would react. *Probably terrified and knowing she can't resist the ... what did Delaine call them, political police? Well, and I've the terrified bit of that with no problem at all.*

"*Sei still*," Reinacher said, the meaning clear from the shake he gave her arm.

They stopped at a hatchway. Reinacher held her arm while the other man slid the hatch open then Reinacher flung her inside. Alexis stumbled and fell after a few steps. She recovered her footing and looked around. It was definitely a meeting room of some kind, with a small sidebar in one corner and a pair of couches facing each other across a low table. The far wall was the outside bulkhead of the station. Most of it was a clear material offering a spectacular view of the planet below.

Reinacher slid the hatch shut, leaving the other man outside, and walked to the sidebar to pour a drink. Alexis edged toward the door, but stopped — even if it were open what could she do? Run through the reception hall with Reinacher in pursuit and a guard outside? No, she'd have to see this through, whatever he had in mind.

Reinacher raised his glass and said something quickly in German. *Well, I've heard it often enough myself. I might as well say it.*

"*Que?*" she asked trying to fix her face in an innocent yet puzzled expression.

"*Excusez-moi*," Reinacher said. He took a sip of his drink. "Or we should use your English, yes?"

A chill went through Alexis and she tried not to react.

"*Que?*"

"Do not play me the fool," Reinacher said. He spoke in rapid bursts, each accompanied by some gesture or movement. "I have little tongue —" He pointed at his mouth. "—for languages, but I have an ear —" Another gesture to the side of his head. "— for accents."

He turned back to the sideboard and poured another glass. Alexis edged toward the door again. Perhaps it would be better to take her chances running.

"Locked," Reinacher said without turning. "You speak French, but not with an accent of the native." He turned, carrying both glasses and held one out, finger extended to point at her. "No, you have an accent of New London in your French." He smiled. "You arrive —" He stepped toward her holding out the glass. "— on a ship called *Röslein*, which we know is *Marilyn*, whose records say is captained by *Herr* Federmann, who we know is Dansby." He raised his eyebrows and gestured with the offered glass.

Alexis took the glass and held it gingerly.

"We know he smuggles, and we allow this." Reinacher shrugged. "Times being what they are. So when you are introduced as Marie Aubert, I must ask myself: How does this French Marie Aubert from the Berry worlds come to be on not-*Herr* Federmann's ship the not-*Röslein*?" He took a sip and smiled. "Drink, please. It is a fine *schnapps*."

Reinacher waited smiling, with eyebrows raised, until Alexis took a small sip. The drink tasted of peppermint and Alexis thought she might enjoy it if she wasn't becoming more and more certain that it would be her last.

I would much rather my last drink taste of peat and smoke, not candy, if at all possible.

"The answer, of course," Reinacher continued, turning and walking back into the room, "is that she is not Marie Aubert." He spun and put a finger to his temple. "But this ... brings only more questions. If she is not Marie Aubert, then why does *Leutnant* Theibaud, a trusted, loyal man, introduce her as Marie Aubert? Has she deceived him? Has she —" He smiled. "— worked wiles upon him?" He shook his head. "*Nein*, no, it makes me think there is more to this ..." This time his smile showed teeth. "We have the saying, 'layers to the onion', you know this saying?" He waved his hand dismissively. "Of course you do. So now I think that under not-*Herr* Federmann is this Dansby and under not-*Röslein* is the ship *Marilyn*, but are these the final layers? Have we peeled these enough?" He grinned widely and Alexis was reminded of a shark. "What might I discover if I peel these things and see the next layer? Hm?"

Alexis remained still, not trusting herself to speak and not sure what she could say in any case.

"Still you say nothing?" Reinacher shrugged. "I will peel a layer of what I know for you and we shall see." He placed his glass on a table and pressed his hands together, fingers at his lips. "I know the men I am to watch, do you see? And so I see *Leutnant* Theibaud walking in the morning —" He gestured at Alexis. "— with a lady and I know that this is not *Leutnant* Theibaud's habit. Since he has come to Dietraching, *Leutnant* Theibaud will smile and *Leutnant* Theibaud will dance and *Leutnant* Theibaud will charm the *frauleins*, but *Leutnant* Theibaud goes to his rooms or ship alone at night."

Alexis' heart fell and she swallowed hard as she realized what Reinacher was saying. She'd given it away, just by her very presence and having spent the night with Delaine. If she'd sent him back to his ship and gone herself to *Röslein*, then Reinacher would never have seen them together. If she hadn't been so terrified, she might have spent more time thinking about what Reinacher said, that Delaine went to his ship alone at night, and that her fears about his feelings were misfounded, but she forced those thoughts aside and concentrated on what Reinacher was saying.

"And I think of the reports that came with this fleet from the Berry worlds," Reinacher went on. "Prisoners who escaped and how *Leutnant* Theibaud was said to have spent much time with one of them." He narrowed his eyes. "A small, pretty *leutnant zur see*." He looked at her and pursed his lips. "Some might think so, I suppose."

Reinacher sat on a couch and spread his arms wide.

"And so *Leutnant zur See* Alexis Carew, will you now speak?"

Alexis' mind was racing as fast as her heart. It had seemed quite a simple plan when she'd started this. Find Delaine, speak to Balestra, sail home — but she'd given little thought to what might happen if she was discovered. She'd known it was a risk, of course, but an abstract one. She'd not really believed it would happen, so hadn't planned for it. Now she was faced with Reinacher, a man Delaine said she had cause to fear, and what was she to do?

"I'm not."

"*Nein, fraulein*, please. Do not deny what I know."

Alexis swallowed hard, took a sip of her drink to stall for time, and inhaled deeply of the schnapps. The scent of the drink seemed to clear her thoughts a bit. What other reason could she have for following Delaine here?

"I'm sorry," she said, moving into the room and sitting on the other couch opposite Reinacher. "I meant I'm not what you called me ... *leutnant zur see*, was it? Does that mean midshipman?"

Reinacher nodded. "Yes, the young officer not yet *Leutnant*. Your midshipman. So, you do not deny that you are this Alexis Carew?"

"No, sir," Alexis said, "only that I'm not a midshipman. Not anymore." She took a deep breath and looked down at the floor as though embarrassed. "I resigned my commission, you see." She glanced up without raising her head to see Reinacher regarding her with raised eyebrows. "I never wanted to be in the Navy in the first place, you understand," she went on quickly, speaking in a rush. "I only did because ... well, because my grandfather was trying to marry me off to whoever'd have me. So I ran away and signed aboard ship."

She couldn't tell from Reinacher's expression if he believed her or not.

"Then I met Delaine," she said, "Lieutenant Theibaud, and I ... well ..." She squared her shoulders and met Reinacher's eye as though defying him to challenge her. "I quite fell in love with him."

Alexis felt sick to her stomach at what she was doing. She wasn't certain what her feelings for Delaine were, but using what they might be in this way, speaking those words for the first time as part of a lie and to Reinacher, made her feel like she was tainting something good and special.

Still if I don't manage to talk my way out of this, no matter how distasteful the telling, we'll neither of us have much of a future to find out what feelings we do have.

"I would have stayed on Giron to be with him," she went on quickly, "but my captain insisted we flee. And when I was back in New London, aboard a ship, I realized that I didn't care about anything else. So I resigned my place and ..." She glanced down again

241

as though embarrassed. "Well, I took what money I had and found that Mister Dansby. He's quite disreputable, I know, but I couldn't just book passage on any ship to come here, now could I?" She gave Reinacher a pleading look. "I needed someone who could find where Delaine was stationed now and who could get me here from New London. It took most of what I'd managed to save, but I did get here. To be with Delaine ... nothing more, *Herr* Reinacher, I assure you."

He regarded her for a moment with pursed lips, nodding, then began to slowly applaud.

"Very nice. Very nice, yes. Almost, I believe you."

"*Herr* Reinacher —"

"*Nein.*" He held up a hand to stop her. "Please. The tale needs no more protestations. It is the best of lies that has so much of the truth. Still, there is the part I believe is true and the part I do not believe is true." He pointed at her. "You have layers to you." He sat back and crossed his legs, reaching to his boottop to pull forth a thin knife. "And I must peel from you the real truth."

Reinacher tapped the knife blade against his lower lip and stared at her intently.

"So," he said, eyes narrowing, "first I will peel away the truths of what you have said and you will see that you cannot lie to me. I have dealt with many accomplished liars, *Fraulein* Carew, and you, while you show promise, are not of their skill." His frequent gestures were now made with the hand holding the knife and Alexis' eyes followed it. "I think it true that you are not *leutnant zur see*, but your voice when you say you have resigned, it does not have the ring of truth. So ..." He bowed slightly. "... I congratulate you on a promotion, I think." He smiled and waved the knife at her face. "Yes! You see? I know the lie from the truth."

Reinacher stood and began pacing. He made his way behind the couch Alexis sat on and walked back and forth, tapping the blade on the couch behind her as he went.

"I do not believe that it is you who have made arrangements with *Herr* Dansby-not-Federmann. You are too young, too much the naïf still. You would hesitate to have dealings with such a man. Still, though ..." He stopped pacing and tapped the knife blade rapidly in one spot. "You and he are much the same in many ways, I think."

Reinacher resumed pacing. Alexis felt an urge to comment or question his comparison of her to Dansby. She felt rather insulted that he'd dare say she was at all the same as Dansby in any way, and the offense had broken her out of the paralyzing fear she'd felt. She clenched her hands in her lap. They were trembling and she didn't want Reinacher to see that, nor did she want to give him any more information to work with by speaking again. What he was doing with the little she'd told him so far was frightening enough.

"You say a grandfather wished you to marry, so this means that your parents are dead — I believe this. But —" He went back to the other couch and sat facing her again. "— you do not speak of him as one who was forcing you to this marriage. There is too much affection in you."

Reinacher crossed his legs and sat back. Alexis eyes followed the knife blade as he rested his arms on the couch's back.

"Affection," he mused, smiling slightly, "has so many uses. Curious, though, that you say you love *Leutnant* Theibaud ... so much that you will give up your life in New London and follow him here, and yet I do not believe this. You care for him, certainly — and he for you, else he would not have dared lie to me — but your face is uncertain when you say it."

He leaned forward and slid the blade of his knife along his other palm.

"Many uses, *fraulein*, you will see. I do not think it would be easy to peel the truth from you. But this Theibaud, he may not bear watching me make the attempt."

Alexis closed her eyes and breathed deeply. She wished yet again that she'd found some way to hide a weapon in this dress. She heard the compartment's hatch slide open behind her — that would be Reinacher's man and likely meant Reinacher was done with whatever game he was playing at and about to begin questioning her in earnest. She felt he was likely correct — neither she nor Delaine would be able stand silent and watch him harm the other. They'd tell him what he wanted, if only to make it stop.

Reinacher was staring at the hatch behind her. His eyes narrowed and he nodded.

"And so it is bigger than the two."

Alexis turned her head and saw Commodore Balestra sliding the hatch closed. Balestra, face impassive, turned from the hatch and took three steps into the compartment.

"I am curious what you have done with Heinrich," Reinacher said.

Balestra frowned. She pulled her tablet from a pocket and ran a finger over it.

"My man at the door?" Reinacher prompted. He was still bent over, elbows on knees, running the blade of his knife over his palm.

"There was no one at the hatchway," Balestra said. She looked at Alexis. "So, *vous*."

"You know *fraulein* Aubert, commodore?" Reinacher asked with a smile.

Balestra kept her gaze on Alexis. "From the blade in your hand, I think you know she is not."

"Your purpose here, commodore?"

Balestra ignored him. "What Delaine has told me, *Lieutenant* Carew, it is true?"

Alexis started to reach for her tablet in the little bag she held, but stopped. There wasn't time for Balestra to view the messages or review the figures and timetables, nor was she asking for that. She nodded.

"It is."

Balestra raised her tablet and spoke into it.

"*Allez.*"

In the same breath, she pulled a flechette pistol from her jacket and trained it on Reinacher.

"So," Reinacher said, "it is more than a *leutnant* or two who is disloyal."

"Drop the blade, *Herr* Reinacher, *s'il vous plaît*, and place your hands atop your head." Balestra waited until he'd complied. "Stand slowly."

Reinacher remained still. "I think not. There is much for me to ponder in this. I had thought it was only Theibaud taken in by a woman, but now ..."

Alexis stood and slowly edged her way around the couch to Balestra's side.

Reinacher looked from her to Balestra. "Much more than *leutnants*, and more than a fleet, I think." His eyes narrowed.

"Shoot him," Alexis whispered, seeing the man's mind work on the puzzle of her purpose here and Balestra's involvement, as it had on her own story for being there.

"*Kommodore* Balestra does not like to kill, *Leutnant* Carew. I know this about her." He smiled thinly. "But now I have learned another of your layers."

"Stand," Balestra repeated, gesturing with the flechette pistol, and the gesture was all the distraction Reinacher required.

He straightened, standing, but at the same time twisting and launching himself over the back of the couch he sat on, disappearing from view.

Balestra fired. The flechettes tore at the couch's cushions, shredding them. Balestra grabbed Alexis' arm and dragged her to the floor behind their own couch just as Reinacher's arm appeared wielding a laser. The bolt snapped through the space Balestra had just occupied.

Alexis shared a look with Balestra and glanced around for some sort of weapon. It didn't appear that Balestra's flechette pistol would penetrate the couch's back, while Reinacher's laser likely would. A suspicion that was proven true a moment later as there was another *snap* and a smoking hole appeared in the back of the couch near Alexis' head.

Balestra raised her flechette and hosed the other couch with a stream of tiny darts as Alexis continued to look for something, anything, she could use as a weapon. Their only advantage lay in the fact that Reinacher would have to replace the capacitor in his laser with a fresh one after each shot, and that would take time.

A disturbingly short time, she noted as another smoking hole appeared in the center of the couch's back. He might have two pistols and could have one at the ready while he reloaded the other, which would make rushing him after a shot disastrous for one of them. Her eyes fell on the sidebar.

When next Balestra raised her arm to send a stream of flechettes in Reinacher's direction, Alexis sprang for the sidebar. She scooped up the icebucket and an armful of bottles before scrambling back to shelter. Balestra gave her a confused look, then jerked back as a hole burnt through the couch near her nose.

"That is not so much space to hide behind!" Reinacher called out. "I will find one of you — it is best, I think, to end this now."

"I couldn't bloody agree more," Alexis muttered. She dumped out the ice and unscrewed the bottles, pouring each into the bucket. The scents reached her nose as she poured.

Peppermint ... cinnamon ... peach ... what are these people thinking?

"What do you do?" Balestra whispered.

Alexis shook her head; anything she said might be heard by Reinacher. She heaved the empty bottles, one by one, over the couches.

Reinacher laughed. "I would allow you a last drink, *frauleins,* never fear."

She waited for the next *snap* of Reinacher's laser, then stood and threw the contents of the bucket over the back of the other couch. Balestra rose at the same time and fired another stream of flechettes. Alexis caught her lip between her teeth and motioned to Balestra to be ready.

The next *snap* of Reinacher's laser was a accompanied by a *thwump* and a scream. Alexis and Balestra both rose, the commodore firing and Alexis grasping the now empty ice bucket.

Reinacher was standing and flailing about. His left arm, from wrist to shoulder, was aflame, as well as his hair. Balestra fired, but Reinacher was moving so rapidly that the flechettes barely caught his arm. Reinacher spun and dashed for the side of the compartment. Balestra fired again and Reinacher staggered, but made it to the bulkhead. He flung open a hatch hidden there and disappeared behind it.

Alexis and Balestra rushed after him. Alarms began sounding as they reached the bulkhead and when they opened the hatch the corridor beyond was filled with jets of fog. Balestra slammed the hatch shut, coughing.

"We have to go after him!" Alexis yelled over the alarms.

"*Non!*" Balestra shook her head. "The fire! In the smaller space, it is enough — we cannot breath the gas!"

Alexis reached for the hatch, but Balestra stopped her and as she did the alarms stopped.

"That must mean the fire's out. We can go after him!"

Balestra held the hatch closed. "The service corridors of a station, they are a maze, *Lieutenant* Carew. Reinacher is well gone and we must be as well." She examined her flechette pistol. Alexis could see that the magazine was almost empty. "We would soon be weaponless, in any case."

"But —"

"*La Baie Marche* fleet, it is in *révolte*. That is the message I have sent. *La mutinerie* has begun. Even now my officers fight for control. I must return to my ships."

"The message? '*Allez*'? That was to have your officers take over the ships? How can you have made plans so quickly?" Alexis asked. "I only told Delaine last night."

Balestra grasped her arm and pulled her toward the main hatchway. "*Lieutenant* Carew, *La Baie Marche* fleet has plans for this since *ma grand-mère* was *l'aspirant* ..." She paused and Alexis looked at her. Balestra's eyes were filled with generations of pain and hope. She shrugged. "We have waited only to know we were not alone."

THIRTY-SEVEN

THERE WAS a rapid knock on the compartment's hatchway. Alexis and Balestra looked at each other.

"Reinacher's man," Alexis asked, "did you leave his body out there?"

Balestra frowned. "There was no one." She frowned further. "You think that I have killed this man?"

"Well, I assumed you'd done something with him. Reinacher left him to guard the door."

There was a second, louder, knock.

Alexis scanned the compartment. The flames had burned out on the couch Reinacher had hidden behind. Luckily its material wasn't flammable and the compartment was large enough that the little bit of heat and smoke had not set off the fire suppression system as it had in the service corridor. Still there was no way to hide the damage fire, laser, and flechettes had done to the room. Or to her dress, she realized, as she saw that a seam had split all down one leg from hip to hem.

I don't even remember that happening.

Balestra gestured with her flechette pistol. "You beside the hatch and I will have a clear view as they enter," she said.

But before Alexis could move, the hatch was slid forcefully open. Alexis looked around for anything to use as a weapon and Balestra raised her pistol, but it was Delaine and Dansby who rushed into the compartment, both holding pistols of their own. Alexis noted Balestra and Delaine in their uniforms and Dansby in his formal wear, all with plenty of places to conceal weaponry. She grasped the side of her dress, trying to keep the torn pieces together.

It was lovely, but I do miss a uniform.

"Reinacher?" Delaine asked.

"*Disparu,*" Balestra answered. She nodded at the hatch. "We must go."

They decided that Delaine and Balestra would exit first, so that all four of them would not be seen returning to the reception at the same time. The two would collect any officers from Balestra's fleet who had not gotten her message and were still at the reception, then return to their ships. Balestra thought they had, perhaps, an hour before the other Hanoverese ships in the system began noticing something odd about her ships — less if Reinacher was not lying dead in a service corridor and was able to raise the alarm. Both the Berry March fleet and *Röslein* had to set sail as quickly as possible.

Alexis wrapped her arms around Delaine and buried her face in his chest.

"Be careful," she whispered.

Delaine grasped her shoulders and pushed her gently back. He looked around the compartment at the shredded couches, the scent of Reinacher's burning hair still lingering in the air.

"*Moi?*" He smiled and caught her nose between thumb and forefinger. "*Toi!*"

Alexis dug her thumb into his side. "As careful as we may be then, the both of us."

Delaine nodded, kissed her, and hurried after Balestra.

"We'll give them a minute or two to clear the ballroom and then follow."

"Reinacher had a man watching the door," Alexis said. "He may come back."

Dansby shook his head. "Not that one." At Alexis' look, he explained, "I followed along when he took you out of the reception. Waited a bit, then staggered up on Reinacher's man with a bottle in hand, like I was a drunkard." Dansby slid the hatch shut so no one would see the damaged room if they happened to pass by. "Had a knife up under his ribs and in his heart before he knew it."

Dansby smiled and Alexis couldn't find it in her heart to pity Heinrich if he'd chosen to work with a man like Reinacher.

"So there I am," Dansby continued, "one arm holding up a corpse, the other wiping my blade on the gent's jacket, and trying to keep his blood from getting on my finery, when your young Frenchman comes around the corner." Dansby crossed to the sideboard and examined the bottles. "No schnapps?"

"We're right out," Alexis said, glancing at the shredded couch.

"Pity. I like a drop of the peach now and again." He took up a bottle of something, poured himself a glass, and gestured toward the hatch. "Time enough, do you think?"

They left the compartment, making sure the hatch was well-shut behind them.

"Your Frenchman, there," Dansby continued as they made their way out of the reception hall and into the station's main corridors, "was all for breaking his way right in, but he saw the sense of us disposing of *Herr* Reinacher's man first. He helped me drag him down to a maintenance compartment around the corner, but no sooner had we got him there than these bloody Hanoverese blokes come into the corridor." He shrugged. "So we're stuck there while these fellows stand about and chatter. Couldn't very well let them see us coming out of a maintenance closet, so we were stuck. That Theibaud boy was ready to kill the lot of them — didn't like the waiting one bit. Balestra must've followed just a bit after we'd carted the body off."

Alexis frowned. "But what were you doing at the reception to begin with? How did you get in?"

Dansby gave her a pained look. "Have you not learned yet? Getting in and out of places is what I do." He shrugged. "I assumed you'd get in some sort of trouble — didn't expect there'd be so many others trying to get you out of it. What became of Reinacher?"

Alexis related Balestra's arrival and the subsequent firefight with Reinacher. When she was done, Dansby shook his head and muttered a string of oaths.

"What?"

"Do you not see it?" Dansby glared at her. "Shot and set on fire and you let him get away? Are you a fool?" He picked up the pace, hurrying toward *Röslein's* place on the station's quayside. "Did you learn nothing from the business with Coalson? Fail to kill a man the first time and he'll always be back to bite you on the arse."

THIRTY-EIGHT

THERE WAS none of *Röslein's* previous dawdling after leaving Dietraching. Though Dansby gave them no specifics, his sense of urgency communicated itself to the crew and the ship sailed for New London space without stopping. The only deviations from their course were to avoid systems that might slow their journey or expose them to Hanoverese shipping.

Whether anyone from Hanover was actually pursuing them was open for debate. Dansby believed it was far more likely that all of Hanover's attention would be on Balestra's fleet, while Mynatt, after she'd been informed of events aboard the station, thought that Reinacher would be focusing his attention on *Röslein* and Alexis.

"This one has a talent for leaving live enemies behind her," Mynatt said as the three of them dined in Dansby's cabin one evening, "and being set afire is the sort of thing that sticks in a man's mind."

"Assuming he didn't die of the fire or the suppression chemicals in that corridor," Dansby said, "he'll still have more on his mind with a missing fleet than us."

"He's a navy to send after them. This would be personal." She turned her gaze to Alexis. "You should have followed him into the service corridor and finished him."

"I had no weapon and Commodore Balestra's was almost out of flechettes."

Mynatt grunted. "You'll regret leaving that one alive."

If Mynatt was correct, or even if Reinacher was alive, it didn't show in the remainder of *Röslein's* flight from Hanover. They made New London space without incident, though also with no sign of Balestra's fleet.

"Balestra knows where she's to go as well as we do, Carew. *Röslein's* faster than they're likely to be, regardless," Dansby said after Alexis again expressed concern. "And I'd just as soon *not* run across them. They're likely to have a Hanoverese fleet on their tail right to the border."

That last did nothing to alleviate Alexis' concerns.

ALCHIBA WAS A SMALL SYSTEM, newly settled, and quite near the border. They had no station in orbit around the single habitable planet, and the navigation summary in *Marilyn's* plot — all her records changed back to her original name upon entry into New London space — told them not to even expect a pilot boat hovering around the system's Lagrangian points.

Alexis was somewhat surprised, then, when *Marilyn* was challenged by a pair of New London frigates still two days out from the system, and more surprised by the pair of 74s and the 92 that were patrolling *darkspace* around the planet's transition points. She was sad to see that neither of the 74s was *Shrewsbury*, as she was longing to see her ship again. Perhaps *Shrewsbury* was in normal space at the system proper.

Dansby frowned at the navigation plot once they'd transitioned to normal space and were able to see all of the ships in-system. Mynatt joined him and frowned as well.

Alexis had filled them both in on the full purpose of their mission during the sail back to New London space, and now they turned to her with worried looks.

"That's all there is?" Mynatt asked.

Alexis scanned the plot. *Marilyn's* computer had quickly identified and counted the different ships in-system. There were a little more than a hundred transports and over forty warships, including a massive 104, HMS *Impregnable*, in orbit around Alchiba. With *Shrewsbury* close aboard, she noted with pleasure. Mynatt's words struck her.

"What do you mean?"

"She means," Dansby said, "that you led us to believe the entire invasion force was to be here waiting for that Commodore Balestra's arrival." He tapped the plot. "This would appear to be ... not nearly enough."

"Glad our bit's done," Mynatt said.

Alexis frowned. "It's the number of ships Mister Eades —"

"Oh, yes, Eades," Dansby said. He sighed. "War on the cheap and always a plan." The signal console *pinged* and he brought the message up on the plot. "Speak of the devil ..." He glanced at Alexis. "Much as I'm sure you're as sad to see it come as I am, it's time we say farewell. A boat's being sent for you and our business is done."

"Good riddance," Mynatt said. She left the quarterdeck without a backward glance.

"You've about an hour before that boat reaches us," Dansby said. "Just time enough to pack your things."

Alexis felt oddly uncomfortable at the thought of parting. *Marilyn* was in no way the sort of ship she'd like to sail aboard, the crew was still standoffish, perhaps even more so than ever, and she certainly hadn't come to care for Dansby. She eyed him, looking just as uncomfortable as she felt.

"I suppose this is farewell, then," she said.

"It appears so." Dansby shifted his eyes to the plot and cleared his throat. "You'll be back aboard your ship and part of this?"

"Yes. Aboard *Shrewsbury*, just there behind *Impregnable* in orbit." She cleared her throat as well. No, she'd certainly not come to care for him any more than she had at the start, pirate, smuggler, and snake that he was. Still, she thought of the moment when they'd been under fire by Coalson's men aboard the Baikonur station and how the excited grin on his face had exactly matched her own feeling of being fully alive in that moment of danger. "Mister Dansby —"

"I'm sure there's none of us could say it's been a pleasure, Carew," Dansby interrupted her. "Certainly not Anya, what with you shooting her and all." He gave her a small smile.

"Twice, come to that," Alexis said with an answering smile. "I'll speak to Mister Eades about that bounty on Coalson. I'm ... I'm sorry if you receive nothing ... due to my actions with him, I mean."

Dansby shook his head. "No, I think it's best if you mention nothing at all about the matter." He shrugged. "The money would be nice, but I expect they'd find some way to keep it from me. And that was ... it's not a thing you'd be wise to bandy about."

Alexis met his eyes and he looked away. It surprised her that he'd give up even the chance of a bounty. Perhaps he was worried what might happen to him, given her actions. If Eades and the Navy disapproved of what she'd done enough, they might take it out on Dansby as well.

"I suppose you'll be leaving then?"

Dansby shrugged. "I may hang about and see just what comes of this." He cleared his throat. "This next bit of business you're about will be neither easy nor clean." He nodded to the plot. "I hope you know that."

"What do you mean? The Berry worlds are rightfully French and we're to help them rejoin the Republic. If ever there was a proper thing to fight for —"

Dansby shook his head. "Those worlds have been part of Hanover for generations, no matter what language the people speak. There're Hanoverese who've settled there ..." He shrugged. "It's civil war and revolution all rolled into one. There's no good comes of that."

"Mister Eades —"

Dansby cut her off again. "Eades is Foreign Office. He has his own agenda and likely a few more beneath the one he shows you. Don't ever think he has anyone's best interests to heart. Not yours and not those of the Berry worlds."

"No, I'm certainly not so foolish as to think that."

"Good." Dansby looked as though he might say more, but then shrugged. "You should be about that packing."

Alexis nodded and started for her cabin.

"Rikki," Dansby called when she was at the hatch. She turned and raised an eyebrow. "Watch yourself."

"Concern for a mongoose, Mister Serpent?"

Dansby cleared his throat again. "Just be cautious, Carew." He paused. "And for God's sake, stop leaving live enemies behind you."

THIRTY-NINE

ALEXIS RETURNED to her cabin to pack and then boarded the boat from *Shrewsbury* to find Isom aboard with two others of the crew to handle her baggage.

"Civilian clothes," she said in answer to his questioning look at the extra chest she had to be moved. "I doubt I'll have need of them, but find a place to store the chest in the hold if it won't fit under my bunk, will you?"

She carried a bundle with her new weapons. Those she'd transfer to her cabin herself.

Her things were loaded aboard the boat and the boat on its way back to *Shrewsbury* without another word from any of *Marilyn's* crew.

I don't suppose I can blame them for being glad to see the back of me.

Her welcome aboard *Shrewsbury*, though, was quite different. Every hand seemed to have a nod and a smile for her as she made her way from the boarding lock aft to Captain Euell's cabin. He'd sent word that he wished to see her instanter, and Alexis was regretting not having a proper uniform aboard *Marilyn* as she now had no opportunity to change.

The marine sentry at the hatchway announced her arrival and she entered. She saw that she'd have to adjust herself to *Shrewsbury's* time, as Captain Euell was just finishing his breakfast while it had been nearing suppertime aboard *Marilyn*.

"Welcome back, Carew," Euell said, gesturing for her to sit. "Did you have a pleasant cruise? Something to drink?"

"I wouldn't go so far as to call it pleasant, no, sir," she answered, then turned to the captain's steward who was hovering nearby. "Tea, perhaps, Littler? Thank you." She settled herself in her chair. "I believe it was productive though."

Euell grunted. "That Eades fellow's taken himself aboard *Impregnable* and good riddance. Likely still abed, else he'd have had you sent directly aboard there the instant you transitioned." He paused as Littler returned with Alexis' tea. "They've finally filled us captains in on the whole of this plan. Hard to keep it a secret now we've seen so many transports gathered in one place. Were you successful in reaching that Hanoverese fleet?"

Alexis nodded. "Commodore Balestra's fleet left Dietraching at the same time *Marilyn* did, sir. They should arrive here soon."

Euell nodded. "Good work then. We'll be thankful for the extra hulls if this comes to a fight with a Hannie fleet. Finish your tea and then get yourself into a proper uniform. I imagine you'll be called aboard *Impregnable* as soon as Eades is awake and knows you've returned."

"Thank you, sir."

Alexis finished her tea quickly and made her way to her cabin. Isom had already laid out one of her dress uniforms in anticipation of her being called aboard the flagship. She changed into it, the heavy jacket and beret feeling more than a bit odd after so much time spent in civilian dress, but still somehow comforting, then went out into the wardroom.

Nesbit and Hollingshed were sharing a bottle at the wardroom table.

"Is that someone just come out of our spare cabin, Hollingshed?" Nesbit asked.

Hollingshed cocked his head and raised his eyebrows at Alexis. "I do believe you're correct, Nesbit," he said. "Did Captain Euell take aboard a passenger when we weren't looking?"

"Must have. We'd recognize every proper lieutenant who's been aboard with us all these weeks."

"Certainly would," Hollingshed agreed. "Weeks stuck aboard ship together makes a face familiar to you after all."

Alexis sat, looking from one to the other with amusement.

"Indeed," Nesbit went on. "Stuck aboard ship in orbit around this Alchiba place, not allowed down to the planet for fear we'll let loose some secret."

Hollingshed scowled. "With, all the while, thousands of troops being landed on the planet and left at loose ends. As though they could keep a secret, themselves."

"While the Fleet's up here with no liberty at all. Waiting."

Isom appeared at Alexis' elbow with a glass and two bottles of wine from her stores. She cast him a grateful glance, even as Nesbit and Hollingshed went on with their whinging.

"Yet waiting for what?" Nesbit narrowed his eyes at Alexis. "Or whom?"

"Yes, whom," Hollingshed murmured, rubbing his chin. "Could it possibly be that lieutenant we once had? You remember the one?"

"What? You mean the one who was always here again, off again? That one?"

"Yes!" Hollingshed pointed excitedly at Nesbit. "The one who broke your foot with her dancing."

"I never broke a foot!" Alexis exclaimed.

"Shush, you!" Nesbit said, waving a finger at her. "Ship's officers talking here — passengers aren't in it." He turned back to Hollingshed. "Could be that one. Had a sly look about her — just the thing for secret doings."

"Look, you two," Alexis said, opening one of her bottles and pouring herself a cup of wine. "Keep it up and I'll drink these myself without sharing a drop."

"Carew!" Hollingshed cried, spreading his arms wide, but not before sliding his own glass across the table to her. "Welcome back! Didn't recognize you there for a moment."

Nesbit slid his chair around the table and draped an arm over her shoulders, cup at the ready.

"Missed you terribly," he said. "Foot's all healed, no worries. Now, tell us, will we finally be leaving this bloody system?"

FORTY

ALEXIS STAYED near the back of the group as they entered the room, uncertain whether she'd been included as a courtesy or an oversight, but certain she knew nothing about planetary invasions. Once inside, she spotted Delaine amongst the French officers and moved to be near him where he stood against the room's wall. The more senior officers crowded around the circular navigation plot at the room's center.

"You've a new uniform," she whispered. Delaine, Balestra, and the rest of the officers she recognized from the Berry March fleet were now all in light blue and white of the Republic's navy and not the black and grey of Hanover.

"*Oui.*" He straightened the front of his jacket. "We are now of the Republic's fleet. It is a little thing, but means much to us."

Alexis laid a hand on his arm. She started to speak, but the group around the navigation plot had begun their introductions.

"Admiral Leneave," Eades said, "may I present General Malicoat who will lead the New London ground forces and Admiral Chipley, commander of our fleet here at Alchiba. Gentlemen, Admiral Leneave of the Republic fleet, Field Marshal Bonnin, and, of course,

Commodore Balestra, late of the Hanoverese Berry March fleet and now, happily, reunited with *La Grande République de France Parmi les Étoiles.*" He gestured and servants began circulating with glasses of champagne. "Before your efforts begin, may I propose a toast?" He waited until everyone had a glass then raised his. "To the liberation of the Berry March worlds, their long overdue reunion with the Republic, and confusion to Hanover!"

"Confusion to Hanover!" the group chorused.

ALEXIS STIFLED a yawn and put just a bit more pressure on her arm where it touched Delaine's. The talks had been dragging on for hours and the initial toast had been the most exciting bit of it. She'd never imagined that planning an invasion could be so utterly boring. Everything from the least little item of supply to the order of embarkation and debarkation from the troop ships had to be endlessly debated. Of particular contention were the supplies for those forces they hoped would flock to their cause from within the worlds of the Berry March, for those men would be commanded by the Republic and every ton of supplies, from uniforms to weapons, brought for them meant one less ton of shipping available to the New London forces. The French transports which had brought the supplies to Alchiba had offloaded and returned to the Republic weeks before.

She felt Delaine lean into her arm where they touched in response to her increasing the pressure. It was a sort of game they'd come to silently play while they waited for whatever purpose they'd been included in the talks. Leaning into each other, a bit more pressure than necessary where they touched, a subtle brush of a finger — all unnoticed by those around them. Alexis caught one of the other French officers cast a glance their way with a raised eyebrow and a grin. She straightened, flushing. Perhaps it wasn't entirely unnoticed by those around them. She dragged her attention back to the talks at the central table.

"Those men will be untrained, Marshal Bonnin," General Mali-coat was saying, "and it will take some time for them to be useful in any sort of battle." He raised a hand to forestall the other man's objection. "Training takes time, you must admit, sir. Should Hanover counter-attack before yours are prepared to face it, my troops will bear the brunt of the fighting and I'll see them well-supplied for that."

Bonnin nodded. "As you say, *général*, but these men, they are proud and will fight for their homes. We must see that it is their victory, not a conquest by your New London, *oui*? This means uniforms so that they see themselves as one, weapons so that they may face their foe."

"I agree, sir, but I see no reason for them to be so fully equipped at the start. It will take time for them to come to us, time to organize them, and during that time the transports may return here for your material."

"All the while the men of that land will march in what boots, *monsieur*? With weapons they bring from their homes? They will do this while your army stands by with shiny rifles and new boots?"

"Marshal Bonnin, I have a scant twelve regiments of foot here, four of heavy cavalry, another six of light, and only three of air. With transport for barely half of that, I'm told." He gestured to Admiral Chipley, who nodded confirmation. "The Hanoverese are closer, more numerous, and have more shipping available. Should they come before our transports may return with the rest of my men, will your new recruits in fresh boots and with weapons they've never held before be at the forefront?"

Bonnin's face flushed. "If they are true French, they shall —"

"No one is questioning their courage," Chipley interrupted. "I'm certain they'd acquit themselves well. The point at issue is whether its best to equip them first or have a larger force of already trained men."

"Perhaps we should first consider which system from which to base our endeavors," Eades suggested. "That might shed some light on the best course of action. Commodore Balestra? Do you have some thoughts on that?"

"Here at Giron," Balestra said immediately, pointing to the system on the plot.

"Are you certain?" Malicoat asked. "It's rather farther from the border than I'd prefer."

"The border worlds have less peoples," Balestra said. "Those here —" She ran a finger along the systems on the far side of the Berry March where it bordered traditional Hanoverese space. "— have had ... the word, the immigration from *le Hanovre*. Giron is still most *Français*."

"Hm." Malicoat looked thoughtful for a moment. "What size force do you suppose will be raised there?"

"On Giron?" It was Balestra's turn to ponder. "Perhaps twenty or thirty thousands from Giron itself will rise to fight. From these worlds —" She indicated those most central to the Berry March. "— ten each. More from those worlds nearest *le Hanovre*, once they see our numbers."

Malicoat nodded. "I see, yes. They won't rise if we start there, but if we arrive already in possession of a strong, French force from the central worlds, those bordering on Hanover-proper will join us you're saying?"

"*Oui*," Balestra agreed. "They are ... the word, fearful now, but will still wish to be free."

"Is that lieutenant who's been there about?" Chipley asked. He scanned the room and focused on Alexis. "What's your opinion? Carew, isn't it?"

Alexis jumped, face heating. She'd fallen back into concentrating on the heat of Delaine's arm against hers and not really paying attention to the discussion. In fact, she'd been paying far more attention to wherever Delaine's body was touching hers than to anything being said.

"Sir?"

"The people of the Berry March, Carew, your opinion of them? Your personal observations, having been there for some time."

Alexis thought for a moment. She was no expert, but an admiral had asked her opinion. She thought of the marketplace in Courboin and the people there.

"I saw only a little of Giron, sir, but the people were universally kind to us. I found it odd that they would be so, given the war, but came to understand that their relation to Hanover was ... complicated."

"Will they rise in the numbers Commodore Balestra suggests?"

Alexis considered for a moment. "In the time I was there, sir, I think it is significant that after three generations under Hanover I heard not a word of German spoken. For myself, I'm certain they will rise, given the opportunity to win their freedom. As to numbers ..." She nodded. "I found Giron much like my home of Dalthus, sir. We're an independent lot. Were we conquered, well, there'd be no end of volunteers to gain our freedom back."

Chipley nodded and turned away, apparently satisfied.

The talks continued for some time, but in the end General Malicoat gave in. He certainly wasn't happy about it, but it became clear that the Republican leaders, Bonnin and Leneave, were adamant that there must be equipment from the start for those recruits they hoped to raise on Giron.

"I'll leave the air regiments for later, as they take the most transport," Malicoat said. "The heavy cavalry and half the light, as well. We'll have need of all the foot to spread out and make a show for your recruitment, in any case. That should free up space on the transports to outfit your twenty thousand, Bonnin, but more than that will have to wait for the next trip. Will that be acceptable?"

Bonnin nodded. "*Oui, Général* Malicoat."

FORTY-ONE

SHREWSBURY WAS at the tail end of the convoy and fleet, and so had no knowledge of the fleet's arrival at Giron until well after the system had been taken and the landing of troops was well underway. Once they arrived, Alexis learned that there'd been but a single ship in-system, a Hanoverese barque, which had quickly surrendered at the appearance of *Impregnable* and the rest of the fleet's van.

By the time *Shrewsbury* transitioned and took her place in orbit, a goodly number of transports had already taken their own orbits and begun sending boats to the surface with load after load of troops. The remaining transports took higher orbits and awaited their turn in the unloading.

For such a large operation, it took surprisingly little time to offload all of the transports. Less time, in fact, than it had taken to load them in the first place. Perhaps because the soldiers were anxious to leave their cramped quarters aboard ship for the planet's surface and were, thus, far more cooperative than during the loading.

As for the people of Giron, they greeted the New London troops as though they were returning heroes. Alexis found herself in the main port city of Atterrissage more than once as *Shrewsbury's* boats were drafted into assisting with the unloading.

Atterrissage was much changed since the last time Alexis had seen it. Then she'd been fleeing imprisonment and there'd been a single merchantman's boat on the field — a lucky chance for her, that there'd been any boat to steal at all. Now her own boat was one of dozens on the field, and the rest of the field was crowded with the tents and collapsible domes of the army forces.

There seemed to be a permanent parade route through the city, lined with cheering throngs smiling and waving to the newly arrived troops, and there were long lines forming at the recruitment tables set up on the edges of the army's camp.

Word spread over the planet and there were soon young men and women from all over Giron were pouring into Atterrissage to see the French Field Marshal and join in the revolt against Hanover.

All of the transports were quickly unloaded without incident. The people of Atterrissage were so thrilled at the prospect of rejoining *La République*, that they mostly overlooked the slights and liberties commonly taken when large groups of soldiers are encamped around a town. To their credit, the New London forces took to heart their officers warnings, reinforced by sergeants, that the people of Giron should be treated as valued allies.

The transports, along with an escort of frigates, were sent back to Alchiba to return with the rest of the forces and the fleet settled into a routine of patrolling *darkspace* around Giron.

All in all, things seemed to be going even better than planned.

Until, at least, the first New London frigate limped back into the system with reports that their patrol farther into Hanoverese space had encountered an enemy fleet. A large Hanoverese fleet, which had made short work of the patrolling frigate's consorts, but one which, by the surviving frigate's accounts, was still smaller than the combined might of the New London and former Berry March fleets.

Admiral Chipley sent out additional patrols to attempt to locate the Hanoverese fleet and determine its true strength, but most returned without having sighted them, while others failed to return at all.

Finally, Chipley felt he had no choice but to sortie the entire fleet and attempt to find the Hanoverese. It was either that or cede control of *darkspace* around Giron to the enemy, and he was unwilling to do that with the next convoy of loaded transports expected at any time.

THE MARINE SENTRY announced Alexis and slid the hatch to Captain Euell's cabin open. Euell looked up from where he was running his fingers over both his tablet and the images that covered the large surface which served as both his dining table and a duplicate of the quarterdeck's navigation plot.

"Come in, Carew. Do hurry, please."

Alexis did so and stopped near the plot.

"You'll have to excuse me, as we've little time," Euell said. "Admiral Chipley has ordered the fleet to sail instanter. We're off after the Hanoverese as quick as can be."

Alexis felt a quick thrill of excitement at the thought. "Are they so close, then, sir?"

Euell frowned. "I wish I knew ... and so does Chipley, come to that. No, with the transports expected to return soon, we simply can't sit here and wait for them. If the Hanoverese fleet slips around Giron and encounters those transports ... No, better for us to find them first." Euell grinned suddenly. "Besides, Chipley's not one to sit and wait, regardless. Our best estimate is that we outnumber them and Chipley's hot to take them all as prizes."

The captain grinned again and Alexis had to suppress a laugh. For just a moment, with his excitement and exuberance showing through, she could picture Euell as a much younger man, a frigate captain anxious to dash off and capture prize after prize, instead of the respected, staid captain of a Third Rate like *Shrewsbury*, limited to standing in the line of battle at some admiral's command.

Euell's grin fell. "Which brings us to you and a bit of a problem, I'm afraid."

"Sir?"

"We must leave someone here to act as the Fleet's liaison with General Malicoat. As well, you're the closest we have in our fleet to an expert on Giron and the French. Chipley still feels you'd be of some value as an adviser to Malicoat."

Alexis felt a chill. She could well see where this was going and didn't like it one bit.

"Sir, I've been little use in that regard so far. General Malicoat has never once asked for my advice or presence — moreover, I *know* no one on Giron to 'liaise' with." Other than her time with Delaine, she'd had little interaction with the people of Giron, and that not so very memorable, she thought. "A few merchants in the Courboin markets might remember me, or a prostitute or two."

Euell raised an eyebrow and Alexis flushed.

"I spoke rather sharply to another midshipman in their presence," she explained. "They may remember it. But that's neither here nor there to my being of assistance to General Malicoat, sir!"

"No," Euell agreed. "But Admiral Chipley does not wish to give the Army cause to complain, so he'll stick to the letter of that agreement. You're to be available should General Malicoat have need of your advice and that's the end of it. I'm afraid you're to remain here until we return."

Alexis shoulders slumped. She dearly wished to be part of the action, a fleet action, no less, with dozens of ships involved. Her gun crews were shaping up well, she thought. Even young Artley was stepping up to offer everything she could ask. She longed to test them against the Hanoverese fleet.

"Sir, is there no way —"

Euell held up a hand. "I'm afraid not, Carew, but I'm loath to leave you ashore with Malicoat and told Chipley so. He's agreed to not put you through that — his own feelings toward Malicoat having something to do with it, no doubt."

"Thank you, sir." At least she'd still be aboard a ship, not trudging around planetside like the bloody Army. She blinked, suddenly unsure — did she really feel more at home aboard ship than on a planet?

How odd.

Of course it would mean transferring, even temporarily, from *Shrewsbury*. Likely to a much smaller ship, whichever Chipley was willing to leave behind, and getting used to a new captain. But such was the way of the Navy.

"You're to have that *Belial* barque we took on coming in-system," Euell said. "It's not much, but it'll keep a deck under your feet until we return and you may rejoin *Shrewsbury*."

"Thank you, sir, I'll ... excuse me, but 'have', sir?"

Euell grinned again. "Never say I've done nothing for you, Carew. Chipley wants all his ships with him, so it's this *Belial* to be left behind, as she's not a proper part of the fleet. Moreover he wants the fleet's officers to man the prizes he expects, so he's unwilling to leave much more than you. She'll be yours for the duration."

Alexis was stunned and no little thrilled. It might be for only a few days, but she'd have her own command. "Thank you again, sir. I'll do my best for you."

"Yes, yes, I'm sure you will. It's only for the time it takes us to trounce the Hanoverese and return, remember, not like you're to have her permanently, you understand. And you're just to sit in orbit in case Malicoat needs you for anything, so it won't be at all exciting. Not as much as the rest of us will have with the Hanoverese." He grinned again.

"Yes, sir."

"I'll leave you a midshipman and some steady hands," Euell said, already turning back to his tablet. "Do you have some idea of who you'll want?"

Alexis thought quickly. "I do sir. May I have Mister Artley as the midshipman?"

Euell raised an eyebrow. "Are you quite certain?"

"I am, sir." As she said, she found that she was. "Artley's come along quite well. He's far more confident than he was on the way to *Nouvelle Paris* and some time on a smaller ship, with him as the only junior officer, might see him along even further. I think some time without his mates in the gunroom to prop him up might do him good as well."

Euell considered for a moment. "You may be right. Decide on which hands you'd prefer to take and see Lieutenant Barr with their names, then be away before the watch is up, please."

"Aye, sir." She straightened, nodded to him, and managed to keep the wide grin off her face until she'd cleared the cabin's hatchway. A command — a proper, independent command. The excitement was almost more than she could bear.

FORTY-TWO

ALEXIS STIFLED a yawn and stretched her neck side to side to relieve the stiffness.

For the first week Alexis enjoyed the novelty of being in command. She'd commanded ships before, but what was novel this time was that she'd been given *Belial*, not taken her in action, and she was in command for something other than a desperate, neck-or-nothing flight from capture or death.

By the end of the second week orbiting Giron, she'd begun to guiltily wish for someone to come along and chase her in a desperate, neck-or-nothing flight from capture or death. Not even the novelty of having *Belial's* master's cabin all to herself was enough to stave off the boredom.

As her third week in orbit came to a close, she was willing to admit that command, at least of a ship stuck alone in a single system, was bloody boring. General Malicoat apparently had no use for her, as he'd not sent her a single message, not even in response to her own inquiries as to his needs. Those had been responded to with a curt 'not at this time' by one of the general's staff lieutenants. There'd been two visits by fast packets, one hurrying back to New London space from the fleet and another returning, but neither carried news or mail for Alexis or her small crew. There'd not even been any merchant traffic, unusual for so heavily populated a world as Giron, but Alexis suspected that word had begun to spread. With two fleets maneuvering to catch each other in *darkspace* around Giron, merchants would avoid the area for fear of being snapped up by either side.

Alexis paced the quarterdeck and caught her lower lip between her teeth. The boredom was getting to the men, as well. She had two dozen men, not including herself, Midshipman Artley, and Isom. Dobb, a bosun's mate aboard *Shrewsbury* was making a creditable showing as bosun, but the crew simply had too little to do. During the second week of idleness, she'd set the port and starboard watches against each other in competitions, but stepping and unstepping the masts, racing around the hull, and even gunnery drill had quickly begun to pall. There were simply too many hours in the day and those that couldn't be filled with legitimate work bred idleness and discontent amongst the crew. Quarrels amongst the men were growing more numerous and more serious.

"Mister Artley," she called, making a decision.

"Sir?"

"Detail a boat crew, please." If General Malicoat wouldn't respond to her messages, then she'd take matters into her own hands. She'd make a courtesy visit to Malicoat's headquarters, of course, but a trip down to the planet would also give her the opportunity to bring aboard fresh supplies, at the least, and possibly arrange for her crew to take leave, as everything on the planet's surface seemed to be going peacefully and according to plan. "And pass the word for Mister Hunsley."

"Aye, sir."

Hunsley arrived on the quarterdeck shortly. He'd been a purser's assistant aboard *Shrewsbury* and had leapt at the chance to act as purser to *Belial*. Even if the little ship was never bought into the

Service, the experience would make it all the more likely that he'd receive a warrant into some other ship.

"Mister Hunsley," Alexis said, "I'll be taking a boat to the surface shortly and wish you to accompany me and see to fresh stores for the crew."

Hunsley nodded. "Aye, sir, but *Belial's* not proper bought-in." He shrugged. "I've no ship's accounts to work with, just the vats and stores we have aboard."

Alexis frowned. She had a bit of coin in her chest. Not a great deal, but possibly enough for at least one round of supplies. "We'll use some of the hard coin I brought aboard, then. Likely you'll get better pricing with that than with Navy drafts as well."

"Aye, sir, that they will. That army's flooded the market with drafts, like as not, and with no merchants arriving, the folk'll be starved for coin, even foreign as ours is to them. Be a better bargain all around." He rubbed his hands together.

"Mind you," Alexis warned, "I'll want good value for my coin and an accounting." She saw Hunsley's face fall. "Fresh beef for the men. Real beef that was once wrapped in leather, not steel. And I'll want some stores for myself and Mister Artley as well. I trust you'll use your not inconsiderable talents to see that we receive the very best bargains."

"Aye, sir," Hunsley said, shoulders slumping.

"Buck up, Mister Hunsley." Alexis smiled. "There may be no profit here for you, but the experience will stand you in good stead."

Hunsley looked pained, but whether it was at the accusation or the lost opportunity Alexis couldn't tell.

"PHIBBS," she said to the pilot, "keep two of the lads here with you and guard the boat. Mister Hunsley, take the rest and see about finding supplies."

Hunsley eyed the bustle of the surrounding tents with doubt.

"Hadn't thought there'd be so many of these Army-types about, sir. Prices may not be what you'd wish."

Alexis examined the surroundings as well. She didn't know what Atterrissage's population had been before, but it was certainly a good bit larger now. Not only was New London's Army in residence, but she saw more than a few French uniforms. If the recruiting of locals was going as well as General Malicoat had reported, then the town's population must be considerably swollen.

"Do you have a suggestion?" she asked, seeing that Hunsley seemed to be hesitating to say more.

"The smaller towns, perhaps, sir?" Hunsley shrugged. "They'll be sending supplies here, themselves, but if were to go to them direct … cut out the middlemen, so to speak?"

Alexis nodded. The smaller towns might better choices to allow the hands liberty, as well. They might not have a proper landing field for the ship's boats, but setting spacers down in Atterrissage with so many soldiers running about might not be the wisest course. The services had traditional rivalries and it appeared many of the soldiers were as idle as her crew.

"Seek out the best prices you can find, but purchase nothing if you feel they're too high, and we'll give your idea a go." She thought for a moment. It would be nice to see Courboin again, even if Delaine had sailed with the fleet and couldn't be with her. "I may know just the place."

She went off alone in search of where General Malicoat was headquartered and finally got directions she could follow after interrogating several soldiers. Malicoat and his staff had taken over the largest hotel in Atterrissage for their use. She made her way there, though she did take the time to stop at a streetcart for a bite to eat — a sort of thin pancake wrapped around ham, cheese, and a fried egg.

The hotel's lobby had been cleared of its original furnishings and filled with desks. Army officers filled the space, either working busily at desks or rushing to and fro between them. If the soldiers at the landing field had been idle, such was not the case at Malicoat's head-quarters.

Alexis stood, ignored, near the entryway for a time, finally resorting to reaching out and grasping the arm of a soldier hurrying past.

"I'm looking for General Malicoat," she said.

The man gave her collar a puzzled look, apparently unfamiliar with Naval ranks, then seemed to settle on saluting regardless. "Back down that hallway, ma'am," he said. "Last door on the right."

"Thank you."

Alexis made her way down the hallway. There was a harried-looking aide in the outer room who asked her to wait, then went into what she presumed was Malicoat's office.

She heard murmuring, then Malicoat bark out an answer.

"Carew? That Naval person? What does she want?" She wasn't able to hear what the aide said. "Bloody — Oh, very well, send her in."

The aide returned and motioned for her to enter. Alexis was having second thoughts about the venture, she'd meant to call on Malicoat only as a courtesy and it seemed now she was disturbing him.

"General Malicoat, sir," she said, removing her beret.

"Do you have some news?"

"Sir?"

Malicoat waved a hand upward. "Some news of the transports? The rest of my men? Supplies?"

Alexis shook her head. "I'm sorry, no, sir. The last packet from Alchiba reported that they had not yet returned."

"Why am I forever waiting on your Navy?" He went on before Alexis could think of a reply. "Oh, never mind, I know there's little you can do about it."

"I've sent along your requests with every packet, sir," Alexis assured him. "Both to the fleet and back to Alchiba."

"Little good it's done." Malicoat snorted. "Your admiral assured me it was but a fortnight's trip from here to Alchiba and back — it's been twice that now, and no sign of transports or supplies. We don't have forever before the Hanoverese figure what we're doing and send troops of their own to outnumber us. When that happens ..." He frowned, then pointed at her. "I want you to see what I'm facing here and send your own report with the next packet, Carew."

"Sir?"

"Perhaps you'll be able to put it into whatever secret language you spacers speak for your admiral, eh? Put in the appropriate 'avasts' and 'belays' that'll make him sit up and take notice."

Alexis blanched in horror at the thought of an admiral sitting up and taking notice of a lieutenant. Good things rarely came of such an event.

Malicoat sighed. "I desire it impressed upon Admiral Chipley that I *must* have those supplies and the rest of my men." He waved a hand at the walls. "The locals are pouring in to join up, more of them than even that Balestra predicted, and we're out of those French uniforms for them. Out of weapons, as well, and they're making do with what they've brought from their homes. And every day that goes by is another day closer to the Hanoverese finding what we're up to here and bringing in their own troops. I *cannot* hold Giron against a sizable force, not with half my regiments and untrained locals!"

Alexis nodded, though she wasn't sure what help a report from her would do. "If you think it will help, sir, I'll write such a report, but surely Admiral Chipley takes more note of your words than mine."

"Surely," Malicoat repeated. He tapped his tablet and barked into it, "Roswell! Get in here!"

A moment later a uniformed woman appeared in the doorway. She was a full head taller than Alexis, with close-cropped hair and a slight build.

"Yes, sir?" she said.

"Carew, this is Lieutenant Roswell, 451st Light Cavalry. Roswell, Lieutenant Carew — highest ranking Naval officer Chipley's left us in the system, if you can believe it." He looked at Alexis and snorted. "Take no offense, Carew, it's nothing personal. Only that your Navy's right buggered me on this one."

Alexis chose what she thought would be the safest course and remained silent.

"Show Carew a bit of what we're dealing with, Roswell," Malicoat said. "Those new Frenchies, perhaps? See if she thinks they'll be of any use come to a fight."

"Yes, sir," Roswell said and stepped aside from the door.

Malicoat had already lowered his face to his tablet again, so Alexis nodded, replaced her beret, and followed Roswell.

FORTY-THREE

"WHAT IS it exactly you'd like to see?"

Alexis shook her head. "I'm not at all certain. General Malicoat wishes me to send a report to Admiral Chipley on the situation here and his desperate need for the rest of the regiment and supplies for the French."

"Well there's plenty of that to see, no doubt." Roswell resumed walking. "The 451st is staging an exercise with some of the new French recruits outside of town. That's what the general spoke of. Perhaps impress upon your admiral that it takes time and resources to train up an army?"

"Thank you, Lieutenant Roswell, I'd like that very much. I'm sure it will prove useful."

Roswell grinned. "Not to mention give you something to do, eh? One must become bored up there with nothing to fill the days save spin round and round the planet."

Alexis returned the grin. "It has become somewhat tiresome."

They left the headquarters building and Roswell led her to an open square where some of the few vehicles the army had brought to Giron were parked.

"One of the perquisites of being on the general's staff," Roswell said as she nodded to a small aircar parked to the side.

Roswell and Alexis entered the car and Roswell told the driver their destination.

"It's ten or so kilometers from the town," Roswell explained. "We're bivouacking the new French troops out there — more room for their training."

"If you don't mind me asking, Lieutenant Roswell, you said the 451st was your own regiment?"

"Company," Roswell said. "We're a part of the larger cavalry regiment — three companies of light and one heavy. Of course, the heavy was left behind on Alchiba."

"I see," Alexis said, though she really didn't know what the difference might be. She was hesitant to ask too many questions and display her ignorance, but one nagged at her. "Are there many women in your regiment? I ask only because we're so rare in the Fleet — the Fringe Fleet, at least — and I've seen so many with the army here on Giron."

Roswell gave her a sideways look. "You're from the Fringe, then?"

"Yes," Alexis admitted, preparing herself to be treated as a provincial dolt once again. The Core Worlds might be superior in some ways, but she saw no reason for those from them to be forever *acting* superior.

Thankfully Roswell simply nodded.

"I see. Well, the Army doesn't hold to the same strictures as your Fleet does, not when the Core regiments are called up, in any case. The Fleet's out here full-time, visiting all the worlds regularly. Even our Fringe regiments are generally quartered in one place and only called out if there's trouble." She frowned. "I suppose it's thought that if things are bad enough for our boots to hit the ground, the time for catering to delicate sensibilities is a bit past."

She took a moment to direct the driver to a hilltop overlooking a large plain.

"Set down there, if you will."

Part of the plain was covered with tents and the domed structures the army seemed to favor. The western edge of the plain butted up against a long ridgeline and the aircar set down on a hilltop near the southern end.

"That's where we're keeping the French recruits," Roswell said, pointing to the camp on the plain. "We're a bit early. We've told them there'll be a simulated attack this morning, but not from where."

She handed Alexis a pair of binoculars and Alexis scanned the camp. The enhanced image showed her not only a magnified view, but displayed some sort of assessment for everything in the image, attempting to identify which tents and domes were likely used for cooking and which for arms storage. Along the outside edges of the camp there were some fortifications dug, simple trench and berm structures to slow an advancing enemy. These were manned by a few soldiers in French colors, but most of the camp seemed to be going about the business of their day without another thought.

"To answer your question, though," Roswell went on as Alexis scanned the camp below. "The 451st's light companies are mostly women, but only one in ten of the heavy. It's the same one in ten for the infantry, I suspect, but I've never counted."

"Why so many in the light companies?" Alexis asked.

Roswell grunted. "Mightn't you better ask why so few in the heavy?" She shrugged. "It's purely physical. There're fewer women with the strength to handle the heavy cavalry. If one's suit needs repair in the field one must be able to handle the components alone." She looked Alexis over. "You'd not make even the light cavalry, I suspect, but the air corps might have you. Little heavy lifting there."

Alexis felt, rather than heard, a sort of rumbling begin.

"Ah, they're about it," Roswell said. She pointed toward the ridgeline. "If they've stepped up their pace enough for us to feel it, then they're on the upslope and should be just about — there!"

Alexis had no need of Roswell pointing it out to her. The ridgeline was suddenly overcome by a wave of figures flowing over it.

"Good lord," she breathed.

At first she had trouble adjusting to the scale, thinking they were closer to the ridge than she'd originally thought. Then she realized that the figures were larger, almost twice as large, as the unarmored French recruits on the plain below. The mechanical battle suits were four meters tall and the ground shook from their heavy stride as they rushed down the slope.

Below, on the plain, the French recruits in the camp had all stopped, frozen in place as they watched the approaching horde.

"They've likely never seen cavalry before, not out here," Roswell said. "They'll break in a moment."

Some of the French at the berms had weapons raised and appeared to be firing.

"Low power lasers," Roswell said. "The suit computers will determine if it would be enough to do damage. Doubtful, that, though. They're set to simulate the sort of weapons the locals brought with them — nothing but hunting rifles and the occasional dueling pistol. Certainly not what I'd wish to face cavalry with."

"I should think not," Alexis said.

Below them, first one and then another, then a steady stream of French soldiers left the fortifications and rushed back through the camp, some even abandoning their weapons. As they passed, other men in the camp began running as well. Before the attackers were even halfway to the camp, the defensive lines were nearly empty. By the time the armored charge came to a halt just before the trenches, there were only a few figures to be seen still at their posts, and those, Alexis suspected, were simply frozen in terror and unable to move.

Roswell pulled out her tablet and raised an eyebrow.

"They did better than I expected," she said.

"Better?" Alexis scanned the mass of people at the far side of the camp. The rout had slowed and then stopped as the attackers paused and she could hear men calling out orders in the camp.

"As I said, they've never seen cavalry, much less faced it. Some of them fired enough to have realized it really was pointless, rather than simply running at the start." She continued to study her tablet. "The point, I believe, has been made, though. Perhaps they'll realize now that this isn't some sort of lark, and that they'll be facing real, seasoned Hanoverese troops at some point. Oh, look —" She pointed midway up the slope to where a single set of battle armor stood still. "— they actually got one." She raised her own binoculars. "That's Thacher — oh, she'll be wound up over that." Roswell waved Alexis toward the waiting aircar.

Once back in the air, Roswell had the driver circle the French camp. Alexis noted the differences between this camp and those they'd overflown closer in to Atterrissage. While the tents and layout were much the same, the camp below them looked rather slovenly compared to the others. The lanes that ran through it were not as straight, nor were the tents themselves so neatly aligned as the others.

"We've begun ringing the city with these camps for the French recruits," Roswell said. "They're eager, no doubt about that. We've had nearly an hundred thousand come to join up."

"So many?" Alexis was surprised. Even Commodore Balestra had estimated that no more than thirty thousand troops would be raised on Giron. No wonder Malicoat was anxious for the arrival of those transports, if he had supplies for no more than a third of these volunteers.

"Some we send home," Roswell said. "Too old or infirm." She nodded at the camp below. "These are the latest and I expect we'll lose ten or twenty percent of them after this morning's fun."

Roswell had the driver overfly several other encampments around the city, then set down beside *Belial's* boat at the landing field. Hunsley had already returned, with news that the prices around Atterrissage were much higher than he'd like. They determined to seek out smaller towns from which to supply *Belial*. Roswell offered to accompany them with the aircar, saying that it would give her an opportunity to report back to General Malicoat on the conditions elsewhere on Giron.

Alexis suggested Courboin. She was anxious to see the town again, though she wished Delaine could be with her for it.

FORTY-FOUR

Roswell had their driver put the aircar down in a field just outside Courboin and *Belial's* boat settled to the ground just beside it. Alexis was anxious to see the town again, though she wished she'd taken the opportunity to do so while Delaine was still in-system.

"You were held prisoner here?" Roswell asked after they reached the town's market square and Hunsley took the men off to purchase supplies.

Alexis nodded. "In a converted warehouse just down that road there." She pointed. "Perhaps a kilometer away."

Roswell frowned. "A warehouse? They gave you no proper housing?"

Alexis realized that Roswell thought she'd given her parole and would have had the run of the town.

Which I did, to a certain extent with Delaine, but for other reasons.

"The other officers were housed in town." She pointed out the building just off the market. "There, in fact, but I hadn't given my parole and was housed with the men."

Roswell's eyes widened. "I can't imagine what you must have gone through there. With common spacers?"

Alexis fought down the urge to snap at her in defense of the men, thinking of all they'd done for her during that captivity. "Don't you berth with the rest of your company?"

"Well, yes, but cavalry regiments are raised of the gentry and nobility, not the commoners." She looked down the road Alexis had indicated. "That would be like serving in the infantry, and not as an officer."

"It was for the best, regardless," Alexis said, wishing to change the subject. "Come along down this street here. There's a shop that sells the most wonderful chocolates." She paused. "Or should we follow along with Hunsley in case he needs help with translation?"

She caught sight of Hunsley and the men. Her purser was deep in haggling with the owner of a vegetable stall, showing the man coins and flashing his fingers in an offer. The seller threw his arms up and flashed more fingers in return. Alexis smiled. Trust that neither a purser nor a shopkeeper would allow a little thing like language to stand in the way of a bargain.

She and Roswell left the square and walked down the street to where Alexis remembered the shop being, but found it was not only closed, but boarded up. The windows on the upper stories were either broken out or boarded as well. The brick walls of the building bore streaks of soot and the scent of burning wood hung heavily over the street.

"They must have had a fire. I hope no one was hurt."

Roswell snorted. "They'll be lucky to have not been hung."

"What do you mean?"

"Retaliation." Roswell said, nodding back at the building. "See the message?"

Alexis looked back at the building and noticed something scrawled across the boards covering the shop window.

"*Rentrez envahisseurs?*" She frowned. "Invaders surrender, no, get out? What does this mean?"

"We're seeing more of it close to Atterrissage," Roswell said. "Reprisals against Hanoverese who've come to this world. General Malicoat's set up a special camp to keep the ethnic Hanoverese safe, at least those who make their way to Atterrissage and ask for protection."

A chill ran through Alexis. She and Delaine had visited this shop many times. The proprietors were a charming, friendly couple who'd only ever spoken French so far as Alexis had heard, and the shop had been busy. They'd always had a bit of chocolate for a child peering through the window and nothing but smiles and friendly words for their customers.

She looked back down the street to the main market square. Could the people of Courboin really have done such a thing?

"I can't believe it."

"We've started a revolution here," Roswell said with a shrug. "A civil war. There's no reason to expect it won't become just as bloody as that sort of thing always does. Oh, in an hundred years it'll all be speeches and fireworks, but here and now it's a bloody business."

"But —" She stopped herself. The proprietor's name had been Steinach, a Hanoverese name, to be sure, no matter that he'd gone by *monsieur* and spoken perfect French. "His grandfather started this shop," she whispered finally, still unable to believe that anyone in Courboin could do such a thing.

"This sort of hatred takes no heed of generations," Roswell said. "It runs deep and it takes little to set it loose. Look even at New London and New Edinburgh — settled for hundreds of years, allies for generations — but I'm certain there are no few on either planet who'd paint themselves blue and take up arms at some excuse. And *this* —" Roswell pointed at the burned out shell of a building. "This is why we in the Core tolerate the Fringe and all its prejudices. Give that type of fool their own planet and let them have a go at it if they like, just so long as they leave their neighbors alone."

"Not all of the Fringe is like that," Alexis said, feeling she should defend her home world in some way.

"No," Roswell agreed, "most of the worlds are settled by those who just want a bit of space, but even they turn up the odd bit of bigotry far too often. Good riddance to the lot of them, I say."

Alexis frowned. Roswell must have forgotten that Alexis was from the Fringe herself. She took one last look at the burned-out shop before they made their way back to the market. She wasn't entirely convinced that this policy of forcing such hatreds farther and farther toward the edges of humanity's expansion was the best solution ... nor, having seen such a thing rear its head in Courboin, was she at all certain there could ever be one.

The market, when they returned to it, seemed to have lost some of its color and vibrancy. Alexis found herself wondering if this smiling-faced farmer or that grinning shopkeeper had held a torch or a bit of rope the night the Steinachs' shop had been burned.

And what happened to them? Were they killed or have they made their way to some camp near Atterrissage?

She was lost in these thoughts when she felt Roswell grasp her arm and shake her gently.

"Carew? Are you listening at all?"

Alexis shook herself out of her reverie.

"That girl over there seems quite intent on you. Do you know her?"

Alexis looked and caught sight of a girl staring at her. She looked away as soon as Alexis turned in that direction, but seemed familiar.

"I may," Alexis allowed. When she'd been held here, she hadn't really spent time with any of the residents of Courboin for more than shopping; most of her time had been spent with Delaine. Still, the girl did look familiar.

"I'd recommend finding out what she wants, if she's going to be following us all day anyway," Roswell said.

"I suppose." Alexis paused for a moment. If the French were willing to engage in such violence against the Hanoverese, mightn't there be Hanoverese partisans who would do the same against New

London's forces? "I never thought to ask, but are we in any danger? From Hanoverese, I mean."

Roswell shook her head. "No, whoever planned this romp chose a good world to begin on. There's been none of anything like that. If anything, the locals have been too friendly with our troops."

They made their way toward the girl who was watching them and Alexis frowned, trying to place her. There were many people in Courboin she recognized from her time here and many who recognized her in return. As they drew nearer, the girl stopped trying to avoid Alexis' gaze and drew herself up. She seemed nervous and Alexis couldn't understand why. She'd been on friendly terms with everyone she'd met when last here.

Then it struck her. The first time she'd seen the girl had been in the lap of Midshipman Penn Timpson, the berthmate from *Hermione* who'd stopped her messages. The last time Alexis had seen the girl she, along with several other local girls, was leaving Timpson behind after Alexis had all but called him out in a nearby café. She hadn't seen those girls again during her stay.

No wonder she's hesitant, when all she's seen of me is a screaming harridan slapping Timpson in the face.

Alexis tried to put on a friendly expression, while wondering what the girl could want.

"*Bonjour,*" she said as they approached.

"*Bonjour,*" the girl said. She smiled shyly, not at all what Alexis expected. The girls she'd seen with *Hermione's* midshipmen that day had been anything but shy. "Allo. *Mademoiselle* Carew, *oui?*"

"Lieutenant," Alexis said, nodding, "but yes. *Oui.*"

"*Je suis* ... I am, Marie Autin." The girl, Marie, spoke her English slowly and held out her hand. Alexis took it, still puzzled. "The ship ... *Hermione?* It is come back?"

Alexis shook her head. "No, I'm afraid *Hermione* is long gone from here," she said, "gone before my last stay, even."

Marie frowned. "Not ship, but *le officiers?* You have come back?"

"I have, at least. I'm on another ship now, *Shrewsbury*. The other officers from that time, they're ..."

Alexis wasn't quite sure how to explain what had happened and she had no idea where *Hermione's* other officers had been sent. An older woman came out of a nearby shop. She carried an infant, probably not quite a year old, who she held out to Marie. She nodded to Alexis and Roswell, but spoke rapidly to Marie.

"*Oui, Mama*," the girl said, and took the child.

Alexis looked from the girl to the child with sudden understanding. An infant less than a year old and some eighteen months since she and *Hermione's* officers were last on Giron made the connection clear.

Penn Timpson, you utter, irresponsible arsehole.

A simple visit to the ship's surgeon for an implant would have eliminated the risk of this sort of thing. For the crew it was mandatory, but not for officers, and Timpson must not have bothered. Marie must not have bothered either, which was understandable given Giron's low population. Many colony worlds, unless they'd been settled as a religious colony, welcomed as many new residents as they could get and paid little notice to the proprieties. Still, with a war on, Marie might have been in an awkward position. No matter how French the population of Giron considered themselves, it couldn't be thought proper to come up pregnant by the ostensible enemy.

Of course now New London was Giron's ally, if not liberator, which made for an entirely different situation. In addition, with New London forces in place on Giron, Marie could make a case for support. It would be a simple matter for someone on General Malicoat's staff to test the child's DNA against Timpson's medical records and the errant midshipman would quickly find his pay docked no matter where he'd been reassigned.

And serve him right, as well, it would.

Alexis nodded to the child. "He is —" She trailed off with a cough, unsure if it was the sort of thing one should ask on Giron, but

Marie was looking at her questioningly. "I mean to say ... *Aspirant* Timpson's?"

"*Oui*," Marie said with a shrug. She looked at the child and her face seemed to glow as she smiled widely. She took one of his pudgy little arms and waved it at Alexis. "Say 'allo' to *Lieutenant* Carew, Ferrau. Allo. Allo."

Ferrau said nothing. He simply looked at Alexis blankly, pursed his little lips, and blew a bubble of spittle that popped and dribbled down his chin.

Timpson's get, indeed.

Roswell cleared her throat. "I think your men have bought out the market, Carew. Perhaps we should be on our way?"

FORTY-FIVE

"Six bells of the forenoon, sir, you asked for me to wake you."

Alexis opened her eyes at Isom's words. She'd been almost napping, her tablet lying on her chest. A particularly dry treatise on attacking fortified systems was a wonderful sleep aid, she'd found. This document was supposed to be quite the thing, but it was a long slog through.

"Thank you, Isom." She threw her legs over the side of her cot and sat up. *Belial's* master's cabin was small compared to the captain's quarters aboard a frigate or 74, but a luxury after a lieutenant's berth. Nearly twice the size of her cabin aboard *Shrewsbury*, and all for her. The cot itself was so much larger that Alexis found herself rolling from side to side in the night just to enjoy the space.

I could grow quite used to this.

"I brought a bit of a bite for you, as well, sir."

Alexis saw the tray with sandwich, glass, and wine on the cabin's table.

"Doubly thanked, then." She rose and went to the table, which doubled as a large desk surface complete with a repeater of the quarterdeck's navigation plot.

Belial was still in orbit around Giron, still endlessly circling, and with still no sign of the returning transports or the rest of the fleet.

Alexis keyed her tablet to call the quarterdeck. "Mister Artley?"

"Yes, sir?" he responded after a moment.

"Have the bosun pipe *Up Spirits*, if you please, and set the men to their meal afterward."

"Aye, sir."

Alexis set her tablet down and waited for Isom to pour her a glass, as the familiar bosun's pipe sounded over the ship's speakers. She could hear the rustle and tramp of feet even through her closed hatch as the crew responded to the call. *Up Spirits* marked the start of the daily rum issue, and none of the crew would miss that. It was a time to be a bit idle, chat with friends, and settle debts by giving over their daily tot for the man owed to take his sippers or gulpers.

Most of crew was idle to begin with, as she'd ordered yet another make-and-mend day. With *Belial* in orbit for so long, there was little work for the men once the day's cleaning was complete. They'd long ago completed even the least important of maintenance tasks. Alexis had let the ship fall into a routine of three days, where the port and starboard watches alternated liberty on Giron for a day each, followed by a make-and-mend day with all the crew aboard and at personal tasks, such as their hobbies or mending their uniforms.

Still, she sensed the crew was growing restive. More and more their liberty time on Giron was ending in fights with the soldiers, and the injuries from those clashes were growing more serious. The army on Giron was not taking their idleness well either. There were more fights aboard ship, as well. Day after day spent on hobbies was beginning to pall and every uniform and bit of gear aboard had long ago been mended.

Alexis eyed her tablet and the article it still displayed. The treatise on the techniques of attacking from *darkspace* to normal space might be dry, but she imagined the exercise itself would not be so.

She keyed her tablet again to call the quarterdeck.

"Mister Artley?"

"Yes, sir?"

"After the hands have finished their meal, we shall break orbit. And pass the word for the carpenter, if you please."

"YOU'LL TRANSITION THUSLY, BOOTHROYD," Alexis said, indicating on the helm exactly what she wanted the spacer to do. Nearby, Artley looked on as well, his brow furrowed in concentration. "Then you, Leyman," she continued to the spacer on the tactical console, "must sing out as quickly as the sensors come to life."

"Aye, sir," they both said.

"And no sooner have we fired, then it's back to *darkspace*, do you see?"

Alexis saw their blank looks and didn't blame them. This was so different from the sort of action that took place in *darkspace*. There, with no electronics or sensors other than the ship's optics, an engagement at even a kilometer was rare, and most took place with the ships only a few hundred meters apart or even closer.

"They'd never see us," Artley said from his place at the navigation plot.

Alexis looked at him.

"Sorry, sir," he mumbled.

"No, Mister Artley, finish your thought, please."

Artley frowned. "Well, it's that we left the target Mister Oakman made so far away." He ran his fingers over the plot. "We're here at L3, but we left the target almost as far away as Giron, just behind it in orbit here." His brow furrowed. "If that target were a ship, then all it can see at L3 now is empty space, but when we transition ..."

"Go on," Alexis prompted.

"Well, they'd still not see us. That target's almost a full light second away. When we transition, we'll be able to see it ... or how it was a second ago, but it'll take that time for anything from us to reach it. If we can target and fire before they even see us ..."

Alexis nodded. "And then transition back to *darkspace* instanter."

"Any enemy'd be struck before they know we're there and have nothing to shoot back at. By the time the light from our arrival got to them, our fire would be close behind and we'd be back in *darkspace* already."

Alexis clapped a hand on his shoulder. "You have it."

Artley smiled, but then frowned again. "But at such a distance, how're the crews to aim?"

"That's the beauty of being in normal space when we fire, Mister Artley," Alexis said. "We'll have access to all of *Belial's* sensors and electronics once we transition. The guns are all locked in place and the computers will track our first shot to calibrate where they're aimed — after that, we simply need to designate our target after we transition and the computer will maneuver the entire ship so that the guns bear. We aim with *Belial* herself."

Alexis laid her palms flat on the navigation plot and smiled. This would be even more fun than a regular gun drill. There was an element of stealth to it that appealed to her.

"On my mark, gentlemen." She waited a moment, then, "Now!"

Belial transitioned to normal space and the stars appeared on her navigation plot.

"Locate that target, Leyman," she said, but before she'd finished he'd done so and highlighted it on her plot. Alexis designated it as the target and the visual feeds from outside spun and twisted as the computer adjusted *Belial* so that her broadside faced the target.

"*Fire!*"

The order and its execution were still manual. The gun captains on *Belial's* gundeck would still have to mash their hands down on the firing buttons, as well they'd have to reload by hand, but the guns were locked to the deck and *Belial's* computer knew how their fire would diverge and disperse over the many kilometers to the target. The magnified view of the target showed hull material boiling away as at least some of their shot struck home.

"Back now, transition!" Alexis ordered. "As soon as we've fired once it's back to *darkspace*."

Most of the quarterdeck's monitors went dark as her order was obeyed and they transitioned back to the *darkspace*. Only the optical feeds remained.

Alexis grinned.

"Let's do it again, shall we?"

"MATCH OUR SPEED and vector to the target, Boothroyd."

Alexis watched her plot as *Belial* closed with the target, what was left of it after hours of drill. She could have left it drifting, she supposed. Eventually its orbit would decay and it would drop into Giron's star, but she didn't feel it was right to clutter up the system like that. Also, she wanted the crew to see how successful they'd been. The target, fashioned to look like one side of a ship's hull, just a bit smaller than *Belial's*, was pocked with holes where their lasers had blasted through the tough thermoplastic. The force of the plastic vaporizing had set the target spinning and changing vectors after every shot, making their next even more difficult.

"Mister Artley, once we're alongside, detail some men to cut the target into manageable sections and bring it inboard for Mister Oakman." The carpenter would be able to recycle what was left back into *Belial's* tanks for future fabrication. "And inform Mister Dobb that we shall 'splice the mainbrace' on our way back to orbit."

"Aye, sir."

Alexis had to smile at the rustle of anticipation from the helmsman and other spacers on the quarterdeck at her words, but they'd worked hard and deserved it. An extra issue of rum with each man receiving his full measure and without sippers or gulpers for debts owed. The three hours' transit time back to Giron would give them ample opportunity to enjoy their reward.

A soft *ping* from the tactical console cut through her thoughts.

"Transition, sir," Leyman announced. "At L1."

"Belay that order, Mister Artley." A transition at L1 would mean a military ship, as merchants typically used the larger and more stable L4 to transition into a system. The arriving ship was probably a packet, either from the fleet and on its way back to New London, or from New London in search of the fleet. Either way she'd best take *Belial* back to orbit instanter. "Boothroyd, set a course for —"

"Transitioned out, sir," Leyman said.

Alexis frowned. That was what ships were supposed to do when approaching a system without a pilot boat where there might be the possibility of a hostile fleet; transition in and then back to *darkspace* quickly, so as to have a glimpse of what was going on in normal space and be prepared to flee if an enemy was present, but the packets had proven themselves quite lax in that regard during her time at Giron. Most hadn't bothered.

"No signals or colors, sir," the spacer on the signals console reported.

"Leyman, send that transition sequence to my plot, if you will."

She bent over the plot to study the brief image of the ship's transition. Into normal space and then back to *darkspace* in only a second or two. The ship's masts were stepped and sails bent on, but uncharged — useless in normal space, but ready to charge and flee in *darkspace* if necessary. Not only that, but three-masted.

"Not a packet," Alexis mused. More than the masts, the number of gunports piercing the ship's hull spoke to a very different purpose. "That's a frigate.

"Kill the drive," she ordered quietly. She turned to the signals console. "Chevis, no signals at all until we know who this is. Kill the hull lights as well."

"Aye, sir."

Alexis studied the image while she waited. There was something odd about it, but she supposed she'd know soon enough. Likely as not the visitor was a frigate from the New London fleet and she'd receive a dressing down from her captain for hiding like this.

"Your thoughts, Leyman?"

"Hard to say from the angle we have, sir, but look here ..."

Alexis crossed to the tactical console. Leyman had the image magnified and was pointing to the ship's bow.

"Do you see here, sir? How the bowsprit seems to angle up a bit?"

"And the masts aren't quite equidistant," Alexis added.

"Aye, the fore and mizzen are a few degrees closer to the main than a proper frigate's should be."

Alexis took a deep breath and held it. She clapped a hand on Leyman's shoulder.

"Well, and we'll know for certain in a moment when she analyzes what she saw and returns, but I believe you've seen the right of it. That's a Hanoverese design."

She caught her lower lip between her teeth and considered what to do next. *Belial* was no match for a frigate, that was certain, and there was no way of knowing what other Hanoverese ships were about to transition into the system. If she were in orbit, she might contact General Malicoat, but the general would know as much as she did already. The satellites in orbit around Giron would have alerted him to the frigate's transition. Any message Alexis sent now would only serve to betray her position if the frigate returned.

"Transition," Leyman said. "It's back and making way for the planet." He paused and hunched over his console, his description of the other ship, it rather than she, making it clear he'd determined the newcomer was hostile. "Transition — another ship at L1 ... Multiple transitions ... L2, L4, L3 ... multiple transitions, multiple ships."

Alexis turned to the navigation plot as markers for these new ships began appearing, *Belial's* computers marking their locations and courses as the light and electronic emissions reached her. That last, L3, was where *Belial* had spent the day in drill and Alexis was glad she'd left to recover the target when she had. Ships were appearing in a constant stream that made its way toward Giron. L5 was out of *Belial's* sight, behind the planet from her position, but Alexis assumed the same was happening there.

"That first frigate's closing on the planet, sir," Leyman said. He hunched over his console. "I'm losing the signals from our satellite constellation there, one by one."

"Well, that settles their intentions, doesn't it?" Alexis caught her lower lip between her teeth and worried at it. "Can you determine what type of ship the others are?" she asked, knowing the answer but needing it confirmed.

"Transports, sir, the lot of them."

FORTY-SIX

ALEXIS' eyes burned with fatigue. She'd been on the quarterdeck for more than thirty-six hours, counting the time *Belial* had spent in drill. Those drills seemed like an eternity ago, now that she'd spent so much time watching the Hanoverese land their forces. Ship after ship streamed into orbit around Giron, dropped its boats full of soldiers, and then made way back to a Lagrangian point to leave the system. Alexis had lost count of how many, but her estimate of the total number of troops made her gorge rise.

Seventy thousand, at least. Perhaps more.

General Malicoat's New London forces would be outnumbered at least two to one. He'd have an advantage in men if he included the French, but they were untrained and only a fraction of them had been equipped with modern arms.

Malicoat had made only one encrypted transmission after the Hanoverese began arriving and had then been utterly silent.

"If you can get loose, Carew — certain of it, I mean — then hurry word of this back to New London. But only if you're certain. Better for word to be late than never come at all."

And so Alexis had kept *Belial* dead stopped, much as it galled her to do so — and galled her further not to be able to respond to Malicoat. She thought *Belial was* somewhat safe where she was, hundreds of thousands of kilometers from any of Giron's Lagrangian points, and the distance increasing as Giron moved on in its orbit. Without any lights or firing engines, and with the tumbling length of hull material they'd used as a target, *Belial* would likely be mistaken for random debris, if she were even spotted at all.

"Have you seen any more frigates than the five, Leyman?"

"No, sir."

They'd identified five Hanoverese frigates amongst the invading force. One was in orbit around Giron, obviously guarding the transports in normal space. The others appeared and disappeared, transitioning at random intervals and at random Lagrangian points, both Giron's and those of the other planets in the system.

Alexis noticed her fingers were tapping the surface of the navigation plot and forced herself to be still.

Even if we could move unnoticed to a point for transition, one of those frigates would likely be in position to intercept us in darkspace.

She reviewed Malicoat's message again. No, she was far from certain she could escape the system, certain she couldn't, in fact. Not with those frigates about.

She'd have to wait and see what happened when the Hanoverese finished their landing. In the meantime, she had no idea what might be happening on Giron's surface.

IT TOOK three days for the Hanoverese transports to complete their landing. More transports arrived after the first batch. Alexis had tried to estimate the number of troops that might be landing and kept coming up with a number that spelled nothing good for General Malicoat and the New London soldiers, much less the French recruits.

At last, the final Hanoverese ship transitioned out of the system. Alexis was at first surprised that they'd left no warship behind, but with Admiral Chipley's fleet at large in *darkspace*, they'd likely thought protection for the transports more important. There was little one frigate could do here if Chipley returned in any case.

Much as there was little we could do when this lot arrived.

Even after the last ship left, Alexis kept *Belial* still, dark, and silent. She worried that one might return. As soon as she moved and tried to contact Malicoat her presence would be picked up by any satellites the Hanoverese had left in orbit and reported to those on the surface. Finally she thought it was safe and contacted Malicoat.

ALEXIS WATCHED General Malicoat's expressionless face on the screen as she waited for his response. She'd let *Belial* fall back as the planet continued in its orbit while waiting for the Hanoverese ships to leave. The result was that *Belial* was a full six light seconds from the planet.

"No," Malicoat said. "I realize your orders were to stay and support me, Carew, but there's little you can do at this point. I need you to return to New London space and report our situation. I *need* those additional troops." He frowned. "The Hanoverese outnumber us by a decent margin, even taking into account the locally raised troops. And some of the French have been abandoning the idea ever since the Hanoverese arrived in system. I can't say that I blame them.

"The one bright spot in this mess is that I have no fixed position I must defend, and so I'm free to maneuver. Tell whoever's in charge of the incoming forces that I plan to split my force into multiple columns. The Hanoverese have done the same — their plan seems to be to come at us from all directions so that we can't maneuver free. If I keep my force together, their columns will be able to keep us engaged long enough for the others to catch up and outnumber us. I'll split my force in such a way that each can maneuver faster and likely take on any one of their columns — two would be a stretch, but I hope to be able to avoid that.

"Once we've broken out of their attempt to encircle us, I'll be free to bring the force back together and maneuver anywhere on the continent that I like — they're as limited as I am with their ships and boats gone, so we'll all be walking. Don't mistake me, though — breaking free and running is the best I hope for. After that, they'll be able to bring their entire force together and come hot on our heels. It's only a matter of time before they catch up."

Alexis wanted to ask questions, but Malicoat wasn't stopping.

"If the reinforcements aren't coming for some reason — lord knows there's always some sort of cock-up — tell them I need those transports back. All of this is in the report I've sent to your ship, obviously, but you'll have to be my voice in this. And if it's come to that — that they're sending ships to pull us off — then tell them we need enough for the French troops as well. And whatever civilians we can take off with us. We're already getting word of reprisals down here and it's a vile bit of business.

"Whatever you're about to say, forget it, Carew. I can see on your face here that you don't like the idea, but this is what I need from you. There's nothing your ship can help with by staying and you must get word of our situation to Chipley or whoever might be in charge back on Alchiba. Once they've made a decision, I'd admire it if you hurried back here with word of it, though, so I know whether my backside will be going into the pan or the fire."

Malicoat paused and after a moment of silence Alexis assumed he was done. No, she didn't like it — it seemed like she'd be running back to the safety of New London space and abandoning Malicoat and all his men, but she realized he was correct. There was nothing *Belial* could do to help their situation.

"Aye sir." She nodded. "You're right that I don't like it, but ... I'll deliver the message and be back with their response as quick as I may."

"Good girl," Malicoat said.

Alexis couldn't even bring herself to bristle at that; the situation was too dire.

FORTY-SEVEN

THE LONG SAIL back to Alchiba was a further exercise in frustration
and impatience. *Belial* performed beautifully, racing before the *darkspace* winds as fast as any frigate — certainly faster than a ship of the
line like *Shrewsbury* — but neither her ship's performance nor her joy
in sailing her could ease Alexis' mind.

When they arrived at Alchiba, her worst fears were realized. Not
only had the transports never returned to Alchiba, but there was no
Naval presence in the system at all. The next nearest system she
could be sure of having Naval officers was two weeks' sail farther into
New London at Lesser Itchthorpe. Even Dansby and *Marilyn* had
moved on, though she heard that he'd been back and forth to Alchiba
several times since the fleet sailed.

She sent copies of Malicoat's messages and her own report on
with a merchantman bound for Lesser Itchthorpe, along with a Naval
draft for the merchant's captain to sail there directly. She hoped the
port admiral there would honor it and not give him too much trouble
over it coming from a mere lieutenant.

What she should do — sail for Lesser Itchthorpe or some other station herself, remain at Alchiba in the hopes a fleet happened by, or return to Giron to assist Malicoat in some way — she didn't know.

Finally she decided. It came down to feeling she was needed back at Giron. She had no idea what use she could be, but nothing else seemed the right course. To cover it all, though, she sent additional copies of her reports off to Lesser Itchthorpe by yet another merchantman, and one farther along to Penduli for good measure.

If she was to return to Giron, though, and place *Belial* alone in the face of a Hanoverese fleet possibly returning there, she could at least see that Artley and Isom were safe. She wished she could leave her entire crew behind on Alchiba to keep them safe, but needed them to sail the ship. They, at least, were proper Navy. Neither Artley nor Isom should face these risks, she thought.

Isom objected, but accepted her orders when she told him she wished him to watch over Artley for her. As for Artley, she told him that she wanted him there to pass on her reports and his own observations, should a New London force enter the system. He'd be her representative, responsible for seeing that any ships that could do so would come to the rescue of Malicoat and his men.

"You understand what I need of you, Mister Artley?" Alexis asked.

"I do, sir, I suppose ... what you've asked of me, at least. I don't understand the why of it, or why you have to go back. It seems hopeless."

"History is full of times that seemed hopeless." She thought of a few of the examples she'd read about since Eades' humiliating comments on her knowledge of history. "Masada, Thermopylae, Agincourt, Third Rosada, our own ship *Shrewsbury's* original namesake, come to that."

"Seems a few of those were quite hopeless, sir."

Alexis thought hard for a moment. "I think, Mister Artley, that it is the trying which echoes most loudly through the ages. The striving against odds. For in that striving, no matter the losses, comes hope. Perhaps, even, the knowledge that some will fight against those hopeless odds may deter the evil itself at times." She shrugged. "I don't understand it fully myself, but I feel as though my place, *Belial's* place, is back at Giron. Perhaps on the sail there it will occur to me how one ship may be of some use." She gripped Artley's shoulder. "I'm depending on you to send me what help you may."

"Aye, sir." The lad frowned as though still thinking it through. "I'll not disappoint you."

FORTY-EIGHT

"No sign of them at all?"

General Malicoat's shoulders slumped. Alexis had thought he looked exhausted when she'd arrived to give him a report on her journey to Alchiba and back; now he looked simply defeated.

"Nothing, sir. I'm sorry." She waited while Malicoat filled a glass from the bottle of bourbon she'd brought down with her. Supplies for the constantly retreating army were low all around and she'd thought he might appreciate a bit of a drink with the news she'd brought for him. "Our transports never arrived back at Alchiba and there was no sign of them on either leg of our journey there and back. No sign of either of the war fleets. Neither any sign of the Hanoverese transports returning."

Malicoat grunted. "Small favors." He drained his glass and poured another. "Thank you for this. There's hardly a drop left in the camp." He turned to a large display behind him and was silent for a time.

Alexis studied the display. It showed the path the army had taken since breaking through the Hanoverese lines and fleeing Atterrissage.

The line snaked across the continent, changing direction here and there to make the best use of terrain. Still Alexis could see the notations made where the Hanoverese columns had caught up and engaged the army's rear. There were far too many of them for her liking.

"They brought in more transport than we have," Malicoat said as though responding to her thoughts. "We manage to disengage and rush off to gain a few hours' time — as we have now — but they'll always catch up with us." He tapped the screen near one of the marked actions. "They brought heavy cavalry, as well. Caught us here at Sauqueuse — the 451st drove them off, but the casualties ..."

Malicoat reached for the bottle again, but capped it and held it up.

"I'll just keep this, if you don't mind, Carew?"

Alexis simply nodded. There was nothing she could think of to say and if the general wanted to drink in private later on, she'd not gainsay him.

"Thank you. There's more than one lad in the hospital train who'll not say no to a last wet. God knows I can't offer them anything more."

"Is there nothing we can do, sir?"

"You've done what you could, unless you can load a few tens of thousands troops aboard your ship." He shook his head. "No, with no relief coming and no ships to evacuate us, the best we can do is draw it out. Don't get me wrong, that's what I'll do. Especially with the civilians pouring in." He rose and walked to the tent's front to peer out the flap. "More every day — the Hanoverese reprisals have been bloody. Towns razed, executions in the square — before you returned and took down their satellite constellation they were transmitting them planetwide." A muscle in his jaw twitched. "They've said they'll salt every patch of earth a traitor's trod upon ..."

Alexis winced. She couldn't see how it had come to this. They'd been so sure, so certain, back at Alchiba that it would be a certain thing. Eades had been giddy as a schoolgirl at the prospect of the beginning of the end of Hanover. Now the people of Giron were paying the price. Only Malicoat had argued that they weren't bringing enough forces in the first wave ... Dansby and Mynatt had seen it too, now that she thought about it, but no one had asked them.

"You were right," she whispered.

Malicoat nodded. "Small comfort."

ALEXIS LEFT Malicoat's tent and made her way through the camp back to *Belial's* boat. Dobb and the others trailed behind her, but she was lost in thought. There was no doubt that Malicoat's situation was dire. She thought there must be some way *Belial* could assist other than constantly running back and forth to Alchiba crying out for aid.

She must have taken a wrong turn somewhere, because she found herself leaving the military encampment and entering that of the civilians fleeing with the army. If the army's encampment had been less orderly than she'd expected, this was chaos. Tents made of anything that could be strung between two posts, piles of household goods and valuables the people were trying to keep with them and further piles of those discarded as the march grew longer. The makeshift tents were arranged in small groups, some with a fire at the center and the occupants huddled around it.

Alexis stopped to get her bearings, Dobb and the others still following behind her. She supposed they'd thought she knew where she was going or hadn't wanted to disturb her thoughts.

She was about to retrace her steps when she caught sight of a familiar face in the nearest group. She frowned, then approached and knelt down.

"Marie?"

The girl looked up slowly. She had Ferrau in her lap, held tightly to her. Her face was dull and still.

"*Lieutenant* Carew."

Alexis reached out and laid her hand over one of Marie's.

"Are you all right?" It was a stupid, silly question to ask, Alexis realized. Of course Marie wasn't all right. No one on Giron was all right.

"I have Ferrau," Marie said. She looked down and ran a finger over the baby's cheek. "*Mama est mort. Papa est mort.*" She looked back to Alexis and shrugged. Alexis had thought she knew how much the French could pack into a simple shrug, but Marie's brought tears to her eyes. "*Courboin est morte.*"

She lowered her gaze again.

Alexis sat with her for a moment, then rose. She made her way back through the camp to where she'd turned wrongly and headed for the landing field.

ALEXIS SPENT the time in the boat returning to *Belial* with her head buried in her tablet. She was convinced there must be some way for her to help General Malicoat, but couldn't find one for the life of her. *Belial* was designed for combat in *darkspace*, not normal-space, and certainly not for use against a planet-bound army. Even if she were, the Abbentheren Accords forbade it.

Part of her determination was anger and frustration. She felt as though she'd been simply dragged along by events for far too long. Ever since Eades had first shown up and recruited her into his mad scheme she'd been helpless at the mercy of others' decisions. First Eades, then Dansby, and now the Hanoverese army. She was determined to find something, anything, that would allow her to take back some control.

By the time they arrived at the ship, she thought she might have the beginnings of an idea. It might not work, might, in fact, be quite mad, for it surely sounded so to her, but she hadn't found any sure reason that it would not work.

"Pass the word for the gunner, Mister Dobb," she said as she was piped aboard. "I'll see him on the quarterdeck. The carpenter and yourself as well."

"Aye, sir," the bosun said.

Alexis went to the quarterdeck and brought up an image of the planet on the navigation plot. She studied the symbols that represented General Malicoat's forces, as well as what was known of the Hanoverese while waiting for the others to arrive.

"Y'sent fer me, sir?" the gunner asked.

"I did, Mister Starks." Alexis kept her eyes on the plot, brow furrowed. "What would be the effect of firing our guns in atmosphere?"

"On the surface, d'ye mean?" He shrugged. "I suppose there'd be a bit o' diffusion an' that. Beam'd be weaker an' wider, dependin' on t'range, but not enough t'make no nevermind."

"Even at, say, one hundred kilometers?"

"I see what yer thinkin', sir, t'bring the guns down an' support those troops an' all, but there's no man can lay a ship's gun fer that range. A bit o' a degree off an' y've missed entire. There's special guns fer that, what can aim themselves, but we've none of them."

"I understand, Mister Starks, but would the beam still be effective at that range?"

Starks shrugged again. "Bit weaker, bit wider — but'll never hit a thing."

"We shan't be aiming the guns by hand," Alexis said. "The guns will be locked in place, and *Belial's* computer shall do the aiming, just as we did in that drill before the Hanoverese showed up."

"Sir," Dobb said, "we can't fire from orbit ... the Abbentheren Accords —"

"Yes, the Accords," Alexis cut him off. "That agreement which says we must now do nothing from orbit while the Hanoverese down there may burn towns and slaughter civilians with impunity." She took a deep breath to calm herself. "I've just read the Accords." She consulted her tablet and read. "'No spaceborn force may bombard, fire upon, nor otherwise engage any planetary installation nor force of men.' The thing about agreements between nations, gentlemen, is they tend to be quite specific. The Accords define 'spaceborn' as any attack from above a planet's mesosphere." She turned to Oakman, the ship's carpenter. "Which brings us to my next question, Mister Oakman. *Belial's* hull may be quite suited for dispersing the heat and energy of a laser ... how is it with friction?"

FORTY-NINE

Alexis forced her hands to relax where they gripped the edges of the navigation plot. She caught her lower lip between her teeth and worried at it. This was where they'd find if she was mad or not.

Belial's masts had been unstepped and brought inboard. All of their hull fittings as well, even the bowsprit. The massive rudder and plane at the stern, made without gallenium and extending far back from the hull to allow the ship to steer in *darkspace,* had been removed as well. They were far too large to bring inboard, so had been left behind in a high orbit. If a Hanoverese force arrived in-system now, *Belial* would be quite helpless. She'd be able to run within the system, but wouldn't be able to flee to *darkspace.*

All of her guns had been brought to the port side and locked in place. If the men had no need to move them, the guns could be crowded together in the space meant for half their number.

The guns were loaded and run out, spare shot waiting on the racks and the gun crews standing by to fire and reload as quickly as they could.

She hadn't told Malicoat what she intended, for fear he'd forbid it. Technically he couldn't, as he was not in her chain of command

and she was the senior Naval officer present, but she thought she might be relying on enough technicalities that she didn't need to add one more.

Technicalities and theories, to be betting our lives on.

Technically, firing her guns from within Giron's mesosphere would not violate the Abbentheren Accords and result in her crew being executed for war crimes. In theory, *Belial*'s hull would be able to withstand the heat and friction of dipping into Giron's atmosphere to less than a hundred kilometers above the surface. In theory, the ship's computer would be able to twist and angle *Belial* so that her broadside fell upon the Hanoverese columns. In theory, the conventional drive had more than enough power to push the ship back into orbit from that height, so that they'd not plummet to the planet's surface.

Of course Mister Oakman assures me that the ship would break up long before we impacted the ground ... so there's that.

The worst part, as the ship made its way through the last orbit before dipping into Giron's atmosphere, was the waiting. The entire thing, save the firing and reloading of the guns themselves, was under the control of *Belial*'s computer.

And if there were ever proof we've not achieved artificial intelligence, it's that the thing didn't balk at what I've asked of it.

Boothroyd stood by at the helm, though. If Alexis gave the order he'd take control and try to get *Belial* to claw her way back to vacuum where she belonged.

Belial reached the start of her descent. On the quarterdeck, nothing seemed to change; there was just the ship's position noted on the navigation plot. Then the view from the ship's optics began to shake and tremble. Alexis had magnified views of the Hanoverese columns she'd targeted, but it soon became difficult to make them out as the image jerked about. It seemed odd that they felt nothing, but *Belial*'s inertial compensators negated the roughness.

The ship dipped lower, neared the point where she would be beneath the upper reaches of the mesosphere, then passed it.

"Fire," Alexis said quietly, almost whispering.

She knew the gun captains had fired but couldn't tell what effect it might have. All of the images on her plot were a useless jumble. She wouldn't even hear from Malicoat until *Belial* resumed orbit. Something about ionization — Chevis, on the signals console, had tried to explain it, but Alexis had cut him off. She'd learned quite enough new things for a time and it was enough that Chevis said they'd regain contact with Malicoat once they returned to a proper orbit.

Was it her imagination or could she feel the ship trembling now? The gundeck reported that all guns were reloaded.

"Fire."

She was firing by broadside. Perhaps if this worked and they repeated it, she'd have the guns fire as quickly as they could individually, but she had no idea what the effect of her shot would be on the surface. Each shot was only ten or so centimeters across, after all; it was entirely possible they'd hit nothing and this was a wasted risk. Still, by broadside had more effect on a ship's morale. Perhaps it would be the same for troops on the ground.

Time passed. Alexis watched their position and a counter she had running on the navigation plot. She'd calculated that they'd be within the mesosphere and within range of the Hanoverese for only three minutes and she wanted three broadsides in that time, but the counter ended before the guns reported they were ready.

She tensed and felt a pain in her lip, then tasted blood and forced her teeth to let go. Now was the real test, as *Belial's* computer tried to pull her out of the mesosphere and return to orbit.

Finally her optics and other sensors cleared ... well, most of them; some were dead and blank still. Alexis suspected they'd been damaged or burned out and would have to be replaced. The Hanoverese columns were back around Giron's curve, so she couldn't tell what, if any, effect she'd had on them.

"A message to Mister Starks on the gundeck, Chevis, I'll have three broadsides in the next pass or know the reason why."

"Aye, sir."

"Pass the word for the bosun and carpenter, as well. They're to take a crew onto the hull and determine its state." She glanced at her plot. "We have three hours for them to make any necessary repairs before we come around again."

"Aye, sir. General Malicoat is sending, sir."

"I'll take it on my plot, Chevis." She opened the transmission on her plot and found Malicoat staring back at her, red-faced. "Yes, general?"

"Are you mad, Carew? Do you realize what you've done?"

"General, I —"

"You've violated the Abbentheren Accords!" Malicoat yelled. "There are craters ten meters across throughout the Hanoverese column! They'll hang you for this and I might well be on the bloody gallows beside you!"

Craters? Alexis considered that. She supposed it made sense, now that she thought about it. The ground would be far less efficient at absorbing and dissipating her shots' energy than thermoplastic of a ship's hull, and each shot did have a great deal of energy behind it in order to overcome that. Superheated dirt and rock might very well react ... violently.

"Good," she said.

"*What?* Bloody '*good*'?" Malicoat's eyes were wide.

"The craters, sir," Alexis assured him. "I was concerned my fire would have little effect, but it appears to have been an idle worry."

"Get in a boat and get down here, Carew. If I have you shot now they may not hang me."

"General Malicoat, I have not violated the Accords, I assure you. *Belial* was well within Giron's mesosphere when I fired."

Malicoat blinked. "The what? And what difference does that make?"

"The mesosphere, it's ... well, sir, here —" She sent Malicoat a copy of the Accords with the relevant sections highlighted, as well as *Belial's* logs from the attack.

Malicoat looked at his tablet, frowned, brow furrowed, then gestured to someone off-camera.

"*Whitehead!* You understand all this legal higgety-jibbet! Get over here and look at this!" he bellowed. "Look, here —" He handed his tablet to someone. "— and tell me whether or not I have to shoot someone."

He took a deep breath and met Alexis' eyes.

"Assuming you're correct, Carew, and I don't have to execute you ... how soon can you do it again?"

FIFTY

OVER THE NEXT SEVERAL DAYS, *Belial* fell into a routine. If, that is, hours of back-breaking effort to repair damage to the hull followed by minutes of terror and unleashing horrible violence can be called routine.

With every orbit, Oakman was out onto the hull with a crew to examine and repair weakened portions. His fabrication plant in the hold was working full time to create replacement parts, sensors, and hull sections. Alexis allowed him his grumbling that it would be easier and safer to simply build a new ship from scratch, confident that he'd tell her specifically if there was a true danger.

Alexis spent the time while *Belial* dove into Giron's atmosphere each orbit with one hand clutching the edge of the navigation plot in fear and the other caressing it as she whispered promises to her ship that if *Belial* stood just a few minutes more of this indignity, she'd soon be back in vacuum and her crew would see to the wounds inflicted.

Her guncrews met, and even exceeded, her demand for three broadsides in each pass, sometimes managing four, and putting sixty or more shots into the Hanoverese lines. Malicoat sent her images of the destruction that caused Alexis to clench her jaw and harden her heart.

She hated that her strikes were delivered so randomly upon the common Hanoverese soldiers, as it was impossible to identify where the officers kept themselves. Then she told herself that these were the soldiers who would obey the orders to sack and burn a town like Courboin, slaughtering the inhabitants indiscriminately, and readied herself for the next pass.

Alexis stayed on the quarterdeck throughout. She managed to catch a brief nap through some of the orbits, but she kept the deck through each dive upon Giron. Also she kept the guns firing by broadside and on her order alone. She'd not put that on anyone else.

The Hanoverese reacted quickly to this new threat from above. They spread out their columns more and more, so that their soldiers wouldn't be clumped together. But they also learned Alexis' limitations.

Though she varied the length of her orbits, there was still a minimum amount of time after each pass before she could return for another. The Hanoverese would rush forward after each of her passes, coming together again to engage Malicoat's columns, then fading back and dispersing before her next pass.

With each orbit came a short time before *Belial* dove where Alexis would communicate with Malicoat. He'd give her the coordinates to fire on that he thought would do the most damage to the Hanoverese.

Alexis entered the latest set of these and viewed the images of where Malicoat wished her to fire next. Her eyes widened and she keyed them in second time, thinking her fatigue had caused her to make a mistake, but the images remained.

"General Malicoat," she said, "there's active fighting at these coordinates."

Malicoat had grown more and more haggard as time went on, Alexis had noted. His hair was in disarray, smudges of dirt covered his face and uniform, and his uniform jacket was torn in places. He nodded wearily.

"I've a rear guard keeping them engaged," he said. "Not allowing them to fall back and disperse."

"Sir, if I fire on this ... sir, our own men are there!"

"There're fewer of them than it appears." Malicoat closed his eyes and took a deep breath. "They're volunteers and of the French ... most from homes that don't exist any longer." He swallowed heavily. "God forgive me what I thought of them at the start of this ... but those lads have found their mettle and more."

"But —"

"The Hanoverese come closer and closer to overruning us with every engagement. If they make it through our lines and into the civilian columns ... those lads know what's coming, Carew. They understand."

Alexis met his eyes. She could see they were as haunted as her own thoughts.

"Aye, sir."

Alexis confirmed the coordinates to target. *Belial* dove into atmosphere once more. Alexis watched the counter tick down, one hand caressing the navigation plot. She closed her eyes and whispered, promising *Belial* that the burden fell on Alexis herself and not her beautiful, faithful ship.

"Fire."

FIFTY-ONE

"Transition, sir! At L1."

At first, Alexis wasn't sure she'd heard correctly. *Belial's* world seemed to have become just a long repetition of fatigue and butchery. She blinked and made her way to the tactical station. There was little information about the newcomer, just the image of a ship as the light reached them. It was flying no colors.

"Make sure we're flying New London colors on the hull, Chevis," she called to the signals console.

With no masts stepped there as little in the way of signaling *Belial* could do, and she'd never been made a proper ship of the New London fleet, in any case, so she had no number to identify her. There was little she could do to flee, either, with her masts in the hold and her rudder and plane still left at a higher orbit. The best they could do was flee in normal-space.

"Aye, sir."

Alexis studied the plot.

"It's gone, sir, transitioned back out."

Alexis tensed. "Set us a course out of orbit," she ordered. For a ship to transition to normal space and then back to *darkspace* so quickly, it had to be expecting trouble. What they'd do now that they'd gathered enough information to know *Belial* was the only ship in system would determine Alexis' next action — either greet a force from New London, or hope to flee the Hanoverese again.

"Transition!" Leyman called out. "Same ship and it's clearing the Lagrangian point, sir! Still no colors."

Alexis started for the tactical console, but had hardly taken a step before Leyman called out again.

"Transition, L1," he said. "Two masts, square-rigged."

"Mister Dobb, pipe *All Hands*, if you please," Alexis said. "If they're Hanoverese we may ha —"

"Transition ... *multiple transitions!*" Leyman all but yelped. "L1, multiple transitions ... L4 and L5, multiple transitions!"

"Calmly, Leyman," Alexis said.

She rested her hands on the navigation plot and narrowed her eyes. So many ships, so whose fleet was it? Hanover or New London? The hands were rushing to respond to the bosun's call, but Alexis was at a loss for what to do next. If the fleet, whoever it belonged to, was using those three Lagrangian points, then they'd surely be using L2 and L3 as well, or at least have ships there to stop her from escaping. They'd see L3, opposite the moon on the planet's far side, when their orbit took them around — L2 was out behind the moon and they'd not see what might be transitioning there until it came around the moon.

Even if *Belial* could break orbit and escape, though, she had nowhere to go. Her masts were unstepped and her rudders were in a higher orbit. There was nowhere to run.

"Sir, I can't keep up," Leyman said. "They're no sooner transitioning than they clear the Lagrangian point and more come."

"Any signals at all, Chevis?"

"Nothing, sir. No signals and no colors."

There were over thirty ships on the navigation plot, with more appearing every moment as the light from their transition reached *Belial*. Alexis tried to make sense of the plot. If they were

Hanoverese, then *Belial* was well and truly caught. With multiple enemies at each Lagrangian point there was no way they could escape.

Thirty ships ... how so many? Our fleet was no more than forty-five without the transports and Hanover's was no larger ... Is it another fleet of Hanoverese transports?

"Sir," Leyman said, "there's some'at odd about these ..."

"What?" Alexis asked, studying the plot, looking for some way, any way, to retrieve her rudder and planes and then get her ship to a Lagrangian point if the incoming fleet proved hostile.

Leyman hesitated. "It's ... well, sir, there's nary a frigate nor a ship of the line in the lot, sir. It's all barques and sloops and smaller stuff, you see."

Alexis ran her fingers over the plot, bringing up what details *Belial's* computers could determine. Leyman was correct. There wasn't a ship larger than a sloop-of-war in the lot and few of them. Most were pinnaces, cutters, and even smaller. Some were the size of pilot boats, so small they had no business sailing the Dark and should have been limited to intrasystem sails.

What on earth ...

Alexis stared at the plot in awe, watching as the computer's count of ships in-system grew. It was over a hundred already and more ships continued to stream in, each quickly engaging its drive to clear the Lagrangian point for the next.

"I've a transmission from that first one ... it's Mister Artley, sir!"

ALEXIS STARED at the image on her plot for a moment in stunned silence. She wasn't at all certain what was most astonishing. The sheer number of ships — over two hundred fifty filled the plot now — their small size, Artley's presence, or the grinning face of Avrel Dansby behind Artley's in the transmission.

"Heard you had a grand bunch of lads needing a ride, Carew," Dansby said.

"How —"

"Your lad here." Dansby rested a hand on Artley's shoulder. "Pestered every captain of every bloody ship stopping at Alchiba with some utter rot about standing up and doing the right thing. Next thing we know, there's a bloody fleet forming. Stripped everything with sails from a two dozen systems around Alchiba. Pilot boats, ferries, ore barges, the lot of them."

Alexis watched the count of ships in system rise again as more transitioned. Her eyes burned at the sight of all those ships, so many captains and crews who'd left their safe, comfortable trade routes to put themselves in harm's way for others.

She met Dansby's eye on the screen.

"'And gentlemen in England now abed shall think themselves accursed they were not here,'" she whispered.

"Sir?" Artley asked.

Alexis smiled. "We'll have to see about the entertainment options in the gunroom, Mister Artley. A bit of the classics never goes amiss, I think."

"Yes, sir."

Alexis had to smile more at the puzzled look on Artley's face, which only grew more puzzled when she spoke again.

"I'll see you back aboard *Belial* once you've got this lot herded into proper orbits, Mister Artley."

"Me, sir?"

"It's your bloody fleet, isn't it? It's upon you to see they're squared away."

The next few hours were both chaotic and a revelation.

Alexis watched with growing satisfaction as Artley began transmitting orders to the arriving ships, slotting them into orbit with ease.

"It's a bit like stocking shelves, sir," he said when she commented on it, then quickly, "A moment, sir ... *Guide of Dunkirk*, your orbit is ten degrees following *Sundowner*, please fall back."

Alexis hid a smile and put Artley's transmissions to the side of the navigation plot, so that she could continue watching him. He'd certainly matured from the hesitant, unsure midshipman he'd been when *Shrewsbury* had arrived at *Nouvelle Paris*. Though they'd both, Artley and herself, had birthdays since then, so she should expect a bit of growing up from him.

She smiled again, caught Dansby's eye where he still stood behind Artley on *Marilyn's* quarterdeck, and set herself to contacting General Malicoat to tell him the situation might not be quite so hopeless any longer.

FIFTY-TWO

"I NEED SEVEN DAYS," Malicoat said. He frowned as he examined the map board at the rear of his tent, tracing lines and plans on it. "In seven days of hard travel, with your ship pounding away at them as you have been, the army can be here." He tapped the screen along a broad plain, then turned and nodded to Alexis. "It will be difficult, but we should be able to string the Hanoverese out chasing us so that they fail to notice the civilians and the bulk of the French recruits streaming off back to their homes."

Alexis nodded in turn. She understood the need.

No matter the number of little ships Artley had managed to arrive with, there weren't nearly enough of them to evacuate an entire planet's population. There was room for the New London troops and many of the French recruits who might choose to leave with the intent of returning one day with a larger force, but there was no room for the civilians of Giron who'd rushed to the New London forces looking for protection from the Hanoverese.

"It galls me to abandon them," Malicoat continued, "but with no sign of our own transports or fleet there's little good we can do here. I can't run forever, and if another fleet of Hanoverese transports arrives with more troops we're finished. If I had the full forces I'd asked for it would be different, but as it is ..." He shook his head and took a deep breath. "It is what it is."

"I'll do everything I can, sir," Alexis said.

"Seven days," Malicoat repeated.

In the end, they had three.

BELIAL WAS HALFWAY through another orbit, gun crews resting and preparing to feed the guns in another dive into Giron's mesosphere, repair crews on the hull replacing what had been burned away in the last pass.

The announcement of a ship's transition into normal space surprised everyone on the quarterdeck, as the last of Artley's parade of little ships had been slotted safely into orbit around Giron or its moon days before. The announcement that the ship was a New London frigate was met with first relief and then horror as the newcomer broadcast its message.

Both fleets, New London's and Hanover's, were on their way toward Giron, each maneuvering for position against the other, but there was no doubt in anyone's mind, least of all Alexis', what even a few Hanoverese warships could do to the unarmed civilian ships gathered around Giron. Moreover, the Hanoverese fleet was far larger than they'd thought when Admiral Chipley had sailed off in search of it. Perhaps it has been all along or perhaps a second fleet had joined it, but the Hanoverese now outnumbered New London in *darkspace* as well as on Giron's surface.

Malicoat agreed. The risk of the Hanoverese defeating New London's fleet and turning their attention to Giron, or of even a few of their ships slipping around the ends of a fleet action and getting amongst the transports was too great. Far better to evacuate all they could immediately, rather than risk the New London army being trapped on Giron with no transports at all.

Malicoat drove his forces mercilessly toward a new location that would allow the ships' boats to land and load troops.

Alexis drove *Belial* and her crew just as mercilessly to fire on the approaching Hanoverese troops and force them back from the New London columns.

Boats streamed down from the waiting ships and returned full of whatever mixture of troops, New London's and French, were ready to board. Any plan for order in the evacuation was abandoned.

Artley, back aboard *Belial*, was at the signals console continuously throughout, ordering the captains of the civilian ships about as though he were a senior post captain himself and their obedience was nothing but his due.

"Captain Gardy, you'll load when *Belial* orders it and not a moment sooner, sir," Artley said calmly into his microphone. "No, sir, I understand your concern, but your ship is a faster sailer and we're loading the slowest first so they can be off." He paused and sighed, turning from the console. "Sir? Captain Gardy of *Randall's Wand* wishes a word."

Alexis glanced over from her place at the navigation plot to find Artley looking to her. His face showed the fatigue she felt, with dark circles under his red-rimmed eyes. The actual loading of boats had gone on for well over twenty hours now and both she and Artley had been on the quarterdeck throughout.

This Gardy wasn't the first captain to give him trouble over the order of loading, nor the first to demand to speak to Artley's superior. She moved to the signals console where she'd be visible in Artley's pick up.

"Mister Artley has full command of the loading order, Captain Gardy," she said, not bothering to hear what Gardy had to say. "Send down your boats when he orders or break orbit and leave Giron empty. It's entirely your choice, sir."

She turned her back and walked back to the navigation plot. She could understand Gardy's worry, with the Hanoverese fleet growing ever nearer and no guarantee that Admiral Chipley's fleet could bring them to action. She'd expected, in fact, some of the little ships to flee, but none had — and neither would Gardy's, she suspected. The mettle that would drive a man to sail so far for others might be tested by the approaching enemy, but she doubted it would break.

"No, sir," she heard Artley say, "that's Captain Carew." She was called captain as a courtesy by virtue of commanding *Belial* and they'd decided that was how she should be named to the civilian captains. "She's the senior Naval officer in-system, sir ... I suppose you could go in search of Admiral Chipley, if you like." There was a long pause. "Thank you, sir. I'll see that it's your turn to load as soon as possible, I assure you."

Artley sat back in his chair and closed his eyes. Alexis returned to his side and rested a hand on his shoulder.

"Do you need a rest, Sterlyn?" she asked.

Artley shook himself and sat up.

"No, sir, we're nearly done — only a few hours more." He took a deep breath and scanned his console, lists of ships ordered by their sailing speed and capacity. "*Azure Rose,*" he said, keying his console, "proceed to L5 and transition. *Sewall's Folly,* release your boats for the southwest section of the landing field — blue lights mark it."

FIFTY-THREE

THE MAKESHIFT LANDING field was a scene of utter chaos. Boats streamed down out of the sky, landing in any open space as soon as another had lifted, despite any instructions they'd been given. Beside the field, clumps of soldiers were lined up, waiting to embark. Others lined the edges of the field, facing the milling crowds of civilians. Far in the distance there was the occasional sound of an explosion. The last of the little ships were loading and there'd been no word from Malicoat about getting him and his staff off of Giron. Alexis assumed he'd wish to travel on *Belial,* as it was the only Naval vessel in-system. Another frigate had appeared and left again, simply passing along the message that the two fleets were only hours away.

Alexis paused at the foot of her boat's steps and took in the scene.

"Dobb, leave two men with the pilot and have them keep the boat well-closed until we return. I don't like the look of that crowd."

"Aye, sir."

"And open the arms locker — stunsticks and batons for the lads, if you please."

Alexis waited while he complied and returned with the armed men. He handed her a holstered flechette pistol and belt.

"Thought you'd like some'at yerself, sir."

"Thank you, Dobb, yes." Another boat landed and a column of soldiers started for it. Shouts and calls rose from the crowd of civilians. "No, I don't like the look of this at all."

They made their way to the edge of the field and through the encampment to General Malicoat's headquarters, a larger, temporary building amidst the camp.

"I'm here to see General Malicoat if he has a moment," she said to the guard out front. *Or even if he hasn't.*

"*Que?*"

"Malicoat," Alexis said again. "*Le général, s'il vous plaît?*"

"*Oui. Attendez un moment.*"

The guard nodded and motioned for them to wait while he stepped inside.

"Dobb?" Alexis asked. "Do you find it at all odd that the guard speaks French, yet wears a New London uniform?"

Dobb shrugged. "Out o' their own, y'think, sir?"

Alexis frowned. "Come to that, I've seen not a single French uniform since we landed."

A moment later the guard returned and gestured for them to enter. They followed him through the building which, if it were possible, was a scene of more chaos than the field itself. Men and women rushed about, calling to each other in French yet all wearing New London uniforms, apparently bent on destroying every bit of equipment in the place.

The exception to this was Malicoat, an island of relative calm, seated at a desk and applying his thumb to a tablet over and over again. He looked up as they approached.

"Ah, Carew. What can I do for you?"

"Sir, I've sent several messages regarding the evacuation of you and your staff. There are only a dozen or so ships left loading, the fleets are only hours away, and once the last of the soldiers at the landing field board I fear you'll not be able to make your way through the civilian crowds."

Malicoat applied his thumb to his tablet again. "Yes, that." He sighed. "I'm afraid I owe you an apology for not replying to your earlier messages. Wanting to put off a difficult conversation, you see?"

"Sir?"

"I'm sorry to put you in this position, Carew, I truly am. You've shown yourself a good officer and I hate to be the cause of your experiencing your admiral's displeasure, but I'm afraid you'll have to tell Chipley that you've gone and lost me."

"Sir?" She realized she was repeating herself, but the man had thoroughly confused her. What did he mean to be lost when he was sitting right there?

"My staff, most of them, have already gone aboard other ships, but I'm not leaving, Carew. Be staying here. You should run along now."

Alexis blinked. Was the man insane? Spacers often claimed that those in the army were bloody lunatics, and she'd seen much on Giron to support that thought, but Malicoat seemed perfectly serious.

"Sir, the Hanoverese are closing. They'll overrun this position within an hour of the last boat lifting. You have to leave now."

Malicoat applied his thumb to his tablet once more, then set it aside. "Look here, Carew, I'll explain as quickly as I can, but I have a great deal to do and you have a short time to get back to your ship."

"Sir, I —"

"Just listen so that you can explain to Chipley and the others that you saw I'm set in my decision and there was nothing you could do. Those ships up there are a marvel. A bloody miracle that we'd no cause to hope for, but we're still having to leave behind half the French troops raised on this world. There's space for New London's forces and an equal number of French, then we're filling in the corners with civilians as best we can.

"Bonnin and I have sent as many of the remaining French troops as we could to melt away back to their homes, but the rest are our rear guard for this evacuation. Most of them come from towns that don't exist any more thanks to the Hanoverese, and they don't plan to survive the day."

He rubbed his eyes and looked at her, and Alexis saw just how tired he was. More so than she herself was or even her crew.

"Those lads deserve better than that and I intend to be here to give the orders that ensure they don't throw their lives away. Once the last boat is away, there's no reason for the fighting to go on, nor for any of these lads to die needlessly. Oh, there'll be reprisals from the Hanoverese, but I have something of a plan for that, as well." He gestured toward his tablet. "I talked it over with Bonnin and we've agreed he can't do it. The Republic's not yet officially at war with Hanover, so far as we know, only New London is, so his staying would only make things worse. As of this morning, the local lads have enlisted in a new regiment. The 11th Penduli Foot, to be clear. I'm just finalizing their enlistment records here myself." He took a deep breath. "It's a shallow ruse, the Hanoverese will see right through it — not least because there's not a one of the new lads who can speak a bloody word of the Queen's English."

"Sir, is this at all wise?"

"Nothing about this expedition was wise, Carew. It was half-done and on the cheap from the start." He pointed at the men and women rushing about the headquarters. "And it may make no difference — they may still shoot the lot as traitors — but whatever the Hanoverese do to these men, it'll be done to New London soldiers and witnessed by a New London officer — and New London will bloody well hold them accountable for it. There'll be nothing swept under the rug here if I have anything to say about it."

Malicoat rose and offered her his hand. "Go back to your ship, Carew. Get that fleet of bloody miracles you managed back to New London safely with my lads." He smiled sadly. "I shall sleep better here with the thought they might be coming back for me some day."

FIFTY-FOUR

ALEXIS LEFT the headquarters building and gathered up Dobb and the others.

"Back to the boat, Mister Dobb."

"Without the general?"

She started for the landing field.

"General Malicoat will be staying to look after his men."

Alexis looked around, the implications of what she saw being driven home. This really was the last bit of time they had and there were still so many who hadn't made it aboard the ships. She knew the bulk of the army had been loaded aboard and the camp, except near the headquarters and landing field, was virtually deserted, a shadow of its former bustle, but there were still so many.

Not to mention the civilians who'd come along with the army. The Hanoverese had destroyed whole towns they'd suspected of collaborating with the New London forces. What would they do to those found in the camp itself?

That thought brought Marie and Ferrau to mind — what would become of them?

Damn me, but Belial's *my ship until they take her from me. Captains have taken guests on a voyage any number of times.*

She considered. No, she suspected things would not go well here for Marie — a single girl from a rebellious planet. The Hanoverese wouldn't look favorably on her and who knew what they'd do if they suspected Ferrau's father was a New London officer?

"Mister Dobb, detail half the men to return to the boat and make ready. You and the other half with me."

They made their way across the camp to where Marie was housed, but she wasn't at her tent. No one was, and the tents nearby were empty as well. It seemed as though every part of the camp was deserted, save the landing field. Occasionally a messenger drove by, but that was all. Once, as they trooped through the ghost town of the living tents, they did come across a man. He was midway through ransacking a tent, stripping off a French uniform and pulling on whatever bits of clothing he found that would fit him.

As Alexis and her troop of spacers came into view, the man froze.

Dobb made to move toward him, but Alexis grabbed his arm.

"No."

"He's looting and deserting, sir."

Alexis stared at the man, still frozen with one boot off. His uniform jacket and shirt lay on the ground and he'd pulled on a rough workman's shirt, but not yet changed his uniform trousers.

"He's making his way as best he can with what's to come. Leave him," Alexis said, making a point of turning and walking on the far side of the rough lane between the tents. "He's afraid and he's reason to be. Malicoat's ruse isn't even worthy of the name. If he thinks he can make his way better amongst the civilians, then so be it. As for looting —" She looked around. "— I suspect anything of real value is close to hand with those at the landing fields."

They walked back to the fields where there were barely half the boats there'd been when they'd left and no more landing. The soldiers were nearly done loading and some civilians were being allowed aboard.

Alexis checked her tablet for the time and found that there was not much left of the deadline Malicoat had advised. She led her men to the back of the crowd, but didn't see how she'd be able to find Marie in the mass of people, even assuming she was there at all.

"We'll make our way around to our boat and hope for a miracle," she said.

Dobb nodded and they started walking. Dobb and the men scanned the crowd, hopping up from time to time for a better view.

"*Marie!*" Alexis called into the crowd as they walked. "*Marie Autin!*" From time to time someone in the crowd would turn and meet her eyes and she'd add, "*Aidez-moi!* I'm looking for — bloody hell, find? *Trouber? Trouver, Marie Autin!*"

Most turned away, but some would cup their hands to their mouths and add their shouts to hers.

Their boat drew closer and closer, and Alexis had begun to despair of finding the two, when one of the old men repeating her shouts stopped and cocked his head.

"*Que?*" Alexis heard, then, "*Marie Autin? Ici!*"

The man made a come here gesture further into the crowd, then turned and waved at Alexis.

"Dobb —" But the master's mate was already moving, forming the point of Alexis' men as the spacers waded into the crowd, jostling and parting it with elbows and knees until Alexis saw them turn and come back.

When they returned, Marie and Ferrau at their center, Alexis wrapped her arms around the girl.

"*Mademoiselle* Alexis?"

Alexis pushed her away and held her at arms length.

"Do you wish to try and get away, Marie?" she asked, slowly so that there'd be no misunderstanding. "You and Ferrau? Away from Giron?"

"*Oui!* It is why we come here — they say some will be allowed." Marie said immediately.

"Come on, then. Dobb, keep the men around her and Ferrau — this crowd is getting more restless."

"Aye sir."

They made their way a bit away from the landing field, back amongst the tents again, to move along without drawing attention to themselves. The crowd was twenty bodies deep ahead of them as they approached the field near *Belial's* boat.

Alexis moved into the center of the group of spacers with Marie and followed Dobb through the crowd, he and her spacers pushing and shoving their way forward. She clenched Marie's hand tightly in her own and looked back frequently to see that Marie had a firm hold on Ferrau. There were fewer than a dozen boats on the field now and the only soldiers still on the field were those watching the crowds. She assumed they were part of the rear guard who'd be staying behind. Streams of civilians made their way from the crowd to the boats, and Alexis wondered how those who'd leave had finally been chosen.

They were jostled and shoved as they made their way. Struck by elbows, nearly tripped, and all but deafened by the shouts and cries from those around them.

They reached the edge of the crowd, which Alexis saw was far nearer *Belial's* boat than when she left. The soldiers there recognized New London spacers and pushed the crowd aside to let them through. Alexis followed Dobb past the line, but the soldiers tried to stop Marie.

"*Non!*" Alexis spun around and grabbed the man's arm. She pulled Marie around her, placing herself between the girl and the soldier. "She's coming with me!"

The soldier — a captain by his insignia, which was on a New London uniform, so might not have reflected the man's actual rank — reached for Marie again. He spoke, but so rapidly that Alexis couldn't understand, something about lists and not being able to control the crowd, but there were shouts from the crowd, perhaps some of them sensing that someone was getting aboard a ship while they weren't, and the captain turned back to try and close the gap. The crowd pushed forward and the soldiers had to fall back, bumping into Alexis and Marie.

"Hell —" Alexis turned, spun Marie around and shoved her toward the boat, following after.

Halfway there they passed Dobb, who'd stopped and doubled back when he saw they weren't close behind.

"C'mon, sir! I don't like the looks of this."

"No," Alexis said. She slowed. Marie had reached the stairs and was safely onboard. She slowed more, stopped, then turned to look at the crowd. Dobb pulled at her arm. Malicoat wasn't coming, his staff was already aboard another ship, and Belial had room — not much, but some. "No, I don't like the looks of it either, Mister Dobb."

She ran her eyes over the crowd, not seeing it as the frightening, faceless mass they'd just fought their way through, but as individuals, no different or less worthy than Marie. She turned back to Dobb.

"Mister Dobb ..."

Alexis saw that Dobb wasn't looking at her. He was staring past her at the crowd, eyes wide and glistening. He turned to her, blinking.

"No more'n thirty, sir," he said. "Not and have air and water enough for the trip."

Alexis nodded. "Get aboard and have all the lads at the entry port. Tell Phibbs to lift the moment my foot's on the bloody steps, you understand?"

"Aye, sir."

Alexis waited until Dobb was on the boat's steps and then walked back to the line of soldiers. The captain glanced over his shoulder at her approach and he left the line to meet her.

"*Vite!*" he said pointing at the boat. "*Fuir!* Go!"

Alexis grasped his arm and drew him close.

"*Trente*," Alexis said. "Thirty. I can take thirty. *Je peux prendre trente.*"

The captain drew back, eyes wide, and shook his head. He looked from the boat to the crowd. "*Non, je ...*"

Alexis understood his hesitation. Two more boats lifted and a moan went up from the crowd. She wondered herself if this was a bad idea, if she was about to set something in motion that couldn't be stopped. She wasn't sure what she'd do if the whole crowd rushed the boat, nor was she sure that any of the civilians should come aboard *Belial*, not even Marie and Ferrau. *Belial* was a warship. What if there was an action? There'd be no vacsuits for any of them.

But *Belial* was a small ship, inconsequential in the scheme of the fleet actions. Her job would be to herd and harry the ships of the convoy to stay on course and hurry themselves along, not engage other ships. That would be for the frigates and ships of the line. *Belial* would be as safe as the other transports.

The high-pitched whine of a railgun sounded, followed by an explosion from the far side of the encampment. The captain jerked and stared in that direction for a long moment, then nodded to Alexis.

"*Trente*," he said and pointed to the boat. "*Vite.*"

Alexis squeezed his arm. "*Vite*, too bloody right, *vite*," she agreed.

She rushed to the foot of the boat's stairs as the captain called out to his men. He addressed the crowd for a moment. Alexis couldn't hear what he said, but the crowd pushed forward and the line of soldiers firmed. The captain reached past his men and began pulling people through the line, mostly women and children Alexis saw. A man pushed a woman into the captain's grasp and she was pulled through the line despite turning and clutching at him. An infant was handed over the heads of the soldiers, to be grabbed by someone already through the line. Then Alexis had to turn away as the first of the refugees reached the boat.

Dobb had returned to the foot of the stairs with her. Together they helped the running, stumbling people board, shoving them up the stairs to where waiting spacers grabbed them and pulled them inside.

Alexis counted silently to herself as they passed her, she followed Dobb up the stairs when the last had gone by. True to her orders, she felt the boat lurch and lift from the ground before she was inside and might have fallen if strong hands hadn't grasped her arms and pulled.

The passenger compartment of the boat was crowded, so she went forward to join the pilot in the cockpit.

It took but a single glance from the cockpit to make her wish she'd remained in the enclosed, windowless passenger compartment.

Theirs was the last boat lifting and the field was still crowded with civilians. The soldiers there, with nothing left to guard, were streaming away, making their way to the other side of the crowd and through the encampment. As the boat rose, Alexis could see where they were going. To the far side of the encampment where a thin line of their fellows was already engaged with the approaching Hanoverese.

Alexis tried to raise Malicoat on the radio to tell him that the last boat was away, that he could issue the orders to stand down, but there was no response and the enemy columns came on.

Sweet lord, what have we wrought here?

FIFTY-FIVE

Once back aboard *Belial*, Alexis gave orders to make way as soon as the boat was unloaded. Even before the boat's hatch was sealed and the boat itself fully secured to *Belial's* keel, the ship was in motion and heading for the nearest Lagrangian point. Ahead of them, the last few ships of the evacuation streamed for it as well.

They transitioned to *darkspace* and Alexis saw just how close-run things had been. The fleets, New London's and Hanover's, were actually within sight of Giron's Lagrangian points, even now falling into their formations as they closed with one another, all thought of further maneuvering given up now that they'd arrived at their target. The lights from the sails of the evacuation fleet were also visible, a long stream of them carrying off into the distance away from the coming action and towards New London space.

Alexis wanted to put *Belial* about and point her at the coming battle, but knew her ship would be useless there. That was a place for the massive two- and three-decked ships of the line. The smaller ships of those fleets, even the frigates, were forming themselves behind the two lines in order to repeat signals or, just possibly, come to their aid if one of their larger sisters needed it. *Belial* would have no use there.

Besides, I have my orders.

Escort the evacuation fleet, keep them in line and on course, and at least attempt to deal with any stray Hanoverese or pirates they encountered on the way back to New London. Alexis eyed the two fleets one more time.

Unlikely, that. Every Hanoverese must be there and no pirate worth the name would find himself where so many warships are sailing.

They sailed on for nearly an hour as the evacuation fleet beat to windward away from Giron. Once they were well away from the system, the winds would become more variable, but this close they blew steadily toward the system, forcing the ships to tack back and forth to remain on course.

Or wear, Alexis thought in frustration as another of her charges did just that. The captain must not have had much confidence in his crew's or ship's ability to tack across the eye of the wind without being caught aback and winding up in irons, unable to make any way at all with the wind dead on his bow. Instead, he wore ship, turning away from their desired course and falling back to turn and take the winds on his other side, all the while losing precious ground.

"Mister Artley, a signal to *King Orry*, if you please. If she must wear instead of tack, then she is to do so less frequently. It may take her out of the convoy's formation —" Alexis eyed the ragged stream of ships on the navigation plot. "— such as it is — but at least she'll not interfere with the others and will lose less ground overall."

"Aye, sir."

"Lieutenant Carew, sir?"

"Yes, Leyman?"

"You'll want to see this, sir."

Alexis crossed the tactical console. Leyman was watching the impending action of the two fleets and had plots of their movements displayed.

"You see this one here, sir?"

Alexis did and a chill went through her. One of the Hanoverese frigates had hung back, well back from the course of the two fleets as they began to edge toward each other for action. This frigate had fallen far behind them and then turned to cross their sterns on a course that took it directly toward the evacuation fleet.

ALEXIS CLENCHED her fist in frustration. She wanted to pound it on the plot, but that wouldn't change what she saw. The Hanoverese frigate had got around *Belial* and was now to windward of them on the starboard tack. *Belial* could come a bit closer to the wind than the ship-rigged frigate, but not enough to close the distance in any reasonable amount of time. Meanwhile, the frigate's greater sail area was helping it gain on the heavily laden ships of the convoy.

"Roll us ten degrees to port, Mister Dobb, and edge us a point nearer the wind," Alexis said.

"Aye, sir."

The maneuver might gain them another, barely noticeable, bit of speed, but nothing that was obvious on the plot. Meanwhile the frigate had closed to within gun range of the nearest ship of the convoy, *Mona's Queen*, a wallowing packet that had been one of the last to take on civilians from Giron. She must have been having trouble with her particle projectors, for her sails were dimmer than they should be and she was struggling along at the tail end of the convoy.

"Frigate's falling off the wind, sir," Leyman said.

Alexis felt a chill as she watched the plot. The frigate fell of the wind, turned, and presented its full broadside to *Mona's Queen's* vulnerable stern.

Surely not. Surely they'll fire a chaser and let them strike —

"Firing," Leyman announced.

Alexis' hand flew to her mouth as the Hanoverese frigate's guns fired, a full broadside, poorly aimed and most missing their target, but enough finding their mark that *Mona's Queen* all but disappeared in a roiling ball of plasma.

"More than one made it through to the fusion plant," Dobb said. "The bastards."

Alexis blinked to clear her eyes. There couldn't even be any question that the Hanoverese had thought the other ship was armed — *Mona's Queen* not only had no gunports, but there was no way she could have carried even a single gun that would so much as scratch a frigate's hull — but they'd given her no warning and no chance to strike. Moreover, the packet's hull was so thin that it wouldn't have been able to stand up to even a single shot. Even *Belial's* hull offered more protection.

"Coming back to close-hauled," Leyman said.

Having fallen off the wind to bring her guns to bear on *Mona's Queen*, the frigate had now turned back toward the wind to continue the pursuit of the convoy.

Alexis studied the plot. There was no way *Belial* could bring the frigate to action, and even if she could, they'd be able to do no more than delay it a few minutes. A handful of broadsides from those guns and *Belial* would meet the same fate as the packet.

Perhaps more than a handful, if they're all aimed as poorly as that last. Not that it did Mona's Queen *a bit of good.*

"Mister Artley, has there been any response to our signal?"

"No, sir, none."

Artley's voice was strained and hoarse. Alexis went to his side and laid a hand on his shoulder. She could see on his signals console that *Belial* was, indeed, still flying the signals she'd ordered, *Enemy in Sight* and *Require Assistance*, but it was as though the rest of the New London fleet, now much farther away and engaged in action with the Hanoverese, had all but forgotten about them.

They were likely too far away now, but Alexis had hoped for some assistance. Even a single frigate let loose from its duty behind the line would have been helpful.

"They just killed them," Artley whispered, his voice breaking. "They just ..."

"Steady, Mister Artley." She looked down and met Artley's gaze, his eyes were full and red-rimmed.

"What can we do? We have to ... What can we do, sir?"

Alexis wished she had an answer to that. *Belial* was at her very best point of sail, she was sure, and every scrap of sail that might help had been bent on. The particle projectors charging the sails were at their highest setting and would likely burn themselves out if this kept on, but she needed every bit of speed she could get from the ship if she was be of any help at all to the convoy.

And what help can I be?

Belial was outgunned and the frigate's guns were heavier as well. They'd blast through *Belial's* hull with ease.

"*Fenella* has struck, sir."

Alexis gave Artley's shoulder another squeeze and went back to the navigation plot. *Fenella*, another packet from the same firm as *Mona's Queen*, had struck her colors and doused her sails as the Hanoverese frigate approached. She must have seen what the frigate had done to her consort and determined there was no hope but to wish for mercy from the oncoming frigate. She slowed as the morass of dark matter around them dragged at her hull without her charged sails to pull her along.

The Hanoverese frigate closed, never changing course, and at first Alexis thought it would sail by, accepting *Fenella's* surrender. But as it drew level with the packet, the frigate fired.

Again, many of the shots missed, flying wide of the mark or going above and below *Fenella*, but enough struck.

Even one is enough ... they've holed the main deck and more ... and none of those aboard with a vacsuit.

"Murderous bastards," Dobb muttered.

"*King Orry* is tacking," Leyman announced, his voice raw and shaking. "She'll not make it."

Alexis looked around the quarterdeck. Her crew's faces were set, jaws clenched and nostrils flaring in anger.

She looked back down at her plot. *King Orry*, another packet and, if Alexis remembered correctly, from the same shipping line as *Fenella* and *Mona's Queen*, was the next in line on the frigate's point of sail. Alexis could see that Leyman was correct; *King Orry's* tack was too slow, she didn't have the momentum to swing past the eye of the wind and her turn had slowed.

Alexis closed her eyes. She barely heard Leyman's announcement that the frigate had drawn even with the helpless packet and fired yet again. There was nothing, nothing at all she could do. She ran the points of sail through her mind over and over again, but nothing changed. *Belial* might, if she was lucky, be able to bring the frigate to action far up the line of the convoy, but by then how many more ships, along with their helpless cargoes, would be butchered?

Even then, if she were finally able to bring the frigate to action, *Belial* would simply meet the same fate. *Belial* was a warship, though small, and would be able to face more than a single broadside from the frigate, but eventually she'd succumb and the frigate would resume its butchery.

Still, even a few minutes delay would certainly save some of the convoy. Once outside the immediate area of Giron, the winds would become more variable. Instead of blowing steadily toward the system, they might offer a better opportunity for the convoy to escape, even if it meant scattering in multiple directions.

None of which would happen if she couldn't bring the frigate to action.

"Roll us ten more to port, Mister Dobb," she said, "and I'll have a single gun to leeward, if you please."

"Aye, sir," Dobb said.

The Hanoverese would see that, surely. A single gun, fired to leeward, was a challenge. An invitation to fight. Perhaps she could goad that frigate's captain into an engagement.

"No change in course, sir," Leyman said after a few minutes.

Alexis shook her head and examined the plot. The next ship in line was larger than the packets, but just as defenseless. An intrasystem ferry called *Royal Daffodil* — barely qualified to sail the Dark at all and never out of sight of a system's Lagrangian points, but her crew had set off along with all the others in the convoy and now there were over a thousand men and women stuffed inside that thin hull.

She took a deep breath and her rage fell away, a deep calmness settling in its place.

"Mister Dobb, see that all the guns are manned, port and starboard both, if you please."

"Aye, sir."

As the message was passed, Alexis considered what little German she could remember. Oddly, she found that she'd gleaned something suitable from *Marilyn's* crew during their travels.

"Mister Artley, when the guns fire, I want this signal bent on. Put it on both masts and the hull itself, do you understand? I want that frigate to see it easily." She tapped a message on the plot and sent it to Artley's signals console. "You'll have to spell it out, just as it is."

"Aye, sir."

"Wear ship, Mister Dobb," Alexis said. "Put us on the port tack."

Dobb stared at her as he passed the order. Men in vacsuits streamed out of the ship through the sail locker to trim the sails.

Alexis could understand his confusion. The port tack would put them on a diverging course from the frigate, still moving upwind, but edging in the opposite direction. Wearing ship instead of tacking would set them to losing even more ground to the frigate and the rest of the convoy. But it would also put them, for a moment, with *Belial's* stern pointing directly at the frigate.

"Both broadsides, on my mark." She waited until just before *Belial* was showing the frigate her stern. "Fire."

Belial emptied her guns into *darkspace*. While a single gun to leeward might be a challenge, emptying one's guns and showing the enemy her vulnerable stern was a gesture of contempt.

"What's that mean, sir?" Dobb asked, brow furrowed as he studied the signal spelled out on *Belial's* mast and hull.

"*Feigling* means coward, if I remember correctly."

"And the other? What's that, *arschficker*?"

Alexis felt herself flush. "Something somewhat less complimentary. If that frigate's captain has no honor, then perhaps he has some small bit of pride."

Alexis stared at the plot, willing the other captain to react.

Have a shred of pride, damn you, Alexis thought. *At least deal with me before you kill more of the helpless.*

Not that *Belial* was so far from helpless herself, not in comparison to the frigate's guns.

Yet nothing happened as *Belial* continued her turn and settled on the port tack, now widening the distance from the frigate.

Then the frigate's sails seemed to shudder. It fell off the wind, just the tiniest bit, perhaps to gain a bit more speed, and began to turn toward the wind's eye. Its bow crossed the eye of the winds and the frigate fell back onto the port tack.

Away from the convoy and towards *Belial*.

FIFTY-SIX

Alexis kept *Belial* on the port tack as the Hanoverese frigate approached. She could sail closer to the wind than the larger ship and took advantage of that. Though the frigate had started more to windward of *Belial*, the loss of speed in tacking and *Belial's* ability to angle more sharply toward the wind had forced it to cross her path astern.

Allowing that was a risk, as the frigate was able to fall of the wind a bit as it crossed *Belial's* path and fire at her vulnerable stern, but Alexis had noted the Hanoverese's gunnery in the attacks on the transports. In those, the frigate had held its fire until it was quite close and even then many of the shots had missed. She was also confident that *Belial* was more nimble than the larger frigate and she'd have a chance to protect her vulnerable stern.

She looked up from the plot as the hatchway opened and Dobb entered. He made his way to her side.

"I've shuffled them around as best we can, I think," he said quietly. "Some in the engineering spaces, the magazine, and up forward in the hold where it's most protected."

Alexis nodded. She was trying not to think too much about the unsuited civilians aboard *Belial*. She'd promised them safety and then taken them into battle, but she had to weigh those thirty lives against the hundreds aboard each of the transports.

"That Marie and the babe I sent to the magazine."

"Thank you, Dobb."

The magazine was the most protected part of the ship. Deep in the center of the hold, just forward of the fusion plant, and wrapped in a bulkhead just as thick as the plant's. It was where the capacitors in the shot for the guns would be recharged and it was designed to be able to do so even if the rest of the ship were holed and opened to the electronic-suppressing radiations of *darkspace*.

She turned back to the plot, forcing the thought of those women and children from her mind, and watched the image of the frigate, brought inboard by the ship's optics, closely. She could just make out the suited figures of the frigate's crew on the hull, ready to pull on the lines to keep the sails full of wind.

In a moment, there it was, the suited figures began moving, the frigate's sails seemed to shiver as its course began to change.

"Now! Hard to starboard!" she ordered quickly.

The helmsman responded and *Belial* seemed to pivot in place. She fell off the wind, turning toward the frigate.

"Fire!" Alexis yelled just as *Belial's* starboard side squarely faced the frigate.

Bolts of shot lashed out and a moment later the frigate's port side lit up with its own fire.

"Hard to port! Put us back close-hauled!"

"Close-hauled, aye," Boothroyd acknowledged from the helm.

The frigate's shot arrived before *Belial* began to turn back toward the wind, most of it passing above or below and only two of the twenty bolts striking home. Alexis had no time to see where *Belial's* fire had struck, though, because one of the frigate's hits was directly on the quarterdeck's starboard side.

A spot on the starboard bulkhead the size of a man's fist seemed to soften and bulge as the laser spent its energy into the tough thermoplastic of *Belial's* hull. It wasn't enough to burn its way entirely through, but it was enough to soften and melt the spot for a moment. And to form at least one small hole, as the high-pitched whistle of escaping air filled the quarterdeck.

Before Alexis could even speak to give the order, Leyman was in motion. He grasped one of the patches kept around the quarterdeck and rushed to the bulkhead, slapping it in place to seal the breach, then returning to his station as though nothing at all had happened.

Boothroyd, at the helm, had barely twitched at the damage, staying steady and settling *Belial* back on her previous point of sail.

Alexis' lips curved in a fond smile as she looked around the quarterdeck at her crew. They were such good lads, calm and steady at their stations, though she did note that more than one had edged his vacsuit helmet a bit closer to his station. Even young Artley, after an initial jump of startlement, was calmly scanning his signals console.

She thought of those on the far more vulnerable gundeck, going about the business of reloading the guns in the face of a much more dangerous foe. None of them had balked at her orders nor questioned the need to engage the frigate. She couldn't help but feel pride in them, nor feel fear for what she was about to lead them into.

ALEXIS WAS able to dance with the frigate twice more in that way, turning *Belial* with it to take its broadside on her starboard side while returning one of her own. Between each exchange, she returned to sailing as close to the wind as she could, each time opening up just a bit more distance between the two ships. Slow and poor as the frigate's gunnery was, she began to have some hope that *Belial* could delay it for some time.

With that third exchange, though, the frigate was either lucky or more clever than she. The frigate's captain had switched to bar shot, a type that sacrificed strength in favor of spreading the laser's force along a long, narrow line instead of focusing it into one spot as the roundshot did.

Again, most of the shot missed, but one found *Belial's* mizzen mast close to the hull. It failed to slice through completely, but it weakened the mast enough that it began to bow, and Alexis was forced to reduce sail. That slowed *Belial* and, while she could still sail as close to the wind as the frigate, the enemy would be able to outpace her. If the frigate could gain enough room ahead of *Belial*, it could tack and pass in front to rake her bow, while the reduced sail and weakened mast would make it more dangerous for *Belial* to tack in response.

"Let us fall two points off the wind, Boothroyd."

"Aye, sir."

Alexis concentrated on the plot before her. She sought some clever maneuver that would avoid the inevitable, but found none. Now the frigate had the advantage both in speed and how close to the wind it could sail. It would rapidly narrow the gap and, with a shorter range, its gunners would surely improve.

As though in response to her thought, another shot struck the hull outside the quarterdeck and Leyman leaped to patch yet another pin-size breach.

"Mister Dobb, take charge of the men on the sails. If the quarterdeck is breeched we'll lose the helm. I wish you to keep us even with that frigate, even if it means closing the range, but not so closely that they could board us." A boarding would be disastrous, as the frigate likely had a crew of hundreds.

"Aye, sir."

She scanned the plot. They were moving farther and farther away from the main action and still none of the other New London ships had acknowledged her signals, nor were any sailing away from the battle to render her aid.

"Mister Artley, I believe the time for signals is well past. Take charge of the gundeck, please. Fire as you bear, targeting their sails first and the gundeck second. I should admire it if our rate of fire were somewhat higher than that frigate's."

"Aye, sir." Artley rose, pulled his vacsuit helmet over his head, and left the quarterdeck.

Dobb made his way back to her side and spoke softly. "With no one on the signals, sir, what if you should need to signal ... what if we must strike our colors?"

Alexis turned her head and met his eyes. She shook her head slowly. "Every minute we delay that frigate may mean another of those transports well away." She watched his face carefully to see that he understood. "This is where we stand."

Dobb took a deep breath and nodded.

"Aye, sir."

He grasped his helmet and left the quarterdeck.

Alexis ground her teeth together in frustration as she found herself with surprisingly little to do. Boothroyd kept his eye on both the winds and the Hanoverese frigate, adjusting his helm as she'd ordered to keep the enemy ship from closing the distance any faster than could be avoided. Still the range closed though. The guns were firing independently as quickly as they could be reloaded, so she had no need to order the firing by broadside.

With each exchange of fire, a runner came to the quarterdeck to report on damage. Most was not nearly so bad as she'd feared, but the Hanoverese gunners were becoming more accurate as the range closed.

Then, as though the frigate's gunners had found their preferred range, the quarterdeck was struck again. Leyman managed to slap another patch on the bulkhead in short time, but Alexis ordered her quarterdeck crew to seal their helmets. It would make communication more difficult and they'd be uncomfortable from the heat and stuffiness, but they'd be safe from decompression.

Just as she sealed her own helmet, the quarterdeck was hit and breached again. The frigate must have fired in broadside, but Alexis couldn't tell just how many shots had struck. The weakened bulkhead gave way and shot lanced across the compartment, splintering into smaller bolts reflected from any surface that couldn't absorb its energy.

Droplets of molten hull material spattered through the compartment, damaging men and equipment without regard. Some consoles were destroyed by the shot itself, while others simply dimmed and went out from the influx of *darkspace* radiation.

Alexis' helmet went silent as her radio died, leaving her with only the sound of her own breathing. The quarterdeck still had lighting — that was distributed throughout the ship by optics and would only go out if the fibers were cut — but all of the consoles and controls were dead. Men were down all around her, some moving feebly, others still, and those who were uninjured, or only slightly so, rushing to their aid.

Her right leg stung where something had struck her, either a beam splintered off the shot or a molten drop of hull material, she didn't know, but a quick glance showed her that her suit had sealed. Her leg would hold her weight and there were both others more in need of aid and more important tasks.

In any case, *Belial* had no surgeon aboard to see to the wounded. The best that could be done was to take them down to the orlop above the hold and hope they weren't struck again. Anyone who could move at all would be needed on the sails and the guns.

Alexis grabbed the nearest spacer who looked whole and pressed her helmet to his.

"The quarterdeck's lost! Send the ablest to the sails and the rest to the guns!"

"Aye, sir!"

Belial shuddered and Alexis knew that meant there was damage to the inertial compensators. The force of the shot vaporizing portions of the hull was enough to knock the ship about.

Alexis staggered and grasped the navigation plot to steady herself.

Please, she thought to *Belial*, one hand caressing the edge of the darkened plot. *I'm sorry, but it's needful.*

She rushed to the hatchway and grasped the handle, pulling it open to face what had become of her gundeck.

FIFTY-SEVEN

Alexis reached the gundeck just as the Hanovese frigate fired again. Bolts of shot flashed through the open space of the deck. New holes appeared in what was left of the hull, most overlapping with damage that was already there.

The shot went straight through the hull facing the frigate, through the center wall that divided the deck, and out the far side. For a wonder, none of *Belial's* guns were struck, nor any of the remaining crew, though she saw several men flinch back and slap at their arms or legs as droplets of melted thermoplastic from the hull struck them. Their suits would seal behind such damage, if the droplets made it through, but they'd bear the scars.

Even with so much damage, though, the crews were working diligently at their guns, quickly getting off yet another broadside, ragged though it was with no coherent command to fire — the guns were firing independently now, but *Belial's* crews were so well-drilled that they were each loaded and firing again within a second of the others.

That was what had allowed them to last this long, Alexis knew. For whatever reason, whether a lack of training or experience, the frigate's broadsides were coming slowly and poorly-aimed, while

Belial's crews had been drilled to beyond reason. First aboard *Shrews-bury*, with Captain Euell's demands for ever faster broadsides, then aboard *Belial* herself, with Alexis' use of drills to alleviate the boredom around Giron, and finally by day after day of feeding the guns as they bombarded the Hanoverese columns.

Belial was sending two, three, and sometimes four broadsides into the frigate for every one in return.

Alexis scanned the gundeck for who was left standing. With so much damage their suit radios weren't working here either, likely nowhere in the ship — what was left of the gallenium nets that once covered the gunports and kept out the *darkspace* radiation would have been useless even without the damage to the rest of the hull.

Spacers were still making their way to and from the aft compan-ionway carrying shot, so the magazine was undamaged. They'd certainly fired all of *Belial's* ready-shot and would be relying on the magazine to recharge the shot's capacitors. That in itself was a good sign, as it meant the magazine and the surrounding engineering spaces had not been holed, nor the fusion plant.

Of course if the fusion plant is holed, we'll, none of us, either know or worry again.

The survivors from the quarterdeck, those she'd not ordered out to the sails, streamed past her to join the guncrews. She spotted Artley, midshipman's stripes spotted and blackened with burns from splashing hull material, and made her way over to press her helmet against his.

"Sir? You've left the quarterdeck?"

"The quarterdeck's holed, Mister Artley, and we've but one particle projector working for the sails. The guns are all we have to work with now."

Alexis could see Artley's face blanch at the news of how much damage *Belial* had taken.

"Shouldn't we strike, sir?"

"We stand, Mister Artley. So long as there's a gun to fire, we stand."

"But —"

Artley was looking around the gundeck, his eyes wide. Alexis knew what he was thinking and why. In the heat of things, when it was just the guncrews to encourage and assist, one paid little heed to the condition of the ship. Now he'd been pulled out of that and could see the holes in the hull and the still figures dragged to the far side of the deck.

Alexis clapped a hand to his shoulder and squeezed hard.

"Mister Artley!" She waited until his eyes returned to her, then held his gaze until it settled. "We stand, Sterlyn," she said, quieter.

Artley's eyes scanned the gundeck again, but steadier this time, not panicked.

Belial shuddered as the frigate fired again. No shot flashed through the gundeck, but the lights flickered once, twice, and then went out, leaving the deck lit only with the dim glow of the emergency chemical lights. The fiber optics that brought light to the decks must have been cut, and around her she could feel the men pause in their work, but she kept her eyes on Artley's. She needed another officer to help her steady the men on the guns.

"The men need you to steady them, Mister Artley. Every moment we fight may mean another transport well away and who knows how many lives."

Artley swallowed and nodded, his face greenish in the emergency lights.

"A wall, sir."

Alexis nodded.

"Aye, Mister Artley, New London's wall, and we will stand." She gripped his shoulder hard so he'd feel it through the vacsuit. "I need you on the guns, Mister Artley. The men need to see you steady."

"Aye, sir. I'll not disappoint you."

Alexis watched him return to his guns. She felt *Belial* shudder as she was struck once more, then felt her stomach lurch. Around her on the deck, discarded shot casings rolled and some floated up from the deck as the artificial gravity failed. She grasped a canister of shot from a crewman shuffling his way through the dim light, and turned toward the nearest gun. The quarterdeck, lights, even the gravity generators might be gone, *Belial* might be all but dead, but so long as the magazine could charge shot and the guns could fire, she wasn't done.

Alexis' world narrowed to feeding the guns. There were fewer crewmen making their way up from the magazine, whether dead or fled to hide deep in the hold she didn't know, but she took to meeting them at the companionway hatch to take the freshly charged shot and hand over spent cartridges. Then she'd shuffle along the deck, careful to keep her feet always on the surface so as not to float away, to one of the guns.

Belial was reduced to three guns, and then to two as the frigate's shot struck a barrel and splintered into dozens of beams that pierced the gundeck. Men fell and she couldn't tell their names in the dim light. Still fresh shot came up from the magazine. She thought that it was Dobb bringing it up, which made her wonder at the state of the men on the sails, but couldn't be sure, and the remaining guns needed to be fed.

Sweat stung in her eyes and rolled across her lips. Her whole world was silent, save for the rasping of her own breath echoing in her helmet.

She caught sight of the frigate through the gaping holes in *Belial's* hull and marveled at the damage. The space between the frigates gunports had disappeared, leaving an open space that ran the length of the hull. The main and mizzen masts were gone, barely stumps left of them, and the foremast on the frigate's far side had but a single sail visible.

For a moment, she thought they might be able to call an end to this nightmare, but frigates carried large crews. Crews that could repair the rigging and step a new mast in little time, then be off again to catch her convoy. Every moment she could delay them meant another of her little ships might reach safety.

More shot poured from the frigate, more men were struck down.

Bodies, dead and injured both, floated amongst the discarded shot casings in the sickly green light.

She shoved her way through them with fresh shot, then realized that the small, still figure floating before her was too small for a gunner and its vacsuit arms had the distinctive markings of a midshipman

She screamed in rage, sound echoing in her helmet.

She forced her way past and found no one at the gun. She wondered if they were dead or fled, but threw open the breech herself and slotted the canister. Someone grasped her arm, but she shrugged it off and closed the breech. Peered out through the gunport to check its aim.

The Hanoverese frigate was a dark mass against the black background of *darkspace*. Only a few white lights shone here and there on its hull and the stubs of its masts. The sails on its remaining foremast were dark and uncharged. That meant something, she thought, but she couldn't spare the time to remember. All that mattered was to keep the frigate occupied with *Belial*, to allow just a few more moments for one of her little ships — a pinnace, a ferry, perhaps a packet — to escape. They'd already sacrificed so much, too much, to allow the frigate to escape them now.

Alexis raised her hand to the button that fired the gun and someone grasped her arm. She shrugged away and reached again for the gun, but strong arms wrapped themselves around her and lifted her from the deck.

She struggled and sound echoed through her helmet. A new sound. Someone was saying something, but she couldn't understand. Someone was talking and holding her, keeping her from her gun, and in a moment the frigate would sail off. They'd sail off and more of her little ships would fall, more men would die because she hadn't been strong enough or quick enough or clever enough to save them.

"— struck, sir!"

"We'll not strike, damn your eyes!" she yelled. "Get back to the guns and fire or I'll cut you down myself!"

The arms held against her struggles, spun her around, away from the gun.

"Sir!" She recognized Dobb's voice. "It's the frigate what's struck, sir! Not us, *the frigate!*"

Alexis shook her head.

"You're mad," she whispered. "They can't have ..."

Slowly she stopped struggling. The arms around her loosened, tentatively, as though Dobb was unsure of her and prepared to grab her again. She set her feet on the deck, feeling the *click* as the magnets in her boots met the deck. She turned and peered out.

The Hanoverese frigate lay a bare fifty meters away, gunports dark and silent. The stubs of its masts flashing white in surrender.

Alexis staggered back from the port and stared around her, starting to grin with elation at what *Belial* and her crew had accomplished. She stopped, blinked, and her grin fell away.

What little she could make out in the dim glow of the emergency chemical lights was a horror. All the guns but one were overturned, their tubes shattered and breeches twisted. Dobb stood beside her, Oakman and Chevis near the one remaining gun, but the deck everywhere was littered with bodies. Some moved feebly, but most were still.

"Dear lord, what have I done ..."

FIFTY-EIGHT

Alexis made her way onto *Belial's* hull by the simple expedience of stepping through the gaping hole that had once been her ship's gunports. She pulled a small, still figure along behind her and made her way to *Belial's* stern.

She supposed she should leave Artley's body with the rest being retrieved from throughout the ship and laid out on the gundeck, but couldn't bear to leave him there alone. She owed him a moment's time — time she'd not had to spare aboard *Shrewsbury* or even to keep him safe on *Belial,* nor to notice the moment of his death.

She settled into place at the stern and attached one of Artley's lines to the guidewires.

"Damn you, Sterlyn. Why'd you come back? You could have stayed safe at Alchiba. Not ... not come back so I could get you killed."

She settled into place and gazed off past *Belial's* rudder and planes.

Dobb and the others still alive were reviewing the damage, but there was little any of them could do. *Belial* was so holed that Alexis was afraid to try and reach any of the areas that might be undamaged

— the magazine was still aired and only portions of the engineering spaces.

Most of the engineering spaces had been holed at the same time *Belial's* gravity had failed. It was only by some miracle that *Belial* had survived, as the casing around the fusion plant was pocked and creased where shot had struck it, though never quite directly enough to breach it.

Her brief tour of the space had left her sick, as none of the civilians she'd sent there had been suited. Three had been shoved into a small compartment by the engineering crew and had miraculously survived, but the rest were dead. As were all of those who'd remained in *Belial's* hold.

Other than those three only the seven who'd been able to fit into the ship's magazine with Oakman had survived, including both Marie and Ferrau. She supposed she should be grateful for that, but it was hard to be grateful for anything when faced with such devastation.

Of her crew, there was only herself and four others, Dobb, Oakman, Chevis, and Hunsley, left alive. With no surgeon aboard to treat them during the action and with no one to be spared from the guns to take them below, most of those injured had been left on the gundeck where they fell, only to be struck again by enemy shot.

A hundred meters away the Hanoverese frigate sat still and silent as well, battered as much or more than *Belial* herself. A handful of suited figures were out on the hull there, and Alexis had to wonder what their butcher's bill had been. She should send someone over to take charge of it, but there was hardly anyone to send. It would have to wait until the end of the fleet action and for some ship from whichever side won that to come along.

And if there is any justice, her captain will have survived, that I might see him hang.

She hoped *Belial's* logs might be intact, and that the recordings of the Hanoverese firing into helpless, unarmed ships could be put to that purpose.

Alexis left Artley at the stern and crossed under *Belial's* keel to the other side of her ship for a moment. Here the hull was largely intact; only a few of the frigate's shots had managed to burn all the way through the gundeck to exit the far side. That, somehow, didn't seem right — the horror inside shouldn't be hidden like that.

In the distance she could see the lights of other ships and wondered what the outcome of the fleet action had been.

Then, a moment later, she supposed her question was answered. She stood and watched as, to leeward, a frigate beat her way against the wind toward *Belial*, New London's colors bright against her undamaged hull.

Alexis couldn't tell what ship — she was flying her number, but Alexis had no way of looking it up and didn't immediately recognize it — but the frigate's other signal sent her to her knees. First in manic laughter, then in wracking sobs.

Do you require assistance?

THE FRIGATE, *HMS Magnanime*, hove-to to windward of *Belial* and the Hanoverese frigate. Both ships were so damaged that there was no way a boarding tube could be attached to either. *Magnanime* worked her sails to drift and edge broadside downwind until she was close enough for lines to be shot across the void between the ships.

Alexis and Dobb made the lines fast to whatever parts of *Belial's* hull seemed least likely to snap off if force were applied.

No sooner had they made the lines fast than *Magnanime's* crew began hauling the two ships together, but Alexis watched in surprise as spacers from *Magnanime* scrambled across the lines as well, risking exposure to *darkspace* away from the protective influence of the hull.

A suited figure with lieutenant's insignia on his arms reached her and touched his helmet to hers.

"Lieutenant Whitefield, *Magnanime*. Is your captain about?"

Alexis had to work her mouth for a moment to be able to respond.

Her lips were dry and parched, and she'd finished all of her suit's water long before.

"*Belial's* mine." She looked around at the damage and shook her head. "Was mine." She fought down her feelings and tried to focus. "We've —" She closed her eyes and cringed at the number. "We've seven civilians in the magazine without vacsuits. Will you have some sent over so that they may board your ship?"

"You took refugees into action? Against a frigate?"

Alexis' temper flared. "And where were you, sir? Behind the lines playing postman, with never a glance this way to see what was happening?"

Her vision seemed to darken as she spoke and her head spun. She grasped Whitefield's arm to steady herself.

Whitefield looked from her to the Hanoverese frigate and back again.

"Your pardon," he said. "I should not have spoken so. Come, let me get you across to *Magnanime*."

ALEXIS and the others were taken first aboard *Magnanime*, where she made her report to the frigate's captain, Captain Hutchings, and was told the outcome of the fleet action.

Magnanime was not a part of Admiral Chipley's fleet that had come to Giron, it seemed. She was with a fleet under Admiral Cammack, whose fleet and flagship, HMS *Royal Sovereign*, a massive, 100 gun three decker, had arrived at Alchiba to reinforce Chipley, only to find that neither Chipley nor the original transports for the invasion force had ever returned to Alchiba, and that a ragtag fleet of little ships had sailed to bring New London's boys home.

Cammack had set out immediately for Giron, arriving in the midst of the action.

The Hanoverese fleet, now vastly outnumbered, had disengaged and fled.

"Admirals Chipley and Cammack exchanged some signals about the best course of action," Hutchings said. "Admiral Chipley believed an aggressive pursuit of the Hanoverese was in order, while my Admiral Cammack felt it was best to see these transports safely home."

Alexis eased herself in her chair and blinked. She was having a bit of trouble focusing on Captain Hutchings' words. She was dressed in a too-large jumpsuit borrowed from one of *Magnanime's* lieutenants. The smallest of them, but still several centimeters taller than she. Her own things were somewhere in the wreck of *Belial* or in her cabin aboard *Shrewsbury*, which was off with Admiral Chipley.

She'd barely had time to change out of her vacsuit before Hutchings was asking for her and she felt the dire need for a bit of time in the head to rinse the sweat from her body.

And a bunk. I should dearly like to make the acquaintance of one of Magnanime's *bunks. With the crew on the gundeck, even, just anywhere I might go to sleep.*

"Carew?"

Alexis jerked, her eyes springing open. "I'm sorry, sir, I —"

Hutchings waved it away. "No, I wasn't thinking. After what you … I can't imagine." He frowned. "Whitefield!"

Alexis jerked awake again at his bellow as Lieutenant Whitefield appeared in the hatchway.

"Sir?"

"Put Carew in a cabin until we can transfer her to *Royal Sovereign*. The admiral will want to speak with her."

"Aye, sir."

"Captain Hutchings," Alexis said, "I don't want to put anyone out of their cabin."

Hutchings shook his head. "No trouble. We'll be up with the flagship as soon as another frigate arrives here to take charge of the Hannie prize. No more than a watch." He frowned. "I suppose Chipley will have all the prize money if he ever catches up with those that fled. With both Chipley's fleet and mine In Sight here, the prize money for those that surrendered in this action will be spread thin as cucumber slices at tea."

Alexis struggled to smile, knowing it was expected of her at a senior captain's jest. The money for prizes was divided between the crews of all ships in sight of the action when the captured ship struck. With two New London fleets here near Giron there'd be many ships to divide what prize money resulted from the action, including whatever came of the frigate which had struck to *Belial*.

As for *Belial* herself? Alexis winced at the thought. With the damage so great, likely her ship would be scuttled in place, her fusion plant set to be breached and left to devour the hulk Alexis had turned her into.

IT FELT like she'd barely had a moment's rest before she was shaken awake and sent through a boarding tube to the flagship. Dobb and the other survivors from *Belial's* crew, Marie, Ferrau, and the other civilians included, remained aboard *Magnanime,* or possibly were transferred to other ships in Cammack's fleet. Alexis was never sure.

Alexis was whisked straight from the tube to the admiral's day cabin where she again told her story, this time to Admiral Cammack and *Royal Sovereign's* captain, Captain Wixson. There she related her experiences on Giron and during the action once more. Word came from the prize crew sent aboard the Hanoverese frigate, and Alexis learned what had occurred there during her action.

Apparently, the Hanoverese captain, furious that a ship so small as *Belial* was standing up to his ship and that his guncrews were performing so poorly, had left his quarterdeck for the gundeck just as one of *Belial's* broadsides had arrived. He'd been struck down in the midst of haranguing his guncrews. In the confusion after his loss, the frigate's guncrews had become even more haphazard until *Belial's* fire had destroyed fully half the frigate's guns. Further fire from *Belial* had struck the frigate's quarterdeck, penetrating it and killing both the first lieutenant, then acting as captain, and fourth lieutenant. The second lieutenant took command, but, seeing the arrival of Cammack's fleet, had determined to put paid to a bad bit of business and ordered the colors struck.

Alexis listened to the report in silence. She was torn between satisfaction that the frigate's captain was dead and disappointment that he'd escaped further justice for his actions.

Finally she was shown to a cabin and left to rest — and that was the worst of all.

Dobb and the others were quickly absorbed into the fleet's crews. They had the support of new mates and tasks to keep them busy. Alexis was left idle — she had no place in *Royal Sovereign's* watch schedule and no duties.

At least fatigue and having to make her report of the action had kept her either occupied or left her mind muddled. Once she had time to rest and her mind was clear, she found herself left idle and with far too much time to think about the action.

Worse, the other lieutenants aboard the flagship either treated her with kid gloves or avoided her altogether. They seemed unsure of her status or of how to deal with her, which Alexis couldn't blame them for. She'd not only lost a ship, but the refugees aboard and nearly all her crew as well. What did one say to such an officer?

For the most part she stayed in her cabin — *Royal Sovereign's* eighth lieutenant had been moved to a midshipman's cabin and those worthies had evicted a master's mate from his — or alone at the wardroom table. Both Admiral Cammack and Captain Wixson invited her to dine with them nightly, but she was poor company and knew it. Her thoughts were elsewhere.

For hours she studied her tablet, searching for some tactic that would have changed the outcome of *Belial's* last action, but found none. At last, she was forced to admit that once she'd determined to engage the frigate, *Belial's* fate was sealed. As the alternative had been to allow more of the transports to be destroyed, she accepted that she'd had no choice.

That knowledge did little to alleviate the loss.

ALEXIS JUMPED, startled by the sudden rap on her cabin's hatch.

"Come," she said.

The hatch slid open and one of *Royal Sovereign's* midshipmen stuck his head in. There were so many of them about the massive ship that Alexis had yet to keep them straight.

"Admiral Cammack's asking for you to come to the quarterdeck, sir," the boy said. "We've spotted the Alchiba pilot boat, I hear."

Alexis frowned. Why would she be needed on the quarterdeck for that? Still and all, a summons from an admiral was not to be ignored. She rolled off her cot and straightened her jumpsuit. The midshipman slid the hatch open and Alexis frowned as she saw that Dobb, Oakman, Chevis, and Hunsley, all of those, at least who were in the Navy, who had survived *Belial* were also with him.

"Admiral's asked for them, as well," the midshipman explained.

Alexis led the way, more curious than ever as to why they'd all been summoned. They made their way to the quarterdeck and entered.

"Ah, there you are, Carew," Cammack said as they entered. "Come over here, please, all of you." He gestured to the spacers behind her. "Here around the plot, if you will."

Alexis shared a glance with Dobb and Oakman. The space around the navigation plot was generally an officer's purview.

"Pilot boat's signaling again, sir," the midshipman on the signals console announced. Alexis realized she didn't know his name either, despite having been aboard *Royal Sovereign* for so long. "Asking for our numbers and they've added *Imperative.*"

Alexis stepped up to the navigation plot — Cammack had invited her to after all — and stared at it in puzzlement. In addition to the plot of each ship's course, Admiral Cammack had it displaying images of the Alchiba pilot boat and arriving fleet — both Cammack's ships and the hundreds of little ships bearing the evacuees from Giron. She felt Dobb and the others step up beside her.

What's going on?

No wonder the pilot boat had added the *Imperative* signal. None of the ships in the fleet were flying New London's colors, much less their numbers. Their masts and hulls were dark, as though they were all waiting for something. With hundreds of unidentified ships so close, the pilot boat must be wondering if this were the start of an invasion.

"There's little enough we can do to honor your ship and men, Carew," Cammack said. "I'll hope this is a start." He nodded to the signals station.

Alexis frowned and looked down at the plot. First *Royal Sovereign's* masts lit up, then that signal was taken up by the other ships of the fleet — from ships of the line to frigates to sloops to the smallest pinnace that had made the trip — spreading out from *Royal Sovereign* in an expanding wave, each ship displaying the same signal.

Not a ship's number, for the ship named in the signal had never received one. Instead the signals spelled out the name, laboriously, letter by letter.

Alexis' eyes filled with tears and she blinked hard to clear them, wishing so many men could be here to see the honor the fleet was paying them.

Dobb laid a hand on her shoulder.

"She were a good ship, sir."

"And the finest of crews," Alexis agreed, laying her hand over his and squeezing hard.

The pilot boat had asked a simple question: *What ship?*

And the fleet, as one, had answered.

Belial.

EPILOGUE

A<small>LEXIS</small> <small>ROSE</small> from her bunk sweating and shaking. The last tendrils of the dream, nightmare, still had hold of her and even the bright lights couldn't dispel it. She leaned over the small table her compartment sported, one palm flat on its surface, and poured a drink. She noted that her hand was shaking and the bottle's neck rattled against the glass. She'd have to ensure that had stopped before her next meeting with Lieutenant Curtice.

Hopefully the last of my meetings with the lieutenant.

She understood the point of the meetings and the Navy's desire that she be recovered from the events on Giron before moving on to another post, but could not appreciate the lieutenant's prying nature and questions. Could he not see that the best way to put that behind her and move on was to do so? Sitting about talking it through constantly only kept it close to the forefront of her thoughts.

There was a tapping at the hatch, which would be Isom come to wake her.

Isom had come aboard *Royal Sovereign* at Alchiba and resumed his duties as her servant. Then Admiral Cammack had taken *Royal*

Sovereign and his fleet back to Lesser Itchthorpe, leaving a few ships to guard Alchiba in anticipation of Admiral Chipley's return there.

She'd taken rooms aboard the Lesser Itchthorpe station while she waited for reassignment or for *Shrewsbury's* return with Chipley's fleet. Dobb and the others from *Belial* had been quickly sent to other ships. She realized she felt very alone, the more so because, with no word of Chipley's fleet, there was also no word of Delaine and the Berry March fleet that had sailed with him.

Alexis drained the glass, letting the fire of the bourbon burn away the last traces of the dream.

There was another rap at the hatchway.

She quickly wiped the glass dry with a cloth and tucked the cloth into her pocket. Isom had said nothing, but she could tell he didn't approve her drinking first thing upon waking. Still, it was her who had to wake from such dreams and not him.

"Yes, Isom, I'm coming," she called. "Have them start on breakfast for me, will you?"

"SO, lieutenant, how did you sleep last night?"

Alexis smiled at Curtice, but it was a smile that didn't reach her eyes. The lieutenant tasked by the Sick and Hurt Board with watching over her always started with that question.

As though my nights were a window to my soul, she thought.

"Much the same as all the others, sir," she said.

"No trouble getting to sleep?" Curtice asked. "No nightmares?"

"No more than I'd expect, nor than the last time you asked."

Curtice pursed his lips. "Why would you expect trouble sleeping and nightmares at all?" he asked.

"I've little to do with my days, sir," Alexis said. "A day of idleness does nothing to tire me, and so my evenings are restless." She shrugged. "Does not everyone have nightmares from time to time?"

Curtice gave her an enigmatic look but said nothing.

"Nightmares are not so unusual, I think," Alexis said firmly.

Curtice tapped at his tablet. He gestured to his office sideboard. "Would you like a drink?"

"It's quite early. No thank you."

"Hm." Curtice tapped more at his tablet. "I'm told you find no issue with the hour where you keep your rooms. It's not unusual for you to be at table with a bottle before you of a morning, is it?"

"Are you having me watched, lieutenant?"

Curtice shook his head. "One hears things."

"Again, sir, my days are idle and my own at this time. If I choose to have a glass or two of wine, what business is it of yours?"

More tapping. Alexis ground her teeth in frustration. She longed to yank the tablet from his grasp and fling it at the wall. She forced herself to take a deep breath and hold it — she'd been more short-tempered and quicker to anger since Giron, she knew. It wouldn't do to show Curtice that.

"You've spoken little of the Glorious Twenty-second. Would you like to do so today?"

Alexis clenched her jaw again. They'd taken to calling it that, those who reported on the events at Giron. Even the Naval Gazette had taken up the name. The Glorious Twenty-second, for the fleet action on the twenty-second of August, as though there were any glory to be had from it.

"I do wish they wouldn't call it that."

No sooner had she spoken than Alexis wished she could recall the words.

"Why would that be?" Curtice asked.

She sighed. The man pounced on every utterance and worried it like a terrier with a rat.

"What possible glory was there?" she asked, knowing it was a mistake. She should remain silent and give him nothing at all to remark upon, but the absurdity of glorifying the events of Giron galled her.

"A Hanoverese fleet was defeated. There's talk they'll strike a medal for that action."

"The Hanoverese fleet sailed off with Admiral Chipley's in pursuit, and we've heard from neither since."

No word from Chipley, no word of *Shrewsbury*, and no word of the Berry March fleet or Delaine.

"Save General Malicoat, the entire New London force was successfully rescued and returned home," Curtice said.

"We left behind three-quarters of the French forces and tens of thousands of civilians."

Curtice shrugged. "Some would ask what use the French forces would be. The Republic failed to declare war on the Hanoverese, after all — just sent a fleet or two to the border and sailed about in threat."

"Some would be fools."

Curtice raised an eyebrow.

Alexis thought of the French forces on Giron. Untrained and ill-equipped, seeing their homes destroyed and their families killed, calling down *Belial's* fire on themselves to give Malicoat the chance to disengage his forces — fighting against such horrible odds so that the last boat, her boat, could lift from Giron and leave them behind. Her eyes burned and her throat was tight as she spoke.

"The French of the Berry March are not the French of the Republic," she said. "The French of the Berry March —" She thought of Malicoat's words. "The French of the Berry March have mettle and more."

"You're angry," Curtice said.

Alexis couldn't help herself, she laughed and nodded. "I am angry, Lieutenant Curtice."

"What's angered you?"

Alexis shook her head.

The Hanoverese for starting a war. Eades for starting this nonsense. The Republic for failing us. Chipley for sending transports off with far too small an escort. Chipley for abandoning Giron.

Whoever thought to do such a thing on the cheap, without enough of anything to succeed. Myself.

She clenched her fists, digging her nails into her palms. What if she'd said no to Eades or never worn Delaine's insignia to that French reception? What if she'd been less convincing when asked if she thought the people of Giron would rise up? What if ...

Myself.

"What are you thinking?" Curtice asked.

"Am I allowed no private thoughts, sir?"

Curtice resumed tapping at his tablet.

"What's angered you?" he repeated.

"If you know anything at all of Giron and must ask that question, lieutenant, no explanation of mine could possibly be adequate."

More tapping.

"Must you do that?"

"What?"

Alexis sighed. "That taking down of every word I say."

Curtice cocked his head to one side. "I do have to prepare a report for Admiral Cammack, you know."

"I have a meeting with Admiral Cammack this afternoon. He can judge me for himself, can he not?"

Curtice's jaw tightened. "I'm aware of your meeting with the admiral, I assure you."

Alexis watched him carefully and saw some cause to hope. She couldn't help but feel if Curtice was unhappy, then her meeting with Cammack would be to her benefit.

"CAREW."

"Admiral Cammack, sir."

The admiral nodded to a chair and Alexis sat. She bit her lip and waited while Cammack perused his tablet. She assumed he was reading Curtice's report or recommendation and wondered what his decision would be. The time spent waiting on Lesser Itchthorpe had been difficult. She wanted nothing more than to be done with Curtice and his questions, and to be off on another ship and doing something useful with her time.

"Would you like a drink, Carew?" Cammack asked.

"No, thank you, sir," she answered. She wanted a clear head for this interview, with nothing dulling her wits.

"Lieutenant Curtice seems to think you would," Cammack said. "His report reads as though you were a drunkard."

Alexis' jaw clenched and she forced herself to relax. "Lieutenant Curtice and I have found ourselves at odds on many things, sir."

"So it seems." The admiral set his tablet down and rose. He went to the rear of his office where a viewport looked out on the shipping in orbit. "Curtice is concerned about some sort of nightmare, as well, he writes."

"Lieutenant Curtice concerns himself with a great many things that are, in the whole of it, none of his concern." Alexis regretted the words as soon as she'd said them. She knew it sounded petulant and defensive, especially given that Curtice had been set to examine her in the first place.

"I don't know anyone who's seen action that doesn't have the occasional nightmare," Cammack said. "Myself included. Still, I must admit I am at a quandary for what to do with you."

Alexis remained silent. She suspected she wasn't supposed to hear such details of Curtice's report, certainly not phrased so bluntly, and despite his claims to the contrary that Cammack had already made his decision.

"Losing *Belial* that way must have been a hard blow," Cammack said. He gestured to his steward, who poured the admiral a glass of wine. "Nothing, are you sure? Tea? Coffee, even?"

"A bit of tea, perhaps, sir." Alexis wasn't sure how she should respond to his comment about *Belial*. He hadn't asked a question after all. Cammack remained silent while his steward brought Alexis a cup of tea. She stirred in a bit of cream and sugar and took a sip. "Thank you."

Cammack raised an eyebrow.

I suppose he does want me to comment on it. Nearly everyone does.

"It was, sir," she said, "very hard."

"And yet Lieutenant Curtice writes here that you've remarkably little to say on the matter."

"Lieutenant Curtice is very much in favor of talking, sir. For myself, I don't see the point." In truth she was a bit afraid to talk about it. That last action on *Belial* had been horrible and she felt she relived it enough in her dreams that she had no need to speak on it out of them.

"Curtice is exclusively part of the Sick and Hurt Board," Cammack said. "Very modern, that."

Alexis raised her eyes from her cup. Had she detected a note of disapproval in Cammack's tone?

"Knowing now what happened," Cammack went on, "would you do anything differently if you could?"

"Differently, sir?"

"If you could change your actions on Giron?"

Never to have gone in the first place?

She supposed Cammack was talking specifically about her action with the Hanoverese frigate.

"Leave the civilians on Giron, sir, if I'd known then that we'd face an action," she said, then went on, feeling as though she should explain more. "Not that I feel taking them was the wrong decision given what I knew at the time. *Belial* never should have faced an action — not with the fleets there. She should have been ..."

"And what of the action itself?"

"I could wish that ... that I had found another way, sir. Some maneuver, some trick of sail, some ruse ... that I had been cleverer than I was."

She'd been over things often enough in her own head. Could she have chosen another point of sail? Somehow led that frigate a chase instead of engaging it? She didn't know. Anything different she might have done could just as easily resulted in more of the little ships being destroyed instead of just *Belial*.

Just.

She took another sip of the tea to cover the pain thoughts of the ship always brought. Odd how one could come to care about a pile of plastic and metal almost as much as the flesh and blood crew.

Cammack grunted. "Sometimes, Carew, there's nothing for it but to put your ship alongside the other fellow and batter away. Clever wins out at times, true, but others it's just ..." He took a sip of wine. "Just brutality that's the only option for you."

Alexis nodded, unwilling to risk speaking. Lord knew she'd gone over and over the events in her head, trying to see where she'd made the mistake that had cost so many lives. But try as she might she'd failed to see a course that wouldn't have resulted in more deaths.

"So," Cammack said. "To decide what to do with you." He looked at her speculatively "What is it that you most want, Carew?"

"A ship," Alexis said automatically, then paused.

Had she really said that? For some time, she would have said that what she most wanted was to return home to Dalthus, the inheritance laws safely changed, and live toward taking over her grandfather's holdings one day. Yet she'd answered Cammack's question without hesitation.

"I think that you do not mean a lieutenancy in one when you say that," Cammack said with a slight grin.

Alexis took that as license to smile back. "You asked what I most wanted, sir, not what I thought I could have at this time."

"Well, you're a bit young for a command, you know, even a lieutenant's. Being sent off into a prize is one thing, but an official appointment is quite another."

Alexis nodded. She did know that, but still he'd asked.

"Another stint as a junior lieutenant aboard a ship of the line, perhaps a frigate if you're lucky." Cammack picked up his tablet and frowned as he reviewed something on it. "Then a run somewhere as first lieutenant, where you can get a feel for things, yes? That's the way we do things, you know."

"Yes, sir."

"Your men fought quite well on *Belial*."

Alexis blinked at the sudden change in subject. Cammack seemed to be speaking almost randomly and she wondered when he'd get to the point of what was to become of her, not least of which because it would put an end to him bringing up what had happened aboard *Belial*.

"They are ... were the very best I could have asked for, sir."

"Reviewed the log myself, you know. What was left before the power was cut to the recorders, of course." Cammack's eyes were still on his tablet and he spoke absently as though he were simply musing to himself. "Had no marines aboard, did you?"

Alexis blinked again at the change in subject. She shook her head, wondering what Cammack's point was. "No, sir."

"No lobster with his rifle at the gundeck's hatch to keep them from hiding in the hold," Cammack went on.

Alexis remained silent. Many ships, most perhaps, posted marines at the companionways in an action to thwart anyone who tried to run and hide. She thought it was a disservice to the men.

"Not a single man left the guns," Cammack said. "Not even in the worst of it." He raised his eyes to hers. "And the worst of it was the worst I've seen, I'll admit."

"They were the very best crew I could ask for, sir."

"The news feeds are all about that action. All of them, not just the Naval Gazette. Full of how New London's brave Jack Tars stood up against such odds and fought for Queen and Country." He drained his glass and gestured for another. He waited while his steward poured. "They don't, you know."

"Sir?" Alexis was becoming even more confused with where this meeting was going.

"Fight for Queen and Country, I mean. They don't. Oh, they

may join for it, when the recruiters make their speeches and they hear the sound of the drum and fife. Quite moving, that. But when the action's on and they're staring at another ship's open gunports, it's not our good Queen Annalise on their minds.

"No, then it's all in that moment, what's right there, and nothing else. They're fighting for themselves, or their mates — so they'll not look shy to the others on the guns. Sometimes they'll fight for their ship, for her honor if it's a happy ship and a good company." He looked up finally and met Alexis' eyes. "Or for an officer they respect and whose good opinion they value."

Alexis fought not to look away from his gaze. She thought he seemed to be saying that the men had fought because she'd asked them too. If that were the case, she wasn't sure she could bear what that meant, and certain she couldn't avoid it.

"I believe, sir, I'll have that drink, if it's still on offer."

Cammack nodded toward his sideboard and Alexis rose instead of asking Cammack's steward. She felt the need for something stronger than wine and for the chance to turn away from Cammack's gaze for a moment. She poured from a decanter of something amber, unsure what it might be and not really caring.

Cammack returned his eyes to his tablet once she'd resumed her seat.

"In mine, I'm a midshipman again," Cammack said, not looking up. "HMS *Aldborough*, 24 ... she was a small, sixth rate. We won the action ... well, won, yes ... it was a close-run thing."

"Sir?"

"It's different in the dark of night, though, isn't it?" Cammack went on as though she hadn't spoken. "I'm on the gundeck and the fire's coming in. Broadside after broadside ... faster than any ship has a right to fire, mind you ... but we're not firing our guns back. The crews are just standing there, falling one by one as the shot comes in, but not firing the guns. I can scream at them, pummel them, but they never fire. More shot comes in, more men fall. I rush to the guns myself ... and I can *feel* the button to fire the gun through my vacsuit.

My hand's right there *on it*, but I can't press it. No matter how hard I try, I can't fire our guns." He looked up and met Alexis' gaze. "Then I look out the gunport and next broadside is coming in."

Cammack was silent for a long moment, holding Alexis' eye.

She started to speak, understanding what he meant by telling her of his own nightmare — what he was offering her — but she couldn't bring herself to describe hers. She couldn't bring herself to tell him, nor anyone, for fear they'd tell her the shadows were right, that it was all somehow her failure.

Cammack waited a moment longer, then shrugged as the moment passed.

"Still, there's the question of what to do with you. Curtice believes you need some time to yourself, some time to rest. What do you think of that?"

"I think, sir, that Lieutenant Curtice is not the best judge of what I need," Alexis said, glad that the conversation had turned again.

"And what do you think you need at this time?"

"To be busy and useful, sir," she said. It was no more than the truth. "This enforced idleness here on Lesser Itchthorpe doesn't sit well with me."

Cammack nodded. "What I'd wish myself," he murmured. "Still and all, there's Curtice's recommendations I have to take into account and he doesn't rate you fit for another commission here on the border where there's so much fighting still."

So he meant to send her away from the war. To be the junior lieutenant on some ship far from Hanover. Alexis wasn't at all sure how she'd be able to take some time of endless patrols in peaceful space. All because of that damned Curtice. She was so caught up in anger at the man that she nearly missed the Admiral Cammack's next words and it took her a moment to understand their import.

"— *Nightingale*'s commander, Lieutenant Borrowman, is asking for leave ... some sort of family issue, it seems. With everyone anxious to come to the war zone and, frankly, our need of them, it's been difficult to find someone to take his place. Only a lieutenant's command, a little revenue cutter, but far enough from any real fighting that it seems to fit Curtice's concerns nicely."

A revenue cutter? They were such small ships, commanded by a lieutenant and having only a pair of midshipmen as other officers. If she was appointed into that, it would have to be as ...

"Best for you, I think, Carew. Give you a bit of time in command in a more relaxed setting than the neck-or-nothing dashes you've had in those prizes you've commanded. *Nightingale* has a pair of good midshipmen aboard to offer you support and a decent crew ... well, as decent as may be with the war on." He raised his eyebrows. "It *is* important and useful work, you know. Smuggling cuts into the tax base and without taxes there're no funds for the Navy to fight this war, you understand?"

"Yes, sir, I understand. Thank you." Her own ship! Appointed into it properly, even. No matter how small it was still both an honor and a sign of confidence in her that Cammack would do this.

"Oh, and your stars seem to have aligned even further with this," Cammack went on. "*Nightingale's* based out of Zariah — that would make her patrol sector include that Dalthus system you're from, I think. Not often the Navy gives us a chance to visit home, Carew, so best take advantage of it."

Alexis took a deep breath, feeling as though a huge weight had been lifted from her. A command, work to do, and a chance to visit home.

"Settled then," Cammack said. "I'll have the orders cut and forwarded to you. You can be on the first packet going that direction."

"Thank you, sir."

Alexis took that for her dismissal and rose to leave, but she paused at the hatchway. She hadn't felt nearly the same reluctance to talk with the admiral as she had with Curtice. It seemed as though he understood, and she risked asking at least one of the questions she was afraid of having an answer to.

"Does it ever get easier to bear, sir?"

Cammack stared at her a moment and she was certain he understood completely. Had felt what she'd been feeling since Giron.

The admiral drained his glass.

"Given the costs ... I should bloody well hope not, don't you?"

ALEXIS MADE her way back to her rooms. With every step she wanted to pull out her tablet and check that Admiral Cammack's orders were real and not a dream. She was getting a ship, her own ship, and properly assigned into it, not just a prize command — something unthinkably rare for an eighteen-year old lieutenant. Surely it would be a small ship, only a revenue cutter, but still it was a command. And more than that, she was going home. Patrolling the sector would allow her to visit Dalthus every few weeks and spend time with her grandfather. It was like a huge weight lifted from her shoulders.

"Isom!" she called as she approached her rooms. The news was good for him as well. This commission would place them in the same sector for months, perhaps a year or more, and with a regular patrol schedule. There were certain to be solicitors on Zariah they could speak to who could coordinate with Grandy on Penduli and possibly challenge Isom's enlistment by the Impress Service.

"That Mister Dansby was by, sir," Isom said, coming out of her rooms.

Alexis' smile fell. Dansby had followed Cammack's fleet to Lesser Itchthorpe. She hadn't spoken to him, but he'd been constantly about for some reason, always catching her eye. She'd begun to wonder if the man was stalking her.

"Is he still here?"

Isom shook his head. "No, sir, but he left you some'at."

Alexis frowned. "What is it?"

"It's wrapped, on your cot, sir. He left a note, as well."

Alexis hesitated at the hatch to her rooms.

"I don't suppose you thought to scan it for explosives?" She waved Isom away. "No, never mind. That man's clever enough to get around that somehow."

She slid the hatch shut behind her, best to deal with whatever Dansby had left her with before telling Isom the good news. The package, little more than half a meter square, was wrapped in brown paper. She pulled a folded note from its top and read:

Rikki,

I've just heard you'll be captaining a revenue cutter, dealing with the serpents and vipers such as I (was, now utterly and wholly reformed, of course).

Alexis stopped reading and snorted astonishment. How fast the rumor mill worked on-station or on a ship was astounding. She'd barely stopped on her way from Admiral Cammack's quarters, and yet Dansby had the whole of it, and with time to write a note.

Perhaps you'll have need of an ally in your future endeavors — and a reminder of your place in things.

A. Dansby

Alexis frowned and parted the paper from the top of the package, exposing a box made of wire mesh. She jumped backward as a tiny face appeared behind the mesh.

Soft, brown eyes gleamed as they reflected the light and she could make out a lithe, furry body ending in a tail, bottle-brush thick in agitation. The face disappeared in a rustle of movement as a soft *chittering* came to her ear.

"Isom!" she called out, shaking her head. "We'll need to pack ... and I'd admire it did you discover to me what one feeds a bloody mongoose!"

A NOTE FROM THE AUTHOR

Thank you for reading *The Little Ships*. I hope you enjoyed it as much as I enjoyed writing it.

If you did and would like to further support the series, please consider leaving a brief review on the purchase site or a review/rating on Goodreads. Reviews are the lifeblood of independent authors and let other readers know what books they might enjoy.

If you'd like to be notified of future releases, please consider following me on Twitter or Facebook, or joining my mailing list (all of which are linked to at www.alexiscarew.com). The mailing list is limited to no more than one or two updates a month and everyone subscribed will receive a free ebook copy of *Planetfall* the Alexis Carew novella when it's released.

I'd like to take this opportunity to thank my readers who are native speakers of French or German for your patience. I know I've taken some liberties with your respective languages, choosing, in some cases, not quite the best translation in order to make some things more understandable to English speakers via context. And to those English speakers for your patience with so much French and German. :)

Inspiration for *The Little Ships,* and its title, came primarily from the evacuation of British and French troops from Dunkirk in May/June of 1940.

With the whole of the British Expeditionary Force, what remained of Belgian forces, and three French armies trapped with their backs to the English Channel, the Allies undertook the task of evacuating over 300,000 men across the English Channel. Hundreds of boats responded to the call — from the merchant marine, fishing and pleasure craft, and even lifeboats. Civilian and Naval forces worked together to accomplish one of the most remarkable boat lifts in history.

Even the weather cooperated to a certain extent, with cloud cover that kept the German air force from being as much of a threat as it should have been and the Channel itself remaining unseasonably calm.

Those Little Ships, many of which still sail, even have their own flag, the Dunkirk Jack, which can only be flown by civilian ships that took part in the operation.

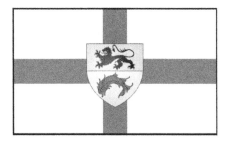

The Dunkirk Jack: The St George's Cross defaced with the arms of Dunkirk

In naming the fictional ships participating in the evacuation of Giron,

I used several from real ships that participated in the evacuation of Dunkirk. Most notably the three packets, *Mona's Queen, Fenella,* and *King Orry.* At Dunkirk, these three ships were among the sixteen vessels from the Isle of Man Steam Packet Company that participated in the evacuation, and all three were lost on May 29th, 1940.

As well, the *Royal Daffodil* was a real ship and made seven trips across the Channel to rescue between seven and nine thousand men — the most of any ship in the campaign.

The reaction to Dunkirk, by all rights, should have been one of despair. The allied armies were defeated, driven not only to the coast, but into the very sea, and had to evacuate across the Channel before a seemingly unbeatable foe.

The people of England didn't seem to see it that way. The soldiers from Dunkirk were greeted by celebrating crowds on their return. The mood was so optimistic, in fact, that Winston Churchill gave one of his most famous speeches, not so much to raise morale, but to remind people of the long, hard war yet to be fought.

We shall go on to the end, we shall fight in France, we shall fight on the seas and oceans, we shall fight with growing confidence and growing strength in the air, we shall defend our Island, whatever the cost may be, we shall fight on the beaches, we shall fight on the landing grounds, we shall fight in the fields and in the streets, we shall fight in the hills; we shall never surrender.

If you'd like to learn more about the evacuation of Dunkirk – Operation Dynamo, as it was called – I strongly recommend Walter Lord's *The Miracle of Dunkirk* as a fine source. Alexis' reaction to the appearance of the Little Ships echoes that of Lieutenant Ian Cox, First Lieutenant on the destroyer *Malcolm,* related in that book:

There, coming over the horizon toward him, was a mass of dots that filled the sea. The Malcolm was bringing her third load of troops back to Dover. The dots were heading the other way – toward Dunkirk.

As he watched, the dots materialized into vessels. Here and there were respectable steamers, like the Portsmouth-Isle of Wight car ferry, but mostly they were little ships of every conceivable type – fishing smacks ... drifters ... excursion boats ... glittering white yachts ... tugs towing ship's lifeboats ... the Admiral Superintendent's barge from Portsmouth with its fancy tassels and rope-work.

Cox felt a sudden surge of pride. Being here was no longer just a duty; it was an honor and a privilege. Turning to a somewhat startled chief boatswain's mate standing beside him, he burst into the Saint Crispin's Day passage from Shakespeare's Henry V.

If you enjoyed the fictional story of *The Little Ships*, I urge you to read the historical events, for they were far more impressive, as it relates the individual stories of many of those incredibly brave men who risked everything for others.

In addition to Dunkirk, I drew on the 1793 Siege of Toulon. French Republican armies — including, notably, a young artillery officer by the name of Napoleon — surrounded the town, which the British had previously taken and which had become a haven for French Royalists. As the British evacuated they took with them some 14,000 civilians, but still had to leave many more behind — some of whom were summarily executed by the Republican forces.

There may also be some parallels there to more recent conflicts, regardless of your thoughts on the right or wrong of them, and the question of what debt is owed to local forces and civilians who assist or rise up with an expectation of promised support.

J.A. Sutherland
  New Orleans, LA
  August 1, 2015

ALSO BY J.A. SUTHERLAND

To be notified when new releases are available, follow J.A. Sutherland on Facebook (https://www.facebook.com/alexiscarewbooks), Twitter (https://twitter.com/JASutherlandBks), or subscribe to the author's newsletter (http://www.alexiscarew.com/list).

Alexis Carew

Into the Dark

Mutineer

The Little Ships

HMS Nightingale

Privateer

Dark Artifice

Of Dubious Intent

coming early 2018

ABOUT THE AUTHOR

J.A. Sutherland spends his time sailing the Bahamas on a 43' 1925 John G. Alden sailboat called Little Bit ...

Yeah ... no. In his dreams.

Reality is a townhouse in Orlando with a 90 pound huskie-wolf mix who won't let him take naps.

When not reading or writing, he spends his time on roadtrips around the Southeast US searching for good barbeque.

Mailing List: http://www.alexiscarew.com/list

To contact the author:

www.alexiscarew.com

sutherland@alexiscarew.com

DARKSPACE

Darkspace

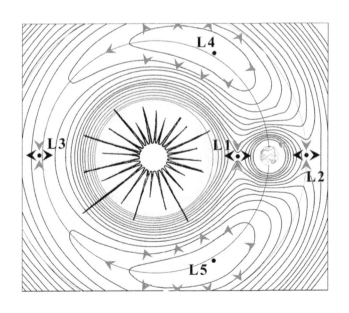

The perplexing problem dated back centuries, to when mankind was still planet-bound on Earth. Scientists, theorizing about the origin of the universe, recognized that the universe was expanding, but made the proposal that the force that had started that expansion would eventually dissipate, causing the universe to then begin contracting again. When they measured this, however, they discovered something very odd — not only was the expansion of the universe not slowing, but it was actually increasing.

This meant that something, something unseen, was continuing to apply energy to the universe's expansion. More energy than could be accounted for by what their instruments could detect. At the same time, they noticed that there seemed to be more gravitational force than could be accounted for by the observable masses of stars, planets, and other objects.

There seemed to be quite a bit of the universe that simply couldn't be seen. Over ninety percent of the energy and matter that had to make up the universe, in fact.

They called these dark energy and dark matter, for want of a better term.

Then, as humanity began serious utilization of near-Earth space, they made another discovery.

Lagrangian points were well-known in orbital mechanics. With any two bodies where one is orbiting around the other, such as a planet and a moon, there are five points in space where the gravitational effects of the two bodies provide precisely the centripetal force required to keep an object, if not stationary, then relatively so.

Humanity first used these points to build a space station at L_1, the Lagrangian point situated midway between Earth and the Moon, thus providing a convenient stopover for further exploration of the Moon. This was quickly followed by a station at L_2, the point on the far side of the moon, roughly the same distance from it as L_1. Both of these stations began reporting odd radiation signatures. Radiation that had no discernible source, but seemed to spring into existence from within the Lagrangian points themselves.

Further research into this odd radiation began taking place at the L4 and L5 points, which led and trailed the Moon in its orbit by about sixty degrees. More commonly referred to as Trojan Points, L4 and L5 are much larger in area than L1 and L2 and, it was discovered, the unknown radiation was much more intense.

More experimentation, including several probes that simply disappeared when their hulls were charged with certain high-energy particles, eventually led to one of those probes reappearing — and the discovery of darkspace, along with the missing ninety-five percent of the universe.

Dark energy that moved through it like winds. Usually blowing directly toward a star system from all directions, pushing those systems farther and farther apart, but sometimes coming in storms that could drive a ship far off course. Dark matter that permeated the space, slowing anything, even light, outside of a ship's hull and field.